INTO THE DEEP

The Haven

V. E. Rosswell

Pith, n. [AS. *pitha;* D. *pit,* pith, kernel.]
1. the soft, spongy tissue, consisting of cellular tissue, in the center of certain plant stems . . . 6. in anatomy, the spinal cord. [Rare.]

Pith, *v.t.*; pithed (pitht), *pt.*, *pp.*; pithing, *ppr.*
1. to remove the pith from (a plant stem). 2. to pierce or sever the spinal cord of (an animal) in order to kill it or make it insensible for experimental purposes.

Webster's New Twentieth Century Dictionary (Unabridged) Second Edition

ARCHIPELAGO PRESS

Campbell, California, United States of America
email: pelago2000@aol.com

This book is a work of fiction. The characters, names, incidents, dialogue, and plot are the products of the author's imagination or are used fictitiously. Any resemblance to actual persons or events is purely coincidental.

Library of Congress Cataloging-in-Publication Data

Rosswell, V.E.
Into the deep : the haven / V.E. Rosswell - 1st ed.
p. cm
ISBN 1-893335-04-6 (alk. paper)
ISBN 1-893335-03-8 (pbk. : alk. pa
1. Title
PS3568.O84914I5 1998
813'.54—dc21

98-50339
CIP

ISBN: 1-893335-09-7

Printed in the United States of America

Dedicated

To my mother

Acknowledgments

There were those in the beginning who didn't laugh when I set out on this journey and to whom I therefore owe special thanks: my patient mother; her friend, Helen Lippman, and also Georgia Baciu—all of whom read the first draft and encouraged me to go on. Sincerest thanks also to my brilliant editor, Kathleen Laderman, who understood what I was attempting and whose fierce intelligence made it possible for you to want to go on. I am deeply grateful to Connie Deronde L. for her astute eye and to Barbara I. for her praise and benevolent criticism, and to Steve J. for his upbeat support. To all of you, my deepest thanks—and my fondest regards to the mavens, wherever you are.

Foreward

Although the characters are wholly fictional, their adventures take place in the early Seventies—a time which has been, with one notable exception, faithfully reconstructed. It would thus be helpful to recall two compelling economic realities of that era: The purchasing power of the dollar was then many multiples of what it is now, but the top marginal federal income tax rate was so high—70%—and so quickly obtained, that people of means often resorted to foreign trusts in order to preserve their estates from the erosion of income and estate taxes. These foreign trusts (all perfectly legal when properly created) were usually established in tax havens—most of which impose little or no tax at all—because the United States, unlike most other developed nations, taxes the worldwide income of its citizens and residents. There were also some unique provisions to be found in the Internal Revenue Code; for example: a "non-resident alien" investing in the United States stock market would not be subject to U.S. taxation of capital gains. Many tax attorneys were quick to realize the unique opportunities these esoteric laws offered to their more adventurous and astute clientele.

Under the tax laws of the early Seventies, a properly drafted foreign trust—even though established by a United States citizen or resident and funded with United States assets for the purpose of benefiting United States citizens or residents—could legally escape the imposition of tax because it was treated as a "non-resident alien" for U.S. tax purposes, thus the correctly administered foreign trust could accumulate its gains wholly free of any tax. Kindly note, however, that the United States tax laws that blessed these means of avoiding taxation were extinguished long ago.

As mentioned above, and as a function of the artistic license that percolates throughout all works of fiction, the notable exception to the context of reality into which this intrigue is set consists of some elements of computer technology unavailable to the general public until the early Eighties.

THE HAVEN

HIGHRIDGE, Bay Area suburb Monday a.m. - February 25, 1974

The clouds parted and a slash of bright winter sunlight fell across the shoulders of the tall woman who leapt up the steps to the Highridge Library. The sudden brilliance seemed to annoy the woman because her shoulders hunched even higher as she marched toward her wobbly reflection in the glass of the double-doored entrance. Rubbing her hands together in the cold, she appeared anxious to plunge into the golden gloom of the quiet sanctuary.

And indeed, today she was truly in need of its semi-darkness because she had to quickly find a hiding place where she could privately stuff her fury while putting a stop to the runner taking off in her brand new pantyhose. Just a moment ago, while perched on the hard edge of the wooden chair in the bank next door, she'd felt something pop—followed by that always ominous creep down the inside of her leg—and then she'd had to sit hunched up and still, like a prayerful supplicant at the altar of that pallid young jerk of an assistant manager.

Mrs. Clare inhaled deeply and forced her shoulders down. She knew she had better get the rest of herself completely composed before heading out for her office because she couldn't afford any more of her little accidents, especially on a morning like this.

The library, immediately next door to the Highridge Bank, would provide a perfect refuge, she thought, especially since it had always been the scene of her most Magellanic and magical discoveries. Just why this was so, she hadn't the foggiest. Maybe the place was charmed, or maybe *she* was charmed, because whenever she faced a deadline and was desperately in need of a quick fix to a particularly thorny tax problem she knew she could always find it right here. She would slip downstairs to the law library, and after heading for the region where she suspected the answer lurked, she would wander aimlessly through the stacks, stop without knowing why, and then reach out and blindly grab the nearest book. Then she would close her eyes and insert her fingernail into the pages, crack the book open, and *lo!* there it would be: the information she needed, smiling up at her from the page. She'd done this five times already.

This never happened in her law office or anywhere else. Only here; reaffirming her belief that magic had its own special place—and it certainly added some spice—in an otherwise orderly, rational life.

Today, more than ever, she needed some reaffirmation of her powers, especially after having just been made to feel so small. And she was still boiling with anger, not because of her pantyhose, or the soggy prospect of having to return home to change into another pair, but because of that puke-faced banker next door. She wanted to kill him. The jerk who thought he could jerk her around. A small, bloodless murder would be nice, thought Mrs. Clare, and she instantly conjured up a handful of Mama N'dobah's needles and drove one of them deep into the pulpy midsection of the asexual-looking young man whom she knew was still lording it over his desk. He had humiliated her something awful.

Yes, he was going to die young, Mrs. Clare again said to herself, and she didn't care if she was a white woman dabbling in the darker arts—Mama N'dobah had taught her well. She drew another sharp needle from Mama

N'dobah's basket, this time even longer, long enough to transfix his pale Adam's apple and then, just as the proper image of his scrawny neck was framed in her mind, she felt her right shoe catch against the top step.

The tight pump did not leave her foot, instead, she felt its slender high heel give a sharp crick. Had she torn it off? Was it a fatal? Mrs. Clare did not want to look down, instead, she quickly stomped down on it, hard, and felt the heel click back into place. She took one more step to test the heel and was relieved to find it was going to hold—she'd just better keep in mind not to make any fancy fast moves in this pair of pumps, was all. Moving a bit slower now, each step a firm rap on the concrete, she approached the door. She would not return home. Going home now for any reason would make her feel thwarted, and she hated that feeling most of all. Especially now that she was all packed and ready to go. She was determined to move forward, onward and upward; never backward.

Pleased that she'd so neatly avoided a problem with her shoe, Mrs. Clare's thoughts immediately returned to stapling the young banker to the top of his desk. It was at that very instant, when she had him pinned down, that the brass door handle slipped out of her grasp and she felt her fingernail break. "Oh no! There really *is* a God," she wailed to herself, "and He's warning me to lay off the thought-crimes!" Mrs. Clare, never one for organized religion, still thought about covering her bases and crossing herself, just for good luck. But she didn't, of course. Instead, she pushed on the cumbersome door and felt it move easily under her hand. This came as no surprise because, after working out at the gym for a year, she was now very strong.

The librarian at the front desk didn't bother to look up as she slipped inside and made for the stacks. She would not go downstairs to the law library. Since she was the only woman lawyer in town, she knew all the men downstairs would want to stop and stare at her. She would have to remain on the main floor because what she needed was absolute privacy. The runner had to be fixed at once before it ran any further . . . she'd already seen its sharp tongue poking out from under the hem of her power-suit when she was sitting down.

Mrs. Clare glided toward the end of the row of shelves in the row marked "G" and when she reached the wall, she turned around, pulled out a shelf rest where she could set her purse and then rummaged around in it until she found the bottle of clear nail polish she carried with her just for problems like this. Retrieving the bottle, she carefully twisted it open and set it up on the book shelf, next to her nose. She looked around, then hiked up her skirt. The runner, beginning somewhere high on her inside thigh, had only reached a point four inches above her knee. She was saved. Placing a dab of nail lacquer on the tip of the runner's pointed tongue, Mrs. Clare now only had to wait until it was dry.

Having managed to dodge this small catastrophe, Mrs. Clare paid more attention to the books on the shelf. Directly in front of her nose sat a slim paperback volume and the words on its spine said: *Lafcadio's Adventures* by *André Gide*. What's this? she wondered. Holding the wetted nylon away from her thigh with one hand, she plucked the small book from the shelf with the other and then stood there while the polish was drying to scan its back cover: "André Gide *Winner of* THE NOBEL PRIZE *for* LITERATURE," it said.

Now that's promising, said Mrs. Clare to herself. She skipped to the paragraph at the center of the back cover and read: "Gide's preoccupation with *the idea of the unmotivated crime* here achieves its most extended treatment, and Lafcadio—one of the most original creations in all modern fiction—is the instrument of the crime. This is Gide at his best . . ."

Forgetting all about the lacquer drying on her nylons, Mrs. Clare let them go so she could insert her broken fingernail into the pages, then she opened the book to see what enlightenment would spring up at her from the randomly selected page. She blinked expectantly, then met Lafcadio head on:

Lafcadio was in a passenger compartment of a train hurtling through the dark countryside. He was not alone. Another man sat near him and Lafcadio was entertaining the thought of destroying him. Literally. By opening the door and pushing the man from the train. Why would he do this? wondered Mrs. Clare. She read on and divined that this Lafcadio was obsessed with the idea of committing a crime for no reason, simply to see what would happen—especially to him—for Lafcadio was thinking: *"A crime without a motive . . . what a puzzle for the police . . . It's not so much about events that I'm curious, as about myself."*

Who was this Lafcadio? wondered Mrs. Clare. Obviously a man. Obviously full of guile. But young or old? Rich or poor? Ugly or handsome? Mrs. Clare was drawn on, fascinated that she should find herself standing with a potential killer on the threshold of the crime which he was about to commit. She drank in Lafcadio's preliminary musings about perhaps being observed, and his flippant dismissal of all such concerns: *"Pooh!"* Lafcadio was saying. *"If one could foresee all the risks, there'd be no interest in the game!"*

It seemed incredible to Mrs. Clare that her very first encounter with this notorious Lafcadio should be exactly when he was in the midst of his ruminations about committing this senseless act—a murder without motive—for it now seemed clear that Lafcadio was not acquainted with his victim. She examined his further thoughts which poured forth on the following page as he moved toward the ultimate act: *"Here, just under my hand the double fastening—now that he's looking away and not paying attention—upon, my soul, it's easier to undo than I thought. If I can count up to twelve, without hurrying, before I see a light in the countryside, the dromedary is saved. Here goes! One, two, three, four (slowly, slowly!), five, six, seven, eight, nine . . . a light! . . ."* With that, Lafcadio unfastened the door, gave a push, and sent the poor camel flying into his final dark night.

Killing merely for the sake of self-exploration. How wasteful, thought Mrs. Clare. Then she wondered: Would such a killing be regarded as the act of a mad man? Could such a crime be made to seem devoid of *mens rea*? Without malice of forethought? Somehow lacking in specific intent? Something like this was not to her liking. If *she* were to kill, it would be with oodles and oodles of malice and intent to spare. And she knew just whom she wanted to kill. That damned twit banker sitting right next door. Yes! thought Mrs. Clare. Intent! Malice! And plenty of forethought. *That* was for her!

Mrs. Clare closed the book. She wanted to know more about this Lafcadio—there were so many questions she needed to ask of him—and for a moment she thought about shoving the book into her handbag. Or tearing out the book's pages and leaving behind only its cover. But she couldn't. Although she harbored no qualms about thinking about killing, she refused to countenance any ideas about stealing or even defacing a library book. She turned the spine of the book toward the back of the shelf and proceeded to shove it deep between the other books where it wouldn't be seen so that it would remain available for her and her alone to retrieve as soon as she returned from her trip.

It was only then, while she was reshelving the book, that it occurred to her to wonder what it was she had stumbled upon, for if this book was an answer, then what was the question supposed to be?

Mrs. Clare's thoughts were abruptly interrupted—something was moving, glittering like a bright snake in the corner of her eye. Slithering slowly down the entire length of the metal shelf post. Then she caught a strong whiff of acetone and spied the overturned bottle of nail polish.

Oh God! What a mess! A small pool of nail polish gleamed on the shelf and another on the floor. Now she was in for it! Linnell pawed frantically in her purse for tissues or a handkerchief to mop it up. There were none. There was no alternative: she'd have to leave things the way they were and hotfoot it out of there. Mrs. Clare looked longingly at the book, then filled to the brim with *mens rea*, she grabbed her purse and ran, not toward her husband—certainly not toward him!—but toward Charles. She needed to bury herself deep in his leathery embrace. Oblivious to the dried polish that now plucked her thigh with every quick step, Mrs. Clare hastened from the library and down the steps toward where she knew her beloved Charles would be waiting for her.

Highridge, California **9 a.m. Monday - February 25, 1974**

"So you wanna 'nother cup of coffee, Harold?"

Harold Dolphe, the most junior of the associates poked his head out of his cubicle. His heart gave a little thrill because, like never before, Margarita's tinny voice sounded so anxious to please. Then he glanced at her out of the corner of his eye and caught her sticking her tongue out at him.

"Just checking," Margarita smirked. "You want coffee? Go get it yourself!"

Harold glowered at the secretary and the impudent woman grinned back at him and began making those hyena-like, hooting sounds he hated so much. With his freckled face flushing as red as his hair, the young man rudely signaled for her to be quiet because he could see that the door to the big tuna's private office was now standing wide open. Margarita, letting her jaw drop inside her closed mouth, just widened her eyes and kept staring at him as if he were a moron.

Harold crept warily out of his cubicle.

So! he thought. Margarita wanted to be a bitch? Fine. Let her be a bitch. Besides, he wanted to check things out for himself, and going to the kitchen would give him another excuse to pass by Mr. Ivener's private office. Harold knew something was coming down because every day for the last five days—he'd been counting—Mr. Ivener had kept his drapes pulled shut and his door tightly closed, as had the two doddering senior associates, Ivener's rubber-stamps, whose offices adjoined Ivener's on either side. That is, they had until early this morning, when Harold, detecting another flurry of activity, had seen the two seniors departing in haste—books and boxes in tow. No explanation for this had been offered, but something important must have happened earlier this morning because the inexplicable tightness that had been souring the air for weeks now seemed to have vanished entirely.

Pointedly ignoring Margarita, Harold cast his eyes all about the law office. Papers oozed in great sheaves from the shelves of the pricey antique armoires that lined all the halls and every interior wall of the two-story hundred-year-old building—a tastefully refurbished Maybeck-style mansion.

Once the residence of a successful gold prospector, the shingled manse crouched high inside its nest of gnarled wisteria, and with its vine-covered upper balustrades reaching out over the palms like paws, it invariably reminded Harold of a begging dog. So whenever Harold looked at the office from afar, he liked to imagine that the entire structure was making ready to leap over the trees for a chase down the freeway to a more sophisticated city, San Francisco. He also knew that the building would acquire an almost comical expression of walleyed puzzlement should the heavy brocade draperies be drawn halfway across the two round top floor windows—a look which belied the more serious, sometimes desperate, endeavors being conducted inside its vine-guarded belly. Sometimes Harold would even sneak up to the top floor and arrange this himself. His little joke when Mr. Ivener, the senior partner, would get too demanding.

Actually, there was no need to escape Highridge. The town had everything one could want, just on a smaller scale than San Francisco. And despite its faint aura of hicksville, it was now seen as one of the more glistening pearls on the hem of the bigger-city-on-the-bay. Highridge had its origins in a small stagecoach watering station in the late 1880s. The station gradually grew and then after WWII it suddenly blossomed into a model of perfect municipal harmony. Now it sported its own small city hall, its own newspaper, and its very own coterie of back-scratching bureaucrats and businessmen, all served by a solicitous squadron of blatting lawyers who industriously curried favor with same. And just like a tribe of great apes, they were all accustomed to the polite daily grooming they received at the hands of the eager event-coordinators who passed for reporters at the Highridge Daily News. Imitating the wealthier residents of nearby Atherton and Hillsborough, Highridge's increasingly wealthy denizens took great pride in seeming to live quietly and in near anonymity.

Harold, whose attention was ordinarily devoted to plotting how he would become the greatest ape of them all, was at the moment more interested in local matters of ingress and egress than his eventual place in the simian hierarchy. For instance, he knew that the two offices—formerly bedrooms—flanking Ivener's quarters had closets whose doors allowed passage into the senior partner's inner sanctum. This allowed the three old gents to hunker down together without the staff getting wind of it. Harold had kept this to himself. A firm believer in knowledge as power, he had made it his first order of business to learn when the closet doors were left unlocked, and now he was wondering if they would remain in this happy state given the sudden departure of the two senior associates.

William E. Ivener's private office was the best in every respect. It faced south, overlooking the street, and his Louis XV desk was placed at an angle next to the brocade-draped windows, which allowed the old slasher to simultaneously keep a watchful eye on both vehicular and office traffic. A long-standing rumor had it that all the front windows were plated with bulletproof glass, so the first thing Harold did when he arrived at the firm was to ask whether old Ivener hadn't developed a touch of paranoia—which had prompted old Ivener to laugh not too kindly and to wonder aloud if young Harold wasn't too late in developing a small touch of paranoia for himself. But since this was a tax firm—a flamboyant firm that was proud to joust regularly with the Internal Revenue Service—Harold soon learned that paranoia in any amount was no cause for shame, thus his impertinent questioning was allowed to pass without the imposition of any official discipline. In fact, as he had later come to realize, paranoia was the very key to survival in any tax firm. Everybody here exhibited it in good measure—all, that is, except Willy Ivener, it seemed. And as Harold knew all too well, Ivener was always eager to give the IRS another picture of his arrogant backside. As for the windows, Harold still didn't know if they were bulletproof because the staff had made it a game not to tell him.

Willy. That's what the senior partner preferred to be called. Harold had regarded such familiarity as the phoniest of affectations, but since Mrs. Clare, "Call me "L.C." "—the femme law associate who had once worked here—had found it so easy to address the senior partner by his first name, he'd decided he wouldn't. Besides, Willy was a name that felt hairy on his tongue. So, for him it was always "Ivener" and sometimes even "Mr. Ivener." And he was glad that L.C. had left the firm. Glad and relieved.

Returning from the kitchen with a cup of coffee in one hand and two donuts in the other, Harold strolled slowly past Ivener's open door and saw that the great man was now sitting behind his desk. Harold slid his eyes sideways to take in as much as he could without actually stopping to gawk. There was the ubiquitous world time-clock found in every cubicle—even the clerks'—except Ivener's was larger and far more elaborate. Prominently displayed on Ivener's desk was a sterling-framed photograph of his second, or maybe it was his third, wife—a big-chested, narrow-waisted blonde, packed into tailored pinks and sitting stiff-backed astride an Arabian. Harold stared at the photo hungrily and bit off a full three-quarters of the donut. He could tell that she was the genuine article and he had to admit, she certainly lent the old man a touch of panache. Lucky Ivener—even if all he could do now was look.

Harold shoved the remainder of the donut in his mouth and the symphony of soft melting sweetness that flowed over his tongue was echoed by the expression of bliss that slowly stole over his face. It was all just too wonderful—because someday, yes someday he, too, would be able to afford a woman like that.

His eyes next fastened greedily on the huge Baccarat ash tray holding Ivener's Buccellati cuff links and Patek Philippe watch—solid gold, not merely plated like his—and automatically took inventory of Ivener's apparel. Every now and then, apparently just to liven things up, Ivener would appear in something mind-boggling. Only yesterday, and the first time in months, it had been the hand-painted Pucci silk shirt—must've cost $2000—tossed over a butt-hugging pair of white satin flares. And those red velvet Turkish slippers! It was crazy. Things like this made him worry about what was really going on in the old man's head. But then, when Ivener wore a suit, it was comforting to know that it would always be something normal, always the very same sort of conservative, dark gray, Savile Road pin-striper. Today, Harold was relieved to see, it was the suit; the jacket now hung from the high corner of Ivener's maroon, tufted glove leather chair. The style: casual luxe. Yes, he could do that number, and better than Ivener, Harold assured himself. And he would, too, just as soon as he got his raise.

Harold slowed, then forgetting himself, stopped dead in his tracks. "If something's been eating at him," thought Harold, "it sure doesn't seem to be bothering him now." Biting off half of his second donut, Harold again eyed Ivener's possessions covetously, then scrutinized his lord and master. Ivener, who was never one to delegate when it came to significant matters, was speaking rapidly into the receiver—then he began to scribble furiously, his spatulate, translucent fingers working rapidly across the top sheet of an enormous yellow pad. Probably setting up a schedule of bank-wire transfers, Harold guessed.

Clearly intoxicated by the aroma of wealth that wafted from the senior partner's environs, Harold sniffed the air while he stared at the top of Ivener's bowed head and the pale boiled egg scalp he saw peeking at him from between Ivener's colored strands suddenly inspired him to wonder if a candling of Ivener's skull would reveal just what sort of monster was squirming inside. Then something new caught his eye: the soft web of swollen vessels that now tracked the bony indentations at Ivener's temples. Harold's nostrils suddenly flared with excitement. This most recent wave of tremors—might they have had something to do with the senior partner's health? Harold considered this for a moment, then smiled—maybe, just maybe, Ivener's pallor was due to a life-shortening bout of anemia. A bleeding ulcer perhaps?

But Ivener's energetic demeanor belied his cadaverous appearance. His firm hand when he set the phone in its cradle, the animated manner in which he snapped off the scrambler and his satisfied air as he rolled down his cuffs proclaimed that all was well in the world of Ivener.

Harold was startled by Ivener's voice. "Why don't you come in here, Harold?" Ivener addressed Harold without looking up. Ivener then raised his head to stare back at Harold and Harold saw the furrows running down from each side of Ivener's thin nose suddenly deepening into grayish creases.

With his hands full of coffee and the crumbling donut, Harold remained frozen on Ivener's threshold. He squinted even more intently and was relieved to see that Ivener was apparently smiling at him.

"That's quite *all right*, Harold. Stop your snuffling, you can finish that in here." Ivener spoke with his usual humorless grin, showing Harold a complete set of sharp ivory-colored teeth.

Harold knew better. He shoved the remains of his donut deep in his mouth, washed it down with a big gulp of coffee and then reaching out without looking, slammed the half empty cup down on Margarita's desk. A split-second later he heard dollops of liquid smacking paper. *That* would teach her to torment him.

Harold stepped forward. He couldn't resist. He had to see what the boss was up to. Choosing the chair closest to Ivener's desk, Harold sat down and began to blink rapidly to make it appear that he wasn't trying to scan the yellow ledger that lay under his nose. With each glance, however, he was able to take in more information. The ledger itself was unique—it was not the usual compendium of boring figure-filled columns, but rather, a map—a map of the United States, the Caribbean, and the Far East—criss-crossed with long arrows with numbers to show the chronological order of the international bank wire transfers that looped from city-to-city and bank-to-bank. Today, all arrows were aimed toward the center of the Caribbean. Harold's eyes glazed when he saw the amounts jotted along the trajectory of each arc, and he almost forgot to blink when he saw that Ivener had been operating his system on behalf of a client noted only as "The W."

"Someday . . . soon, I hope . . . you'll come to understand what all of this means," Ivener murmured, pulling the ledger sheet from its pad. With a deliberate air of mystery, eyes twinkling, he slowly folded it in half and fed it into the shredder under his desk.

Harold kept a straight face while he listened in frustration to the sound of grinding secrets; he couldn't afford to let Ivener in on a little secret of his own: He already knew, or at least, he thought he knew what Ivener was up to . . . and for whom. Smiling ingenuously, Harold replied, "I just thought I'd drop in to see if you still want me to take that little trip you mentioned last week."

Ten minutes later, Harold emerged from Willy Ivener's private office smiling an entirely different sort of smile which he carried triumphantly toward a sullen Margarita.

"I understand you have some tickets for me." Harold spoke smugly, managing to sound more like an arrogant child than the *senior* law associate—Ivener had bumped him up over all the rest of the associates—he'd just become. Then his smile broadened into a moist grin. It had worked. All of his brown-nosing and puppy-like fawning had paid off—and far sooner than he'd expected. Harold stuck his hand out over Margarita's desk, palm up, his fingers stopping inches short of her lumpy, unsmiling face.

Not bothering to reply, Margarita reached for a packet in her out-basket and slapped Harold's airline tickets to the Cayman Islands on the outside corner of her desk. Harold noticed that one end of the packet was soggy with coffee and now regretted that he'd added so much sugar.

LUCK

HIGHRIDGE **9 a.m. Monday - February 25, 1974**

Woe, woe unto woman;
For she shall not succeed
To the lands of her noble ancestors,
Nor to the fruits of the golden tree.

Woe, woe unto woman;
For she shall possess no things
Except through the dispensation of a man,
And her issue shall take nothing
through her by descent.

Lex Salica—*Clovis,* ca.510A.D.*(paraphrased)*

Intending to head for her office, Mrs. Clare drove like an automaton, deep in thought. When she finally came to, she realized she had driven, instead, toward the law office of William E. Ivener, her former employer. She was now only a hundred yards from his door.

"No!" Mrs. Clare spoke aloud. Willy Ivener was the last man on earth she wanted to see. She quickly turned the wheel with one finger and sent her Jaguar sedan around the corner and then, without braking, let it glide through the pale bars of pollen-filled sunshine filtering down through the palms.

She looked all around her, astonished. She had lived here in Highridge for almost ten years and yet she had never been on this street before. How surprising it was to find this wonderful residential neighborhood, lush with foliage and manicured lawns only one block away from the main drag of town! Letting her sedan roll to a stop at the curb, Linnell Clare cut the engine, dropped her car keys into her handbag, and let her head fall back against the padded headrest. She was at last feeling the full effect of getting only four hours of sleep the night before.

A small groan of exasperation escaped her lips. Then she yawned and caressed Charles' leather-clad steering wheel. Sometimes it felt as if her car was her only friend. Her husband, Bear, had surprised her with it on her thirty-fifth birthday, and now, six months later, her fragrance, with its light note of freesia, had combined perfectly with the libidinous scent of its glove leather upholstery. Thinking of it as a "him," she had named her car Charles, and every day when she greeted her precious Charles, she would recall that for one fleeting instant she had actually considered refusing the gift out of fear that should Bear ever ask her to close her office, she'd be obliged to obey. Now, however, she was glad she had not given in to such dismal thoughts, because Bear had *really* surprised her: He'd produced no such ultimatum and had made no demands. None whatsoever—although she sometimes had a sneaking suspicion that some might be coming.

But never mind about that. Right *now* was what mattered. And right now she was utterly miserable, alone with Charles—a machine. The only male she could handle, she thought ruefully. Well, that's how it seemed, especially after what had just happened to her at the bank. Mrs. Clare was still trying to blot it all out of her mind. She lifted a fine-boned hand to shade her eyes while she looked around. For a Monday morning, the streets seemed surprisingly busy. But what would she know? She hadn't been out of her office—especially this time of day—for such a long time that the whole town looked unfamiliar. She felt like a stranger. Nonetheless, Willy Ivener still was the last man on earth she wanted to bump into. Especially the way she felt now: frazzled and just this side of a flaming rage, but barely.

Willy was the one who had warned her. He was the one who had said: "You want to leave to set up your own law office? Well, that's fine, but you'll see—it's not going to be so easy, m'dear."

She had submitted her resignation to him anyway. That had been over a year ago and now she knew he'd been right. Even so, she was *not* going to give him the satisfaction of letting him see her sweat.

Besides, as far as she was concerned, nothing ever came easy, especially if it was something she really wanted. It was always work, work, work! There seemed to be some kind of rule of thumb about this, something about how it took only 10 percent of the lawyers to sop up 90 percent of the gravy—which left only very thin pickings for the rest of them. To escape this dilemma a young lawyer had to establish a niche, some kind of specialty, and she was working on one for herself right now. In any event, she now understood why so many lawyers high-tailed it to Washington. It wasn't the law that drew them to politics so much as it was the security of the per diems, the taxpayer-funded pensions and medical plans, the lucrative speaking fees, and all the rest. Maybe that's where she should have headed, she thought, because now, here she was—a tax attorney—one who was hot on the trail of some really big gravy, and now caught up in what could become a really big mess. Worse yet, one entirely of her own making.

Mrs. Clare suddenly froze and her hands turned clammy: What if it were true? That life was really nothing more than a joke? A big, long, bad joke; one she was forever destined to never get. Maybe that's what her husband really meant when he said that she just didn't "Get it"—which was something *he* all of a sudden apparently did, now that he was so firmly plugged into The Wei.

"The Wei! Sea urchins! Me! Bear! It's *all* so ridiculous!" Mrs. Clare exclaimed angrily. Then she jumped out of her car, flung open the rear door, and felt her skirt twisting as she slid across the back seat.

Mrs. Clare—Linnell Leigh Clare—"L.C." to those who knew her professionally and just plain "Ma" to her husband—now sat slumped in sweaty discomfort on the soft caramel-colored leather. She couldn't trust herself to sit behind the wheel a second longer because she was still in such a killer mood that she feared she just might reach out, turn the key, rev the engine, and send Charles' three hundred horses flying back to Main Street so he could hurtle straight through the plate glass door, across the shiny marble-floored bank lobby and over the desk of the worm who had just turned her down.

All she had asked for was another bank account—and he had refused! He had looked at her smugly and replied no-can-do. No can do! The phony snot—ten years her junior, too—had even grinned at her over the steeple he'd made of his thin milk-blue fingers. He'd smacked his wet lips and then told her that she would *not* be allowed to establish another bank account unless she brought him her husband's written consent. When she had pointed out to him that there was a new law called the Women's Property Rights Act, he had laughed. Right in her face. Then he said he'd never heard of it and that even if there was such a law, this didn't give her any right to come marching in there, yelling about how they should run their bank.

She hadn't yelled. She had been very polite. And she'd had no chance at all to make a scene because he'd cut her off with his little lecture: The bank had its policies, and one of them was that a married woman, even if she was a lawyer, had to obtain her husband's written consent each and every time she opened a new bank account. *Every* time. No exceptions. And the fact that Dr. Clare could establish as many accounts as he liked, and without her consent, made no difference to him. And furthermore, he'd rattled on, the fact that her husband had already consented to her having a business account for her law office was "Not of itself a sufficient basis to warrant any exceptions to their rules." He must have seen the rage flickering in her eyes because he'd quickly jumped up to hand her an account application and then, with a yank to his vest, he'd let her know in no uncertain terms that she'd better be leaving.

He expected her to hop to it, did he? To scamper back to her husband with the worm's little square of white cardboard clutched tight in her hand? To hold out her bowl like a needy waif and beg her big daddy for just one more scoop of approval? No way! Linnell fought back tears of frustration. She'd wanted a new bank account because this was where she had been planning to bank-wire the profits from the secret venture she'd been plotting and scheming and slaving on all this past year. She'd wanted to surprise Bear on his birthday. She'd had this big dream of slipping Bear the spanking-new bank book at his birthday dinner and then blushing modestly. Yes, okay, the money would be their community property and it would still belong to the both of them, but the account was important! It would be a tangible sign of their equality and not incidentally, her talent and skill. Of course, and this was something she had to keep to herself, it was all part of a much larger scheme and a grander plan. And now this hitch! It was truly infuriating!

How had she ended up like this? Having jittery fits in Charles' back seat? Well, the answer to that one was: luck. Good and bad.

It had all begun as an impetuous gesture. In the beginning, all she'd wanted was to do something wonderful for Bear. Something so grand that it would compensate for all those years she'd spent grinding over her law books. But most of all, she'd wanted to do something to surprise him so she could see, once again, his still handsome face lighting up with genuine pleasure. The way it once did before he became so immersed in that damn dental practice of his. But then, as her secret project became ever more complicated over this past year, other motives had somehow crept in. An element of cunning, for one. And then pride—because as things became increasingly difficult, she'd become even more determined to prove that she had what it took to succeed. And finally, over the last several months, as Bear, the primary beneficiary of all this hoped-for largesse, appeared to be withdrawing from her, a pinch of desperation was added to this already too-complex melange.

The plan, her top-secret scheme, had begun by accident the year before, over Easter break when Benjy and Bear accompanied her on a trip to the Caribbean to visit Grand Cayman Island—where she now went every quarter to attend to her client's foreign trusts. This family vacation had been made possible because, happily, with her very first case she'd collected enough fees to pay for everything—air fares as well—and thus for the very first time the three of them were spending the entire Easter vacation together.

And her good luck had begun the afternoon they took their first hike on the beach, although this wasn't immediately apparent at the time because, while they were splashing through the shallows in front of their hotel, Bear pierced his toe on a sea urchin quill. He'd screamed and then shocked her by throwing a terrible tantrum, making it clear to her and everyone else on the beach that as far as he was concerned, the entire trip was a flop. After calming him down and seeing him up to their room so he could recover, she and Benjy had the rest of the day to themselves.

At first she'd been depressed by Bear's angry behavior, but as the day wore on, her spirits improved through her efforts to entertain Benjy. She took him snorkeling in the shallows in front of their hotel and they had ended up marveling at the huge skeins of sea urchins—glistening black, big as baseballs, with long lethal spines—that appeared to stretch for miles and miles immediately off shore. She and Benjy estimated that no less than two million of them inhabited the waters just in front of the hotel. In some places the urchins were so densely packed that they had piled into ominous underwater reefs. Benjy caught one and very cautiously cracked it open to see what was inside and when she saw what there was, her eyes almost popped out of her head.

A mound of glistening dark beads. Treasure! Sea urchin roe!

Bear, apparently still uncomfortable, wanted to stay in his room that evening, so she and Benjy ate dinner outdoors at the beach bar. Benjy told the waiter all about the millions of sea urchins he'd seen and then the waiter informed them that he had no love for urchins. They were a menace, he said, and likely to ruin their business because for the first time in years, they were invading the waters where the guests liked to swim. The guests had begun to complain about injuries and the management was worried.

As soon as Benjy ran off to play, Linnell found the manager and asked him whether he'd made any plans to get rid of the sea urchins. The instant he said no, she offered to solve all their problems and thus that same evening she acquired the exclusive right to harvest the sea urchins in front of the hotel. Linnell knew what others had apparently failed to grasp: that sea urchin roe was a prized delicacy in Japan. It had been her good fortune to be the first to recognize that she could export them to Tokyo, where sea urchin roe—not to mention the meat—was now fetching $20 *per ounce*!

Trouble was, she didn't know exactly how she was going to get the prickly things out of the water let alone all the way to Japan. Nonetheless, as soon as she returned home, she'd shared her plans to become an international exporter with her secretary, Karen. They dubbed the new enterprise "The

Project," code words she'd chosen for the sea urchin caper. Using code always made things seem far more exciting than they really were and besides, you never could tell—there always were troublemakers and snoops, eager to stir up some difficulties in order to force you to give them a free ride on your coat tails.

In the beginning, she had tried to tell Bear what she was planning to do. But he had just glanced at her with that faraway look of his, then gone back to staring at television. That was what gave her the idea not to tell him at all so she surprise him with it as a gift on his birthday.

After overcoming the first hurdle—finding a Japanese broker willing to do business with a woman—she'd attacked the more mundane matters of obtaining permits, leasing a warehouse, solving the refrigeration problems, developing harvesting methods and conservation policies—not to mention her $3000 phone bill. All this merely to get the project off the ground. And since she was determined to go the whole nine yards, she'd also hired a dive master and paid him a large advance to ensure that his diving crew, twenty in all, would be ready to get to work the instant she set foot on the island.

She'd come up with a plan for harvesting the sea urchins. So far, and although it still was all theory, her faith in her ideas had been unwavering—until today, when for the very first time she had allowed herself to admit, at least to herself, that she didn't know whether her brilliant ideas were going to work. But if not, if she failed, she was going to be stuck with thousands of dollars of useless dredging equipment, which would be followed, she feared, by a bitter divorce.

For the last twelve months, almost all of her income had gone to pay for the sea urchin project, and she'd told Bear one story after another to cover things up. In fact, she'd become so engrossed in trying to make The Project a success that she'd ended up scarcely paying attention to anything else. "Prioritizing," was what she called it, which helped save her sanity while she was so busy keeping everything secret and under control. But just lately she had begun to wonder if being so focused had been a mistake, because sometimes she would get this strange feeling that something odd was going on right under her nose. Then she'd dismiss it, simply chalk it all up to her imagination. How could something be going on? Impossible. She knew Bear—he was always so busy with his practice. And when he was home, well, things always were so predictable, the boredom was literally stifling. But still, being so bored was vastly superior, she supposed, to the lot of some other wives. In fact, she knew one wife in particular whose husband thought nothing of sneaking around.

But there was absolutely no reason for her to worry about Bear. At least not about something like that. Because day in and day out, he could always be found slaving away at his office, and almost every other night he attended The Wei. He had enrolled in all of their programs—*life-training sessions*—usually held at the Highridge High School Gym. His dental practice and The Wei. And yes, television. They seemed to be the only things that held his interest these days. She knew that she hadn't tried very hard to talk to him lately, which made her feel even more guilty—and guilty she felt, because more and more this past year, and while she was plotting to give her husband her monumental surprise, she had begun to entertain these small fantasies about how to escape him.

Maybe it was the stress—but the idea was always there, looming behind all her thoughts about tax law and sea urchins. She would think about cheating. With this man she was slowly constructing inside her head. He would have a great body—muscular shoulders, good hands and legs—and most important, he would not be as tall or as broad as Bear because she wanted a man she didn't have to climb. She hadn't gotten around to fashioning her dream-lover's brain, or for that matter, his eyes; she was saving this part for last. But still, committing thought crimes was as far as it ever got. And she had always taken the greatest pains to never, *ever* give Bear even the slightest reason to worry about her.

Struggling to make herself comfortable, Linnell yanked the tails of her blouse out from under her, flapped them like fans and then slid farther down in the car seat. She was relieved that all of this complicated business was about to come to a head. Because if she was lucky tomorrow—not *if,* she reminded herself to think positive, but *when*—then they would at last have enough money and then both of them could leap off the treadmill and start living a real life together. Yes, together. After fourteen years of a hectic, nose-to-the-grindstone marriage—time had passed so swiftly—they would finally be able to afford to take all the time they needed to *really* get to know each other, and then there'd be no more of this stupid "You-Just-Don't-Get-It" stuff.

That's why she had to follow through with the project. It might have begun as an impetuous gesture, but it had become a most serious undertaking . . . and this was because she simply couldn't go on the way things were now. She just had to change things, especially on the home front. And she knew that she could, because Linnell Leigh Clare was a woman of action. Hadn't somebody described her as: *The One Most Likely to Do Something About It*? . . . Yes, somebody had. In her college yearbook. She could have just as easily been described as ". . . the owl; the brain; the girl most likely to be found in the library on a Saturday night." Mercifully, instead of this, a classmate had scrawled a few words that had left her feeling secretly flattered that someone saw her more as an action hero than the earnest student she'd been in those days.

Yes, without question, the whole thing had become rather complicated; but still, The Project was an altogether clever scheme, and if she had Bear figured right—and this was the part that was cunning—her gift would also serve to persuade him to do something he had so far stubbornly refused to do: Tell her the truth about their finances.

People might think her being a lawyer meant that she had a handle on everything, but the truth was—and it was a rather embarrassing truth given that she was a tax attorney—she had no idea how much money they really had. For all she knew, they could be tottering on the brink of bankruptcy. Highly unlikely, of course, but still, if you got right down to it, she hadn't a clue. However, whatever it amounted to, it was hers, too. That is to say, half was—including the debts—because this was a community property state, which meant that each spouse had to pick up the tab for the other, especially if they were living on borrowed money. It was only recently that the law had been changed to give the wife any say about how their property was managed. Unfortunately, there weren't any laws to compel a husband to reveal what they really had, and personally, she worried about this because they were living very grandly now, and she'd feel a whole lot better if she knew they could actually afford it.

Bear liked to say that money was power, which no doubt explained why he worked all the time. She'd had a slight taste of this sort of power herself, but only indirectly, through her clients, so it wasn't the same. She didn't know if money could buy happiness—she'd never had enough of it to try—although it had been her experience that money could certainly buy a whole lot of relief from pain. Bear had a different way of putting it: *Money is power . . . 'cause people will kiss your ass if you got the bucks.* For a college grad, he sure knew how to talk rough. Of course, she knew he was just joking around in order to divert her, which he usually did whenever she wandered into such touchy subjects as the state of their finances. But it was his stubborn secretiveness that made her even more curious about how much they really had and what sort of power their money bought. And most important of all, she wanted to have some power in her own right, because right now all she had was the little derived through being a wife—and this was obviously very little, as had been made so painfully clear to her, earlier this morning.

Power. And learning how best to use it. That's what she *really* was after. It wasn't the money, or the things she could purchase with it that intrigued her half so much as the effect it would have on her and the people around her. She was curious: Did a man regard, and thus *use* money differently than would a woman? And if she had her own money, would she get the same bang from a buck as a man? And really, why *shouldn't* she have power? What was the problem here? Why did Bear fear he'd have less if she had more? And that snotty little banker! What was *his* problem? All she had asked him for was a stinking bank account! It just wasn't fair! Linnell Clare looked down and saw that she was holding the bank's signature card and that she'd dog-eared it beyond recognition.

For the first time in all these past twelve months, she felt her confidence slipping. Painfully aware of this tide of self-doubt, Linnell took a deep breath, then feeling even more sticky and uncomfortable, she tore off the jacket of her navy-blue power-suit and yanked open the droopy silk bow that stood in place of a tie.

Her good luck had held all this past year, things had been running fairly smoothly—until last night, when her luck had begun to change. And not for the better. Thus, after twelve months of driving herself, slaving and swimming and working out at the club so she'd be strong enough to keep up with her divers, and the night before she was set to embark on the grandest, craziest gamble of her entire life—the night she had been *counting* on to get some much needed sleep—she'd ended up getting barely four hours, and this spelled disaster. Linnell yawned; just thinking about it made her eyes water.

Like any respectable tax attorney, she had stayed up past midnight to read some late-breaking tax law because she was still putting some finishing touches to her soon-to-be-published tell-all tax article about foreign foundations, an undertaking that held out the promise of changing her life. Well, that's what she hoped, although this was putting it a bit too dramatically. The article's intended effect was simply to enrich her still-fledgling law practice by drawing a new class of well-heeled clients to her door. She had written it cleverly, thus her article was riddled with detailed warnings about how the IRS might go about taxing foreign foundations—even though they were established offshore—and then she had laced it with alluring hints, suggesting that she already knew the best ways to circumvent all the terrible problems she was bringing to light. She'd completed her research around 1 a.m. and then after finishing her kitchen chores, she had slid into bed, only to find Bear lying in wait for her.

Yes, last night, for the first time in months, in fact, after four months of sulkily dismissing her entire repertoire of romantic overtures—all of a sudden, hurrah!—he had wanted to "do it." More precisely—amid much grunting and panting—he had tried. And tried and tried. Had he succeeded? Had anything actually happened? She wasn't quite sure because by the time he was ready—he had fiddled and pulled, even whacked—she'd been close to unconscious. Actually, she didn't want to remember because it had been that awful. Was something wrong with him? Or, like he said, was it all her fault?

Linnell squirmed with embarrassment—she had this vague recollection of him clawing at her new silk pajamas and mumbling a few words about her being a klutz. Yes, he'd actually said that. She had wanted to bat him, but instead, she'd said nothing because she hadn't wanted to get a fight started on her last night home before leaving for Cayman. And now that she thought about it, there was something else that puzzled her even more. Even if they hadn't actually done the deed, just how had Bear managed to suddenly find all the energy it took to attempt his crude efforts, such as they were? He usually was bushed from standing on his feet all day long, which was what he usually said. But last night there was something about him that was different. And if she didn't know better, she'd have to wonder if he'd gone back to running on dexies. Like when they were cramming for finals during their senior college year and he would give her those little dextroamphetamine pink valentines that keep you buzzing for days. They were called "hearts," and they'd cracked them in half to make their supply last through finals. But since then he'd sworn off them; she knew this for a fact because he'd promised her he would never again use anything stronger than coffee. So maybe last night—same as she—he was just running on nerves.

Linnell strove to recall something more. She was sure something else had happened, earlier that morning, but the harder she tried to recall what it was, the more it escaped her. This always happens, she told herself, when you try too hard. Linnell made a conscious effort to stop trying—more often then not things seemed to come her way just as soon as she stopped searching, especially if she pretended not to care.

This was not entirely true. There was One Big Thing she wanted very much, cared about very much, and there was no way she could pretend otherwise. Because, if they didn't do it last night, it meant that they hadn't done it for over three months. Maybe longer. Poor Benjy, dear Benjy—too wise for his years—he had been pestering them for a little brother or sister. Well, at this rate it sure looked like he wouldn't be getting one any too soon. Linnell sighed deeply. Like everyone said—the clock was ticking.

What she did remember from earlier that morning had to do with Bear and his strange rituals: Like usual, like clockwork, as if he were following a script—every morning he always did the same thing: He would rouse her at 6:30 a.m.—not because he needed to give her any kind of meaningful message, but apparently only for the sake of stirring her up. He'd poke at her until he knew she was awake and then he would tell her he loved her and then, when she would reach out to touch him, he'd run. Simply run away, as if he were a little boy—straight down the hall and out the front door. Then she would lie there, alone and seething with resentment, until the feeling subsided enough for her to fall back to sleep.

This routine had begun shortly after Benjy was born—and every day thereafter it had been the same. Exactly the same. Same words. Same moves. Same time. Like a terrible, unvarying, frozen script. And he would also call her office every day, shortly before noon, to tell her he loved her—he never had anything else to say and he never had time to meet her for lunch. Too busy, he'd say. At one time this had led her to believe he was having an affair and she had borrowed a car so she could hide outside his office and see for herself what he really was doing. And that's how she'd discovered he was telling her the truth—he really was too busy to see her, because as she saw, there were scads of patients—mostly men—streaming in and out of his office during their lunch hours.

But today, this morning, she was positive something more must have happened, something different from every other morning . . . because here it was again, this faint trace of the event, pieces of it floating loose inside her head, pecking on the membrane of her memory as if desperate to break in. What was it? Why couldn't she remember? Was she blocking something? No! Linnell shook her head and told herself she was just over-tired.

But she *could* recall what had happened later on. After she'd fallen back to sleep, Benjy had awakened her at 7:30 with his horrible new trick, the only trick Bear had ever bothered to teach him. Yes, it was easy for her to remember something like this because she simply *loathed* spiders. In fact, just thinking about them, especially the huge ones that hid in the tops of the eucalyptus trees, left her paralyzed with revulsion. So Benjy-the-spider-man, finding her fast asleep instead of up and stirring his Cream-o-Wheat, had run his little fingers across the back of her neck, causing her to wake with a wild shriek—poor Benjy had jumped ten feet. Yes, poor Benjy; she had understood—he was just in need of more attention.

Well, she'd be making it up to him as soon as she returned from her trip.

And she had a lot of making up to do.

After all, she was the wife, and the rules said that it was the wife's duty to go the distance no matter what; to be the helpmate and so wherever possible, to pour oil on troubled waters, and whenever necessary, to sell herself in order to buy the peace. And she had Benjy to think of—what would he do without a father and a nice place to call home? And how would she make it as a lawyer without her large husband? After all, it was her being half-a-couple that gave her some clout. This was the essential key, she was sure, to keeping the nastier of the Good Ol' Boys from doing worse than just talking dirty. Yes indeed, when it came to dusting it up with so many combative, testosterone-pumped men, being married—and to such a big man—certainly was a big help.

But sometimes she felt torn, as if her feet were planted on different continents, continents that were drifting ever more swiftly apart. There was the familiar old world of the Fifties—her mother's world—under whose rules Linnell had been raised. And then there was the exciting new world of the Seventies, with its determination to smash the tablets and *burn-baby-burn.* Maybe this explained why, more and more, she felt like an alternating current, switching instantaneously between love and hate whenever she thought about Bear. Well, she'd better try harder to put a cap on things, not let this sort of thinking get out of control, because the rules also said that it was up to the woman to hold things together. And that she should stand by her man. And of course, she would—she'd given Bear her word about that. And furthermore, she couldn't forget that since she was a lawyer, people would be counting on her to uphold the rules.

Linnell looked at her watch and panicked. She'd better put a swift halt to this pity party because she still had to get everything organized at her office before she could take off on the red-eye for Miami—and now she was so tired she couldn't even see straight! Maybe she ought to catch a few winks right here in the car? Linnell thought about it, then realized she actually could.

Linnell yawned drowsily. Onward and upward, she thought. She had already packed her bags, they were in the car trunk; all she really had left to do was to go to her office to pick up her briefcase, then head for the airport. And she'd already arranged to have Helene, her savior, pick Benjy up from school and stay at the house while she was gone. Linnell looked at the window—it was open a crack—then she rubbed her eyes and yawned so uncontrollably that her entire body shook. It was shady here under the palms, and she could use her purse as a pillow. Linnell's leg gave a jolt, as if her body was already well on its way. And then she heard the metallic slosh of keys and the contents of her coin purse spilling onto the floor mat. No need to look. Her handbag. She'd kicked over her handbag. Bear was right. She was a klutz. And that was no Helen of Troy, no powerful Queen Boadicia staring back at her from Charles' fogged-up mirror. It was just plain ol' Ma. The unadorned. The unadored. What on earth had gotten her to thinking that she could pull everything off?

Leaning sideways to roll down the window, Linnell felt another fingernail break and then she became aware of the warm tears that were rolling down her cheek and across the bridge of her nose. She saw one splash onto the soft leather upholstery, where it left a dark stain. Then losing her balance, her arm slipped out from under her and by the time her cheek touched Charles' warm upholstery, she was fast asleep.

HIGHRIDGE **8 a.m. February 25, 1974**

Bear sat in the padded restaurant booth and leaned forward over his breakfast in order to shift the weight from his ankle. It finally occurred to him that he might have twisted it earlier that morning while walking through the gravel on the way to his garage. Bear anxiously rubbed his tender ankle and then his right leg and tried to obliterate the inexplicable pain by forcing himself to think only about his garage and what it now held.

Converted from a ten stall horse stable, the two garages—one for himself, the other for Ma—were extra wide and their graveled aprons broad, so that if he ever felt like it he could with little effort back his car into his parking space when he returned home at night. But no, this was something he never did and would never do. He always, but *always,* drove in hood first so that the Cadillac's sharp chrome fins would present an aggressive barrier should anyone get any funny ideas about trailing him up to his house. Ma always fought with him over the way he parked, she wanted him to back in at night so he could leave more quietly in the morning when she wanted to sleep. But he'd simply said no, that *this* was the way he liked doing things. The same with the new home security system—he wasn't going to explain that to her, either. But he had his reasons: Should anyone dare to sneak up on him, or try to trap him in his garage, he'd hear them coming and then he could ram them the hell off the hill with a couple of taps of his heavy rear bumper, thus sparing his engine from getting wrecked. He'd learned *that* trick from watching the late-night TV movies.

This morning he had used his new hand-held remote clicker to turn on the light so he could take a look at the tower of boxes stacked in the corner. Satisfied that they appeared undisturbed, he had swiftly backed his Cadillac into the turn around area even before the garage door had begun its slow downward progression. He'd even paused for a second to make sure that the light was off and the garage door closed tight before grinding noisily across the gravel-covered apron. Yes, like usual—and except for last night's fiasco with Ma—everything had been in perfect order when he'd left the house. Now all he had to do was get the alarm guy up to the house one more time to install a security system for his garage. He could get this done while Ma was away.

Bear was aware that his breakfast was getting cold, but this morning he didn't dig in like he usually did because he was so engrossed in thinking about Ma. He seldom thought about her after leaving the house, so why was he thinking about her now? Why? Because she was always so brim full of energetic disorder? The lint on his lapel? The smear on the collar of his otherwise beautifully organized life? No. That wasn't exactly why. Bear fiddled with his fork, rolling it between a surprisingly delicate-looking thumb and forefinger while he sought an answer. He stared at his plate. Maybe it was the eggs, the two of them staring up at him from the waffle like that, sort of reminding him of her eyes. Always looking up at him. Asking him to explain to her what he was doing. *That's it!* he thought. More and more, this is what he hates most. Eyes staring at him. Questioning him. Asking him to explain. But nobody had any right to question him, least of all, Ma. Because he was the King. And a King didn't have to answer to anyone.

While waiting for his side dish of bacon to be served, Bear began to grumble about his wife: *Ma! She's been so full of surprises these last coupla years. Yeah! Like passing the bar, for one.* It had been three years already but he still hadn't gotten over it. And even though he was the one who had let her go to law school—she'd given him her sacred word that she'd never leave him if he'd let her attend—he had been counting on law school to knock the starch out of her. Absolutely counting on it! *And then she goes and shocks everybody by actually passing the bar exam. And this morning! This morning she goes an' scares the hell out of me! For crissake! Whatsa matter with her? She's driving me nuts. But . . . it looks like everything's gonna turn out okay because she still doesn't know anything. She thinks she's so smart . . . always reading and studying those law books and scribbling in that little black book of hers. Poor Ma . . . guess she's not so damn smart after all.*

With that, Bear sliced through the eggs and watched the yellows run into the small square hollows of his nicely browned waffle. He forced himself to take a small bite and then licking his fork, he began to dream about his big white-walled house. The best one in Highridge. On the highest knoll overlooking the town, crammed to the rafters with all the hottest new stuff. He'd thought of everything: the trick lights; the locks; the new security system—right down to the deep layer of gravel in the turnaround area. A perfect touch, the gravel. Put there to give him plenty of warning about the presence of strangers.

Bear exhaled with a whistle; he felt a lot better. Much better than he'd felt earlier that morning: so slow, like a lead sinker being dragged underwater. But here! Here he was safe. Here was where he could do no wrong. Here was where he was given respect along with a special breakfast fit for a king. And now that the Percs were finally beginning to kick in, he knew that very soon now the grays would be melting into halos of glowing color and the terrible past would soon merge into the future, squeezing the here-and-now until it became a tolerable pinpoint of glowing light.

Yes. Oh please yes. And soon.

But he wasn't too worried about *soon* because after much trial and error he knew that the yellow pills were the best way to jump-start his day. His little sunshine nuggets. He loved them because they could be counted on to melt every dull gray thing into beautiful warm pools of shimmering Jello. And he knows that as soon as this happens, he'll be immediately swept up into a widening tide of color and sound that will lift him higher and higher, up toward a glorious light, and then at the very top . . . at the very top he will be held in delicious suspense as each cooling molecule sets up into a brand a new pattern. Oh, it was always so wonderful because just like a two-stage rocket, when enough of them jelled there will be this *click* and then he will be kicked high into orbit, launched into a whole different world where everything smoothly spooled like a brilliant Technicolor movie, faster and faster, until everybody would be left far behind and only he could keep up. He needed that moment. *That click.* It was like being born into paradise all over again.

But where is it?

Then just as he raised his cup, and with a profound sense of relief, he finally felt the click and saw the bright pinpoint swiftly transformed into a golden flower that bloomed behind his eyes. The rush had finally begun—just a tiny bit slower than usual, that was all. Bear kept his eyes closed to give himself time to bask in the light of his inner sun. *Everything is being compressed; time is collapsing into itself.* Then he forced them open, held up his cup so his waitress could see it, and watched her as she grabbed up a fresh pot of coffee on her way over to his table to serve him his bacon. As if from a great distance, he observed her filling his cup before setting the crackling-hot side dish next to his plate. He could feel her heat too, and he was aware of his servant's tender smile as she carefully picked up one crispy strip of bacon and laid it across the top of the perfect circle of mounded food he'd pushed so neatly into the center of his plate.

After she turned away, he took a large bite and felt time expanding again and when he ground his food between his teeth he could hear a faint rumbling in the back of his nose. But he could tell, thank God, that it wasn't the voices; it was just the hollow sound of a sinus infection. Another one. These infections seemed to be occurring more frequently. He'd better tell Manny, his pharmacist, to get him some stronger antibiotics. Bear crooked his little finger as he lifted his coffee to take a small sip and again let himself float while he rested the thick cup against his mouth. Looking inward, he forgot about everything else in the world and dreamt only about the pleasures he'd planned for later that morning.

Without willing it, Bear felt his feet touching ground.

A soft landing. He'd come back to earth without missing a beat. Yes. He was back and it was a damn good thing too because he had so much to do. But first, right after breakfast, he had to take his usual nap at Margo's while she ironed his lab coats before going on ahead to set up his office. He would have her send the flowers for him, too, and she would still have plenty of time to get Debbie prepped so that everything would be ready for him at exactly 10.

Thank God for Margo-the-office-manager! She'd gotten rid of the last girl—that humorless, skinny broad. But from the looks of this new girl Debbie—he'd only caught a quick glimpse of her when Margo was parading her through his office—he could tell she was a nice, placid sort, though maybe just a little bit broad in the beam. But hey, that was okay—just so long as the girl liked taking orders. Bear suddenly produced an involuntary low-pitched groan, almost a belch; fortunately it was not so loud that anyone would want to turn and stare. And then he realized with a start that he hasn't heard such a sound since he was a boy. Something wasn't quite right. Something heavy, something new, something that didn't quite belong was turning inside his chest. Bear looked around, wondering what had changed. But it all looked the same. Then he studied his watch and willed himself to relax. *Slow down. Slow down.*

There was no need to rush. He had plenty of time. He could stay here and flirt with the waitresses who would always say the same thing: "C'mon, have s'more coffee, Doc. Have you heard this one yet?" And then, like usual, they would flutter around him like butterflies, filling his cup while they caught him up on all of the latest jokes. They adored him and they all called him "Doc" while they bowed and scraped and treated him like a king. Les Droit de Seigneur—the Rights of the King—how satisfying it was, to know that he ruled over this land of the brilliant sun, a place where everything was under control.

SAN FRANCISCO **9: 30 a.m., February 25, 1974**

"So, Jordan, what you think?" August Rizzo could be described as an energetically nosy kind of guy and Robert A. Jordan knew that getting anything past him was going to take some work.

Rizzo had just been appointed Chief of the Special Services Section. It was a new unit of the Intelligence Division of the San Francisco Office of the Internal Revenue Service which had been organized the year before for the specific purpose of investigating United States lawyers, accountants and their clients who were suspected of using tax havens to evade federal tax. Jordan had asked to be transferred to Rizzo's unit because it was part of his plan to find a way out of the fog and into some sun.

To avoid confusion, Robert Andrew Jordan now went by his surname only since there were two other agents in his office with the same first name. Robert—he'd always wondered if it had been Robert Taylor or some other bedroom-eyed movie star responsible for turning on all the fertile women of the mid-Forties, because practically every other guy in his age group had ended up with the same first name and for some reason this always bugged him. Andrew or Andy didn't cut it, either. And he was no Robbie.

He was deep-chested and his shoulders were solid and maybe that explained why the other guys in his unit seemed to feel a need to come up and tap him—apparently just to see if he really was as solid as he looked. He was, and he'd had to literally pick up one guy in the I.D. office and sort of flatten him up against the wall to get him to knock it off. He didn't like having to do that sort of thing—not unless somebody really punched his buttons. Jordan absent-mindedly fingered the short scar that sliced vertically down the left edge of his chin. He'd missed a few hairs in the crease this morning when shaving in the dark at Joanne's.

Maybe it was the scar. Probably made him look like street fighter. It was really just an accidental memento from his younger brother who had collided with him on their last ski trip. Head on. He was lucky to still be alive. So now he was Jordan with a jagged edge. And just like the guys who needed to test him, sooner or later every woman he'd ever slept with seemed to get this irresistible urge to remind him that he was marred. With oh-so-soft fingers they'd stop and they'd reach up to stroke his scar and then raise their eyebrows without actually saying anything. Or they'd interrupt things just to ask him how he got it. Why? Why did they always have to do this? To remind him that they knew he wasn't perfect? Yeah. Well he already knew he wasn't perfect so he didn't need reminding. But maybe doing this made them feel better about not being perfect themselves. Maybe they didn't understand that he didn't need, or even want them to be perfect. He just wanted them to be sexy and smart and to make him laugh. So all this did was spoil the mood. And then they'd do it again and end up turning him off for good.

"Hey! You still here?" Rizzo's rumble was friendly but fuzzy-edged.

Younger than Rizzo by twenty years, Jordan leaned against the door and watched Rizzo reach in his pocket and pull out his tie. Rizzo was the kind of guy who liked to look sharp when he visited a taxpayer's office. Jordan studied how Rizzo tossed it around his collar and then buttoned his shirt with one hand.

Rizzo began to hum flatly, as if he were figuring something out in his head while he waited for Jordan's reply.

"Yeah, Sure I'm here," Jordan finally replied. "I was just wondering what put you onto Dr. Clare."

"Well, as you're soon gonna see for yourself, it's the little things that usually give a guy away."

Jordan could tell that Rizzo—unlike some other pricks in the Intelligence Division—was taking pains to avoid making him feel like a greenhorn. The man was genuinely interested in his work; this was infectious and Jordan had come to enjoy hanging out with him.

"Our Dr. Clare's no slouch," Rizzo continued. "But he's screwed up on a coupla important details. Like how his expenditures on his injection sets relate to all that gold he's been buying—supposedly for crowns and bridges—and then there's the mystery of all that nitrous gas he's using. But I'm getting a little ahead of myself here, so let's start at the top: What I noticed first was the fact that his profit and loss statements were showing disproportionately high expenditures for what he describes as *dental supplies.* So, when I reviewed his supporting invoices, I saw that he's been buying enough nitrous to gas the whole county.

"Furthermore, the amount he says he's spending on his dental laboratory is astronomical—he supposedly uses his lab only for fabricating crowns and bridges—and most of his expenses are for gold. Strangely enough, and I think this is where he really slipped up, I found a partial invoice for gold issued to him by that crazy bank I told you about, that outfit in the Cayman Islands. So now I have to ask myself, what kind of a dental practice is that? And to top it all off, I see that his purchases of injection sets and what he pays for linen and laundry are *way* too low for a crown and bridge kinda practice. You see, we can count the number of towels and injection sets from his invoices, and this clues us in to how many people are going in there to have him work on their teeth. So right off the bat I saw that his invoices for his expenses are presenting a contradictory picture about the *kind* of traffic that's passin' through his office You see what I mean? It looks like a helluva lot of people are going in to see Dr. Clare, but perhaps it's for something else besides dentistry. Then, when we served a second notice on him to produce documentation and his canceled checks for all that gold he's been buying, he failed to respond, which means he has to be hiding something. We still haven't seen any supporting checks for the gold . . . and this gets me to thinking that he's been paying cash for it—cash that's not being run through his books. See what I'm getting at here?"

"Well, what exactly? Something more than just tax evasion?" Robert Jordan wondered if he looked as puzzled as he felt.

"Yeah. I think so. See, you gotta look at the picture from every angle. Take Clare's annual gross receipts, for example—they show he's doing better than other dentists are doing in this district—yet according to the number of towels he uses, he's only seeing a couple of patients a day. I mean, a dentist has to use towels. You know, the little ones that go 'round each patient's neck. Like I said, these you can count from the invoices over that same period. Things don't jive, and I think a whole lot more cash is passing through that office than our Dr. Clare is reporting, but I just can't prove it yet. At least, not beyond a reasonable doubt. I need some more info, that's why we're on our way over there now."

HIGHRIDGE **8:45 a.m. February 25, 1974**

"Oh what a wonderful morrrrrnning," Bear sang aloud while he admired his high cheek bones and small straight nose in his rear-view mirror. He was on his way to Margo's apartment. Now that things had snapped back into place, he was feeling no pain—and he had to admit, he was looking every bit as

good as he felt. His sun-lamp had given him an even dark tan and his eyebrows had fixed themselves into a knowing tilt. His skin, bronzed to a patina of glowing good health, set off his sparkling gray eyes—the whites were so clear today, thanks to the new eye-drops Manny had just given him. Yes, he was looking good, everything was wonderful. Manny adored him. Margo obeyed him. And his circle at The Wei, everybody there, they all loved him too.

Bear grinned at himself and a perfect set of matched dimples appeared. Wasn't he just the picture of prosperity! And with the sunshine back-lighting his hair like this, creating the effect of a halo—he appeared otherworldly, almost divine. Bear held his grin so he could admire his white teeth while fluffing his curls, then licking his fingertips, he smoothed a few unruly strands with his fragile-fingered, broad hand.

It was just like Ma said: He was a handsome bear of a man. Other women thought so, too. "Cute as a teddy bear, but such a big bruiser," that's what women would say. He had to laugh—he certainly *was* a clever, handsome, bear of a man. There was no doubt about it.

Bear turned the wheel and a shaft of bright sunlight cut suddenly into his clear gray eyes. Squinting, he reached into the glove compartment and fumbled for his dark glasses. Oh-oh. His $300 gold-filled Vuarnets. He knew where he'd left them—the third pair he'd bought in a month. Somewhere in the dining room. No big deal. He could always stop by Nordley's and pick up a new pair on the way to his office. Bear gave a little snort of happiness. Financially, things certainly had changed for the better. And soon they'd be better still.

He was grateful for these moments alone, when he could cut loose without having to fear what others might think. Narrowing his eyes against the light, he began to chant his mantra, the special one created for him by his encounter group at The Wei: *I am the King, the flow goes through me. I am the King!*

The mantra had been created both to honor and calm him and Bear sang the words, rounding out every vowel, just like he'd been taught at his Wei training sessions. Inhaling deeply, as he'd been instructed, he exhaled loudly because he knew this would stifle the voices. The voices—rude interlopers into his otherwise perfectly organized world—he knew who they were. They were unruly troops of angels and demons who had for years been content to live quietly hidden, deep in a closet at the back of his head. Friend or foe? He couldn't yet tell—sometimes it seemed they were both. But whichever they were, he'd always known they were in there somewhere. Lately, however, they had been creeping up on him. He couldn't understand why they were trying to test him, always trying to escape and feed on his brilliant thoughts. The last few months had been a terrible struggle. But he was going to win; he would conquer them because he was the one who was born to rule. As if to prove him right, the voices whispered discordantly and scattered into the darkness.

Bear concentrated on singing scales in his resonant baritone—and then he abruptly stopped when he saw how the passengers in the adjacent Cadillac were staring at him openmouthed. He quickly flashed them his boyish grin and they immediately waved and smiled back. Yes, all it took was one of his smiles and everybody would fall all over themselves trying to see things his way—that much hadn't changed.

Thus returned to the realities of surrounding traffic, Bear concentrated on the tasks he had planned for that morning: Besides his patients, there was the no small matter of training his new girl, Debbie—the former Mrs. Brillis. Today was her first day on the job, her initiation so to speak, and he was just as eager as she to get everything right. But he really needn't worry too much about that; Margo would teach the new girl what she was supposed to do. He could always count on Margo. She understood him better than most and as much an any woman ever could. In fact, it was the always dependable, unflappable Margo who had found this girl for him, sparing him the aggravation of having to advertise for a new one. Margo had also volunteered to iron the white nylon lab jackets he wore over his clothes. Ma had laundered some over the weekend and he had stuffed a couple of them in his new leather briefcase.

Bear reached out and gave it a pat. He'd bought it for himself—a leather one, the same as Ma's, with expandable pockets and neat little locks—at the same store where Ma had bought hers, and he had already begun to fill it with things he needed to stash, a task which would be a whole lot easier once she left on her trip. As for his prescriptions? He could use Margo's phone to call them in, and then he'd be able to sack out. Good old Margo. She'd told him that doing a little ironing for him was "the least she could do now that the wife was making herself too busy to take care of his needs."

It was strange, really strange, the way women were always so eager to please, so ready to drop whatever they were doing in order to make a big fuss about "meeting his needs." As for Ma? She was the same, except more so. Even though it got her exactly nowhere with him, it still impressed him to see how much energy she was always so willing to invest in her sorry attempts to get through to him, to try to discover what he was thinking or how he felt.

"I can't seem to get through to you," she'd always complain. "You're just like a wall." Then he'd always snicker and reply: "Oh now Ma, I'm *here* now, aren't I? What more do you want?" That always seemed to shut her up. Most of the time he wasn't thinking anything. And lately, especially, he was just listening to all the new sounds in his head. But he never talked about this. Ma wouldn't understand. And besides, he didn't want her to.

Anyway, you'd think that after all these years, and as smart as she was, that she'd finally get the drift. But no, not *this* woman. This woman—who had so much smarts that she could simply turn herself into a lawyer—somehow this woman couldn't get it into her head that she wasn't going to get any closer to him than she was on the day they first met. And for crissake! Why would she want to? He gave her everything a woman could need. Furthermore, he didn't want anybody getting too close to him because this made him feel sticky. Except for the bed, where being close was okay; then, when Ma got herself all worked up, when he saw her lying next to him with her eyes all watery and her shoulders tensed up—that was usually all that it took to get him turned on. Then he'd roll over and give her rape-shape a little poke; she really didn't need much more, a little poke seemed to hold her. Except for last night. Last night was different. Last night it wasn't working and it was all her fault. Well, he'd spoiled her rotten, so what could he expect? But soon—very soon—things were going to be different.

Suddenly filled with elation, Bear began to sing as if he were doing scales: "Oh-me-oh-my-oh-Ma-on-my-birthday! I'm gonna wait till she gives me my gift and then I'm gonna give her the surprise of her life! I can't wait to see her face!" Bear's throat opened so his joy could pour forth: "Oh yes everything. Everything is going to be changed," he crooned. Then his voice deepened. "Louis," he called. He was testing. *"Looooie—Loooooie,"* he called again, this time softly. *Orrrrrry-gorrrrrreeeee,* the voices whispered back in unison. But softer, and this time from far away. Good. They were going to leave him alone. Today—he could already tell—things were going to go fine.

HIGHRIDGE **Monday morning - February 25, 1974**

I've got fourteen years on ol' Doc, thought Margo. At five foot four, Margo Callahan stood on her tiptoes so she could examine herself very closely this morning to see how much this might be apparent to others. "Not bad. Not bad at tall," she assured her reflection. "Anyone with a tad of sense could tell I was a real swell looker when I was a chick. Oh Nuts . . . would you just look at that!" Margo exclaimed at the small opening that gaped at the seam underneath her left arm. She dropped her arm, then let her belt out a notch to keep her waist from bulging over the buckle. Inhaling to expand her chest even more, she sucked in her stomach while she admired herself in the mirror and then after a sidelong glance at Doc to make sure he was still asleep, she leaned into the glass and baby-talked to her reflection, "Gotta drops some pounds—no more booze you bad girl."

Margo held her mouth open while she applied her false eyelashes, taking care not to smudge her frosty-blue eye shadow. Spitting on her mascara palette and stirring furiously with her eye-liner brush, she completed her toilette by thickening the black line that swooped out from the corners of her bulging blue eyes. Her eyes did the trick—they always made her look brimming with energy even if she really was half asleep. Then spinning around in front of the mirror, she looked over her shoulder to examine the new uniform Doc had just given her: a pink nylon ensemble with long sleeves that closed at the wrist, a zipper down the front, and a wonderful skirt that rustled whenever she moved.

Tugging at the material until it was tight over her enormous breasts, she pinned the nurse's insignia she'd found at the flea market precisely two inches upslope from the tip of her huge bosom. Doc always liked looking at her big bazoombas and the pin gave her a nice professional touch—pretty good for someone who'd never finished high school, she thought. Margo adjusted the zipper until exactly three inches of cleavage showed. "Perfect," she whispered, "there's nothing about me that's anything like the wife."

However, on this early spring morning, Margo Callahan did have one thing in common with Mrs. Clare: Her thoughts were focused on the very same man. This wasn't all that strange, since most of the time he was on her mind. She could remember everything from the time they first met. She had first visited Dr. Clare's office in response to his ad for an office manager, and even though seven years had passed, she could still recall how close she'd come to making a dive for his zipper the instant she saw him ogling her blouse. She had never before met such a good-looking man, so tall, so handsome, so obviously interested, and she had barely managed to play it cool. Good thing she had, though, because after another five minutes she'd had him pegged: he was just a great big baby. And that was when she decided he was going to be hers. Margo now turned to look at Dr. Clare's sleeping form. *He still looks just like a movie star with that tan and those great big gray eyes. Yes, and those dimples and perfect white teeth!* Margo sighed. He was one big piece of work—a baby, all right.

During her interview she'd told him that she'd just left her third husband. (Ol' George was her fourth and he was six feet under, but she wasn't about to get into *that*.) She'd even told him she needed the job. Of course that wasn't quite true; what she was really looking for was some excitement. She was ready for a new man and a dental office promised good pickin's—a guy who could afford to take care of his teeth was just the sort who'd make a great George the Fifth. Fortunately, she wasn't hard up because when good ol' George the Fourth kicked the bucket, he'd left her with a big wad of insurance money. In fact, as she had correctly guessed, she was in far better shape than her poor handsome dentist—until *she* arrived on the scene, he'd barely been making a living.

She'd let Doc have a sample early on—they'd had a couple too many one night after work and they'd ended up rolling around on the floor of her apartment. But after that evening, she had stopped the music. Now that she thought about it, she still wasn't sure whether she ought to feel grateful or miffed that Doc had simply taken her decision in stride. But still, she had felt it was smarter to cut him off, and for two very good reasons: The first was that when it came to sport-fucking, well, she really needed a man—not some overgrown puppy who thought making-out meant dry-pecking her nipples. And second, she needed to keep a firm grip on her long-range plans.

She wasn't a kid anymore; she knew what she wanted. And if she was going to retire with lots of money then she'd better make sure she stayed top dog. Margo smeared another layer of lipstick on her thick lower lip and thought her usual thoughts about him. *Screwing him was at least useful—It showed me that what he really wants is a mommy, and I give good mommy. That's what I do best. And all those young girls? They mean nothing. They are nothing. They can come and go and I don't give a damn, 'cause I know they'll never get anywhere with him—and besides, I'm the only one who knows how to keep him in line.*

Margo took stock of what she had done to keep a handle on Mark Clare: *She* was the one who had first called him "Doc," and then after observing how flattery would puff him up like a fish, she had decided to "doofer him." And so "doofer him" she did, way beyond all of his wildest dreams. She was the one who helped him skim cash—showing him some slick tricks even he didn't know. And *she* was the one who had kept the wife's little snout from poking around in their business.

But, best of all—*she* was the one now in charge of their "games." This had all come about by accident. Yes, one day she had walked in on him while he was spanking it . . . his little man, and being careful not to show any sign of shock or disapproval, she'd simply told him that he wouldn't have to do that anymore. She'd get him a real dolly to play with, she'd said. And that's just what she'd done. She and Doc—they made quite a team. And she'd made it seem like they were merely playing lighthearted sex-games, and Doc clearly loved to play any game she invented because he'd put her entirely in charge of them now. She was beginning to worry, however. Doc had begun to creep a little too close to the edge. Daring was okay. But reckless? That would be stupid, and they couldn't afford to be stupid because this place was a gold mine. And she wasn't about to let everything get all screwed up just because he felt like swinging—and besides, a big share of this gold mine was really hers. She'd brought this office to where it was, and she'd settle for nothing less than her share. And that was exactly what she intended to get: A *big* share.

Margo glanced at the couch to see if Doc had awakened. She smiled even more broadly; he was still zonked out. And she really meant it—she was truly happy to see how safe he felt, putting his feet up in her little apartment. *See?* she told herself. *He knows this is the only place where he can be himself. He can't relax in that big fancy house with that damn-fancy woman. Only here, with Big Momma . . . that spoiled wife of his has no idea how to take care of a man like him.*

Margo tiptoed over to the table next to the couch. She would give him enough time to rise from his stupor and get to the office by 10 a.m. sharp. Margo set the alarm and carefully placed Doc's freshly ironed lab coats where he would be quick to spot them, tied on her white oxfords, and then with pink skirts rustling deliciously, headed out for the florist to do his bidding.

Margo pulled into the parking lot at exactly 9:45 a.m. and saw Deborah Brillis' old clunker parked outside the dental office. The girl must have been there for at least twenty minutes, waiting for her to arrive. Margo was amused to see how nervously Deborah paced the pavement. "Good," said Margo, under her breath. "She's a real eager beaver all right, but, oh my! she's *such* a doofus."

She'd heard the sad story, how Debbie's old man had dumped her, leaving her with all their bills. "Same old, same old . . . happens all the time, but not to me," Margo thought. "I 'spose I'll have to show her the ropes. Get her shaped up—but that hair still looks like a frizzy ol' dust bunny." She had just that morning arranged to get Debbie connected up with some cash so the poor thing could afford to do something about it, maybe go to the beauty shop and get a real permanent.

Margo had met Debbie, the newest face on the singles scene, two months before, in the cocktail lounge at the Red Dog Inn. She knew how to read people, so she knew that the girl was literally down on her uppers. And, sure enough, Debbie had proved her right by confiding that she'd spent her last dime on enrolling in The Wei, assuring Margo that it was well worth the price because "The Wei Process" had given her the courage to get out there and look for a miracle. In fact, Debbie told her she was hoping to find one at the Red Dog Inn—and that was when Margo decided to make sure Debbie did.

After they next met for drinks, Margo was sure that ol' Deb was just who they needed, so she had carefully explained the duties the girl would be asked to perform, in fact, she even promised to get Doc to pay her $250 a month until Debbie was properly trained—and a $100 bonus if things worked out to Doc's satisfaction. Margo had chosen her words with care, so that Debbie would understand that it was she, Margo, who ran the office. And when she saw that Deb's little head had grasped that fine point, she allowed Doc to have the girl's name and address so he could have her checked out. Margo also gave Debbie a tour of the office; actually, the real reason for this was to let Doc sneak a peek at the girl. Debbie's overawed expression—the office was plush, and there was even a computer—further convinced Margo that Debbie would work out all right.

Margo welcomed Debbie with a bright smile. "Hi sweetie, you ready for the big day?"

"Oh Margo, I'm kinda nervous, y'know?" Debbie whimpered in a tremulous voice. "I sure hope I'm gonna do everything right."

"Well buck-up honey, you're gonna be swell. All you have to remember is what I told you, and you be sure to move everything *exactly* the way I showed you, and also . . . always act *real* confident. He likes that," Margo reassured. "And lookie-here, you be sure to always call him Dr. Clare even if *I* call him Doc. I haven't told you about the wife, we'll talk about that later—*she* calls him *Bear*, but we don't do *that.* Never! Now, let's go on in. I'll get things set up and you can go on in and get ready. That's a good girl. You got plenty of time."

Of course no one calls him Bear! Margo thought. *Not in here, they don't. Doc takes the credit for that one, but it was really my idea. We worked things out so only that little family of his calls him Bear. That's how we screen our special patients . . . 'cause anyone who lets on they know Dr. Clare as Bear is someone who for sure knows his wife, and then we kick 'em out, 'cause we don't want anyone like that in here.*

Debbie shuffled anxiously at the door, watching Margo digging around in her purse for her keys. It was a large set and Margo grumbled about them, which was her way of letting Debbie know that the office had a security system and that since she ran the show, that she had a key to it too, as well as a key to each and every one of the many drawers and cabinets. Margo finally seized the right one, and then, after keying off the alarm and letting them in, she bustled about the office, first lighting the ornate crystal lamps in the carpeted reception area and then flipping the switches in the operatories that opened onto the carpeted hall. Then she stood back to watch Debbie's face.

Debbie, huddled awkwardly inside her none too clean rain coat, gave every appearance of feeling useless and out of place as she watched the fluorescent operatory lights flicker and then suck the color out of the rooms as one after another, they blazed on. Blinking her eyes, she remained standing in the reception area and waited for Margo to tell her what to do next.

"Now Debbie, you go on into the Ladies and get changed. There's a brand new uniform in there and it's for *you*, sweetie. And here, honey. Take this." Margo handed Debbie a small flat box wrapped in gold paper, then cooed, as if she were comforting a very slow child. "This here is something special from *me,* so you be sure to put it where it belongs." Margo winked at the girl and then added: "Now, you be a good little girl and give me your purse. I'll take care of it for you."

Debbie, staring at Margo like a freshly clubbed cod, quickly removed her cosmetics kit and handed over her shabby purse. She stood in the hall and watched Margo's pink skirts as they swished away and then she ducked into the back bathroom to change into her white nurse's uniform. A pair of white oxfords, her size, sat waiting for her on the floor. They were clean and they had new laces, but Debbie could tell they were not new; she wondered what sort of woman had worn them before.

HIGHRIDGE **10:00 a.m. February 25, 1974**

Linnell woke to the sound of a horn honking. Her eyes flew open, but she still couldn't move. Her mouth was dry and she felt like a helpless fish, rising ever so slowly, up from the depths, to gulp at the glazed surface of an alien world. Her eyes finally focused on the small chrome light fixture above her head. Still half-paralyzed, she finally realized where she was—flat on her back, on the back seat of her car. She recognized the sound of a car door—first opening, then slamming shut. She automatically tipped her head back and looked up in the direction of the sounds she'd just heard and found herself staring into a pair of large hair-filled nostrils now floating above her head.

"Darlin? You okay?" A male voice boomed.

Linnell shrieked. The large head bumped against the top of the car window and jerked away.

Linnell sat up, turned, and stared into the shiny officer's medallion on the belt buckle of the man who stood next to the car window. She slid closer to the window and rubbing her eyes with the tips of her fingers, she peeked between them and saw the lambs wool collar of a black leather jacket and then a tanned face with large white teeth, leaning in her direction. The officer—who appeared to be grinning madly—yelled, "Hi Honey! *Love* that new car of yours!" and then pulled off his mirrored aviator sunglasses.

Linnell stared as if she were still in a trance, then she finally recognized him. She dropped her hand. "Chief Sommers! That *you*?" So! It was Captain Marvel himself! She'd heard rumors about him; that Sommers, whose wife had died the year before, was back on the prowl. She wanted to smart off and ask him if he was hitting on her, but before she could, his expression changed: Now he looked almost shocked—as if it were he, not she, who had been taken by surprise.

"Well, L.C., don't you get yourself all shook-up. I was just checking to see if you were okay." Chief Sommers' face now sagged.

"I'm okay. I just fell asleep." Linnell rubbed her neck.

"Well, okay then. You take it easy." With that terse remark, Chief Sommers backed away, quickly climbed into his patrol car, and just as swiftly, gunned his engine and peeled out.

And rather rapidly, Linnell thought, turning her head to stare; even for a cop.

Shaken but relieved that it was only Sommers, Linnell pressed a button and her window rose.

"Oh *God!*" thought Linnell. "Have I blown it? How long have I been asleep?" She looked at her watch and was greatly relieved. It was 10.15. She'd been asleep for only an hour. And then she looked down and saw the large runner in her new pantyhose had become an ugly ladder running all the way down to her shoe. "Oh Lord!" She groaned. How exasperating! She hadn't packed any pantyhose for her trip, and she couldn't run around in these for the rest of the day. Bear was right. Look at her! She was an absolute klutz! And now she'd have to waste even more time going home to change.

Controlling her temper, Linnell Clare picked everything up, pushed the seat forward, hiked up her skirt, kicked her shoes off so as not to mar Charles' upholstery and crawled into the front seat. She slowly pulled away from the curb, and when she looked in her rear-view mirror she could still see, in the distance, Sommers' patrol car zooming off in the opposite direction. Linnell headed in a direction that would take her away from Ivener's office and as soon as she saw a service station, she pulled in to find a pay phone. She needed to call Karen, her secretary.

Linnell finally got the correct change, and then for a minute, couldn't remember the telephone number for her own law office. Now near to tears, it finally came to her; she plunked in a dime.

"Karen! I fell asleep in my car. Can you believe?"

"Hey there! Nice going, L.C."

"And I put a runner in my pantyhose so I'm going home to change."

"*That*-a-way spaz! *Really* good work." Karen laughed. "Well, at least things are under control at the office. In fact, I'm typing your magnum opus right now."

"Magnum opus?" Linnell took no offense at Karen's good-natured jibes.

"Yes. Your *manuscript*—remember? You know, all that foreign foundation stuff. It's pretty interesting, especially that insider-info you just wrote about the CIA!"

"Oh, *that*. Right!" Karen was talking about what Linnell's research had revealed about the tax privileges Congress had given to the government's off-shore agencies—the most notable being the Central Intelligence Agency. Linnell had included this small touch of mischief in the hope it would spark her treatise on foreign foundations with a touch of pizzazz.

"It's gonna keep me busy through lunch," Karen added. "By the way, your editor called. He's only willing to give you another month which means you've got until March to deliver it to him. And I'm logging the hang-up calls—there were a couple of them earlier this morning. And I've already sorted out all the stuff you need for your trip. Why don't you take a few hours for yourself? You know, there's no reason for you to rush on in here. It's only 10:30 and you've actually got plenty of time—you could even go to the club. And I want to ask you a favor, but it'll keep till I see you later this afternoon."

Linnell listened to Karen appreciatively. Despite her breezy manner and her teasing, Karen always had such a tactful way of getting her straightened out. And taking some time for herself sounded pretty good to her, too.

Linnell returned to her car and pulled up to the gas pump. Although she felt better, physically, than she had for months, the uneasiness that had haunted her earlier had already crept back. What was it? Linnell rubbed her eyes and then told herself that she was simply reacting to Karen's news about the hang-up calls. It seemed that after having stopped for a couple of days, the caller—or callers—were at it again.

HIGHRIDGE **10:00 a.m. February 25, 1974**

Margo swiftly unlocked and entered Doc's private office. His enormous mahogany desk stood between her and the double-doors that separated the office from his elaborate bathroom. The bathroom, fully equipped with shower and bidet, was actually a small annex that had been added to the building after she had arrived; the wife had never been in it. Since Margo was the one who had helped Doc design it, she knew that the broad-basined marble sink would stand immediately opposite Doc's desk when the bathroom doors were pulled open. But the desk, with its elaborately carved trim, had come from the estate of the wife's grandfather and this was a sore point with her. She'd asked Doc to get rid of it, but he had refused, telling her that it was too valuable. She not only hated its size—it forced her to swivel her hips in order to avoid its sharp corners—she hated it most because the wife had given it to him, and it was shortly after Doc had proudly moved this so-called treasure into his inner sanctum that she had made it plain to him that no other tokens from the wife would be tolerated on the premises.

Today, she was once again satisfied to see that no photographs of the wife or the child could be found anywhere on the premises. After dropping Debbie's purse on the desk, Margo swung open the bathroom doors and grunting, got down on all fours so she could inspect the underside of the basin, which for their own special reasons had been installed a bit lower than usual. As soon as her eyes were adjusted to the dim light, Margo was able to locate the small microphone partially concealed by the wooden moulding. Satisfied that no wires were visible, she tried to rise, and then, with ankle bones popping and creaking, she gripped the edge of the sink and pulled herself up. Standing on tiptoe, she next opened the upper cabinet and removed a new bar of translucent glycerin soap and a long white cloth which she folded lengthwise and laid on the polished marble counter. After arranging the soap so that it lay square in its dish, she gave the large mirror and the gold-plated faucets a final inspection to make sure that everything was spotless.

Sorting through her keys, Margo returned to Doc's desk and unlocked the top right-hand desk drawer. She attended to Doc's desk every day, and then she would check it again, at night, to make sure he had remembered to lock it up when he was finished. The bank of drawers on the left side of the desk were keyed separately, however, and Doc kept these keys hidden, even from her. This was why she was so certain this was where he was stashing the hundred dollar bills—she knew he was collecting them, because almost every other day he trusted her to take the smaller bills to the bank and exchange them for hundred dollar bills—he would give her a ten for each trip. Probably just to keep her from pilfering, she thought. Doc had already given her two tens and a five for today—but this was for Debbie; he'd only given her a ten-spot for herself. After folding the tens and the five and tucking them in a plain envelope, Margo opened

Debbie's purse to inspect its contents. Only one lonesome dollar remained in the girl's musty wallet. Margo dropped the envelope in the purse and then set the purse, open, on the outside corner of Doc's desk so that Debbie would be sure to notice it right away. The poor thing would be grateful for this handsome spiff.

Margo was pleased with herself—she had talked Doc into making this welcoming gesture. She paused, and then fished in the envelope and took the five. Having unlocked the top right-hand desk drawer, Margo now pulled it all the way out so she could inspect the tape recorder that had been pushed to the back. She clicked in a new cassette and flipped on the switch. Whistling softly, Margo watched how the capstan turned, but only so long as there were sounds to record. Fascinated, she tested it again, and it worked just like magic. A sound-activated tape recorder—hard-wired into the telephone system! Doc must have wired it himself. He was so clever! Such a good-looking man. And he sure wasn't chintzy when it came to spending money on the latest and most advanced electronic gear.

Margo returned to the bathroom to look in the mirror and adjust her white nurse's cap, then she stepped back to admire her handiwork. Everything looked so clean and nice. Doc sure was lucky to have someone like her. Margo left the heavy curtains closed and the door wide open, and then, as a final dramatic touch, she dimmed the lights to a golden half-glow. It was almost 10:00. Time for her to get back to her station at the front desk.

HIGHRIDGE **10 a.m. February 25, 1974**

Debbie looked at the clock in the hall before closing the door to the small back bathroom. She'd already wiped off every last trace of mascara and fluffed up her hairdo, and now she stared at her mouth in disgust. She simply had to apply just a smidge of pale lip-gloss even though Margo had warned her that Doc didn't like his assistants to wear any make-up. She noticed that her hands were already shaking—she had only a minute left to get to her station and into position! She wondered how she was going to get through this. Then she ordered herself to feel confident. She strode briskly past Margo's desk to show off her new uniform and getting a quick nod of approval, she stood for a moment in front of Dr. Clare's private office, took a deep breath and cautiously entered—and then caught the tip of one of her rubber-soled white shoes and stumbled, almost falling face-down on the plush woolen carpet. Her heart suddenly raced; she was about to meet Dr. Clare and this next part was crucial. She *had* to make the right impression on him. Think of the money, she kept telling herself.

Without looking to either the left or the right, Debbie walked a straight line to the splendid bathroom, stood in front of the marble sink with her feet exactly four inches apart, then took a long last look at herself in the mirror to be sure that she had her bearings. When she was sure she was oriented, she found the folded white cloth and tied the blindfold tightly over her eyes as instructed. The next thing she heard was the sound of a door opening. It had to be Dr. Clare. Her hand found her zipper and she slowly pulled it down until her blouse was open to her waist. She already knew—she'd rehearsed it with Margo—that if he was standing next to the counter, he would be able to view her in the mirror by looking through the door that Margo had left open. As instructed, the moment she heard Dr. Clare greeting Margo, she pulled her blouse open with both hands and bent forward until her extended elbows touched the outer edge of the low marble basin, and then she began to wiggle and shake until she could feel herself falling out of her brassiere. He needed to see her exposing her nipples. This was important to him. After recovering from her shock upon hearing this from Margo, she had listened to Margo explaining to her that he would be watching them in the mirror. It's nothing, Margo had said. Just something he likes to do. They could not lie, she had said.

But Debbie did not stop with this; there was more. Arching her back, she continued to posture and bend until her plump buttocks resembled a white nylon valentine hovering high in the sky, and the instant she heard Dr. Clare entering and closing the door—the signal for her to begin—she reached down with both hands and then following her instructions, slowly lifted her skirt up and over her round white cheeks, now encased in the gossamer stretch-panties she'd found in the little gold box.

Debbie guessed Dr. Clare was now standing behind his desk. He would be inspecting her presentation. She counted to ten and then she stretched out her arms, folded them so that the tips of her fingers touched the tops of her shoulders, and then bending even lower, she carefully touched the tips of her elbows to the edge of the sink. She was not to move or to make any sound. And she was not to make any attempt to look at him, ever.

Bear sang to himself. Tentatively: Louis. Then—*Looo-ie—Loooooie*—Looooowah. He had to see if the voices were going to tease him. There was silence. Good. Then he could proceed. Bear kept his eyes on the girl as he walked behind his desk to stand and look at the view. He was impressed by the way she was offering herself. Properly. Patiently. Like an obedient servant should. He was the source, the king, the sun. He was the reason why all the best women were always hoping and yearning, waiting just for a chance to offer themselves. Except he much preferred this more utilitarian approach. It had become his way. There would be no distractions. No annoying chatter. No reproachful eyes. And having her waiting for him, like this, would fill the room with such a palpable aura of nervous excitement that it had become his favorite means of arousal. Even now he could feel a faint stirring, somewhere way down there between his legs. Oh, when he was finished with her, she would join all the others who thought he was king.

Quickly. Now he had to get to it quickly. Bear unlocked the left side of his desk and pulled out a small packet of white powder. He tapped it expertly and then tipped its contents into the barrel of a syringe. This was a splendid new idea. It was very tidy and better than using some dirty C-note like he'd been doing. Expressing the air from his lungs, he inserted the tube in his right nostril, blocked the left one with his index finger, and snorted up the cocaine with a mighty inhalation. When he was finished, he stood dazed for a second and then he swept everything into the drawer and locked it again.

Now he would have to move fast. His head was exploding, and he could tell from the way the new girl was breathing that she was listening to his every move. He headed for her around the desk and when he was close enough to reach out and touch her he spoke the familiar opening lines of the carefully prepared script:

"Mrs. Brillis, do you really think this is a good idea?"

"Yes, Dr. Clare. I do. I think . . . I guess I need to be trained. And you can call me Debbie."

Hyper-aware, Bear could detect the uncertainty in her voice. And she'd fumbled her lines. He demurred. "I don't know. I'm not sure about this. I need to hear you tell me very clearly what you want." Seeing that the girl didn't flinch, he was so confident of receiving a favorable reply that he popped open the briefcase that sat on his desk and removed Mr. Wattaman, who was lodged in his soft flannel sack. Bear let him slide out and then dropped him into his waiting hand so that he could slip a condom over his bulbous nose and roll it down the length of his rubber torso. He slapped him lightly against the palm of his other hand and then waited for Debbie's reaction. She needed to have enough time to wonder about all these interesting sounds.

"I want to be trained." This time Debbie spoke loudly and firmly.

Bear addressed her in a pleasantly clinical tone. "Are you sure?"

"Oh yes. I *need* to be properly trained," she replied, and then added for good measure, "by *you,* Dr. Clare." This time she remembered to chirp her lines with a perky bravado.

◆❖◆

That vulgar witch Margo had told her, repeatedly, explicitly, that he wanted a girl who was hot to trot. But she had read the witch's underlying message: The Nouveau riche shmuck needs to see that she understands she's only here to be used. That his money can buy her. That he is special because he can afford to do this to her. In her own mind, Deborah saw that there was also a certain measure of danger here, and to tell the truth, this was the only part that made it exciting for her. However fake it might be—she would fake it for him since he was, after all, only a handsome but harmless, fantasizing fool.

And then she remembered the words: "You can do it . . . It won't be so bad. There's nothing that a little soap and water can't later clean up . . ." She thought of her future and then told herself to think only about the money. And yet, despite herself, she could not fail to acknowledge the heat that was flowing toward the destination where Dr. Clare was eager to go.

Bear felt a faint sensation of fluttering. Miles below. Somewhere in the area of his crotch. Oh good girl. She was beginning to give him some gusto. Despite his recent travesty with Ma, it felt like maybe his Big Thing wasn't dead. Bear leaned down through the clouds to see if he could see himself in the mirror and then he felt, rather than saw, himself beginning to re-assemble. Now he was more aware of the girl's heavy breathing. Bear deliberately matched his breathing to hers, he could tell she was nervous and still listening to his every move. Her excitement was contagious. He stopped breathing and then, without any warning, he aimed Mr. Wattaman's nose at the exquisite heart of the valley and with a quick thrust led him on a quick walk not into but along the entire length of the eager crevasse and with just enough pressure to leave the sheer fabric caught between the white peaches. He looked down from the Olympian heights where he was now floating and there, far below, he could see them looming up at him. White pillows. From a great distance it seemed, there had come a faint yelp, a gasp of surprise perhaps. But otherwise no movement or flinching. This was a strong and sturdy one.

He intended to pause for a moment; he wanted to search in the mirror to see if her nipples stood proud, but then, at this exquisitely crucial moment, there was a burst of static and Margo's strident voice ricocheted throughout the room:

"Doctor *Clare*! Two gentlemen are here to *see* you . . . The IRS! . . . They want to talk to you . . . right NNnnNOWwww!" The volume had been cranked up too high and her last word ended with a discordant out of control squeal.

Bear saw bright flashes of light leaping before his eyes and then twinkling stars began to pepper his vision. He jammed Mr. Wattaman into a trouser pocket and leaped toward the telephone. Snatching up the receiver, he punched the button of his line to the reception desk and spit into the mouthpiece. "Get *off* the damn intercom! And boot up code two! Tell 'em I'll be out to see 'em in a coupla minutes!" Bear cut Margo off and clicked on his other line and frantically punched in the numbers for the law office of Buster Hosterman.

"Get Buster! Now!"

Buster immediately came on the line and this time Bear was glad to hear his adenoidal, mid-western drawl.

"Hiya Doc. So what's up?"

"The IRS! Two agents! In the office. Right now. Code Two on the computer." Bear's voice sounded strange, even to him, and he too late realized he'd mentioned "Code Two." A mistake. He hadn't intended to do that.

"Now, just cool your jets, Doc. You're talkin' too fast. Gotta ask a few questions. First, did you tell L.C. 'bout me?"

"No. She doesn't know *anything.*"

"Good. Been thinking about that. Works to your advantage." The lawyer's voice was dry and devoid of emotion.

Bear suddenly came to his senses when he looked up and saw Debbie's rump. She hadn't budged. *Stupid cow*, he thought, *got to get her out of here.* "Hey!" he barked. "That'll be all for now. Zip it up and get out there with Margo." Then he stared, fascinated by Debbie's response to his orders: Debbie, who hadn't bothered to remove the blindfold, now slowly turned around to face him. First she fondled her wonderful pink-tipped melons, then lifting them up, she pressed them together and pointed them in his direction before forcing them back into the huge satin cups. Bear was astounded. While he straightened his tie and finished locking up his desk, he kept his eyes glued on Debbie while she pulled herself together; but he managed to notice that her slim ankles and smooth rounded calves were the same as his Ma's—and she was the same height, too.

Debbie pulled off her blindfold and glanced at him with a smile, and then seeing his furiously intent expression she blinked her eyes and smoothed her hair but made no move to leave.

He waved his hand wildly, as if to say "out," and said, "Uh, you're fine, Debbie, and close the door when you leave." He had calmed down enough to return the smile she shot him as she walked out the door. Good. It looked like Margo had found him a hot one this time. But he'd still have to start her all over again from the very beginning, because he had to be sure she could pass his test.

"Who's that you talking to?" Buster's voice sounded peevish.

"New office chick. Just checking her out."

"Now see here! This is no time for you to be foolin' around, Doc. Now you listen up! There's *two* guys, you say? Well, that means special agents. Could be there's a criminal investigation comin' down. You ask them what they want. If they say they just want to have a little look 'round your place, then you tell 'em to show you the search warrant. If they don't have one, then you tell 'em to get the hell outta there. And make sure they know your wife's a tax attorney. Tell 'em she handles everything. Lay it on thick. You tell 'em she's one of those tax-haven lawyers. You hear? Then kick 'em out, and call me later." Buster clicked off the line without saying good-bye.

For a split-second, Bear's mind sprayed like shrapnel. He recited his mantra for an entire 30 seconds to make the panicky feeling subside. He'd forgotten all about the audit! And he hadn't said a word about it to Ma because he sure didn't want her to volunteer to help him and then start nosing around in his records! He wasn't quite ready for that. At least not yet. His hand automatically groped for the telephone and he swiftly dialed the unlisted number of one of his special patients—the one he'd been cultivating for just such a time as this—the chief operations officer of the Highridge bank. He'd already paid him off with a big contribution to the officer's charity drive; but no sweat about that, he'd simply used Ma's money—money that she'd earned over the years which she'd been giving him to invest. As soon as he heard the voice of the operations officer, Bear curtly announced that he wanted to bank-wire the funds in all the Clare savings accounts to the bank he'd selected in Montreal, to be placed at interest for ten days, with instructions to follow.

Speaking rapidly, he told the operations officer to set up the new account in his father's name, Markus Clarichevik; then he reached in his briefcase and pulled out a small piece of paper where he'd written the numbers. After reading them to the operations officer, he gave his instructions: The numbers were to be used as a key to the new account so that nobody could access it unless they had this code. Bear listened to the operations officer confirming his instructions. Then he cut off the call and slipped the paper into the back pocket of his briefcase, which he quietly closed and slipped under his desk.

Bear finally began to breathe a little easier. He checked out the room to make sure all the drawers and cabinets were closed and then he decided to leave Debbie's open purse on his desk to give the agents something to look at. After closing the doors to his bathroom, he stepped out to the reception area, leaving his office door ajar to show he had nothing to hide. The two agents, he saw, were standing next to the reception counter and Margo stood hovering over the computer on the other side. Bear gave them a bland, dimpled smile.

The older agent spoke first, flashing his identification. "Dr. Mark Clare? Hey! Good to meet you. I'm Mr. Rizzo, August Rizzo, and this is my associate, Mr. Jordan. We just thought we'd drop by to get acquainted with you."

The husky younger agent remained standing at Agent Rizzo's back and looked at Dr. Clare with a friendly air before turning his attention toward Margo. Margo immediately sidled over to the young man. Batting her eyelashes rapidly, she made a wet rosebud mouth as if to blow him a kiss and then grinned at him boldly.

"Well. It's good to meet *you*, too." Bear fixed Rizzo with a level stare. "I wish I had more time for you, but I have a patient waiting for me right now. You folks have anything special in mind?"

"Well, we hope *you* don't mind . . . We just wanted to stop in, maybe take a little look around, that's all. I see you keep your records on a computer. That right?" Rizzo nodded toward the bank of patient files that filled the wall behind Margo's counter.

"Oh . . . that. Yes. You'll have to talk to Ma, I mean, my wife about that. Well, uh . . . you see, she's handling this here audit . . . she's a tax attorney, y'know. She takes care of all the paper-work and that sort of stuff. I don't get involved much in paper-stuff 'cause I'm just a plain, wet-finger dentist, if you know what I mean." Bear chuckled and then gave Rizzo a wide, dimpled grin.

Rizzo threw his head back and laughed, then he pulled a tissue out of his breast pocket to dab at his eyes. "Pardon me. That's a good one," he guffawed. "So, your wife's a lawyer, *your* lawyer? Hey! That's good, too. We'll just give her a call and get things cleared through her office today. Then we can meet with the two of you right here. How 'bout this afternoon. Sound good to you?"

Bear quickly interjected, "Uh, Ma, my lawyer, excuse me, I mean L.C., that's what most people around here call her. . . well, you see, she's going out of town. Sometime later tonight, I guess. Going off to the Cayman Islands again. Business I suppose, she doesn't really tell me much about what she does. But, she'll be back here in about a week. She's *big* into that tax haven stuff, y'know."

Rizzo gave a mirthless smile to no one in particular. "Well, that's very interesting. So, you think she'll have time to meet with us before she leaves?" Rizzo's voice was now soft and teasing, as if he were trying to charm the neighborhood pit-bull.

Bear saw the younger agent's eyes suddenly come alive.

"Well, to tell the truth, I think she's actually leaving sometime before lunch." Bear was aware that Rizzo was hoping to work him, so he hoped he sounded cool and unconcerned. He needed the agent to think it was too late for them to get in touch with his wife today, which would be nice because this would give him more time.

"Okay. If that's the case, we can wait until your lawyer returns," Rizzo replied genially. "A week's not going to make much of a difference here. We'll have staff call Mrs. Clare's office and leave a message for her. You say she's leaving *tonight.* Right?"

Bear blinked his eyes as if he hadn't heard and then he shuffled and smiled and did his best to make himself look fat, dumb, and innocent. He was so busy pretending, he failed to notice that the agents hadn't bothered to ask him for his wife's law office telephone number.

"Well, it's no problem. There's no big rush. And it's been good to meet you," Rizzo said.

By the time Bear thought to extend his hand to say good-bye, the two agents were already half-way to the door. He wiped his hand nervously on the back of his nylon jacket.

◆❖◆

Standing in one of his patient operatories where he could peek at them through the shuttered blinds, Bear watched the agents as they drove out of the medical center parking lot. Not to worry, he thought. He'd fox them good and by the time they returned he'd have everything in order. When he was sure they were gone for good, Bear slipped back to his private office and fished Mr. Wattaman out of his pants and tucked the dildo safely away in his briefcase. Then he sat down behind his desk and stared at the panels of his bathroom doors. It was at times like these that he wanted his Ma. Good Ma. She was always there for him like nobody else. And that explained why he was always so careful never to let any part of his body touch the privates of any other woman. Of course they were free to touch his—that was different. Besides, that's what they were here for.

Bear leaned back in his chair and folded his arms behind his head while he arranged his thoughts. "See? It's not so hard to think like a lawyer".

That's what Ma always said she was doing, and now he was doing it too. So, technically speaking, he was still a good husband as any good lawyer would hasten to point out. And as a good husband, he had every right to demand total fidelity from his Ma—despite what Margo officially referred to as their "office games." Games were different; games were games and that's why they didn't count, and just because Ma was always so serious didn't mean that he couldn't play. Yes, he never touched them. And nobody could say that women didn't come to him of their own free will. He couldn't help it, women just did, and besides, nobody forced them to work here if they didn't like it.

Bear rocked back and forth in his chair, telling himself what a good husband he was and reassuring himself about the future, when suddenly and for the very first time, he began to feel himself splitting away from his body. He could see himself, actually see himself, as if he were watching himself in a movie projected on the panels of the bathroom doors—and he was lying next to his little brother Stevie in the narrow bed they slept in that night when he was only thirteen. As usual, the details were still very sharply defined and he could see them now, growing brighter and brighter until they were spiked with black zig-zags of electricity.

He had gotten up that night to complain about Stevie, and how he kept grabbing at him and keeping him awake by making this rattling wet purr when he breathed. And even though Stevie was burning hot, that penny-pinching, self-pitying rum-dum of a father of his had refused to call a doctor that night. Instead, he had ordered Mark to get back to bed. Mark knew better than to disobey, he'd already learned that his father liked to discuss things with his knuckles. As usual, his mother had taken Stevie's side—her efforts, however, were confined to a few seconds of useless whimpering and hand-wringing—and then his father had rolled over on the living room couch, refusing to listen to any of them. Later that night, sick of the lot of them, sick of breathing the stale, re-breathed, rat turd air of their tiny flat, he had wrapped the dirty sheet around and around his brother's head and then he had packed Stevie hard away in the bedroom closet so that he could get some sleep.

A tear slowly rolled down Bear's bronzed cheek. He could still see himself lying there, all by himself. Yes. He could see himself now. Poor little Markie Clarichevik. He felt so sorry for him because he could see that this poor little Markie wasn't given any choice.

He had awakened early the next morning to the sight of his brother's exhausted, cave-white face—Stevie had somehow managed to work his way out of the sheet—disgusting yellow stuff dried in his nostrils, mouth agape, lips cracked and darkly speckled with what Mark knew was dried blood. He ran away, into the kitchen. Hungry, and under the pretext of making some for his father, he gobbled up Stevie's share of the sour gray mush—a mixture of flour and stale oats—and then he waited until his father cleared out before making any attempt to call for help.

The social worker visited their unheated tenement later that day, and then after a feeble fuss from his mother, Stevie was carried out on a stretcher under the same sheet that little Markie had used to stifle the rasping sounds that had come from his brother's mouth.

After that, it wasn't too long before little Markie realized how wonderful it was to be an only child and he'd played it for all it was worth. From then on everybody paid lots of attention to him and even sometimes his mother did too. His teachers at school called him "precious" and "special" and they favored him with lots of extra help so his grades steadily improved. And he got lots and lots of praise for being such a brave and smart little boy.

Bear wanted to forget, but he couldn't and he tried to banish the vision by pressing down on his lids with the tips of his fingers until he saw silvery stars, but the vision got stronger. With his eyes still closed, he reached for the telephone and dialed his home number. He needed help. His Ma was supposed to be there for him, waiting for him to call. He let the phone ring three more times before reaching out with a short round finger to cut off the call. He had remembered, just in the nick of time, that she wasn't home. Ma was at her office, taking care of her clients. Not taking care of her Bear. Fine. Ma didn't know anything. No one knew anything. And nobody ever would. Bear suddenly was filled with a towering rage; he could scarcely breathe. Shaking, he pressed his hands on either side of his ribs and then squeezed them as if they were bellows until he finally caught his breath. If anything happened to him, people should know that Ma was to blame. She was to blame for everything.

If eyes could have somehow penetrated his walls, they would have found an entirely different man. His face, now gray, had become that of an animal. His ears had actually flattened to his head, and his eyes, drained of all that made them seem human, were flat and cold. With a grimace, Bear picked up the telephone and slammed it down in front of him. He punched the buttons over and over again, each time listening, first to the sound of it ringing and then to the voice on the other end. Then he set the receiver down and unlocked his desk drawer for what seemed like the millionth time. He didn't need Ma. He didn't need anyone. All he ever would need was right *here.* Bear picked up the receiver again and listened with distant disdain to the voice on the other end of the line repeatedly saying hello, then sent a murderous thought down the line and cut off the call. And finally, with his thumb and forefinger poised like an insect's delicate pincers, he reached into the drawer and picked up a yellow pill.

Once he kept track of how many he took every day, but now he no longer bothered.

Tossing the pill up high in the air with a practiced flick of the wrist, Bear tipped his head back and caught it in his open mouth. He stood up, then lurching toward his bathroom, he yanked open the doors, crouched over the sink, and drank from the golden faucet. Wiping his mouth with the back of his hand, he stood straight and took stock of himself. He was the biggest, tallest man in town. He wore two-inch lifts in his boots to make sure of that. And he still was as handsome as any movie star. People, especially other men, needed a big handsome guy like him because they identified with him, they wanted to look like him, they wanted to follow his lead, and that was why he was The King. Filled with renewed confidence, Bear squared his shoulders and straightened his lab coat and after a quick squirt of breath deodorizer, marched out of his office to begin the onerous task of tending to patients. In five minutes he was feeling much better and actually enjoying his work. He made sure his patients heard all the jokes he'd learned at breakfast so they would think of his office as a fun place to visit.

Finally, when he'd finished his regular patients and the reception area was cleared of waiting patients, he instructed Margo to complete the Code Two drill and then to get on the phone and reschedule his afternoon appointments. He had to apply himself to all the extra things he needed to do now that his tax audit was picking up steam. Back in full command, he told Margo to find a way to keep the new girl busy—maybe the office games should be put off until later on in the week?—and then he remembered that he'd better make an appointment with Buster.

Placing the call on a different line to keep Margo from snooping, he set up a Tuesday afternoon consultation with his lawyer, Hosterman. Finally, he was ready to place his last call: to the local pharmacy. He asked for Manny, and said the two words: "Code Two," which to Manny would mean *extreme caution required until further notice.* Manny was one of the two other people on earth who knew what this meant, but Manny would never be a problem, because he, too, had too much to lose.

◆❖◆

Margo spent the rest of Monday morning hunched over the telephone rescheduling the afternoon appointments. When she was through, she left the phone off the hook so she could work on the computer without interruption. She needed to double-check the Code Two program and make sure it was operating properly. She had already used it earlier that morning, when the young IRS agent had approached the reception counter, but now that he was gone, she wanted to run through the program again to make sure everything tallied with their deposit slips for that quarter.

By using a macro—a programmed set of instructions which she'd used earlier that morning—a punch of only one button would let her produce an entirely different set of accounting records for the past three months. Of course, these new records were phony. They were intended to be substituted for the real records that detailed all the business that actually passed through the office. They referred to the real stuff as the "Code One" data, which was actually a ledger of all the "medications" Doc ordered for his "special" patients and what the patients paid for them. Then, with one more punch to the keyboard—any key would do—the Code One data would be transferred onto a floppy disk which she could remove and easily ditch. "If," as she frequently liked to say, "push ever came to shove."

This disk, which she had generated earlier, had already been slipped through the slot of the locked drawer underneath the reception counter, where it would remain until Doc wanted to see it. As an added precaution, there was another button—located under the edge of the reception counter—which controlled the "dumpster." If pressed, the bottom of the drawer holding the disks would simply pop open and the disks would slide to a small hole underneath the floor. It would take a demolition crew to get under there if they ever wanted to retrieve the disks.

And why didn't they simply destroy all their records? And why did she have to go through all this crazy business of setting up a phony set of books? *She* knew why: because the IRS required all businesses to maintain a set of books and to keep them available for inspection. And what would happen if they didn't? Well, the IRS could charge them with tax evasion, that's what! So they had to give the IRS *something*, and it had to be something that really looked good.

Margo punched a few keys and ran through the Code Two program again to see if their receipt records needed to be corrected. Doc could always send her to the bank with enough cash to deposit if for some reason the Code Two records showed a shortfall, but it was always more economical for her to simply take a little time and alter the records themselves, which no longer was a major task because of this nice new computer. Computers were wonderful, she thought, because as soon as she got the data on the screen to add up the way she wanted it to, she only had to give the print key a little tap and then Doc would have himself a nifty new set of records to give to the IRS.

Margo felt confident. They had always been prepared for an IRS visit; she and Doc had rehearsed their plans over and over, so today, when those IRS agents dropped in on them like that, they weren't the least bit nervous. And all the agents wanted was to "look around." Big deal. Let 'em look. Nothing to worry about. The storm would blow over without doing them a lick of harm.

Margo hit the enter key, and the screen went dark.

And now, what to do with their new sex toy? Margo thought about it for a minute, then she decided to keep the little ninny out of their hair by putting her to work in the back laboratory. Debbie might as well make herself useful—she was perfectly capable of cleaning dental trays and sterilizing instruments until Doc wanted to use her again.

After Margo completed her tasks she looked at her watch and saw that it was time for her daily meeting with Doc. She pulled at her uniform zipper and lowered it just a few inches more. Entering his private office without knocking, she walked over to his desk and sat on the corner of his desk and crossed her legs. Leaning toward him to give him a view, she handed him the office appointment log, whispered, "Okay Doc, what's next?" and waited for his usual appreciative reaction. It was always nice to know that she still had what it took to take a man's mind off his business.

◆❖◆

Bear leaned back in his chair and swung his feet up on the opposite corner of his desk. He let Margo know with his eyes that he'd seen her main events, but then he decided to play her a different way today: "Did you take that envelope I gave you to the florist and get the flowers sent off to my lovely wife?" He spoke softly and let his eyes fall half-closed, as if he were pleased to treat Ma to this little surprise. But even with his eyes half-closed, he could tell it had worked—he could hear Margo huffing angrily at him for reminding her that he had a wife and another life, but it was even more amusing to see how fast she yanked up her zipper. She was always so predictable. There never were any surprises with Margo, and that's what he liked best in a woman. If only they were all like her.

Ordinarily, he would have joked around with her, pretending that she was being stingy with him, but there was no time for that today because figuring out how to keep a handle on Ma was more important. And time was important. He needed just a little bit more of it with Ma, so he could get things organized, and he knew that a few dozen roses and a little money would suffice to buy the additional time he needed. Bear chuckled to himself. He knew what Ma thought: that he was too dull and too straight to lead a double life. Take that car, for instance. Her big birthday surprise. Expensive, yes. But it hadn't really cost him a thing. She'd actually paid for it herself—he'd merely spent some of the money she'd given him over the last couple of years. In fact, none of his tender gestures really cost him that much compared to what he spent on himself. No. Never in her wildest dreams would she think he was capable of what he had done and what he was planning to do.

"Sure the flowers were sent. Took care of that early this morning." Margo spoke irritably and immediately changed the subject. "So, what about the new girl? She goin' to work out?"

Bear ran his hand through his curls and stared blankly at Margo to keep her from thinking he was in any way obliged to her for this treat. "I dunno," he replied. "It's really too early to tell because of all these damn interruptions. Well, now that we're in Code Two, just have whats-her-name come in here a coupla hours a day. I'll leave it to you to keep her handy. Oh yeah, and here's her purse." Bear handed it back to Margo.

"Her name's Debbie. You know that!"

Bear grinned, full of a little boy's mischief. "Awright. So it's Debbie. Okay! Here. Give this back to her now, and I want you to get her out of here early. Get the special patients rescheduled before you start on the files. Those files are important! So keep working on them and you'd better stay here till seven and then you should lock up 'cause I'm leaving early to go to The Wei. You heard what those agents said about getting the wife involved in my audit? Don't you worry! I know how to head that one off." Bear grinned and looked up at Margo. "You know why?"

Margo shook her head.

"I never made her a corporate officer of this here dental corporation, so she's never even once seen its tax returns. And just keep this one under your hat—I took a room at the club for a week so I can work on things while she's gone . . . I don't want Benjy or anyone else to see what I'm doing. So don't worry, I'll have everything squared away by the time she returns."

It sounded to Margo like Doc had everything under control, but then, when she inspected Debbie's purse, she could see his wet palm-prints still glistening on the scruffed-up vinyl. He was now sweating heavily, at least his hands were, and he seemed to be acting a little too crabby. Maybe he wasn't feeling so good? Or maybe he was overdoing it with all those pills—the ones she'd been seeing him sneak lately. Margo wondered what she would do if anything ever happened to him. Maybe she'd better start thinking about some plans for herself instead of always worrying about him. In any event, it looked like she'd better keep Debbie out of the picture until she was sure Doc was feeling okay.

His voice interrupted her thoughts: "You've still got a lot of calls to make, so you'd better get out there." Margo quickly obeyed and carried Debbie's purse to her desk behind the reception counter. She was pleased to see that the envelope was still there; then she peeked inside and saw the bills—well, no one would be any the wiser . . .

BECAUSE IT IS WRIT

HIGHRIDGE **10:30 a.m. February 24, 1974**

After treating Charles to a full tank of high-octane gas, Linnell drove home and parked him at the end of the walkway leading up to the house. She let herself in, and meaning to disarm only the front door, she accidentally disarmed the entire security system. This time, instead of berating herself for her mistake, Linnell took the time to study the panel's blinking lights so that she wouldn't repeat her mistake again. Then she headed for the kitchen—a big cup of coffee would set her right.

She disrobed on the way and examined her pantyhose. Ruined completely, she saw. Linnell piled her clothes on the counter and retrieved the bag of Kona she'd put away the night before. The house was so quiet—too quiet, she thought—and so terribly tidy that she felt like an intruder. Standing half-naked, alone in the kitchen, she suddenly felt ill at ease—but then, after admiring the pristine white walls and the spotless Mexican tile pavers of the kitchen floor, her uneasiness disappeared.

It was a solid house, solidly planted at the top of the hill. "It's my safe haven." She spoke aloud to reassure herself. Then she wondered why she was even thinking about this. She knew why. Lately, and for some unknown reason, she'd had the feeling that somebody was shadowing her; keeping track of her every move. This seemed to begin—it was hard to describe exactly what told her so—as soon as she left the house. But there was no point telling Bear; she already knew what he'd say: He'd say she was simply imagining things. Linnell hugged herself, then threw open the kitchen window and stood before it in her bra and panties, luxuriating in the breeze that fanned over her face and shoulders. Rain from the night before had cleared the valley of smog and the sight of the chartreuse-green buds on the sturdy live oaks spoke of future promises. The sap was rising in the Monterey pines, its piquant top note floating over the honeyed fragrance of the early-blooming almond trees.

How could anything go wrong in the midst of such beauty? Linnell inhaled deeply. Spring would be here in full glory when she returned from her trip. Really! Instead of worrying so much about things that in all probability didn't really exist, she should fall on her knees and give thanks for having such a beautiful—albeit predictable—life here at home. And for being doubly blessed because she had a marvelous international tax practice which allowed her to escape it.

Linnell exhaled and sent a prayer-balloon rising above her head: Thank God for Grand Cayman Island. That mysterious hook of tan bark, floating with its two small companions in a bowl of electric-shock blue. Cayman. Her house of the spirits! Her land of illusion and smoke and mirrors, where nothing was what it seemed. Whatever it was to others, it stood for freedom for her, because it allowed her to be whoever she wanted to be. Here, at home, she only knew who she was supposed to be. Her fault—she had passively allowed herself to play only the roles others wanted: Fix-it Lawyer and Mop-up Mom. Her fault, too—that Bear thought of her only as "just-plain-ol'-Ma." She was a proud mother all right, but to Benjy, not Bear—so this "Ma" stuff was another thing she intended to change, and she would, too! Just as soon as she returned.

But she was leaving! And just thinking about how soon she would be hiking the island's powdery beaches and dipping into its warm gin-clear waters was all that it took to send her spirits soaring. Restored by the thought of her imminent departure, Linnell Clare floated back to the counter to measure the coffee. Just then, the telephone rang and her hand automatically shot out to catch the complaining instrument before it could ring again.

Cradling the receiver under her chin, Linnell said hello.

There was no reply.

She said hello once again and heard only a click and then—just like what was happening at her law office—the dial tone. Was this a wrong number? Or was the same thing beginning here? Linnell carefully set the carafe in the coffeemaker and rubbed her neck, uneasy. She had a slight headache now. Well, a couple of aspirin would fix things, she thought. Linnell padded out of the kitchen and headed down the hall for her own bathroom. They had separate bathrooms—Bear's was adjacent to their master bedroom, while hers, smaller, was across the hall. She entered and found the aspirin in her medicine cabinet and then shook the bottle in disgust when she saw that only one tablet remained.

It must have been the sound of the lonely pill rattling inside its container that did the trick, because instantly, memories of what had happened to her earlier that morning came flooding back. Pills! It all had something to do with Bear and his pills. Yellow pills. Leaning against her sink, Linnell closed her eyes and envisioned what she'd seen early that morning, shortly before daybreak.

She had for some reason awakened before Bear. Desperate for more sleep, she'd slid entirely under the comforter to play possum, hoping against hope that he'd leave her alone. But he'd done his usual routine of noisy things: He'd banged his medicine cabinet; opened and closed his towel bin; turned on and off the faucet and so forth, and then—*now* she could remember—she could actually see it happening all over again:

While she had lain hidden in darkness, peering at him from inside the dark cave of the comforter, he'd stood in his brightly lit bathroom in front of his medicine cabinet, pulling on its mirrored door until it was so perfectly aligned she could see his eyes in the glass. Which meant that except for the darkness enveloping her, he would have been able to see her eyes, too. His eyes had glittered gray and bright at first, but then, as they focused in her direction, they slowly turned cold and baleful. The expression on his face had made her stiffen with fear. His eyes. They were the eyes of a lizard. Flat and evil—as if they were coldly calculating the distance between the tip of his tongue and a hapless fly—and then she knew, don't ask her how, but she *knew* what he was thinking: That *she* was the fly that he had in mind. Yes. It was crazy. But she had known, beyond any doubt, that he was thinking this. About *her*. His helpmate.

She'd only caught a brief glimpse of all this because he had immediately reached out with his hairy high-arched foot to push on his bathroom door until it was half-closed. This was followed by the familiar sounds of him fumbling around in his medicine cabinet, and she could recall herself wondering if he was trying to find the vitamins she always bought for him at the grocery store. Then she had heard the very distinct sound of a pill bottle. Rattling. A pill bottle rattling as if it were almost empty.

He had astounded her with what he did next: He had leaned over backwards while slowly rotating his head in her direction to squint madly at her—the lump under the cover—from around the edge of the half-closed door, and then, after shooting another murderous look in her direction, she had seen his mouth suddenly fall open and three yellow pills leap toward it from behind the door. He'd looked grotesque, and if not for the frightening expression on his face she might otherwise have laughed aloud at his weird gyrations. Staid Bear. Dull Bear. A man of unshakable and steadfast routine who liked all things predictable. But this morning—this morning he had looked like evil incarnate, a demon. But only for that one fleeting instant because a second later he straightened up and then shoved the door with his foot until it was closed. She could even remember his large white toe with its yellowish toe nail. This had been followed by the usual hypnotic sounds of water, drumming against the walls of his shower. She must have nodded off at that point because the next thing she knew, he was waking her to say good bye—and his face wore its usual expression again: a blank pleasantness that bespoke no emotion.

But he had been carrying a briefcase—this was different—and she would've sworn it was hers if she didn't know for a fact that hers was still in her office. But yes, he'd had a briefcase—a brown leather one, with those clever little locks, just like hers, and he'd stood at the side of the bed with it dangling just opposite her nose and she remembered the scent of new leather, and then, like usual, he had bent over her to kiss the air above her head.

Linnell jerked. Now she could remember the rest!

They'd had this strange exchange: She'd suddenly sat up in bed, apparently startling him, and had asked him if he was taking his vitamins. He'd said no, that he was just taking something for his headache. Some odd-sounding preparation. She hadn't quite understood because he had mumbled the words, but it had sounded to her as if he'd said: "Jessum perco." He'd explained that the pills were new, something his detail man had just given him the day before. Then he'd said something even more puzzling: That she ought to take some, too. That he thought these pills would do her some good. When she had tried to get him to explain what he meant, he had dimpled blandly at her like he always did and then he had fled. He had actually run down the hall and then, like a flash, out the front door, crying, "I love you. I looove you! I'll call you at noon like usual."

Jessum perco. That's what he'd said. What on earth was he talking about? Well, now that she had the time, she was going to find out! Linnell raced down the hall and stalked into Bear's bathroom to look for the flying pills. She suddenly realized she hadn't been in this wild kingdom for years, not since he took it for himself and ordered everybody else to stay out. Well, she'd had no interest in his private space, so "staying out" had never been an issue for her—and besides, she had the greatest respect for an individual's need for privacy.

"Well, to hell with *that*," Linnell said to herself. She opened Bear's medicine cabinet and looked on the shelves. Surprise! There were no vitamins, none whatsoever. She stood there, puzzled; she was sure she'd heard a bottle rattling. Hadn't he said he was taking something for his headache? Something his detail man had just given him?

After sorting through all the debris on his shelves, she finally found a small plastic vial. She picked it up and shook it and it made the same sound she'd heard earlier that morning. "This is it," she thought, turning it over in her hand. She read the label: "Percodan. #30 — 250 mg." The date on the vial showed that "Dr. Mark Clare" had prescribed the pills two weeks before for a person named "D. Brillis." She knew who that was—it was his new chair-side assistant. The one he'd just hired. Debbie. Debbie Brillis. She could remember him mentioning that name. Linnell could see with a glance that only four pills remained out of the original thirty. She replaced the vial exactly where she'd found it, then opened the laundry bin. The stench of molding towels rose to tickle her nose and she sneezed noisily. Holding her breath, she rummaged toward the bottom of the bin, finding, along the way, one empty plastic vial after another.

After lining up all of them on the counter—there were fifteen altogether—she examined each one. All the labels said the same thing: "Percodan. #30—250 mg."

". . . Huh!" she exhaled. "They're all prescribed by Dr. M. Clare for Margo Callahan! That old witch!" Linnell swept the empty vials back into the bin, shoved the dirty towels down on top of them and walked back to their bedroom. She didn't understand. What did all of this mean?

Ordinarily, she would have stood there trying to figure things out, because if there was one thing she couldn't stand, it was an unexplained puzzle. But before she could give the matter any more thought, she was distracted by the blinking red light of the answering machine that sat on her bedside table. Some calls must have come in earlier that morning while she was at the bank. Linnell punched the replay button and listened to the beeps from a series of hang-up calls. Then she flushed with irritation. Not because of the calls—like usual they were just hang-ups—but because she had just spied another Benzedrine inhaler. Bear had done it again! He'd simply dropped it on the carpet for her to pick up. Why couldn't he use the waste basket? Linnell walked over to the small tube and kicked it into Bear's bathroom. Then chucking everything in favor of coffee, she grabbed one of Bear's huge short-sleeved T-shirts and slipped into it on her way to the kitchen.

While her coffee was cooling, Linnell stood at the dining room window, trying to make sense of the pills and wondering why Bear would want to look at her with such an evil expression. But nothing figured. Nothing made any sense whatsoever. Frustrated, Linnell ended up scolding herself: Why did she let herself get so upset about such trifling things? Why couldn't she simply think positive? Just look at her now! Here she was, standing in this magnificent house. Filled with everything. New this and new that. And yet no matter how good things really were, she always had this neurotic need to peek under the bandages. Why did she have to do this? Was there something wrong with her?

Or was it him?

It's him, whispered the little voice which she now recognized as the remains of her instinct. "Oh, shut up." Linnell replied to the walls. As an act of contrition for feeling so ungrateful for all the wonderful things that she had, she picked up a dish towel and polished the kitchen counters. And then to show her appreciation for having so much, she lined up the cutlery in the drawer so that all the sharp edges were turned to the left, the way she knew Bear liked to find them. *Really, it's him,* the small voice insisted. Well, perhaps this was so.

Linnell thought guiltily about their last fight, when she'd finally blown up. He had been ragging at her, trying to get her to do meaningless tasks—like what she was doing now—such things as re-setting the table and re-folding the towels so they'd be "just so." She had resisted. "Why? It's a waste of my time!" she had screamed.

First, he had replied, "Why? I'll tell you why! 'Cause I work hard all the time. And *you* should, too." Then, in an apparent attempt to soften his remark, he had tried to joke her into seeing things his way, and he'd said: "Why? 'Cause it's *written,* that's why." Then he'd chuckled, "Like, y'know—preordained—and besides, it's what *I* like, so you better get used to it, kiddo." Of course she always wanted to do things to please him, but whenever he used that tone of voice on her, she'd simply lose it and the fight would be on.

The few who knew about this side of their marriage—just her sisters, really, not counting Mama N'dobah, who was too far away to count—would tell her that she'd better "get with the program," just do what he said, "because the price was right." They'd always take his side, then point out how good she had it. Here she had this handsome husband who'd bought her this magnificent house in the best section of Highridge—never mind that he'd purchased it without consulting with her, thank-you-very-much!—and she was complaining? He was such a *good* provider, they'd say. And it was not just the house. There were the new cars. The country club. "What's the matter with you?" they'd ask.

Okay, so maybe her sisters had a point. And maybe she *should* try harder. She knew things looked splendid. At least on the surface, they did. But nobody, not even her sisters, knew about what was really happening, or rather, not happening, between the sheets. Whom could she tell? Nobody. Not her mother. Not her sisters. Nobody except the too-far-away Mama N'dobah wanted to know anything about things like that. So what could she do? She'd read every book and magazine she could lay her hands on for clues to "Unlocking the Secrets of Making Your Marriage Work," and "How to Put the Sizzle Back into Your Sex Life," but to no avail. Nothing worked with him. Nothing she did seemed to make any difference. And Mama N'dobah's solution was to her mind a bit too extreme.

Oh God! She had better face up to it: If the thrill had ever been there, it sure was gone now! Take last night for example. Before rolling on top of her with a grunt, he had once again felt compelled to declare that he was going to *bake his big meat loaf in her hot little oven*. Why did he *always* have to say this! Did he think this was foreplay? Or funny? Maybe once, years ago, when he'd first said this, she'd laughed. Big mistake. Because now every time he came near her he'd say the same thing. She'd beg him to stop, and sometimes he would, but then the awkward silence was even worse. It seemed that underneath that pretty-boy exterior there dwelled a stubbornly repetitive, meanly compulsive, pile of meat and potatoes! And besides that, his hair always smelled of thymol, the solvent he mixed into the paste used for setting gold crowns.

Is this all there is? Linnell thought of Peggy Lee's mournful complaint and heard the sad melody in her head. Maybe having that second child wasn't such a good idea after all. Intending to really think about this, Linnell carried her coffee into the dining room. When she was settled, she saw something dark, sitting on one of the dining room chairs: a pair of sunglasses. She had the frames folded and placed on the table before realizing that she'd found an entirely different pair only the week before. The lenses were so terribly dark she had to wonder just how Bear could see through them, and then for the first time it struck her that his eyes might be bothering him. She felt guilty immediately, this time because she had come so near to forgetting how much stress-filled, detailed, close-up work he had to do in order to make a living for them. Perhaps this accounted for all those headaches he had. Really, she really was being much too hard on him. Linnell carefully polished the lenses, then set them in the middle of the dining room table where she was sure Bear would find them.

Sipping her coffee, Linnell thought about how it had all begun. With his eyes, that's how. And it unsettled her to think that these were the same eyes that had scared the wits out of her earlier that morning. But long ago, when she first saw them, they had been luminous with yearning, earnest moonstones fringed with heavy dark lashes. And they must have shorted out her brain completely because she'd never been able to recall what he'd first said when they met.

They'd met calamitously, the first day of their final college semester. He'd slammed into her, sending her books sailing across the floor of the Econ building, and then he had stopped to pick them up, all the while keeping his eyes glued to her face instead of her legs, a reaction which immediately set him apart from the rest of the guys. It had been the sheer physicality of him that had done her in. His hair—he was one of the first guys on campus to let it grow long—and that smile. His white teeth, framed by a set of matched dimples, were perfect. Tall and cocky, he had rocked back on his heels with his hands jammed deep in the pockets of his black leather motorcycle jacket, and she'd come to just in time to hear him urging her to sneak off campus to meet him after dark. That same evening they got together at a smoky jazz joint at the beach, and by the time she'd emptied her first cup of coffee—she had refused to trust herself to anything stronger—she knew she'd found herself a diamond in the rough. A brilliant savage with a hint of danger.

She had been helpless before his charisma, because, like all the rest of the girls in her class, she had been deeply inoculated with the then popular notion that her real purpose in life was not to attend school to learn but to find herself a big bad wolf and then save him from self-destruction through her purest love and her unswerving devotion. And how would she know any better? Like all the rest of her classmates—they were called coeds then—she'd been shipped off to college with no armaments beyond a cashmere sweater, a pointed bra, and a warning from her folks that she'd better graduate with an *MRS.* as had her two older sisters. It was also a given that after landing her man she would want to drop out, do children, and spend the rest of her life as a proper housewife.

As for Mark, he'd seemed totally flattered by her attention. He told her about himself on their first formal date and that same night he'd explained that he'd changed his last name when he left Chicago at the age of eighteen. This name-change was merely a symbolic gesture, "a more pronounceable name would make it easier for him to build a new life for himself," was what he had actually said. Although she hadn't quite understood what he meant by "symbolic gesture," still, if he preferred "Clare" to "Clarichevik," so what? After all, this *was* California, where so many here did the very same thing.

But why had his penchant for symbolic gestures extended so far into the present? Why, for example, had he insisted that she start calling him "Bear"? Linnell caught herself. The truth was they hadn't actually discussed it. Some years back, Mark had simply told her he wanted her to call him *Bear* and then he had stubbornly refused to respond if she or Benjy called him anything else. So really, what was it with him and his names?

However, now that she thought about it, when it came to changing - names, what was it with her? She'd started out in life as Linnell Anne Leigh; but then, when she married, she became Linnell Clare, which didn't last too long, because shortly after that, she'd been given a nickname, "L.C.", and then later, Bear had reduced her to just plain old "Ma." If this was a natural progression, it was very possible a day might come when she'd disappear altogether. But then, who was to blame for this? She'd gone along with this, hadn't she? She had to admit—yes, she had.

Linnell considered her husband's nickname. *Bear.* Actually, this suited him. He *had* put on pounds, and sometimes, especially when he was nervous, his hands curled up into round hairy bear-paws . . . too bad The Wei couldn't help him with that. In fact, come to think of it, he was antsier now than he'd ever been. And just recently he'd formed a new habit that was even more distracting: He would sniff distractedly and then scratch his arms, especially in his sleep. For instance, just a couple of nights ago she'd been awakened by his frantic scratching and for the first time ever, she'd heard him talking in his sleep. He must have been dreaming about his work, because he kept babbling—over and over, all night long—weird passages that must have had something to do with royalty. Louis-the-Sun-King?—and then he would rant about gum surgery: *Orry-gorrry-cutting-fuzzzzy.* It had been very bizarre and upsetting because he'd seemed so distressed. Poor dear. He really did need to get away from that office.

But this wasn't all, there was something else that seemed a little bit strange: Nancy, her closest friend at the country club, had told her she'd heard Bear telling all kinds of stories to people at the club about Linnell and her trips to tax havens. His interest in tax havens and offshore tax planning wasn't at all surprising because it was a terrific game—a game in the fourth dimension, to her mind the only one worth playing—and she was hooked so he probably was too. No, it was his bragging about *her* that was odd. It was so unlike him.

As for off-shore tax planning, he knew *plenty* about that, because, while she was learning the ropes at the Ivener firm, she'd always kept him abreast of the incredible things she was learning; so much so that after a while she had begun to wonder if she hadn't made a mistake and told him too much. Because now look at him! Bragging. Well, bragging about *her* was okay, but about what she did? *That* was unacceptable, not only because it was such bad form to boast about "going offshore," but also because these days any talk about tax havens seemed to attract the wrong sort of attention from the IRS and God knows who else. What else was he doing? Giving complete strangers curbside consultations about offshore tax law? Linnell shuddered at the thought. But what she thought was even more strange was the fact that when she told him about what Nancy had said, Bear had promptly replied that Nancy was nuts. He had denied everything.

And then, as if he were deliberately trying to make matters worse, he absolutely refused to address her by name. She'd told him a thousand times to stop calling her "Ma," but he'd just look down at her, his gray eyes turning cloudy, and he'd say: "Whatsa *matter,* Ma? Don't you *love* me anymore?"

It was all so aggravating! And it left her feeling so perplexed and confused and so sort of crazy that sometimes her eyes would well up with tears and her heart would sink and then she'd long for the days when they were just a penniless young couple. Just plain Mark and Linnell.

Linnell absentmindedly stirred her coffee and thought back to their first date. That was when Mark first told her about his family, which was how she had come to understand that he didn't much like his father. His mother, however, was a different story. She'd died when he was only sixteen, he'd said, leaving him a small inheritance—just enough to send him through dental school, he'd assured her. And then he'd confessed that he'd never really known his mother at all because she'd spent most of her life in a make-believe world behind her mountain of movie magazines.

Strangely enough, after all these years, what she remembered the most about this particular conversation was the odd expression he'd had on his face when talking about his mother: Blank of eye, wholly empty of feeling, yet stealthy. As if he were lying about something. It was sort of like this morning, except this morning that stealthy look of his had been amplified to a new level of . . . of what? Loathing? Hatred? Did any of this have anything to do with those pills? Percodan. And just what was this Percodan, exactly?

Linnell made a mental note to investigate this, then returned to the past.

They graduated from college together and that very same day he'd simply dropped his leather jacket on her shoulders to announce their engagement. Her folks had been plenty excited. So much so that she had gone along with it all without any questions or qualms. Why had she done this? Oh yes, she knew why; she was still painfully aware of why: In those days the curse on the head of the "Nice Girl" was that she had to either marry the man she slept with or else run the risk that the next guy would treat her like dirt. "Sloppy seconds" was how a woman was described if she had any kind of a healthy sex life, and even women slandered each other this way because of the fierce competition over landing" a husband. So Mark, by letting everyone in on the secret that they were a "couple," became, as he himself liked to say: "Her destiny; her inescapable fate."

He was accepted to a Bay Area dental school the week after their engagement and the first thing he did was to shear off his glorious mane, leaving his hair cropped so short that his head had resembled a honey-dew melon set with white-walled tires.

Stunned by this sudden change, she had begun to toy with the idea of trying to escape. Maybe he'd guessed as much, because he immediately packed her and all their meager belongings in his ratty old car and then, like a traveling flea-market, they had rambled north, pawning their goods along the way, until they arrived in San Francisco and without further ado, got married at City Hall. It all happened so fast, she'd had no time to think. But still, she'd raised no objection, because after all, getting married was what a girl was supposed to do.

Actually, an elopement had been fine with her because tradition or no, good girl or no, she had decided long before meeting Mark that she was not going to be handed off from one man to another as if she were chattel.

In those days, nobody would have imagined her capable of entertaining such revolutionary thoughts—but still, early on in her life she had promised herself that she was going to *own* property, not be it, and an elopement spared her from having to argue this point with her parents, who had always wanted to "give her away" at a big formal wedding.

Distance put her on a par with Bear as far as their families were concerned. He had only his father and her family was too far away to stay closely in touch; besides, she and Mark saw themselves as pioneers, marching hand in hand on a new frontier. But after a couple of weeks in San Francisco it became painfully clear that Bay Area living was going to be a far more expensive proposition than Mark had imagined, so both of them took menial jobs that summer in order to make ends meet. Thus it had come to pass that her summer of love—the indolent, passionate Summer of Love she'd been longing for all her life—was over before it ever had a chance to begin. And now, after their fourteen years together, she could look back and see that their marriage was just like a prune: at its best, it provided only a dry taste of sugary contentment, but now, regrettably, there was no tang left of what must have once been a plum.

Nevertheless, she had wanted a child, and so had Bear—until Benjy came along, and then Bear lost all interest in being a father. Though it seemed a bit crazy, she sometimes thought Bear saw Benjy as the competition. Bear spent so little time with him now. And except for teaching him that awful spider trick to play on her—for which Benjy had seemed almost pathetically grateful since it meant he was getting some fatherly attention—Bear seldom spoke to him. Dear Benjy, he was such a gorgeous child, with his apricot cheeks and shiny head of blond hair—and he was so clever, so amazingly tolerant and aware for a seven year old. In fact, just the other day they'd had quite a conversation. Benjy was playing. Then he stopped, raised his head to give her a piercing look and asked her a remarkable question: He wanted to know if he was still *baby glue.*

"Baby glue? What's that, darling?" she'd replied.

"You know, Ma . . . stuff used to hold your marriage together."

All she'd managed to reply was a rather startled "Oh!"

And then he had really knocked her for a loop. He'd turned his head away, and then still looking at her out of the corner of his eye, he'd said, "I'm not a baby anymore."

Maybe it was this, combined with her strange early morning episode with Bear, that was making her feel so inexplicably uneasy. Linnell shook her head. No! She refused to think it could even be possible that while she was knocking herself out to get the project together, everything else in her life was coming unglued. No! Impossible! she reassured herself. Linnell rubbed her neck to fight off the tension and told herself to think positive thoughts, like a winner should. Linnell stiffened her back and sat up straight in her chair. She needed to change her attitude. Yes, from now on she was going to try harder to look on the bright side and think about things in a more positive light.

Feeling a bit more satisfied with herself, Linnell took another sip of her coffee and escaped into the scenery. From one side of their hill she could see clear across the valley through the lanky trunks of the eucalyptus trees and into the cracks of the far lavender-gray hills. But in the opposite direction, far beyond the thick row of dark hedges that guarded the path to their door, lay her favorite vista. She loved it the most because it encompassed the town and at dusk the sight of the gently sparkling nightscape lent an aura of sensual longing to the warm summer evenings. Their lushly landscaped swimming pool lay in the foreground—now glittering like broken glass when the wind skimmed the surface. Linnell shivered involuntarily at the sight; the water had to be freezing because she had turned off the pool heater for the winter season. Then she thought about what it would feel like to slip and fall in and goose bumps immediately sprang up on her bare arms and legs. Linnell hunched her shoulders and nervously rubbed her arms. *So, here I am . . . all cold and alone, and that's how I got here . . . and now I've been settled . . . Oh God! It feels like forever.*

Nowadays it felt as if the needle of her emotional compass could swing only between two unpleasant points: the haunts and the guilts. As for the haunts—this strange feeling she had, that she was being watched—most likely it was all in her head. She sure hoped so. And the guilts? She couldn't help it, she always felt guilty. And she knew why, too. Deep down she always felt that she wasn't quite up to snuff when it came to being a good wife. Although Lord knows she tried. Couldn't Bear see this? Even though he liked having his dinner on the table at six p.m. sharp. Lately, however, she simply couldn't get to it till it was seven, sometimes even eight. But what could she do? She was too deep into the project to quit, and she couldn't very well provide any explanations without ruining her surprise—besides, telling Bear, especially at this late date, would surely lead him to putting a stop to her export adventures. So—not having leveled with him, she'd ended up feeling guilty, instead.

"Okay. Enough of this whining!" Linnell exclaimed. "It's like Bear says—you *do* let your imagination get the best of you and right now you're being a big pain in the ass!" Practical, routine-driven Bear had told her more than once that she wasted too much of her time yearning for things that did not exist. He was probably right. It seemed as if she was always hoping to find something that didn't exist. But what was she was trying to find? She couldn't say exactly. Adventure, excitement—possibly a little taste of the plum? Perhaps. But what she most wished for, right now, was to meet with success so that Bear would no longer feel that he needed to work himself to death.

Linnell sprang to her feet. She was a lawyer and a good lawyer was both logical and practical. In which case, she'd better *do* something practical instead of just sitting here dreaming. Like, for instance, she should make a real effort to get past that horrible guard dog, Margo. She really needed to hear Bear's voice, she needed some reassurance from him, especially after what she'd seen of him earlier that morning. Linnell looked up at the wall clock and saw that it was almost 10:45 a.m. Startled at how long she'd been daydreaming, Linnell whirled about and the back of her hand clipped her cup. It tipped over and then all she could do was watch in horror as the surge of brown liquid spread across the table; she could hear it dripping over the edge and onto her nice clean floor.

Her second large mess of the day.

After mopping up, Linnell Clare hurriedly dialed her husband's office and was greeted by an angry busy signal. She dialed again. Another busy signal. And then, feeling daring, she tried his private line, but that, too, was busy. She knew he would be upset at her for calling him when he was so busy but she couldn't help it; she had to talk to him. After ten minutes of listening to nothing but busy signals, Linnell finally gave up.

Well, she thought, now that she was home and had all this time to herself, she'd better see to those few little odds and ends she'd been too busy for earlier. Moving carefully now, Linnell opened a kitchen drawer and retrieved a small roll of transparent tape and stuffed it into her handbag, then she grabbed her clothes and headed for her bedroom. Catching sight of herself in her bathroom mirror, she stepped into the room and stared at herself. Being plain wasn't the problem here—it was just that Bear liked to see her dress down. But a lawyer's looks *should* make a statement, she thought. Linnell opened the drawer that held her collection of unused cosmetics and found a virginal tube of mascara. Black. "Take Them to Daring Lengths!" the package offered in swirly script. Bear hated makeup. Linnell picked up the tube, twisted it open and smelled it to make sure it was fresh and then with fierce motions brushed mascara on her lashes, layering it on thick until they stood out stiffly from her tilted brown eyes. She wouldn't be seeing him for ten days, so why not?

So, really . . . was something wrong with her? Linnell examined her face. Could it be that he was turned off by the dark shadows under her eyes? Or the tiny crow's feet that emerged whenever she laughed? She could still see her little wrinkles underneath her nicely blackened lashes. If only Bear would *tell* her he thought she was beautiful. "Now you just stop it! You're being vain and shallow so snap *out* of it," she scolded her reflection. Didn't he love her? Of *course* he did, and she would be a whole lot happier if she could just accept the fact that her man thought marriage was more than enough sustenance for any woman's ego. Why did men get this way? she wondered. Then, as if she were apologizing to her absent husband, Linnell pulled her long hair into its usual pony tail, which was the style he liked most, and looked at herself. She didn't like it this way—it made her look immature, not youthful, and at thirty-five, this certainly was not the way she wanted to see herself.

"He calls me Ma and then likes to see me looking like some kid—go figure," Linnell signed, then she sighed again while she reminded herself for the umpteenth time that she didn't have it so bad. After all, didn't he call her every day to tell her he loved her? And every year, didn't he buy her a splendid gift for her birthday? And this year, on her thirty-fifth, hadn't he displayed a generosity that had astounded everyone; her, most of all? Yes, yes, and yes—he had given her Charles. She had better not forget about *that*.

Well, thank God for Cayman, Linnell thought; then she tightened her stomach and measured her waistline to see if she ought to pack her new bathing suit—the one Bear had never seen—the daring, lavender, ring-bikini. Happily, her waist was exactly 25 inches; then she measured her hips. Linnell gasped. *Thirty-six inches! But, not to worry, I'll probably drop five pounds by tomorrow night.* Then she remembered the lipstick she'd bought at Christmas. She had been saving it for this trip and she'd almost forgotten to pack it. She found the tube and dropped it into her cosmetic bag. As an afterthought, she added a bottle of her favorite perfume. She hadn't worn it for such a long time. She had stopped using it the instant Bear told her it gave him a headache.

HIGHRIDGE **10:15 a.m. February 24, 1974**

As was their custom after "visiting a site," August Rizzo and Robert Jordan returned to their car without speaking. After they rolled out of the parking lot, Jordan turned to Agent Rizzo and spoke. "Well! I'll bet you've got something to say about *that!*"

"You first." Rizzo was now laughing out loud.

"It's like you guessed," Jordan said. "Our Dr. Clare is a player. Did you dig the look on the face of that chick? No question about what *they* were doing in there."

"And did you see his torpedo? I guess we broke up the party before he could get it launched. In fact, it stayed hard the whole time we were there." Rizzo snorted with laughter and then his voice sobered abruptly. "But tell me, what else you pick up on?"

"Well, I was wondering about his wife, Linnell Clare. Did I hear right? Didn't he call her "Ma"? Is this 'cause she's older than him, or what?"

"You heard right. Well. I dunno about him. Maybe the guy has some kind of fixation, because they're exactly the same age, thirty-five, and let me tell you something—she's no dog. You can see for yourself. Her photo's in the file."

"He says everybody calls her "L.C." . . . and I picked up on that stuff about her business in Cayman. Did you know she was a haven-maven?"

"Oh sure. Very interesting that her old man was so keen to mention something like that. You'd think he'd want to keep it under his hat. As for her going to tax havens? We've been tracking her same as we do all the others . . . At first we just open a file, get a background on 'em. That's routine procedure which makes it easier for us to catch up with 'em if they turn crooked. Mrs. Clare got into the tax-haven game at the Ivener firm. Willy Ivener . . . now *there's* a story. But her? I'm not sure what the scoop is on her. Hope it's not the same as Ivener's. Well, we'll just have to wait and see. *Very* interesting. Yes, from what we've seen so far we'll have no trouble getting a warrant to tap their lines, but it might be a helluva bigger picture than we first thought. So we'll start looking into that picture today and we'll have a tap on their lines by tomorrow morning. We should tell the head office in Miami to put a tail on Mrs. Clare when she passes through Miami International and we can courier her bar roster photo to the agent on Cayman. There's only one outbound flight from Miami to Cayman tomorrow morning and she'll be on it if she's leaving San Francisco later tonight. "Also, I want you to call her office. Line her up for an appointment when she returns. That should get the mice up and scurrying about, which is good, because then we can watch them. And given the new laws about privacy, you'd better notify all IRS divisions that Mrs. Clare is her husband's tax attorney, that way she can have access to everything he's filed with the IRS, including that dental corporation he set up. This will keep her from pulling a stall and it might also give us insight into the areas that she's concerned about. Also, I want you to order copies of their telephone records for all of their phones—the last six months should do the trick."

Agent Rizzo fell quiet, then changed the subject. "Did you happen to look at the wall behind the counter?"

"Yeah," Jordan replied, "he must have way over five thousand files back there. Color tabbed."

"You noticed. Good. I was wondering if you would pick up on that. And let's assume he also maintains his patient files or some other records on that computer. You might not know it, since you've only been here for a couple of months, but our Dr. Clare was the first in the area to get a computerized office system. Given the other discrepancies, what might that suggest?"

"Well . . . that he's massaging two sets of books? A computer would be ideal for that." Bob Jordan scratched his chin in puzzlement. "Or are you suggesting something else?"

"I think we're soon going to find out. By the way, did you notice what Mrs. Callahan was doing behind the reception counter? I thought I saw her hovering around the computer."

"She didn't look any too surprised when we identified ourselves, so it looks to me like they've been expecting us," Jordan replied. "She picked up the intercom and announced our arrival. Oh yeah, she punched something on the computer keyboard but I couldn't see the screen."

"Very good. And what else do you know for a fact?"

"Clare's got a wife who knows how to hide the money."

"Excellent. You're doing fine, kid. And if I can get my hands on some evidence that she's squirreling his skimmings in some secret bank account in the Cayman Islands, well then . . . I'm gonna have her head on a platter and her license on ice."

"Yes. But what if she *doesn't* know anything about what he's been up to?"

"Oh, you're wondering if she might raise the innocent spouse defense?"

"Yeah."

"That's not going to be so easy for her to do. It's not enough to show that you never knew about your spouse's tax evasion. For the defense to work, you've also got to show that you didn't benefit from it, either." Agent Rizzo ran his hand over his graying buzz cut and grinned broadly as he turned onto the freeway toward San Francisco.

HIGHRIDGE 11:00 a.m. - February 24, 1974

Linnell attacked her chores with vigor. Her plans hadn't changed—she'd still go straight to the plane from her office. She repacked her suitcase, adding more street clothes, her pumps and a new pair of pantyhose, then arranged everything so her bathing suit would be lying on top and easy to grab when she next opened her bag. This way she could leave her clothes unpacked when she arrived at her destination, something she knew would annoy the spooks who had been pawing through her clothes during her last several trips. What did they expect? That she was going to make it easy for them?

On a sudden impulse, she decided to take Karen's advice and put in an hour at the club. She hadn't been there for over a week and she wanted to see if there had been any more developments in the Baron's interesting marital situation. Linnell pulled on her navy-blue warm-ups and stepped into her tennis shoes and then after double-checking the house to make sure all the windows were locked, she called Helene and gave her the codes for the new security system. Helene reassured Linnell that she'd be at the house in time to meet Benjy after school, and then she wished Linnell good luck and said her farewells.

Now, at last, Linnell felt she was free to leave.

After re-setting the latch mechanism to allow the door to lock behind her, she glanced over her shoulder—she thought she'd just seen something move near the lower corner of the fireplace screen. Something dark. Or was she just imagining things? Most likely she was still feeling jumpy from Benjy's trick. She certainly hoped it was only that. *Spiders!* Linnell shuddered. *You can't see their eyes so there's no way to tell where they're going to run!* She shuddered again, then punched the buttons of the security system and when it began to chirp softly she knew she had only 15 seconds to exit before the alarm would go off. Linnell sprang through the door, slammed it behind her and dashed down the path toward the garage area—where stood their converted stables, one for her, one for Bear, each with its own side entrance and remote-controlled garage door.

Halfway down the path, Linnell slowed and lifted her eyes to the surrounding hills. The weather was exhilarating and it seemed as if all the trees on the hill had changed overnight. The fat pink buds of the flowering almonds and wild plum trees always filled her heart with such poignant yearning. But for what? Didn't she have a good solid life? Wasn't this a good, solid home? As if in response to her queries, thin high clouds drifted in front of the sun and the temperature dropped. Suddenly cold, Linnell hastened toward her garage and with a click of her key, she was through the side door and into her car; then after only another two clicks and a fumble, the engine was humming, the garage door swooshed, and she was on her way!

She flew down the hill. Charles would be perfect were it not for his unpredictable electrical system, thought Linnell. Lifting her foot off the gas to feel the engine's compression, Linnell Clare guided Charles around the gentle bends in the winding road and descended toward town—she knew if Charles was going to cut out, he would most likely cut out now. Better here, where she would be close to a telephone, than on the freeway, she thought. But today, all was fine; Charles behaved like a dream, and a minute later she was heading down Main Street toward the club.

They had joined the country club at the urging of her best friend, Nancy Seith, whom she'd met shortly after moving to Highridge. As for the club—now the newest and largest one in the county—it had materialized on the heels of a demographic study declaring the Bay Area one of the fastest growing regions in the nation. *Electronics, transistors, silicon wafers, hardware, software, vaporware,* these were the latest buzz-words on the street and since Highridge had more than its share of nouveau riche engineers and entrepreneurs, some investors from Texas had apparently decided Highridge needed a new place to play. They had designed it to meet a Texan's taste for excess because it offered everything the upwardly mobile was supposed to desire: twenty-four new tennis courts; a tricky eighteen-hole golf course with velvety greens and a lavishly equipped gym that led outdoors to an Olympic length, ten-lane pool.

There was absolutely nothing "old money" about the club. What with its two enormous bars—one restricted to club members, the other a disco open to the public—the place was known far and wide as a wide-open meat market. And every now and then, on those special summer evenings when the moon was full and the nights stayed warm long past midnight, it would seem as if all the pot-fields of the Marin Headlands were wafting up in blue clouds of smoke from the parking lots surrounding the main club house. The Highridge News had noticed this too. In its usual purple prose, it had described the club as the "throbbing heart-beat of the Seventies-sexo-revolution." This time Linnell had to agree with the newspaper because it seemed as if every cock-eyed tax-shelter, every bizarre real estate deal, and every scandalous divorce up and down the peninsula could be traced back to the various playing fields of the club. However, as far as she was concerned, the best thing the club had to offer was not its gossip but rather its very large membership which had made it easier for her to find a circle of friends quite apart from Bear's.

The facilities, though, were marvelous indeed; the pool was maintained year-round at a comfortable temperature and the large gym was clean and fully equipped with the newest weight-lifting machines, all of which made it less of a chore for her to maintain her strict training regimen. She knew she had to be able to lift at least half her weight if she wanted to keep the respect of her diving crew, so for almost a year now she'd been going to the gym three times a week. The results were amazing; her small bulges had smoothed into long lean curves and she hadn't bulked out—in fact her waist had tightened and her abdomen was now hard as a plank—and she could tell she was at least twice as strong as was before having Benjy. Her friends had noticed this too, and now Nancy was lifting weights and Linnell knew that her days as the only woman in the gym were over because all the rest of the "Cs" would soon be following her lead. But best of all were the two unanticipated dividends her regimen had produced: her lung capacity—she had smoked all through law school—was now back to normal, and despite her constant sleep deprivation, her new fitness allowed her to get by with less sleep.

Linnell pulled into the Highridge Country Club parking lot and rejoiced. She could tell her good luck had returned: for the first time in months an empty parking space awaited her, right in front of the entrance, too. Linnell eased Charles into the spot and hopped out. She hoped her three pals, the "Cs"—Nancy Seith, Elsie Baron, and Cecile "Cee-Cee" Dickenson—would be there so she could see them before she left.

Her three friends spent more time at the club than she, because she could only squeeze in a couple of hours in the afternoons on Monday, Wednesday, and Friday. Nancy, who had just landed a part-time job at the Highridge Bank, still swam regularly, and the other two played tennis every afternoon. Since she was the last of the four to join the club, her entry into their clique was by invitation. At that time they'd all said, and Cee-Cee had been especially interested in this, that with her as an addition they had become a perfectly matched sorority because they all looked so much alike. And Cee-Cee had delighted in her nickname, too, because it expanded the rhyme they'd made of their names, which eventually led everyone to know them as the "Four Cs."

This had seemed fun at first, but now it was all just so cute and cozy that it was sometimes too much for her to stomach, but since Benjy played tennis doubles with Elsie's son, and since the boys were the same age and were now such good friends, Linnell never complained, at least not aloud. As the "Four Cs," they had also created a loopy Laurel-'n-Hardy routine in order to even the score with the old geezer who chaired the club's board of directors. A grizzled member of the "doggone-skeedaddle-dag-nabbit" generation, he had become fixated on them. He would spread gossip about them, using such curious terms to describe them as "those four floozies . . . the *hors*-ies."

They were *Hors*-ies? Or was it *Whore*-sies? Old gramps said it in such a way that it sounded as if he were struggling to invent an unfriendly double-entendre. This sounded rude enough to make her and Nancy want to look into this further and sure enough, when they got to the bottom of things, they learned that the old half-blind fool, mistaking one of them for the other, had launched a false rumor that Elsie had been "stepping out" with Cee-Cee's husband—he had even gone so far as to describe them behind their backs as a "wild band of husband-swapping hoydens." Although his quaint insults were a scream, they'd decided to punish him nonetheless. Nosy old fart! And so they'd made it their pastime to stalk him. And when they had him corralled in their midst, they would tease him and run their hands through his hair while they moistly spit their names in his face so he would make no more mistakes about who they were.

Sometimes Linnell would worry that Bear would hear about their silly behavior and get the entirely wrong idea about what they were doing. But so far so good—he'd given her no signs of having heard any rumors, which was a very good thing because just recently she and Nancy had discovered there was an even larger and more serious problem: One of them *was* having an affair—Cee-Cee—she was slipping around with the club's tennis ace, Larry, who worse yet, just happened to be Elsie's husband.

Larry Baron was loaded with dough and an irrepressible jerk who carried tennis balls in his pockets in order "To cover up for *HIM!"*—which he liked to crow—of course, out of Elsie's earshot—while grabbing his crotch as if he had a wild snake in his pants. So, strangely enough, as things turned out, the old geezer had been on to something after all. She and Nancy were still shocked—just as much by Cee-Cee's wretched taste as her bold deceit. Larry! Of all damn people! Here Cee-Cee had managed to con them so coolly they'd almost failed to grasp why their looks had always been of such special importance to her. It had apparently always been on her mind that their similar, in fact, near identical likeness would someday be useful to her as a beard for her prowling—if she were ever caught sneaking around, well, she'd be able to shrug it all off as being nothing more than a case of mistaken identity.

Now she wondered how much longer The "Cs" were going to last if Cee-Cee didn't cut the nonsense. It's only a matter of time and the whole club's gonna know about these dumb fools, said Linnell to herself. Disbanding might not be such a bad idea, she thought. Linnell, thinking of Benjy, immediately re-considered. Well—to borrow a few words from The Wei—maybe she'd better just go with the flow and stay out of it. Shouldn't she? After all, they were all adults, weren't they? And it was really none of her business what Cee-Cee did—just so long as she wasn't doing it with *her* old man.

Linnell rationalized as she climbed the stairs to the lobby and as soon as she stepped through the door, she stopped because she could tell all the rest of the "Cs" were there. She could hear them, and then, as she moved past the reception desk, she could see them on the other side of the potted palms. Like usual, they were garbed all alike in their short tennis whites and they all sported shiny blond pony tails, just like hers. But today there were cameras and helium-filled balloons. She'd forgotten—today was Elsie's birthday!

It was apparent that Elsie—always the most vivacious, invariably the loudest, the one who most got on her nerves—had some terribly important news to share, because Nancy and Cee-Cee were pressing around her and she was squealing for joy. With a face flushed with excitement, Elsie looked up and caught sight of Linnell. Elsie immediately jumped up and bounced over to meet her, her new tennis shoes squeaking loudly against the polished hardwood floor.

"So, what's with all the noise? Something happening?" Linnell asked.

"You'll never believe! I can't wait to show you my birthday present!"

Linnell caught a warning look from Nancy and realized it was a good thing they'd kept their mouths shut about Larry.

"C'mon, you've *got* to take a look!" Elsie grabbed Linnell, whirled her around, then dragged her back through the entrance, down the steps to the parking lot and around to the side of the clubhouse.

At the side of the building, parked far away from the other cars to protect its shiny new doors from being dinged, stood a resplendent white Jaguar sedan. For a second Linnell was confused, she clearly recalled parking Charles in front of the entrance. Elsie continued to drag her toward the marvelous vehicle and Linnell blinked her eyes when she finally grasped that what Elsie was raving about so excitedly was a car—identical in every respect to her darling Charles.

"What d' you think about *this*?" Elsie burbled excitedly while her fingers lovingly caressed the streamlined hood ornament. "Larry just blew me away! Isn't he just the most *wonderful* man? So, L.C., now honestly, *tell* me. You're not pissed at me 'cause they're exactly the same? Tell the truth!"

Linnell pressed her nose to the car window. The butterscotch leather upholstery was the same. The gleaming inlaid console was identical. Everything was the same. And from now on every day would be the same, with the two of them getting their cars mixed up—aggravation forevermore. She wanted to scream. Damn Larry anyway! thought Linnell. This was either his guilt-gift—which would have to mean that Elsie was still in the dark, or else it was a peace-offering, in which case Elsie knew the score, but Larry was doing his best to patch things up. What could she say?

Linnell laughed to cover up her irritation. "Angry? Because we have the same car? Oh, come *on*." Turning away so that Elsie couldn't read her face, Linnell added, "This is great!"

As soon as the words were out of her mouth, she felt like a hypocrite. *No, no no! What I want to say is this: That wild dick-head husband of yours has no sense whatsoever. And I'm sick of you copy-catting me! I want it all to stop! Right now. Immediately!* With her smile stuck to her face like a crooked bandage, Linnell tried for just the right combination of cordiality and nonchalance. She managed to produce a few more insincere words: "Well. Glad you scored big . . . it sure is a surprise, all right. And happy birthday, old thing. Now let's go back inside and we'll do something to celebrate your birthday. Maybe we can get in a set, too."

"Thanks L. C. But let's do it another day, really, I'm sorry . . . I've already got something planned."

Linnell caught a secretive expression on Elsie's face and then she realized that she must have been looking at her like the grand inquisitor because Elsie grinned sheepishly and explained, "Oh. It's nothing, just another birthday surprise. . . . uh, now that I've got this big white thing here with all this tan leather, I'm gonna go out and get me a big hunk of something in black leather that's tan . . ." Elsie winked slyly at Linnell, unlocked the Jag and jumped in and then, without so much as a fumble, had her key in the ignition as if she'd been doing it all her life. Elsie gunned the engine, braked suddenly, gave Linnell a small smirk and rolled slowly away while Linnell stood looking at her, simply aghast.

◆❖◆

When Linnell Clare finally arrived at her office late Monday afternoon, she sensed that Karen had been waiting to tell her something. Just like Elsie, she, too, was grinning and smirking, making her wonder if Karen was setting her up for another one of her practical jokes. *What's it going to be now?* Linnell tried to guess.

"So what's up?" Linnell asked, looking at Karen with suspicion.

Without taking her eyes from her work, Karen flashed her another pearly-toothed smile and nodded her head in the direction of Linnell's private office. "You'd better see for yourself."

Karen, taller than Linnell, the shade of cafe' au lait and with hundreds of sparkling gold beads braided into her corn-rows, had perfectly manicured talons that produced a red blur when they flew over the typewriter keyboard. Generously endowed, this statuesque offspring of a Swedish actress and a prominent Jamaican politician had recently married an aerospace engineer named Ray. Ray, sweet and funny and a really good guy, stood six foot five, and since he was too tall to be an astronaut, he now worked nights at Moffett Field in the South Bay Area where he headed up a secret aerospace research division. This left him free to come in during the day, and Karen would sometimes put him to work when he dropped in on them on his way to his office.

"Hey Karen! How can you *do* that with those damn long nails?" Linnell challenged.

"Hey baby, it's not *my* fault you can't walk and chew gum at the same time," Karen shot back without missing a beat.

Linnell studied Karen's impish expression. She could get away with murder, that woman. Like the time Karen had frozen the cushion of her new leather chair. That had led to war, with escalating terrorist tactics on both sides. They had spent two whole days just playing practical jokes and laughing and screeching before calling a truce. Was it going to begin all over again?

"L.C., I know you're stalling. Just go on in there and take a look at what's on your desk! Hurry up, you know I can't stand it. Who did this? Bear? Or are they from Bermuda? God! My old man should kiss *my* ass like that!" Karen sighed theatrically while she continued to bang even more furiously on the typewriter.

Linnell had no idea what she was talking about until she walked into her private office, the only room that wasn't crammed to the ceiling with boxes of client files and stacked with books and rainbows of papers. She was amazed—reaching out from the green bubble-glass florist's vase that now stood on the corner of her desk was a huge bouquet of magnificent scarlet roses. A long plastic fork, holding a white envelope, was tucked among the fragrant blooms.

Who had sent them? Bear?

"No way!" Linnell said to herself. "He never sends flowers. Why would he suddenly make such an extravagant gesture? Especially after last night. Maybe they're from my client in Bermuda, thanking me for the case I just won. Or . . . Maybe I've got a secret admirer?"

The thought of a secret admirer sent thrills of excitement up and down her spine; Linnell stood next to her desk without touching the envelope and counted to ten in order to prolong the suspense and then feeling the most exquisite pangs of curiosity, she snatched the envelope and ripped it open. Hastily unfolding the plain white card, she read the typed message:

"From Dr. Clare. Here's something for you so you can have fun."

"Oh!" Linnell gasped. "Since when are we on such formal terms!" Then she realized that he must have had Margo type the card. "That jealous old sow," thought Linnell. "I know what she's up to here, even if Bear doesn't."

Truth was, she was slightly deflated. And Bear hadn't even bothered to sign the card, let alone take the time to write the message himself. Then Linnell saw that something had been tightly rolled and taped to the bottom of the card. When she removed it she was astounded to find a hundred dollar bill. This wasn't like him at all—he was usually so stingy when it came to her spending money on her offshore trips. What a marvelous surprise! Really! She had to stop picking on Bear. She sang out to Karen, "Hey! You're right! They're from my husband. Get him on the line for me. I've got to talk to him before I leave."

Then she pulled the hundred dollar bill off the card and was amazed to discover there were two of them stuck together. She unrolled them and after tucking them flat in her wallet, she saw that her fingers were smudged with white powder. Linnell absent-mindedly wiped her hands on the drapes before placing her call to the IRS Records Division. While waiting, she discarded the envelope in her waste basket and stuck the card back in its holder so that Karen could read it. Still waiting to be put through to a clerk, Linnell pawed through the stack of papers on her desk until she found what Bear's accountant had sent her the week before: An IRS audit notice addressed to Mark Clare, the president of the Mark Clare D.D.S. Dental Corporation and the IRS envelope it had come in; their accountant had simply stapled them together and for some unknown reason had forwarded everything to her office—probably so she could give her husband a nudge. Linnell read the notice: *Second Request for Additional Documentation—Audit of the Mark Clare D.D.S. Dental Corporation.* "Oh-oh! IRS sent it by certified mail—here's Bear's signature on the carbon receipt. Oh boy! This is the second notice . . . which means he got the first one over a month ago. Oh dear! He's been trying to put things off by ignoring the matter . . . the first mistake everyone seems to make. I'm surprised at him! He ought to know better, especially since he's the one who likes everything to be so neat and predictable."

Linnell admired the roses, then burying her nose in the fragrant blooms, inhaled their fragrance and was quite overcome by a sudden wave of tenderness—he had remembered after all that she was leaving today. Her irritation at Bear evaporated instantly. This was quite a first! She should encourage this marvelous change in his behavior by reciprocating in spades. Of course! Why should he have to *ask* for her help? She would get everything lined up in advance so that she could jump on Bear's audit, first thing on her return.

When the IRS clerk came on the line, Linnell asked for copies of the tax returns for the Mark Clare D.D.S. Dental Corporation—for the most recent three year period—to be sent to her law office. And then, on impulse, she asked for some copies of their personal tax returns—the 1040s they filed jointly—for the same three year period, just in case she couldn't find the copies Bear had already given her to store in her archives.

Linnell wondered why Bear had never shown her the tax returns for the dental corporation. She'd mentioned it once, and he'd told her he would, and then when he didn't the whole thing simply slipped her mind because she'd been so busy establishing her own practice. But now that she thought about it, she could vaguely remember Bear telling her that he had retained an attorney to incorporate his dental practice while she was in law school. Furthermore, she'd never had any reason to worry about it, since Bear always gave her copies of their joint tax returns which showed her essentially the same information about the salary he received from the dental corporation.

But now, thanks to the audit, she would have to pay some attention to the damn dental corporation. Oh-oh and double-bind! This could spell trouble. Since she was neither a corporate officer or Bear's legal counsel, she no longer had any right to receive any copies of the corporation's tax returns—even if the dental corporation was their community property—because of the stringent new privacy statutes. What if the IRS clerk was hip to the new law? Well, maybe the clerk would send her the tax returns anyway. That could happen, in fact it happened a lot since it was very difficult for the clerks to keep up with so many changing rules. Linnell was so engrossed that she didn't hear Karen.

"L.C.! Can you hear me? I've tried three times to get through to your husband, but his line's been busy. I'll try later. We've got to organize the trust documents! And how do you spell it?—is it *S-a-l-i-a-n*? Or *S-a-l-i-c*?"

Linnell yelled back. "They're both correct." She could tell from the question that Karen had been reading one of her research memos.

She had engaged in this particular line of research merely to satisfy her curiosity. She had been scouring the law library for some case law and this had taken her into a dark corner where by chance she'd stumbled upon some copies of old texts that she found quite unusual—the Sixth Century codes of the ancient Germanic rulers, a tribe known as *Salians*. Intrigued, she had read all she could find on this subject and then she had written a memo. To her mind, the Salic laws were an important key to the puzzle of money and power and why women had ended up with so little of both.

What the early Sixth Century Salic Laws meant for mid-European women was devastating: They barred women from owning or inheriting property, or, if they had any, it forbade them to pass it on to their heirs. At first more akin to informal "understandings" than hard and fast laws, they had gradually solidified during the Dark Ages when roving bands of men would as soon slaughter each other over a bucket of wheat as a choice parcel of forest or farm land. However, even in the days when Might made Right, women still stood half a chance of keeping the family property—which some women managed to do with the aid of her children and relatives. But for the most part, land usually passed to the oldest or strongest male in the tribe.

During those brutish, bloody years, the all-male church hierarchy—wholly engrossed in worldly affairs and working hand-in-hand with the powerful land-owning barons—soon combined with the wealthiest of them to make things easier and safer for themselves by fixing these vague understandings into laws which they hoped would give them an unassailable edge when the best of the baronial lands came up for grabs. This they did at the expense of the "weaker sex" who couldn't be expected to wield a broadsword and who were already at a severe disadvantage since women were already barred from holding any churchly powers. Thus when the holy fathers and barons cut a deal to save their own skins—with the gratifying "incidental" effect of adding to their riches—they did so at the expense of women.

As a result—since the Salic Laws barred women both from inheriting property and passing it on to her heirs—over time, vast numbers of women, the serfs and the servants, came to be passed from man to man—like chattel—along with the land. Meanwhile, those women who were so fortunate as to be royal were used by their families as bargaining chips. For its part, the Holy Church, unseparated from State and governed by avaricious nobles, often accused those few women who still held on to their property of heresy and witchcraft. And then these unfortunates would be ordered condemned and burned at the stake, which permitted their lands to be seized by the Church and the Crown.

Women soon learned that if they wanted to survive, they had no choice but to place their fate in the hands of men. No love was lost in those days, and romance between woman and man was a rarity, because when people courted, it wasn't for love but for property rights.

Linnell was fascinated by all this; it helped her understand her own rebellious instincts, which so far she had only tepidly displayed through avoiding the ritual of being "given away." With some melancholy now, she recalled how she had concluded her memorandum on the middle ages: "True love, so rare and so menacing to the social order that it became the stuff of legends, did not lay the foundation for powerful hierarchies . . ."

"Hey L.C.!" Karen was yelling.

Startled, Linnell's thoughts jumped from the Sixth Century back to the present.

Karen placed a stack of documents on Linnell's desk. "Looks like you're going to make overhead on this trip. You've got five trusts to set up, and need I remind you of the contract?"

"The contract I know all about, but what's this about five trusts? I thought I only had four." Linnell was thrilled to have four. Her fees were lower than what Ivener's firm liked to bill for establishing foreign trusts and she knew she was making substantial inroads into a field that Willy had mistakenly thought was his exclusive territory.

"Nope. It's *five*." Karen first looked at her impishly, then grinned. "That is, if you'll do me a really big favor. I don't expect you to comp me, because if anyone knows how much work you do on one of these trusts, it's me. I don't just type, you know, I *read* them."

Although Linnell's firm was the smallest one to practice in the rarefied field offshore tax planning, Karen knew Linnell Clare was as good as the best and an expert in the legal use of tax haven trusts. She also studied Linnell's client memos, so she knew Linnell was warning her clientele about proposed changes in law which would clamp down on their creation. Thus, when her father offered to give her a substantial sum of money for her wedding gift, Karen already knew that a foreign trust would be the ideal way to go because it would allow her father's gift to be invested essentially free of all tax—and better yet, since it was a legal trust, she wouldn't have to live in dread that the IRS might come after her sometime in the future.

Her father had already bank-wired the funds from Jamaica to Cayman, along with a power of attorney so that Linnell could settle the trust on his behalf. She had spent the morning adapting one of Linnell's precious trust documents and a *Letter of Wishes* to instruct the bank-trustee to receive investment instructions. Best of all, a carefully worded foreign trust—such as those that Linnell had drafted—would allow Karen to profit from trading securities on US stock exchanges. Legally, and entirely free of US tax.

"Now I get it! So *that's* why you were so busy this morning!" Seeing Karen's grin, Linnell laughed. "Well. I'll be happy to do this. But, I don't expect you to *pay* me."

"Oh, you *have* to be paid. Because my father's your client and he insists. And surprise! Here's his check for your fee." Karen laid her father's bank draft on Linnell's desk.

Linnell blushed. "Thank you. Tell your father I'm pleased to have his business. Now let's make absolutely sure that your father's trust includes all your unborn children as future beneficiaries."

Karen knew she had done the right thing—the money her father had bank-wired to Cayman for her wedding gift—fifty-thousand dollars—could grow to a quarter-million in no time at all because unlike trusts in the United States, the foreign trust could compound its gains without paying any tax.

"Oh, I almost forgot, I need some information," Linnell said. "I don't have time to read it now, so just make a copy. And Karen . . . there's something else I have to talk to you about."

Detecting a trace of unhappiness in Linnell's voice, Karen stopped shuffling papers.

"Karen, it's near miraculous that we've managed to keep the Sea Urchin Project a secret from Bear. Anyway, we've got to start handling everything else the same way. I don't know why I've waited so long to do this, but, I've *got* to stop sharing information about my practice with him. I know he likes to carry on as if he were my partner, but he's not. And if I don't stop him from poking around in here, some day I'm going to be sued by an angry client."

Karen nodded her agreement so emphatically that her corn-rows tinkled and blazed like a lit chandelier.

"So, from now on, *don't* let him quiz you. Tell him, if he tries to pressure you, that you've just learned about the Rules of Professional Conduct, client privacy, that sort of stuff. Do you think you can get a handle on him for me?"

"No problem. I can handle him. Makes me feel more comfortable too. I guess Bear is really interested in what you do, because he sure acts like I owe him an explanation whenever he calls. He's so *intense* . . . Now, what's the info you want me to get for you?"

"You'll find a large book on the top shelf, in the library, the Physicians Pharmaceutical Desk Reference. Copy the page on Percodan and stick it in my briefcase. I'll get to it later."

"Anything special going on here?"

"Well. I don't know. I just discovered that Bear's been taking a whole lot of whatever it is, so I was just wondering what it's supposed to cure, that's all."

When Karen was finished packing Linnell's briefcase, she placed the airline tickets in Linnell's purse along with a roll of quarters knotted inside one of Ray's black socks—just in case Linnell needed a blackjack for protection at the Miami airport. And then she remembered. "Hey L.C., I almost forgot! The IRS called! Something to do with Bear's audit. By the way, has Bear said anything to you about it?"

"No. Not yet. But knowing him, he will. He'll wait till the very last minute and then he'll tell me to drop everything and hop to it for him. So this time I'm getting things all lined up in advance. I've just ordered a whole bunch of copies of our tax returns from the IRS, so keep an eye out for them."

Linnell stood at her desk, still looking at the stale audit notice.

No. I'm not surprised by Bear, just concerned, Linnell thought. He's so busy, maybe he's hoping the IRS will just go away if he pretends they don't exist. Silly Bear. Anyway, it just goes to show how certain he is that there's nothing to worry about.

With that, Linnell dropped the audit notice on top of the pile on her desk.

"What was it the IRS wanted from me?" Linnell asked. "Anything special?"

"A Mr. Jordan was looking for you. I told him you were leaving this evening and that you'd be gone for a week. I didn't mention you were heading for Cayman. He said he would call you when you return. Just something to do with Bear's audit, that's all."

"Did he leave his number?"

"No. He just said he'd be getting in touch with you soon."

"Well, it'll have to wait until I return. Put a note in the file so I'll have a record that he didn't ask me to return his call. As for the hang-up calls, just continue to log them. Maybe we'll see a clearer pattern developing. Do you think it's only one person calling and hanging up like that?" Linnell continued her conversation with Karen while she unlocked her desk drawer and removed her black leather rudder book and hid it in her handbag.

"*I* think it's one person and that it's someone you know," Karen replied. "That's probably why he—or maybe it's a she—never says anything."

Because of the mysterious calls—they called them *cat-calls* now—Linnell was beginning to hate the telephone. Nowadays, when she heard the phone ring, instead of feeling a thrill of excitement at the thought of it being a prospective client, she felt a lead weight churning inside her stomach. Sometimes there would be as many as a dozen cat-calls over a five minute span. Then the calls would just as suddenly and mysteriously stop, only to begin again a few hours later. They had begun to log the cat-calls to see if there was a pattern to them, and despite her best efforts to pretend she was taking it lightly, the cat-calls were finally taking their toll.

They also made her feel totally stupid; in fact, she was galled at herself for having been so slow on the uptake—it had taken several weeks of this harassment before it had even occurred to her that some sicko out there had this relentless need to mess with her head. Why on earth would anyone want to do this to her? That was the real mystery. But, she'd find out. Sooner or later she'd find the tenacious nut and crack his head open to see why they had to pull stunts like this. In any event, even though these calls had her worried, right now she didn't want to share her distress because she didn't want to leave Karen feeling on edge. "Mm-hmm," was all Linnell replied, "you're probably right. Most likely it's someone we know. Well, I'm ready to leave. At last! While I'm gone, I need you to finish typing my article so I can send it off as soon as I return, and if you feel like taking off during the day, then come in here at night to catch up on things. Just be sure to set the alarm and keep my magnum opus locked up. I don't want anyone in here except you—not even Bear—while I'm gone. Okay? And if you ever feel uneasy about anything, you be sure to call the cops. By the way—that article's going to open up an entirely new avenue for my practice and I can't afford to have anyone—and especially not another lawyer—see it before it's published because then he'll get the jump on me."

"L.C., you *always* worry too much. Just get out of here—and have a good time! You better get a move on before I decide to go with you!" Karen crossed her fingers and waved long red nails at Linnell. "Break a leg!"

"Thanks. You'll find your pay check for next week on my desk, and I'll be back a week from next Wednesday."

Despite the heavy briefcase that banged her knee and the purse that cut into her shoulder, Linnell felt weightless, as if she were skimming the ground on the way to her car. "I'm free," she exulted. "Let someone else hold the rake and the broom for a while.' She knew exactly how Alice in Wonderland must have felt when she stepped through the mirror, because now, at long last, she was finally on her way to Looking-glass land.

HIGHRIDGE **Monday evening - February 25, 1974**

Debbie, still wearing her dirty rain coat, slipped into the oldest drug store in town. She was in the oldest drug store because she was looking for something old: a straight edge razor and the blades to go with it—something not likely to be stocked in any of the newer outlets. She stood next to the dusty display rack holding toiletries for men, quickly checked it out, and on the lower shelf spied what she was looking for. Now she had to decide whether to purchase it, and run the risk of being remembered by the clerk, or to palm it and run the more dangerous risk of getting caught. The matter was decided for her when the clerk turned his back. Debbie dipped so that she could slide the razor up her sleeve, made as if she were adjusting the strap of her handbag and then slowly shambled out the door without looking back.

HIGHRIDGE **Monday evening - February 25, 1974**

Bear had a tight thing going with Harold, his Wei trainer, who had promised to meet him at the program tonight. Harold had assured him that he'd be leaving for Houston at ten that evening and Bear needed to give him some more information before he took off. Harold had suggested that it would be better if he kept his path from crossing L.C.'s; so instead of taking off from San Francisco International and giving her a chance to spot him, he'd volunteered to drive down the peninsula and catch a late flight to Houston from San Jose.

Helluva guy, that Harold Dolphe, thought Bear.

His mind was now racing so fast he had to force himself to slow down so that he could perform the simple task of turning down the air conditioner in the Cadillac. It seemed that lately he could never find a comfortable temperature. Bear tapped the lever tab impatiently and then pulled it up. It came off in his hand. He glared at the console and swore. Maybe he should have kept the Jaguar for himself and given Ma this old tub instead. When would he ever learn? Bear pitched the broken tab on the floor, then pulled open his collar. What had he been thinking about? Oh yes. Harold. He had offered to pay Harold's air fare and Harold had refused to take his money, telling him that his costs were already being picked up on his expense account. Harold could have kept his mouth shut and pocketed the extra money—but no, Harold wouldn't do something like that because Harold admired him too much.

However, he'd better not forget that Harold *had* said: *"If I do a good job for you bro, then I'd welcome a few bucks as reimbursement for costs and maybe one of those nifty gifts you're famous for giving to those special patients of yours."* That's how Harold had put it, perhaps thinking that he was being tactful. He'd had to tell Harold to shut his face and to never talk about him like that. Harold, no slouch, had gotten his point immediately, which made it possible for them to come to an understanding about what Bear really wanted from him.

Bear had early on recognized Harold's native talent for pitching sales, and he had decided to hire him as soon as he was established in his new line of business. Harold would do very well on the retail side of things. But first, he had to sort out a few things with his stubbornly career-minded wife. It was bad enough that she had her own office—but still, she was a tax attorney, and she knew so much about international money transactions, so there was still a chance for her to become his ace-in-the-hole. But it was just as likely that she could become a dragging anchor around his neck. He had to find out which, and just as soon as possible, because he was just about ready to make his big move.

Bear parked his Cadillac and looked around. There already were more than 200 cars in front of the meeting hall. A terrific turnout for a Monday evening. Tonight's program was right up his alley—a session oxymoronically entitled by some twisted wit as: "Getting The Wei of Zen Aggression." Bear tipped his head back and this time downed a Dexie before passing his ticket to the freckle-faced kid who stood at the door. The lights had been dimmed for dramatic effect, but it wasn't so dark that he couldn't find Harold's rusty-red tufted head, bobbing and weaving as Harold noisily worked the crowd.

The hall, actually a gymnasium, had hardwood floors and concrete walls which amplified the sound, causing even whispers to reverberate, although it looked entirely different now that it had been decorated. It reminded him of some kind of medieval bull ring. He liked the effect of the chairs. There were hundreds of them, folding chairs set up in concentric circles around a cleared space in the center of the gym. They were matched by an equal number of banners—fluttering in the rising body heat, high above their heads. Each bore a green willow branch bending on a field of white, the symbol of The Wei. The volunteers had risked their lives to hang them in concentric circles from the rafters of the high ceiling. Bear nodded his approval—Harold had told him that the loyal Wei-farers worked without pay. They sure do a good job, Bear thought. What a slick operation! A low overhead and a staggering cash flow—the Wei-farers paid in advance just as if this were a pricey rock concert at the Fillmore—and it looked to him like The Wei would rake in a cool $18,000 for this evening alone. He'd better look into this—see what it would take for him to get in on the ground floor of this new self-empowerment game.

A ceiling spot flared into the center of the ring, and Bear kept one eye on Harold while he slowly worked his way toward his chair that sat in the innermost ring. The din slowly began to subside. Looking around the auditorium, Bear could see that a lot of his special patients had turned out. They exchanged quick nods and then, just as he was about to sit down, he caught sight of a sharp profile that seemed vaguely familiar to him.

The man was standing all by himself. At first Bear couldn't place him, and then it finally dawned—it was his wife's former boss—the man who promoted himself as the best tax attorney in the United States. Bear felt a warm surge of satisfaction upon seeing that the man's smoothly slicked-back hair had thinned, and noticeably, since he last saw him. As he stood there rubbing his own thickly curled head and wondering what the lawyer was doing at The Wei, he couldn't help noticing the respectful way people seemed to give Ivener his space. As if they could sense that here was a man too important to be toyed with. Bear scowled in Ivener's direction. He'd disliked him the instant he'd first laid eyes on him—he was a shit-head, that's what he was. The truth—and he didn't want Ma to know it—was that he didn't want her spending so much time around a man with his attitude, a man who thought he was so damn superior to everybody else. He'd finally managed to pry Ma out of Ivener's office by promising to pay for half the cost of setting her up in her own little place. That, and a hint of an ultimatum had done the trick. As for Willy—that's what Ma always called him, which still made him wonder if there hadn't been something going on between her and the sonnavabitch—he hadn't really met him. He'd only heard about him from Ma and he'd only seen him once before, at the law firm's lavish Christmas party.

There he'd gone to all that damn trouble of taking Ma to this big shot's ostentatious bash—where *she* got all the attention—and then the arrogant jerk hadn't bothered to come over and show him some respect. Ivener owed him. After all, he was letting his wife work at Ivener's firm instead of making her stay home and take care of the house and the man hadn't even bothered to come over and thank him. What that man really needs, Bear thought resentfully, is a good swift kick in the pants.

Bear had just shifted in order to get a better look at the bony backside of Ivener's head when Ivener spun around and locked eyes with him. Bear was startled into giving him a mirthless grin. The sight of Ivener's ghostly dry face, with those moist eyes staring levelly at him, was oddly disturbing. It made him feel as if something very alert but not quite human was studying him from deep inside the angular skull of a python. Ivener's expression, however, did not convey any sign of recognition.

The lights slowly dimmed and in the velvety half-light, Bear thought he saw Ivener's wet teeth grinning back at him from the shadows. But before he could tell for sure, the lights were abruptly extinguished and the room fell into total darkness.

A tenor voice, vibrating with manic excitement, suddenly boomed from the center of the circle. After congratulating the audience for attending, they were asked to give him a moment of silent meditation. The room quieted down immediately. Just as soon as Bear's eyes became adjusted to the dark, all the lights in the hall flared on, leaving everyone gasping and blinking. The bright lights hurt Bear's eyes and rubbing them with his finger tips, he turned to where he'd last seen Ivener. He was surprised—Ivener had vanished like an apparition. The lights slowly dimmed once again, the spotlight flared, and a Pat Boone-faced youth with a huge head of peroxide-blonde curls and a dark Palm Springs tan leapt into the circle and stood at its center like a glistening archangel in the column of light. Trim hipped and broad shouldered, he was dressed all in white—white shirt, white chinos and spotless white shoes—reminding Bear of an ambulance attendant.

With the joyous howl of a television evangelist, the archangel began to work the crowd. "We're here tonight!" he yelled into a round of applause. "To proooooove! Once again! That when a Wei-farer *Gets It* there will be ab-so-looootly NO limits to what he can do!" There was a rapt silence while he paused, and then, as if the entire idea had come to him only at that very instant, he ordered everyone to take off their shoes and socks. "That's *right.* You heard me! Get-'em-*off!* I want to see your bare feet!"

A buzz filled the hall because the Wei-farers were accustomed to having their programs begin with hugs and embraces, which they had been taught to describe as getting their *warm fuzzies*. A few groans could be heard—they wanted their warm fuzzies—but soon all of them were removing their shoes and pulling off their socks. Harold patrolled the room like a stormtrooper, locking the doors and making sure that everyone obeyed orders. Bear resented the fact that he had to do it too. None of the Wei trainers were required to go barefoot, so why did he have to put his clean bare feet on the cold dirty floor? Nevertheless, and despite the rising din of whines and complaints, he and all the rest of the Wei-farers dutifully followed orders.

The archangel ordered them to simmer down. "We're going to begin now!" he yelled. He sounded mean. There were a few giggles when the overhead lights illuminated the cloud of spittle that flew from his lips. He ignored the audience and looked around, and then with a loud whoop of joy, pointed to a slender young man who sat slumped in a second row seat, smiling uncertainly. Perhaps it was his shy demeanor and his slight build that had prompted the group leader to choose him to be first in the ring. Grasping a narrow wrist with his other hand, the youth swiveled his hips to avoid the chairs and padded uncertainly out to the center of the circle, leaving behind a moist trail of footprints.

The group leader slumped and then imitated his smile so perfectly that an ominous titter rippled throughout the room.

"Hey *you*. Tell us your name, sonny boy." The group leader turned to his audience and rolled his eyes heavenward and smirked, inviting more laughter.

"I'm Dennis," the young man squawked. He was fresh out of his teens and the look in his eyes hovered between a desire to please and absolute panic.

He's stoned, thought Bear. Or maybe he's gay and just doesn't know it. Bear watched with rapt fascination.

"No you're *not.*" The group leader bellowed into his victim's face. Dennis flinched, he tried to jump backwards but his foot remained stuck to the floor; then he tripped and fell hard, twisting his ankle. Instead of helping him up, the group leader continued to bellow at him as he lay on the floor: "That's where you belong, on your weak worthless ass, you fuckin' wuss."

Stunned by this unexpected onslaught, the young man's lower lip began to quiver while he struggled unsuccessfully to get to his feet.

The group leader placed the sole of his white-buck shoe on the young man's forehead and pushed him down slowly. "Look at him waving his ass in the air. Hey. Hey! Pussy. I'm talking' to you! You can't hide from us. We know what you are, so come out and admit it."

Dennis sat on the floor and cried openly now, rubbing his ankle.

"You don't *get* it, do you?" the group leader said in an soothing voice. Dennis looked up at the ceiling spot as if that could help him, shook his head, and everyone stared at his startled, woebegone face. The audience collectively held its breath. Bear loved moments like this, when the crowd reacted as one.

"I said, you don't get it! Do you! Look at me and answer, you shit-faced fag! Look! Or else you won't get my permission to leave. You get it now?" The group leader stood over Dennis in a threatening pose and hooked his finger under Dennis' chin to keep the boy from looking away.

"No. I don't get it," Dennis replied, shamefacedly.

Cupping Dennis' chin, the group leader crowed to the invisible mob, "*He* doesn't *get* it. You hear that? Now let's all of us give our little wuss here a great big hand."

While the audience broke into a mixture of cheers and jeers, the group leader yanked the humiliated Dennis up to his feet and with a hard slap to his rump, sent him limping out of the circle. Few people saw the small pool of urine Dennis had left on the floor because everyone was laughing and clapping, while a group of Wei-farers rushed over to pull Dennis back to his chair.

"You *get* it?" the group leader yelled.

"We *get* it!" the group roared in reply.

"You sure? Hey, *you* there. *You* say you get it? Come here!" The group leader chose a bespectacled, chubby-faced woman whose dimpled pink cheeks were still blubbering with excitement. The loud center of her circle of friends, she had been shrieking and clapping wildly. Having been summoned, she now smiled with a slightly befuddled air, as if she were surprised that her applause hadn't bought her better protection. Cutely tossing her curls as if she were Shirley Temple, she stepped into the circle. She wore a high-necked, puffy sleeved, full-skirted dress of uncertain green material and she flounced her skirts as she walked, beaming and oblivious, through Dennis' small pool of urine; then she slipped and almost fell because although she wasn't wearing her shoes, she still wore her nylons which for reasons she was about to understand were now slippery against the floor.

Thanks to Harold, Bear could guess what was coming.

The angel-faced group leader caught her by her plump arm as if to steady her and waited for her to stop blushing. Then after the room quieted into silent expectation, he pronounced her an overfed relic, a leftover from the Fifties. "A no-class canned ham, that's what you are. You! You *stu*-pid, *fat*-assed, *plas*-tic sow! Can't you follow a few simple directions? Barefoot! You're supposed to be barefoot! Get those offa you *now*!" With his face leaning down into hers, he lectured her until her face was beet-red and her glasses were fogged with perspiration.

The plump creature seemed unable to escape. She had a choice: either put her huge white thighs on display, or be hooted out of the auditorium. Dark green stains of perspiration could be seen spreading out from her armpits as she tried to decide. Although her embarrassment was almost too painful to watch, she chose the Wei-farers—and, grunting and wiggling and sweating copiously, she pulled down her nylons, first releasing the soft fat pads hanging from her dimpled knees to the scrutiny of the chanting crowd, then exposing her pendulous fuzzy mound to their whistles. That done, the group leader seemed to lose all interest and giving her a sharp nudge between her plump shoulder-blades, he sent her thundering back to her chair. She was immediately followed by others, who were systematically badgered and humiliated before being released, while the group leader continued to howl: "Do you get it?"

With each passing victim, so far there were five, the crowd—which obviously didn't know what to "get"—continued to applaud, although Bear could now sense that many of them were puzzled and some, afraid. Despite the rising tide of tension and the Dexedrine, he was getting bored; he nodded and rubbed his eyes while he sat waiting for the group leader to call him into the ring. He was confident that the group leader had no idea that Harold had already clued him in.

"Okay. Let's do this big guy here. You say you *get* it? Well, let's see what *you* got." The group leader, hands on hips, stood in front of him now.

Bear lumbered to the center of the floor and blinking, stood tall. For the first time in his life, his audience was hidden from him by the bright lights. But still, he could hear very well, and he knew that a few Wei-farers were making ready to jeer him. Standing barefoot next to the group leader, he was surprised to find that the young man, who had looked so tall from the side of the ring, was almost a foot shorter than him.

The group leader looked up in his face with a puzzled expression, as if he didn't quite know where to begin. Stepping out of arm's reach, he said, "And who do you think you are?"

"*I'm* Doc Clare. A dentist here in town." Bear replied genially and rocked back on his heels.

"That's not what you are, that's just what you think!" The group leader tried to stir up some laughter but he was greeted, instead, by an expectant silence.

Bear turned slowly to face the group leader. "Hey punk. Go *fuck* yourself. " He spit the F-word in his inquisitor's face.

It was obvious to all that the group leader was shocked and offended. Wei-farers were forbidden to use profanity with anyone above the rank of trainer. That was part of the contract they'd signed, and there were *stiff* fines for this kind of acting out. The group leader looked behind him to make sure his back-ups were standing close by.

"Hey, you heard me pretty-boy!" Bear, emboldened, now roared. "You too friggin' stupid to find your own ass?" Placing his hands on his hips, Bear glared menacingly at the group leader and then he turned and grinned triumphantly at the audience; the Wei-farers gasped as one and then burst into cheers.

The group leader, fast on his feet, decided to cover. He lunged for Bear's arm, and then holding it up as if Bear were a champion, he yelled: "*He* gets it. See? He *gets* it."

The two men stood in the spotlight, and the group leader told Bear to take a bow. Bear turned on him and whispered, "You think I was joking?" He ruined the group leader's charade by tearing his arm from the group leader's grasp and headed for his chair. He scooped up his shoes and put them on. He felt good. He felt like a winner. He had just had a little taste of the power that would be coming to him.

He knew the real purpose of tonight's session—Harold had told him—it was meant to condition the donkeys to responding, on cue, to given orders. It was really incredible. The idiots were willing to pay for this stupid brain-washing. What a racket! Glancing back at his field of conquest, Bear saw that the Wei-farers were still clapping and chanting and that the group leader was still leaping around, trying desperately to make it appear as if he were leading them.

Bear finally caught Harold's eye. Harold walked to the door at the side of the hall and waited for Bear to approach.

"Congrats. You did good bro." Harold's voice sounded a little fearful.

"Yeah, and it's like you said. What a crock! Do you *get* it ? Hah! Who thinks up this bullshit anyway? But thanks for the tip. I appreciate. So, you wanna know what *I* got tonight? I gotta feeling that if people are willing to spend big bucks on crap like *this*, then they're gonna be spending a fortune on my new line of business. You still interested?"

"Sure. Sounds good to me. Just tell me when and where and I'll be there for you, brother," Harold replied.

"Oh, I almost forgot to ask," Bear whispered. "Wasn't that Ivener I just saw in here earlier? You see him?"

"Yeah. That was him all right." Harold whispered back. "But he disappeared before I had a chance to talk to him."

"Well, have a good trip. As for me, I won't be staying at home this week. Here's where you can call me at night and the name of the hotel where she's staying." Bear handed Harold a piece of paper. "I have a few things I have to do tonight so I'm leaving early. See you later, bro." Bear patted Harold's shoulder.

Harold Dolphe unlocked the side door and let Dr. Clare slip out.

SAN FRANCISCO **Monday evening - February 25, 1974**

Linnell felt absolutely euphoric! Giddy with anticipation, she maneuvered her way through traffic on the way to San Francisco International Airport.

Relief. I'm out of here for ten days. The longest I've ever been away from home! I'll call Helen from the airport to make sure everything's okay. I can't wait to go to the beach!

When she pulled into the traffic corridor leading under the terminal she found herself humming: "Hi-diddle-dee-dee, I've-got-a-week-for-me." Annoyed that she couldn't shake the tune, Linnell turned on her radio and switched to the news and then just as she rolled down the ramp to the underground parking garage, the reporter's concluding remarks caught her ear: " . . . this evening . . . indictment of . . . handed up as a result of the . . . successful Project Tax Haven Mavens . . . criminal investigations. KXWA reports that . . . on the . . ." The rest of the broadcast was blanked by static because she was now too far underground. Linnell checked her bags and went straight to the airport cafe to wolf down a hamburger on San Francisco sourdough bread. Then she called Bear's office again and was again greeted by a busy signal. Now anxious because she'd been unable to reach him all day, she called home to check on what was happening at the house. Linnell was greatly relieved to hear Helene report that Dr. Clare had just called to say that he'd be staying at the country club all this week "so he'd be out of her hair," and that he had also asked her to convey the message that "everything's fine." Helene added that Bear had told her he would be coming home after dinner to pick up some clothes.

"Oh! I guess that's why I couldn't get through to him, he must have been talking to you. Well, I'm glad everything's okay." Linnell said good-bye. She felt flat. Why would Bear want to stay at the club? Didn't he like Helene? They had always seemed to get along in the past. She was puzzled by this.

She had selected Helene—who was old enough to be her mother—to help her run the house because she was warm and shrewd and possessed a pragmatic optimism that had rescued Linnell on more than one occasion. Helene had cared for Benjy since he was a baby, and although she could sometimes be bossy—maybe that's what bothered Bear—she was also a born peacemaker.

Less anxious now that she'd received word from Bear, Linnell relaxed over a newspaper and read every page, looking for more information about "Project Haven Mavens." Finding nothing about it, she dismissed the matter—perhaps her mind had been playing tricks on her. Then, with nothing to do until her departure, she decided to change into her jeans and boots so she could go straight to the bank the following morning.

After changing clothes, Linnell still had another twenty minutes to kill. Finding an empty table next to the gate, she dug out her new National Geographic Map of the West Indies and Central America and managed to get it open without tearing it at the creases. Linnell smoothed it out on the table next to the gate and then turned the map around until she was looking at it upside down, with Nicaragua at the bottom and the Antilles at the top.

"Excuse me. But why are you looking at your map upside down?" The onlooker spoke in the open manner that traveler's get when they know they're just passing through.

"Oh, I dunno, I'm just killing time," Linnell replied with a smile. She liked his friendly face and feeling equally expansive, she decided to share her fantasy with him. "Look at this. Isn't this marvelous? I can see an outline of Erzulie on the map . . . sometimes, when I think about Her I call her by her other name: Ba-Abaloah. We have a side-view of her here, so her hair and her back are outlined by Hispaniola and Cuba. And this is her crown." Although Linnell didn't expect the man to understand, she nevertheless swept her finger across the map from the Virgin Islands to Grenada.

"Well, what do you know! Erzulie, the mightiest Loa . . . the Goddess of Love," the stranger exclaimed. "Well, regardless of what you call Her, you're quite right. If I squint my eyes, I can see Her image outlined on the map. How do you know about Her? Are you a student of Obeah?" He was referring, Linnell understood, to the Jamaican form of Voodooism.

"No . . . well, I don't know that much about it, really," she stammered, thinking about her secret friendship with Mama N'dobah and Mama's warning to always admit to less than what she actually knew. "But, I'm on my way back to the Cayman Islands which is where I first learned about the veneration of the goddess Erzulie and the other deities. When I was first went there, three years ago, I learned that the Loa are the sacred expressions of God who rise up from the bottom of the sea. So, how do *you* know about Voodoo?"

"Well, I go to Jamaica and the Caymans, too, so I know enough about it to tell that you've got quite an imagination. However, it seems you've only been looking at the surface of things. So now I want to show you something more." The man laid his finger on Linnell's map. "More than four and a half *miles* beneath the surface—in this region, here—there's an even more fascinating tale. I am a marine geologist, and what most fascinates me about the Caribbean Basin is the possibility of finding an active rent at the bottom of the Cayman Trench."

Linnell had never heard of the Cayman Trench; intrigued by this information, she saw that his finger lay on an area immediately south of Grand Cayman Island.

"That," he said, "is the deepest point in the Caribbean Sea—almost 25,000 feet—in fact, the Caymans are an outcropping of an undersea cliff so huge that the walls of the Grand Canyon are puny by comparison. The Trench itself is more than 900 miles long, it runs East to West and it's part of a large fault formed by the moving plates of the earth's crust.

"You said something about a "rent" in the trough. What do you mean? Is the earth splitting open down there?"

"Yes. That's it exactly, and that's what we intend to explore. The rent, or rift, is indeed like a crack in the earth's crust. This one runs at right angles to the Cayman Trench and we'll soon be going down there to look for evidence of recent underwater volcanic activity. But don't worry—this has been going on for millions of years."

Linnell saw her boarding sign flash and began to fold up her map. "I think it's amazing to meet someone like you. I hope the great Goddess Ba-Abaloah brings you good luck and that I'll hear more about you in the future," she said.

"Ba-Abaloah. I like that, and thank you," the man replied. He reached in his wallet and handed her his card. Linnell read what it said on her way to the gate: *Woods Hole Oceanographic Institution, Massachusetts.*

The jumbo jet boarded passengers at 11:30 PM and Linnell walked through the cabin until she found a row of unoccupied seats where she could stretch out and sleep. All she needed was a couple of hours and then she'd have enough energy to run the length of the Miami terminal and catch her flight to Cayman. Linnell turned on the light over the seats and rummaged through the overhead compartment for blankets. After making herself a nest, she climbed in and fastened her seat belt and fidgeted restlessly until the plane had gained altitude, then she unfastened her seat belt, leaned back, and watched the other passengers lighting up their cigarettes.

Whenever she lifted her hand into the overhead beam, it appeared to flutter in the smoky air like a blue moth in a strobe light, and then her thoughts suddenly skipped back ten years, to the time when her husband had first begun to practice and people still referred to him as "the new dentist in town."

They had attended a mixer held by the Highridge Chamber of Commerce and had separated upon entering in the hope that this would double their chances of attracting more people to Mark's fledgling practice. Later that evening, when Linnell caught up with him, she found him standing in the midst of a cluster of people who appeared to be hanging on his every word. He stood tall at their center, and Linnell thought he looked like a king holding court. Orbiting on the periphery of his circle of admirers, Linnell finally stood on her toes to see what he was saying and that was how she caught him inventing an entirely new story about his background, which he was recounting to his enraptured audience: "So tired of my family's business," he'd said. "Yes . . . they're filthy rich, in banking. Yes, I grew up in Beverly Hills . . . I'm a dentist because I want to give something back to humanity. Of course, I'm no different than a physician because I can prescribe . . . I came up here to blaze a new trail in Northern California. Sure I played football . . ." were but a few of the curious inventions that had spilled from his mouth. Then Mark, finally appreciating what must have been the look of astonishment on her face, had shot her a warning look, which she knew meant: *"You'd better be quiet!"*

As if it had just happened yesterday, Linnell could remember it all so clearly: At first she'd felt embarrassed for him because everything he'd said was a lie, and then, for a moment she'd felt dizzy because he seemed such a stranger to her. Later on in the evening, while they were walking together and Linnell was sure no one could overhear, she had whispered to Mark. "With your circle of new admirers, you looked like a king holding court—but, what on God's earth was *that* all about? Those stories! What's gotten into you?"

By way of reply, Mark draped his heavy arm over her shoulders and while crushing her slightly he'd spit in her ear: "Hey! You wanna be rich? You gotta *learn* something: Those who *get* are those who *got.* So I gotta look like I already have it! You better get *that* one straight in your head!" Then he had cupped his hand under her chin and turned her head toward the women who stood gaping at her with apparent envy. Then with his eyes fixed on his bank of admirers, he'd planted a cold wet kiss on the side of her neck.

Linnell reached up and wiped her neck with the back of her hand. After all these years, she could still feel that frigid kiss, and she had never really forgotten her astonishment at her husband's ability to play to the gallery with a desperation as cold as a cave. It had been truly amazing. However, and despite that charade—or most likely, because of it—the word soon got around that they were rising stars, a well-matched young couple. But that night, and for the very first time, she had begun to wonder about what she had done with her life.

Feeling uneasy, Linnell counted on her fingers to see how many years had passed since then, and then she realized there was more to remember from that night. Linnell raised her hand and fluttered her fingers in the light. Yes! Of course! There was *another* memorable event that same evening—with the short balding dentist who had asked her to dance.

The man, with an oily scalp, had been much older than her and had worn such expensive apparel she could even now recall the luxurious hand of his thick cashmere jacket. And the first words out of his mouth were about his divorce. He'd said he had just "laid off" his wife of 25 years and had just "bought himself a new one. Did she want to see?" Then he'd swept Linnell across the dance floor to show of his "new model"—who appeared to be even younger than she. She had asked him to tell her why he had divorced his first wife and he had explained that men always divorce their first wives because of their hands.

"Their *hands*?" she had replied. "What on earth do you mean?"

"Yep. Their hands. See? The first wife does all the work in the marriage. You can just take a look at those old weathered hands of hers if you wanna know what I'm talking about. They're wrinkled. They're tired. Comes from holding onto the plow for so long. But y'know, when a man works, it's different. *He* becomes a success and then—you see?—he's not gonna want a woman who's worn out from all that plowing." The old dentist had chuckled smugly and then pressing his moist lips to her ear, had whispered: "So let me tell you a little secret, honey . . . this new one's gonna be havin' it *easy*. Know why?" He'd paused for effect, then pulling away from her in order to better observe her reaction, he'd happily wheezed: "Cause the *first* one worked so damn hard!" Erupting into a self-satisfied snorting fit he then lifted her hand toward his bared little teeth as if to give her fingers a playful nip. And he'd almost had them in his mouth when she decided to put a stop to his antics. She'd first coughed in his face, then yanking her hand away, she'd made it look as if she'd only accidentally whacked him across his cheek.

A sudden jolt brought Linnell back to the present; the aircraft had slammed into turbulent air. As the aircraft bounced and lurched, it suddenly occurred to her to wonder if she had ever really, truly known where the ground was with Bear.

But he calls everyday to tell me he loves me.

When she reached up to turn off the overhead light she fluttered her fingers, then looked more closely at her hand. Yes, it was still young, and still smooth despite all the hard work it had done. Linnell Clare closed her eyes and tried to sleep, but she could still see Bear's furious eyes glaring back at her. Staring at her. Spinning her around and around through a darkening mist until she finally disappeared into a gray tunnel of sleep.

INTO THE DEEP

MIAMI, FLORIDA **6:30 a.m. Tuesday - February 26, 1974**

Five miles beneath the ruffled iridescent skin,
Ba-Abaloah, immortal Efik of the deep did sleep.
Slowly parting every now and then Her lips,
Slowly grinding Her magnificent jaws,
Spewing fiery plasma between Her teeth.
Pressing sulfurous molecules into life,
At depths where mortals
If so foolish as to venture there,
Would be compacted
swiftly senseless
into spheres . . .

Crackling with static, the pilot's disembodied voice floated over the intercom to greet the passengers aboard the one-hour flight from Miami to Grand Cayman Island. The tail section was already full by the time she'd climbed aboard, so Linnell felt herself lucky to have two vacant adjoining seats for herself in the front row of the aircraft. And that was where she now sat, reviewing the files she would need at the bank where a crucial meeting would be taking place as soon as she landed.

After breakfast was served, the svelte Cayman Airways flight attendant said hello to Linnell and then dropped into the seat next to her to tell her the good news: Because of its foreign registry the airline had been granted the right to pass through Cuban airspace on its outbound flights. Then bestowing an air-kiss above Linnell's cheek, the stewardess sprang to her feet to continue her upward climb toward the tail as the craft began a slow dive toward Matanzas de Cuba. A few minutes later, the pilot announced he would be slow-flying so that all the Norte Americanos aboard could see the famous Cuban sugar cane fields. The craft dropped altitude and for a disconcerting second or two it felt as if all forward momentum had ceased while row after row of lush dark-green foliage marched toward them and then passed in great rippling waves underneath the stubby wings of the twin-engine prop-jet. Then the engines roared, the nose went up, and the daredevil pilot reassured the passengers: "Hokaaaay, folks! Keep your seat-belts fastened. We're already halfway there."

Linnell fixed her eyes on the sapphire waters below and thought about why she had come to love international tax law. *It's so complex and absurd, so wicked and insane . . . it's a marvelous Alice-in-Wonderland double-speak world where things are quite different from what they seem. It has given us a reason for Cayman and accounts for what Bermuda knows how to do best.*

She might be uncertain about a lot of things, but there was one thing about which she was absolutely certain: As much as she yearned to have her own money, she would never allow herself to become one of those sleaze-ball lawyers who blew into the Bahamas to pick up dozens of tax haven shelf-corporations to hawk at a ten-fold mark-up as "A sure-fire way to bury your income and beat your taxes." These schemes were utterly useless and if you were caught using them, you would be busted. In contrast, the tax planning that a maven did was the sort that could be revealed in broad daylight—if such should ever be necessary—because the know-how of an international tax attorney was based upon some very strange but real laws. That was the reason why she didn't care if anyone thought she was odd for spending so much time poring over thousands of pages of tax statutes. She knew things others didn't want to know: that the Internal Revenue Code was a vast road-map of the convoluted trails laid down by the wealthiest and most brilliant influences in the United States; it was a complicated script of a vast soap opera that would reveal to its knowledgeable readers a long history of power and greed. That was why her knowledge was worth a fortune: because it could save a fortune in taxes. The life of an international tax attorney was never easy, but it certainly was always crazy—especially when millions were at stake.

Haven mavens are an extremely peculiar breed, thought Linnell. She knew that even if she didn't look the part, she was born to be one. And she had had Willy Ivener to thank for recognizing this. Thus no matter what she thought of him now, she still owed him a debt of gratitude for taking her under his wing, especially after every other lawyer in town had made it plain that they wouldn't be laying out any welcome mats for a "lady lawyer." But Willy had taken a chance on her and she would never forget it.

The law firm of William E. Ivener was renowned throughout the United States and like all the largest tax firms in New York and Chicago and Denver and Dallas, it was especially keen to provide off-shore tax-planning for its more sophisticated clientele. She had first heard about Mr. Ivener when she was in law school—rumor had it that he had never lost a tax case. So, being her idol, she had ultimately become one of Ivener's underpaid, overworked associates. Her bubble of adoration had popped soon enough after that.

Ivener got a big kick out of passing himself off as an everyday kind of guy. He was nothing of the sort. However, and as part of his charade—in actuality, a gesture intended as an extreme manifestation of reverse snobbery—he projected a laid-back image for the firm, and thus everyone in this supposedly egalitarian outfit were under similar orders to conduct all their business on a first-name basis. In fact, Ivener had so often reminded her to just call him "Willy"—"And just remember that it's Willy with a *Y*, he would say—that one day, out of curiosity, she had looked up his name in the firm's OED and was surprised to find that *Willy* was actually the Old English word for *willow*.

Very apt, she thought, since his pale hide, stretched taut over a narrow landscape of sharp cheekbones and temples, gave him a close resemblance to his namesake tree. As thin and as deathly white as a peeled stripling, with his ubiquitous gray suit the slippery bark, Willy was a wily and mercurial being, a flexible gray eminence who delighted in concocting endless schemes, more for the purpose of confounding the IRS than to serve his nonetheless worshipful clients. Moreover, the slim-shanked elegance he liked to affect—both in himself and his luxurious surroundings—was frequently belied by his voice. A sometimes frightening voice which could flick in an instant from soft velvet strokings to shocking street-wise vulgarities. And there was something about his tough spareness that made Bear's great bulk seem merely pulpy. In fact, when she compared her husband to Ivener—which she seldom did, and then only in secret—she would come away with the uneasy feeling that should there ever be a contest between the two men, Ivener would prove to be the stronger of the two.

Shortly after she'd arrived at his firm, Ivener's devoted secretary, the lumpkin Margarita, had made a big thing out of letting her know that Ivener was married and lead a very "private" life. A warning, she supposed, to let her know that he was "off limits." An entirely unnecessary admonition as far as she was concerned—there was nothing about Ivener that could possibly interest her insofar as he was a man. Nor for that matter was she the sort who'd ever dream of using the casting couch as a way to get a leg up the ladder.

However, and even though Willy had never said anything directly, she knew that her quitting his firm had made him upset. He probably still was upset, perhaps even more so just recently, because she was in direct competition with him now. Nevertheless, and thanks to Bear's persuasion, she now had her very own, albeit small, law firm. And despite her initial misgivings—and Ivener's warning that she would have a difficult time making it on her own—she was actually doing okay. So far, she had won two major tax cases and she had also acquired some significant clients. This was the main reason she had warned Karen to stop telling Bear what was going on in her office. Now that Bear was bragging, there was a chance her new clients might get wind of her confiding in Bear, and this would have a chilling effect upon her reputation. Bear knew she had begun to clam up on him, and he had certainly let her know that he was miffed at her about this, but she had used his refusal to tell her what he was doing at The Wei to justify her recent reticence. But soon, soon all this sparring would disappear because her surprise would make Bear so happy. Linnell smiled out the window. She was thinking very positively now, even though she felt a chilly ripple of fear and excitement up and down her back.

She rummaged in her purse for her diary—the daily log book which she had first begun to keep during her initiation at the Ivener firm. It was not just a diary of her professional exploits—it did contain some personal information—it was actually a *rudder,* because, like those kept by the Caribbean navigators who had first written them during the 1600s, it was an ever-enlarging record of all the highly confidential information that a modern-day offshore explorer would need in order to navigate safely through the shoals of the Internal Revenue Code.

Staring at the glowing horizon, Linnell clutched her rudder and felt a thrill of danger as she tried to imagine all the sleek pirate ships and treasure-laden galleons that had fought in the very same waters she was looking at now. Thus, if the Internal Revenue Code was a prescription for imposing taxes, then her rudder was the antidote, because it held her summaries of IRS rulings and regulations, code-names, unlisted phone numbers of useful contacts, blind post box addresses, sophisticated tax plans and translated excerpts of the Dutch tax treaties between the United States and the Netherlands Antilles—not to mention all of her plans for her Sea Urchin Project as well.

Linnell thumbed through its marked-up pages and found the information she needed: the telephone number for the shipping line and the unlisted address of a certain fisherman's warehouse on the outskirts of Georgetown. Then she thought about Mama N'dobah, and wondered whether she would see her again on this trip.

Mama was a strange one, all right. Linnell had met her by accident at a very private party she'd been invited to by one of the locals. Linnell had been drawn to her out of curiosity and now knew that Mama N'dobah was not her real name, and from what she'd already learned from her so far, Linnell knew better than to ask. Nor would Mama say where she lived. But Linnell knew that if she were to see a shiny black Lincoln sedan, that Mama would be in it, because most afternoons Mama liked to patrol the roads and refresh herself with the large automobile's air conditioning.

She caught her breath and then to calm her nerves, she recited the chant that Mama had taught her. Her heart pumped at the thought that she was about to discover if her meticulous plans were going to work. And then she forced herself to exhale, blowing out the bad luck the way Mama said she must do. Linnell held the thought of good luck then clearing her mind, made a deliberate attempt to distract herself by thinking of something else. She thought of the mavens, of whom she was the youngest, and then thought about all the games they liked to play on the IRS. One, their favorite, was called Snooker the Spook. It was her favorite, too.

Reflecting the spirit of the tax laws that had spawned them all, mavens would begin to play Snooker on the flight to Cayman or in the Cayman customs shed where everyone queued up to have their passports stamped. Since most of the mavens from the United States came from Florida and Texas on commercial flights—the private jets usually arrived just before sunrise carrying passengers who considered darkness a blessing—the mavens could usually be found amongst the tourists, usually on the earliest morning flight from Miami. This allowed the mavens to mingle with the more ingenuous visitors who were in turn usually wondering aloud why there were so many briefcase toting suits on a tropical island. The mavens, however, were always on the alert for something more challenging than exchanging pleasantries with curious travelers.

As all mavens well knew, there were also IRS intelligence agents, the spooks, otherwise known as "Special Services Agents," loitering amongst the crowd. The spooks used a variety of slightly unsavory disguises. Sometimes they would try to pass themselves off as wise guys, other times they would pose as gamblers looking for a place to stash their cash. Most often they'd pretend to be sleazy accountants or naive tourists looking to score some free tax advice. They hoped to strike up an easy acquaintance with the numerous lawyers and bankers and brokers and political aides who were there to pay their respects to the island's banks. Not so coincidentally, the mavens were also engaged in the very same charade; thus a maven might pose as an awestruck tourist, or a high-powered accountant might pass himself off as a hard-drinking beach bum. The objective was to identify and then secretly uncover an agent—hand him a big line, and then send him flying on a wild goose chase all over the island. This entertained the mavens, who thus gained the opportunity of watching the watcher as he strutted about the island, playing his little IRS games. Usually, by the time the agent discovered he'd been snookered, the mavens would be long gone.

Linnell clapped her rudder shut and shoved it in her purse. This time there would be no time for games. Linnell kept an eye on the horizon as the aircraft increased altitude and droned on a beeline to Cayman. Detecting a subtle shift of color in the waters below the wings, she closed her files and tucked them in her briefcase. She glanced at her watch—another twenty minutes and they would be landing at the small airfield on Grand Cayman Island, grandly named Owen Roberts International Airport. Linnell turned around and searched for familiar faces among the passengers. When she was sure there were none, she reached down and pulled her heavy gold wedding band from her finger, slipped it into her briefcase and snapped it shut. Then she sat back in her seat, closed her eyes, and prayed—just in case there was an all-seeing deity who would punish her for what she had just done.

Okay God . . . it's only a symbolic gesture, so don't get pissed-off and go ruining the weather. I'm just taking it off for a little while so I can feel free. Linnell felt her broken fingernail and then added: *And please God, don't let me slip, or fall, or do any of my clumsy stunts. I can't afford to injure myself or ruin my equipment. I swear I'm not going to be looking for trouble, I just need some rest—a good meal that I don't have to cook, some sleep, a walk on the beach, and then I can go home and put on the ring and the harness again . . .*

She opened her eyes, yawned, and leaned forward. With her nose now pressed close to the window, she drank in the brilliant splotches of blue changing shape in the waters below the wings and then finally, she saw the fluorescent explosion of aquamarine that signaled their approach to the airport over the North Sound of the island. The colors seemed to blur as they began their descent. Linnell quickly cleared her ears then tore off the rubber band that held her pony tail and shook her hair free. Somewhere down there—miles beneath the surface—the earth was stirring, cracking open and spewing its furious heat into the cold sheets of mother earth's bed. That certainly adds a nice touch of tension, thought Linnell; she grabbed her briefcase and held onto it tightly. She no longer was afraid and she couldn't wait to land. Soon she'd be laughing and flirting; again just enjoying being a part of her favorite scene.

The plane landed smoothly and Linnell Clare was the first to disembark. She knew the custom agents would look only at the passports and ignore the bags; they were more concerned about visitors having the requisite round-trip tickets that would guarantee their ability to depart at the end of their stay. Her passport was quickly stamped and then stepping ahead of the crowd, Linnell waved for a taxi so that she could be the first to disappear on an island that was only ten miles wide and twenty-four miles long.

GRAND CAYMAN ISLAND Tuesday, February 26, 1974

The Cayman Islands—Grand Cayman, Little Cayman, and Cayman Brac—sat at the center of the Caribbean like three small blond raisins in the middle of a blue glass plate. Largely ignored for centuries by all except pirates, the small islands finally came into their own during the early Seventies when the Bahamian upheavals sent international financiers scattering toward friendlier shores.

Georgetown, the capital, was an exceedingly friendly place and Linnell ordinarily felt thrilled to be a part of this fast emerging financial center. But today, the only thing that mattered to her was the Sea Urchin Project. However, before she could begin to set it in motion, there was one final hurdle, the most important detail of all: the money. Which explained why her first appointment would be at her bank. Linnell shivered with nervous excitement.

The taxi carried Linnell to Georgetown on a freshly paved road which disappeared entirely at the edge of the business district. She was amazed to see that from this point forward all streets leading to the banks had been torn up by new construction projects. It was hard to believe but, during the four months since she'd last visited, the tiny town had been transformed. The taxi skillfully navigated the dusty maze and dropped Linnell off at her destination. She stood for a moment at what should have been the curb and looked up.

Heavy steel lattices now rose everywhere she looked and new buildings appeared to be sprouting from every patch of available ground. It was a boomtown! Construction cranes, concrete mixers, lumber trucks and beat-up taxies vied for space in what had once been a sleepy square. Linnell looked at her bank, once the only new building in Georgetown, and saw that it would soon be surrounded by its major competitors—well-known US, Canadian, and European institutions. Their signs were already up although their buildings were no more than skeletons. Threading her way through the arches of scaffolding, Linnell finally reached the jerry-rigged wooden walkway that snaked up to the entrance. She was glad she'd had the foresight to change into her jeans and boots because it looked like she would have to climb over a barricade to enter the lobby. Hoisting up her luggage, she passed it to the bank guard who stood at the curb and then she waited for him to help her climb into the newly enlarged, marble-paneled lobby.

The first thing she looked for was the directory board, where Cayman law required all banks to list all the registered companies they sponsored. A newer and larger board, now inside a locked glass-covered case, had been installed to accommodate the bank's rapidly expanding list. She felt a stab of pride when she saw the name of her company: *SUP Cayman Ltd.* Having borrowed one of Ivener's tricks, Linnell had selected the acronym for "Sea Urchin Project" for the company's registered legal name, and the only person outside of Karen who knew that she owned it was her banker—and he was forbidden to tell.

Seeing that the elevator was blocked by a stack of sawhorses, Linnell fought her way through the construction debris and headed for the stairs. With her briefcase tucked under one arm, she slipped through a tarpaulin curtain and took them two at a time. The acrid odor of mildewing sheet-rock and fermented taper's mud hit her nose like a fist, forcing her to hold her breath until she reached the door on the second floor landing. Springing through the door and into the anteroom, she was greeted with equanimity by an older lady with a Canadian accent—her banker's personal secretary—who examined Linnell's credentials and then offered her some refreshment. Linnell waited outside his private office while she brushed off sheet-rock dust and quaffed the obligatory cup of tea. After a proper few minutes, Colin, her banker, ushered her into the inner sanctum where they would engage in the formalities of establishing her clients' foreign trusts. While Colin was signing, stamping, and affixing seals to the trust documents, Linnell inspected the room.

The decor had been completed at last, and Linnell saw that Colin had selected Chippendale chairs and an unusual mahogany desk which so closely resembled the one she'd inherited from her grandfather that she wanted to reach out and caress its ornately carved moulding. On the wall above Colin's high-backed leather chair—now resting on an antique Persian carpet—was an elegant, gilt-framed portrait of a beribboned Elizabeth II in her flower-faced prime. A florid faced, rep-tied Colin sat poised for action beneath Her Majesty's satiny visage—a stout knight of commerce eager to enrich his bank and protect the remaining borders of the Kingdom's once far-flung Empire.

Linnell's eyes darted up to the Queen's agreeable image before settling on Colin. Her Majesty above. He below. Perhaps it was this juxtaposition that explained why British bankers were so much easier to deal with than her own, or perhaps they seemed more agreeable because the Salic laws hadn't affected the British monarchy to the same degree as on the continent—hence the Brits weren't conditioned to regard a woman with authority as something unnatural. Unusual? Perhaps; but unnatural? Never. As for Cayman, the women of the island had always possessed enormous clout because they had for centuries managed the land and local businesses, since their men, renowned sailors, spent most of their lives at sea.

Nevertheless, Linnell still faced some difficult problems and even now, at this very late date, she still wasn't sure her plans to resolve them had actually worked. She would know in a minute. She sat quietly, trying not to look like she was about to crawl out of her skin while she watched Colin shuffling trust documents.

Colin instructed his secretary to hold his calls.

This was it. Linnell coughed nervously behind her hand because she was afraid she might hiccup. Then, with a small flourish, Colin handed Linnell the files for SUP Cayman Ltd.. Almost blind from nerves, Linnell examined them twice and then with a sigh of relief saw that the Japanese broker had not only signed the final drafts of the contract but had also—thank heavens!—bank-wired his funds to the escrow account at the bank in Cayman. Colin was all smiles.

Her scheme had worked. She had met her most difficult challenge: getting the broker to deposit funds in Cayman instead of relying on letters of credit. The matter of international letters of credit had been the most frustrating hitch. Banks in Cayman did not issue their own letters of credit to their customers unless they had large sums already on deposit, and no bank elsewhere had been willing to hold a letter of credit to her benefit without the signature of her husband. "Why not? I mean, what's the big risk here?" she'd ask, and they would explain that this was because she was a married woman. It was merely another version of the same problem she'd encountered at her own bank in Highridge. When she tried to explain that the very purpose of this entire exercise was to surprise her husband, they had in turn informed her that the very purpose of their rules was to forbid a woman from doing any such thing. And then they would say: "We're so sorry, but our hands are tied."

To get around this barrier, she'd finally convinced the broker to put up his own money by agreeing to pay him interest at an annualized rate of 28% for however long it would take for her to fulfill her contract and deliver her load of sea urchins. The prospect of making an enormous profit on both ends of the deal was what had prompted the broker to go along with her. However, unbeknownst to the broker, she'd next persuaded the bank to waive their escrow fees and to absorb the costs of currency exchange, on the grounds that she, not the bank, would be paying the interest on the broker's funds when they hit the bank. The bank had been more than willing to undertake this unusual arrangement because it would have the use of the broker's funds until the escrow was closed. The bank had apparently concluded that it was going to take months for Linnell to effect delivery on the contract.

Now dizzy with excitement, Linnell heard Colin announcing that the brokers' funds had been deposited to the SUP Cayman Ltd. escrow account the day before. This meant that the interest—which she would have to pay—had already begun to accrue. A deal was a deal, and it had been struck so that Linnell would bear all the risk if she didn't perform as agreed—which was as it should be. But what a screwing awaited her if for any reason she should fail to deliver her product on time!

Now that this financial hurdle had been overcome, she still had to decide what to do with her profit, assuming she delivered the cargo. Technically speaking, the profits actually belonged to the corporation. She merely controlled all the shares. This was where her profession stood her in good stead: Because the source of the business income arose in the same jurisdiction as SUP Cayman Ltd., the current rule was that no U.S. income tax would have to be paid on the profit despite the fact that she, as a U.S. citizen, owned all the shares. No, taxes weren't going to be a big problem here. The real problem was going to be finding a way to give Bear his gift without her losing any of the advantages she was after.

She certainly didn't want the shares of SUP Cayman Ltd. to end up in Bear's hands and hoarded the way he hoarded the rest of their property. He had already placed their savings at the Highridge Bank and maintained them beyond her control, and all the bankers in Highridge were in league with him. Especially that little snot she'd encountered the morning before. She knew this for a fact because whenever she called the bank to inquire about their funds—she'd remind the bank that the money belonged to her, too—the manager would shuck her off by telling her that he'd get back to her as soon as he "consulted with her husband."

The manager had never gotten back to her, ever, although he might very well have told Bear she was prying. So, new laws or not, it had been made very clear to her that Bear had no intention of letting her get anywhere near their money. Joking on the square, which he so often liked to do, he'd say such things as: "What's yours is ours, and what's ours is mine." And then on a more serious note, he'd declare: "Women and money? No way! Can't trust 'em with money. As far as I'm concerned, these new laws are dangerous and they should be repealed and the sooner the better!"

Secretly fuming, she had managed to keep her own counsel while she continued to work on the sea urchin project, but, then and there, she'd ruled out giving him an outright gift of the SUP Ltd. shares because this wouldn't get her where she wanted to go. Yes, she wanted to surprise Bear, and yes, and she also wanted to make him happy, but she also wanted to gain an advantage for herself and have a real share in her own largesse and that was why she'd decided to place the SUP Ltd. shares in their foreign trust—the one that Bear had been so eager to establish the year before. She had drafted some rather unique provisions for the trust—not many, just a few were required to achieve her objectives—which Bear had said he was too busy to read. They gave her powers over *all* of their community property in exchange for any asset that she might transfer into their foreign trust. Thus, if Bear wanted to receive any of the benefits from their trust, he would have to consult with her about *everything*. The trust document also required them to stand as legal equals in every other respect as well. Yes, either that or else he'd be required to forfeit all rights to the trust's assets. She knew Bear—as soon as he saw how much money she had earned and that she had placed it all in their trust, he'd agree to just about anything. And if things turned out right, the trust could soon have as much as $400,000—and she would share control over this and all the rest of their finances.

Although Linnell had thought this plan through many times, she now had some serious reservations about surrendering *any* of her control over the SUP Ltd. shares. Bear, and that evil look he'd just given her . . . this still troubled her. Why did he look at her like that? And what did it mean? She first had to know.

She was not altogether surprised to find herself confessing her new sense of ambivalence to Colin. Colin had met Bear the year before and Linnell was sure he must have formed an opinion about her husband. She now had to wonder what it might be because she could see that Colin, always the ever-so-matter-of-fact British banker, did not seem the least bit surprised by her equivocation. Perhaps, as a man, he'd seen something she couldn't as far as her marriage was concerned. Was that it? Her hand rose to grab a lock of her hair and she realized she was twisting it nervously around a finger.

Colin raised his eyebrows ever so slightly and finally spoke. "So, why be in such a hurry, m'dear? Why not simply leave things as they are? Hold onto the shares. Give the matter a little more thought. If you place your shares in trust, you might find it quite difficult to retrieve them if your reservations about your husband prove well founded. *Do* pardon me for inquiring . . . but, does any of this, uh . . . have something to do with the fact that you're no longer wearing your wedding ring?"

Linnell had forgotten all about her ring or even that she'd removed it. She replied just a bit too quickly: "Oh Colin, *not* at all. I don't want to wear it while I'm diving, that's all." She felt a pragmatic family man like Colin would regard her real reason for not wearing her ring as too peculiar, or perhaps a bit too fanciful to believe—but there was nothing sinister here, she had merely removed it in order to enjoy the illusion of freedom during her visit to her island floating in time.

The telephone rang unexpectedly and Linnell was relieved to see that she would be spared any further conversation about her ring or the state of her marriage. It was Colin's secretary, calling to remind him that he was running late.

Linnell left a copy of the contract for the Sea Urchin Project with Colin and kept a signed duplicate for herself, then she blew him a kiss, watched him blush, and headed out for the great do-or-die.

In addition to having the best plumbing on the island, the newest hotel on Seven Mile Beach offered gossip as juicy as the succulent turtle steaks served in its formal dining room. The hotel lounge offered a hardwood dance floor, the largest on the island, and best of all, it now featured the wildest rock-'n-reggae band in the Caribbean. The dining room opened to the outdoor courtyard and at its center could be found the hotel's famous beach bar—a round, hugely thatched open-air saloon styled after those of Puerta Vallarta. "The Beach Bar," with its hundred or so bar stools, was the island's unofficial headquarters—everybody who was anybody dropped in almost every day to swap stories after the banks closed their doors. The rest of the courtyard was filled with comfortable chaises and cocktail tables and ringed with tropical foliage, which parted upon a wide sandy path that sloped gently down to the broadest, whitest section of the beach.

It was her habit to take a room on the second floor, always with a balcony facing the western horizon overlooking the beach. She would usually retreat there at sunset to sit high above the action while waiting for room service to bring her a cocktail. Wearing only her bathing suit and plenty of mosquito repellent, she would prop her legs up on the rail and tip her head back to marvel at the umbrella of colors flying open above her head. She liked her sunsets lurid, and Cayman never disappointed, so while the boys on the beach would be watching her, she would watch the fantastic veils of color flaming out against the darkening azure. There was also the matter of seeing the green light—a sign of good luck for sailors—which was said to flash the instant the sun slipped below the horizon. She hadn't caught it yet, but she was sure that one day she would. Besides, keeping watch for it was an excellent excuse for getting buzzed on a tall rum and orange juice.

But now she was thirsty and dusty and she needed a taxi to take her to her hotel. Linnell stood in a swirl of brown dirt on the boardwalk hoping to find one on the road. By wonderful chance, she looked up just in time to see her dive master, Wee Billy, sometimes cabdriver and full-time capitalist, whom she'd hired for the Sea Urchin Project. He was barreling along, head down, on the opposite side of the street and it looked like he was heading out for the warehouse district where he was supposed to meet her. Linnell yelled. Billy saw her, pulled a U-turn in front of a pick-up truck and managed to reach her without getting smashed. His door popped open, a thick arm reached out, and in a second her bags were in the back seat. Linnell jumped in beside him and then they dodged their way through Georgetown and turned north onto the newly paved road that ran the entire length of the westerly side of the island.

Wee Billy was an easygoing man. Nothing and nobody bothered him, probably because nobody in their right mind would want to disturb this 300 pound mountain of muscle. His arms, twice the girth of an ordinary man's thighs, came with a neck to match, and his long mahogany face was dominated by an English nose that jutted proudly over his thick-lipped mouth. He was a true son of his pirate forebears, and a whiz of a mechanic. Wee Billy had dropped out of high school. He'd explained that being indoors with books was no place for a man like him. Especially when he could be outdoors, working on what he liked, which was anything made of metal with more than two moving parts. She'd seen him rebuild an engine in what seemed like ten seconds flat. He'd done all right for himself even without a high school education, and now he and his family owned most of the taxis in Georgetown. Wee Billy was her blessed savior as far as her valuable equipment was concerned, and catching him an hour earlier than expected was wonderful because now she would have an extra hour for herself.

"Things sure have changed in the last four months," Linnell commented.

"No lie. De whole place it be exploding."

They were about to turn into her hotel parking lot when Linnell happened to glance at the building across the road. The sprawling but well maintained single-story structure was the only bank located outside Georgetown proper. With its many small bins emptying onto its central courtyard, it had the appearance of a fast-paced motel, and as far as she could tell, all of its clerks were little Lolitas.

"Talk about enterprise zones," Linnell said to herself, "this one is the living end."

Linnell turned to Wee Billy and said, "Well, Mr. Billy, it looks like the old whorehouse hasn't changed very much."

"Oh, Miss L.C. you sure do make me laugh. Now, you be nice. Everybody they go there, now it be selling gold."

"Well, I don't care . . . I'll never like that outfit," Linnell replied darkly.

The words, "Ye Olde Banke Builte by Bankes" were emblazoned in gilded Old English script above the entrance. She'd heard the story about the bank's logo—a clever play on words which led people to think it had been established by a consortium of banking institutions. "But in fact," said the man who'd told her the story, "It's named after me. *I'm* Bankes . . . See? I'm the contractor and I built the damn building."

She'd laughed at the story, and then wondered if the bank's customers would be laughing so hard if they knew the score.

Despite the disapproval of the rest of the banks in Georgetown, Ye Olde Banke relentlessly promoted itself without shame. Its weekend sailing parties, hostessed by its young clerks, were legend. Although the island's secrecy laws applied no less to this bank than to any other on the island, Linnell had often heard its girlish clerks bragging openly about the identity of the bank's U.S. customers who were heedlessly violating the Federal Gold Reserve Act by purchasing bullion. Not that the other banks wouldn't sell gold, it was just that Ye Olde Banke took out full page ads in the Cayman newspaper and distributed their flyers at the airport gate to all the incoming tourists from the states.

Linnell quickly filled Wee Billy in on her plans: He should immediately round up her crew, gather up the equipment, and bring the gasoline-fueled water-pumps, the air compressors and most important of all, the rubber rafts and long hoses, down to the beach in front of the hotel. Another crew should start moving the ice to the storage lockers on the wharf. Billy confirmed that he had modified her equipment to her specifications. Her secret weapons were the Venturi pumps, ordinarily used for dredging for treasure, which clever Billy had altered so they would gently suck the sea urchins into the nets—which they would then use as sieves to wash the urchins free of sand while they were being dragged up to the surface and deposited into the rafts that would be inflated underneath each load.

Wee Billy boomed happily: "Right on, Miss L.C., an' all d'boys they be waiting to go. De air compressors here an' de ice, it come jus' fine, it be packed fuuu*ull* to de ceiling. You want, we work all night. But dearie, I think we be all done before tonight. Not to worry, sweet thing, d' ice is *nice*, it be lastin', an' I take charge of all d'nets."

Linnell nodded her agreement, hoping that she had understood him correctly. When he dropped her off in front of the hotel she tried to pay him for the ride. Wee Billy refused, rumbling, "No dearie, you be riding free this trip. This be pay-day. We *all* be rich come tonight."

Now there's a vote of confidence, thought Linnell. Feeling less nervous because of it, she told him she'd meet him down on the beach in forty-five minutes, which would give her plenty of time to set up her room and prepare herself for a day in the water. Linnell almost ran to the reception desk. Ordinarily, when she checked in, she would tip the clerk and then take a long look at the hotel register to see if she recognized any of the guests; but today she was focused exclusively on the weather: She glanced anxiously out to sea. If the water stayed flat, the battle was already won.

Linnell quickly exchanged her money for Cayman dollars, posted her copy of the Sea Urchin contract to her law office, then proceeded straight upstairs to her room to change into her lavender bathing suit. Now that she had some free time, she could sneak her pale legs down to the beach bar and settle her nerves while she waited for the divers to arrive. She quickly opened her suitcase, grabbed her bathing suit, and then left it lying open in the middle of her bed, next to her purse. After slipping into her bathing suit, she slathered herself from head to toe with heavy oil, wrapped a large towel around her waist like a sarong, pinned her room key to her bathing suit strap, and then, as her last step, carefully planted a small red bead inside the clasp of her briefcase. That done, she stuck a few pins along its back edge, set the briefcase on the table next to the window and pushed it until the pins were caught in the loosely woven curtains.

Although all of her tax work was on the square, and even though she was sure the IRS had to have spied on her long enough to know this was so for an absolute fact, she'd still heard all the rumors about the new IRS Special Services agents who'd been hired to keep track of everyone who visited tax havens. She fully expected one of them would soon be paying her a visit during this trip. Just this one small test, she told herself. Then she remembered. Her rudder. She had to hide it! Linnell dug in her purse and pulled out the roll of clear tape, grabbed her rudder, and headed for the bathroom. After hiding her precious daily log book, she memorized the room and triggered the door latch so it would lock when it closed.

The long halls were dimly lit to make them seem cool, and while Linnell was padding her way to the exit, she caught sight of a man peeping in her direction from around the corner at the end of the corridor.

"My God!" Linnell stopped short in her tracks. She thought she'd just seen Harold Dolphe. She crossed her fingers and prayed she was wrong. Better it should be a spook, she thought. She hadn't run into Dolphe since her last day at the Ivener firm.

Harold "the Hyena" Dolphe. She had come to detest him. She still did. He had cultivated the miserable habit of barging into her office, sack of donuts in hand—which he would munch while leaning over her desk so that his greasy crumbs could be sprinkled all over her freshly typed memos. Nothing she said, no insult, no withering stare, seemed to stop him. Since they were the only new associates admitted to the Ivener firm that year, the secretaries had at first jokingly described them as "Beauty and the Beast." Linnell immediately told them to stop it, warning them that any more talk that suggested they were in any way linked—in this or any other fashion—was abhorrent and most certainly would trigger her gag reflexes. She couldn't stand the thought of *any* connection with Harold, neither figuratively, and certainly not literally—the latter being simply too awful to imagine.

She was sure that Harold Dolphe had come to the human race by an entirely unknown evolutionary route. His rusty hair, speckled with coarse dark brown tufts, reminded her of a Hyena, as did his Neanderthal neck, which appeared to expand without demarcation into his sloped shoulders. And since he lacked a well defined bridge over his nose, his domed pink forehead, covered with large reddish brown freckles, appeared to have melted into a broad speckled honker that turned up at the tip to reveal round hair-filled nostrils. And for so long as she'd known him, his eyes—light brown with curious green flecks—had revealed but a single emotion: Hunger. And seeing as how Harold Dolphe had passed the bar exam the first time he took it, Linnell's sense of accomplishment at having done the same thing was for that reason somewhat diminished.

His appetite, especially for fat-fried junk food, was voracious; the secretaries confided that he not only surreptitiously pilfered their snacks, but also crept into the law office kitchen to finish the scraps Willy left on his plate. It hadn't taken her long to learn how to give Harold fits: She would munch potato chips at her desk, rattling the bag so that Harold would hear, and then, when he came sidling into her cubicle with that hungry look in his eyes, she would give him a tiny glimpse of the bag before ditching it under her desk. He'd beg, and then she'd smile sweetly and tell him she'd finished them all.

She hadn't spoken to Harold for well over a year—in fact, the last time she'd had any words with him was her last day at the Ivener firm. He had plummeted into her chair and swung his flat feet up onto her desk to say good bye the same way he'd first said hello.

Linnell would never forget her first day as a practicing lawyer—she'd only seen Mr. Ivener once before, at her interview, and she had been thrilled that a legend like him would want to hire her straight out of law school. She had entered her assigned cubicle that first day, determined to do Ivener proud, and then she'd found Harold Dolphe sitting in her chair, with his size ten double-Ds parked on her desk, trying to make it look like she'd been hired to be *his* assistant. And although he had no authority to tell her diddly-squat, he'd had the nerve to try this old trick simply because he thought he could get away with it.

She had quickly disabused him of that notion.

Instead of saying hello—and more for the benefit of the staff's flapping ears than her own—he had loudly blatted, "You know what my law professors say? They say women lawyers are like crabgrass in the fair lawn of the law. But, hey baby! I'm really surprised—*you're* no hag, so I'm not goin' to mind looking at those stems of yours when you ankle in here with my coffee. I take it with cream and three lumps of sugar—and from now on, when I want you, I'm just gonna whistle for 'Legs.' "

Concealing her shock while imagining that Bear was standing behind her and brandishing a club to bash this idiot back into the ground, Linnell's first words to Harold had been equally loud: "Get your awful fat ass out of my chair you dribbling hyena or I'll give you your three lumps right now! And from now on you're going to address *me* as Ms. L.C."

Hearing her reply, the secretarial staff had howled with laughter. They even took her aside to tell her they loved Harold's new nickname. And when Ivener wasn't around, they addressed him as "Mr. Hootie Hyena." Stuck with Hyena as his new nickname, Harold turned whiny and vicious and from then on he engaged in endless schemes to even the score. Needless to say, this proved beneficial, not only for Willy, but for her as well, because Harold's competition forced her to work even harder to ensure that he'd never get the best of her. In the end, this had made her a better lawyer, and so it went, until the day she decided to placate her husband and leave Ivener's firm.

But, despite Harold Dolphe, and the fractious atmosphere at the Ivener firm, she still had to give Willy plenty of credit. If it weren't for him, she never would have found her way to *any* tax haven. And she wouldn't be standing here now, in the dimly lit hall of a hotel on an island the size of a raisin, with her eyes fixed on the spot where she was sure she'd just seen Harold the Hyena. This is just so much more fun than staying home sorting socks! Linnell thought. Stepping out of her sandals and dropping her towel, she sprinted to the end of the hall. She peeked around the corner—but there was nothing to see except a door closing halfway down the dimly lit corridor. Linnell crept up to the door and stood next to it without making a sound, waiting to see if it would open again. Bracing herself on the door frame, she stopped breathing and pressed her ear to the panel.

Silence. She could hear nothing except the soft *thump-put* of blood in her ears. Pushing herself back from the door, she stepped back and looked over her shoulder. Good. She was glad there was no one around to see her behaving like this. Retracing her steps, she picked up her things and just as she rounded the corner, she spotted another shadowy figure ducking around the corner at the opposite end of the hall.

"What are we playing here! Hide and seek?" Linnell spoke loudly, trying not to sound self-conscious. She listened to the sound of her voice echoing down the empty corridors. Perhaps it wasn't the Hyena after all—probably just a couple of agents whom she'd caught in the midst of their spooking. Flopping her sandals noisily on her way to the exit, she slammed the door to let the gamesters know she was leaving and that they were now free to search her room.

A warm breeze blew gently into her face when she stepped onto the landing. Linnell stopped to inhale and then walked down the stairs and straight to the beach bar. Something cool and sweet would do her some good. She looked toward the beach and saw bronzed muscles flexing against a field of stark blue waters. She counted heads. Only three of her divers were missing, but all the rest of them were busy assembling a flotilla of large rubber rafts. She was immensely relieved; everything appeared to be proceeding on schedule. The ocean shimmered with banners of silver and aquamarine because the wind was down and there were no clouds throwing shadows across the water. The weather was holding.

◆❖◆

Linnell Clare slid into a vacant seat at the circular beach bar next to a good looking young man who wore nothing but shorts and a pair of thick prescription sun glasses. The young man, who looked to be in his late twenties, listened to her asking the bartender for something cold, sweet, and virgin. He swiveled in her direction to give her a slow, sleepy smile.

"Hah. Ah'm Terrance Walsh," he announced. Linnell heard echoes of the *very* deep South. Terrance chugged from a can of Dr. Pepper and then he pushed it her way to let her know that he wouldn't mind some conversation. "Virgin? So what d'yawl get when yuh order that?" The young man pushed his thick shades on top of his head and Linnell got her first glimpse of the saddest blue eyes she had ever seen in her life.

"You know what I mean . . . you get nothing. No booze." She looked him up and down; now sure that he wasn't an agent, she gave him a gleaming smile and volunteered that she'd just arrived from California.

Terrance gave her an equal amount of scrutiny, and then, in apparent approval of what he saw, his serious face broke into a grin. "Swap spits?" he asked.

Linnell gagged and then burst into laughter. This disgusting gibberish had been devised by the haven maven from Atlanta—it simply meant *You tell me yours, then I'll tell you mine.* Only another maven would have the proper response, which was: "You go first."

"You go first." Linnell wrinkled her nose and then gave him her best cat-grin; she had him pegged as either a CPA or tax attorney because of the thick lenses. Definitely not an agent; all the field agents she'd ever seen were blessed with perfect vision.

Terrance nodded back at her. "Well there, so you're in the loop. Glad to meet you. I'm from Memphis. People 'round there call me Terry." Terrance drawled sadly and made no further inquiries about her bona fides. "And I'm feeling poorly 'cause I got myself jammed real good."

Linnell knew what that one meant, too. No wonder he looked so droopy. Sad news. He was letting her know that he was caught between a rock and a hard place because he'd acquired a dangerous client. A picture began to form in her mind: Young Terry, fresh out of law school, hungry for action, taking a generous fee for something easy but not quite right—like opening a bank account in his name to hold somebody else's money—foolishly succumbing to temptation only to discover that he had more or less permanently tied himself up with a client who was now putting some heavy muscle on him to do even more things that could get him disbarred—or worse.

Mavens rarely found themselves in such sorry predicaments because most of them did their best to steer clear of organized crime. But every now and then Linnell would hear a sad tale about another tax attorney winding up at the bottom of a stairwell because he had neglected to check out his client's bona fides. That was why Linnell had made it her practice to take new clients through referral and then only from sources she could confirm as straight up and legit.

"That's really a shame, but I'll bet you'll find a way to get out." Linnell truly felt sorry for Terry but she knew better than to pry into the exact particulars of his difficulties. "So, when did you arrive?" she asked sympathetically.

"This morning," Terry replied glumly.

"That's odd, I didn't see you on the flight from Miami."

"That's because I came in on the firm's Lear jet."

Linnell's ears pricked up. "The Lears! I've never *been* on one. I've often dreamt of going out to the airfield to see if I could hitch a ride."

Terry immediately quashed her ambitions, declaring in a flat voice that his firm's jet was the very last one in the world she would ever want to see, then he pointedly changed the subject by asking her why *she* had come to the island.

To save face after such an abrupt rejection of her hint that he should take her for a spin in his jet, Linnell quickly changed the subject, but instead of telling him about herself, she told him about the Arawaks who had first inhabited the islands, and about Henry Morgan and his band of pirates who had arrived later to camp on the east side of the island.

When she paused, Terry interjected: "I can tell you're a lawyer from the way you jaw, 'cause I'm one, too."

Linnell wondered if she ought to feel insulted. "Yes," she replied, managing to keep a straight face. "I had guessed as much." She watched Terry wiggle a finger into the pocket of his Bermuda shorts and then pull out his I.D. and an engraved business card which he handed to her as an offer of proof.

Brightening slightly, Terry went on, "I'm not trying to pry, I'm just curious—it looks like everybody's coming here now. Why'd you choose this place? I mean, if you can tell me, that is."

Linnell decided that since Terry was a maven, and too young and most likely too inexperienced to be any kind of threat to her practice, that she could safely tell him. "Well, it wasn't exactly my choice," she replied. "The Cayman Islands were actually chosen by one of my wealthiest clients. Unfortunately, he's passed away, but that means I can tell you a little something about him, now that he's gone."

Terry seemed eager for a diversion, so with one eye on the beach, Linnell leaned closer to him. "About a year ago, shortly after I opened my office, a San Francisco bank referred a client just to help me get my practice off the ground. They said he didn't want to consult with my competitor, the William Ivener firm. He was one of my first clients to have any real money, so I'll just call him *Mr. Big*. The only other thing the bank told me about their referral was that they had taken the liberty of setting up an appointment for him and that he would be at my office the following day, at exactly 4 in the afternoon.

"The next day, I anxiously awaited his arrival because I wasn't sure anyone would show up. But exactly at 4:00 my secretary announced that a chauffeured Rolls Royce had just rolled up to my door and that its occupant, a very elderly gentleman, was headed my way. It was Mr. Big, all right, and he made himself at home in my private office as if he owned the place. He wasted no time on formalities. He merely said: ""The bank says you're good. My problem is that my girlfriend just fell and broke her hip."" I must have looked lost because he immediately explained: ""I am 83 and extremely wealthy. I own founder's stock in several South African Gold Mines. Low basis—30 million plus in today's market. I've outlived my two wives, got no children, no living relatives, and it's a dirty damn shame but it looks like I'm going to outlive my girlfriend as well. So, you see? I have no heirs.""

"I interrupted to ask him how old she was, and he curtly replied, ""She's 79. Now let's get back to business, there's no time to waste. I want you to know I haven't liked any president since Teddy Roosevelt and I'll be damned if I'm going to leave one thin dime to the government. I want my money to go where the government can't touch it. Now, what do you suggest?"" "Well, I was so speechless, he almost smiled. And when I finally gathered my wits, I said, and mind you, it was only a guess: ""A *foreign* foundation? Bermuda?"" And he said, ""There! That's it. I want one. Give me your home telephone number so I can talk to you in the evening. I work on my own after my staff gets out of my way and I want to keep this a secret from them.""

"So I gave him my number, and he cut me a check for all of $50.00 for my retainer and then he walked out without so much as a thank-you-good-bye. He called me the very next evening. By then I'd had a chance to look for some published authority to guide me and I discovered there wasn't any—which meant I'd have to develop the subject all by myself, you know, dig into the congressional records, look for unforeseen opportunities, that sort of thing. Of course I told him I'd be happy to take his case. He gave me the go-ahead and from then on we conferred only by telephone. Of course, I was so totally green that I failed to ask him for a larger retainer or any more money for costs, and I was so impressed with myself, I decided that I would simply submit my bill at the end of the case—just like the big boys do in New York.

"We discussed tax havens and I again suggested Bermuda. ""No!"" he said. ""They're too greedy. They already think I'm rich as Croesus and if they find out what I've really got, they'll want to cut themselves in for too big a share. You go to the Cayman Islands. It's a British colony, they'll be looking for business, and more important than that, the fees those pirates want to charge will be lower than anywhere else. You go there and be sure to get me a good deal.""

"So, that's what I did and that's how I got here. Then after I'd completed all that complicated research and had prepared all the intricate documents he needed to sign, he simply stopped returning my calls. You see, he had passed away. But nobody told me—perhaps through his own design. Anyway, I didn't learn about Mr. Big's death until long after the statute of limitations had run, so I was barred from presenting a claim against his estate for my fee—and I had nothing in writing from him. So, instead of battling for years over a few thousand dollars, I decided to extract something of value from this barren case by publishing my original research on foreign foundations. In fact, and you're one of the first to know . . . my article on foreign foundations will appear in the Universal Tax Journal two months from now. So, now you know why *I'm* here . . . Because the old turkey insisted on pinching his pennies."

Terry turned to Linnell with what amounted to a look of awe. "Wow! You actually got it into the Universal Tax Journal! You're lucky, you know. Really lucky. Your practice is made! Well, good for you, and it's a good thing you're not all tied up like I hear some people are."

Linnell wondered if he was referring to himself, or, perhaps, to someone she knew. "What, exactly, do you mean by that?"

"Didn't you just mention the Ivener firm? Since you're from California, I thought you would have heard about it. Willy Ivener—*the* Willy Ivener—he's just been indicted for tax fraud. Forty counts. And the paper says he's the lawyer for The Wei. There's a big IRS tax haven investigation going on right now. He's the first case. Didn't you know?"

"Uh . . . no. It must have happened while I was traveling." Linnell, shocked, barely managed to appear unperturbed by the news. "You hear anything more?"

"No. I just caught it on the news this morning. It's all over the papers in Miami. But, I'm glad for you . . . since you're in on the clean side of the business, you don't have to worry. Well, I guess I have to get back to work." He sighed, and then, as if wanting to impress her that he was a Southern gent, he let his accent thicken for his farewell. "Y'awl take care, y'heah? And ah'll be looking t' read yuh article."

Linnell wished Terry good luck and watched him slide off the bar stool and walk away. Alone at the bar, she sipped her lemon fizz and thought about what she'd heard on the radio the day she was leaving. Something about Project Haven Maven? They must have been reporting the news about Willy's indictment. Linnell tried to recollect everything she knew about Willy's connection to The Wei. What she *had* learned wasn't much—just that The Wei was Willy's largest client.

This discovery had come about as a result of her noticing that Willy liked to use clever acronyms for his offshore companies, so one day she asked him—Hyena was present—if The Wei was one of his progeny; she told him that she had noticed that the name of this entity was the same as his initials. Both of them had stared at her—Willy coldly and the Hyena blankly—and then Willy had tartly replied that The Wei was a Zen expression which meant "The Path" and then he had changed the subject. Even then she had thought this an odd response, which made her even more curious than before. She asked one of the secretaries about The Wei and the secretary told her to keep it a secret, and then she had confided that The Wei was Ivener's client—but, said the secretary, she had never found any of its files. And she'd looked for them, too.

It was obvious to Linnell that Ivener was a man who really knew how to compartmentalize; but then, couldn't the same thing be said about her? She had not only managed to keep the Sea Urchin Project a secret from Bear, but she had never said a word to him about The Wei being Willy Ivener's client. Her reverie was suddenly interrupted by a deep voice floating up from the beach.

"Miss L.C.! Where you be, dearie?" The dive master was calling.

"Coming!" Linnell yodeled back, making heads turn to see where she was heading. It was time to make-or-break. For a moment she felt as if she were rushing to her own execution. Then she took a deep breath and ran down to the beach, tossed her beach towel on the big log next to the water and splashed through the shallows toward her fate.

◆❖◆

Running on nothing but nerves and a couple of candy bars, Linnell Clare worked without stopping for the rest of the day. Her hands and feet had turned wrinkled and white from being in the water so long, and her eyes were bloodshot because she had discarded her face mask. But, by that evening, shortly before sunset, they had loaded close to twelve tons of sea urchins into the rubber rafts. These were then strung together and attached to Billy's power boat, which ferried them straight to the cargo ship at the wharf. The sea urchins were drained and weighed, and then the stevedores packed them in Linnell's secret formula for super-cooled saline. When the last load was finally aboard the freighter, Linnell felt she could breathe again. Her part of the bargain had been fulfilled.

It was an incredible coup—her inventiveness had turned her project into a remarkable success—and she still couldn't believe it was over. Of course, the broker would be earning interest on his funds—and she'd be paying it—until the escrow closed. But the principal—now fixed at $480,000, which was eighty thousand more than she'd anticipated—would be rightfully hers the instant she signed the lading list. Elated, she signed with a flourish. She could well afford to wait until the following morning to inform Colin, and best of all, she only owed two days interest—less than $800.00!

It would hit her later, but for now she was too tired to feel tired. Linnell wound a towel around her head and dragged herself to the log. She sat down, astounded that she had actually pulled it all off in a single day. The divers, however, took it all in stride; now they all lay on the beach, drinking beer and waiting for her to catch her breath. It had all been miraculous. There had been no near-death experiences, no jammed valves, no overturned rafts. Absolutely none of the awkward accidents that so often plagued her when she was home. It must be some kind of enchantment, she thought, a wonderful spell must have seized her as soon as she set foot on the island—because she had won a total victory.

Sensing the restlessness of the diving crew, Linnell Clare finally stood and wrapped herself in the bathrobe that had been laid out for her by the hotel staff. Too tired to change into clothes, Linnell signaled the crew to follow her and dressed as she was, they caravanned back to the warehouse to drink a case of champagne while they hosed down the warehouse. In a final ceremony, Linnell paid her men with bank drafts which she counter-signed on the spot and then she had a glass of champagne to celebrate with them. She was filled with joy; they were matter of fact. It was just another day's work for them.

The air in the warehouse was stifling; but looking out through the open door, Linnell could see the sun turning orange and sinking into what looked like a pool of honey. Her head was swimming and her hands were still cold, part from emotion and part from the effect of the iced champagne. She felt faint. When she shook Billy's hand to thank him, he threw a huge arm around her shoulders to steady her. Linnell leaned on him for a moment and grinned, and then, out of the corner of her eye, she saw a bright flash of green light.

The rare sunset she had been waiting for all these years! How fitting. Linnell laughed with delight. And then she had the silliest notion that it had come from the wrong direction. Or was it just the champagne? Linnell's knees buckled and she sat down on an overturned bucket to watch Billy close up the warehouse. Then she followed him out to his car and climbed in the back seat so she could stretch her legs while he took her back to her hotel. Dazed and sleepy, she gazed through the rear window. Dusk had fallen and the sky was a fading scarf of bright lavender and blue. Linnell finally focused on what she must have been staring at for the last several minutes: A rental car—following them down North Beach Road. It was three full car lengths behind them, but the driver's face, suddenly illuminated by headlights from an approaching vehicle, was unmistakable. The Hyena. He was here on the island. Her head bobbed sleepily. So why should she care? The Hyena was ancient history.

HIGHRIDGE **Tuesday Afternoon — February 26, 1974**

With a not inconsiderable measure of glee, Bear kept track of Ivener's dilemma through the newspapers, which were now portraying the lawyer as "A notorious tax haven operator charged with criminal tax evasion." So! Ivener was damaged goods! The Wei would probably be dumping Ivener, especially now that the whole world knew that the man was a worthless tax cheat. He'd always known he was a better man than Ivener—which reminded him—he still wanted to buy into The Wei. Now that Ivener was on the skids, he could probably buy in at a really cheap price. He'd better stop fooling around and get his man Harold to look into the situation immediately.

Bear tossed the paper aside. He was alone in his office, having let Margo go home early with the files so she could work on them in the privacy of her apartment.

The files for his special patients were tabbed with two colors: yellow *or* blue to prevent the colors from becoming too obvious a cue, and when he actually performed some dentistry, which lately had been less often the case, Margo would add another colored tab—selected at random—to their folders. In fact, at this very moment, she would be attaching a bunch of old discarded X-rays to the yellow and blue color-coded files because it was important to make them look authentic just in case they were yanked for an audit. However, he'd be willing to bet his life that no agent would ever think to ask whether the X-rays actually matched the teeth of his "special patients."

He expected 54 of them tomorrow. These were the ones Margo had rescheduled, in addition to the midweek regulars. They had already been charged for X-rays—income which he had wisely reported to the IRS—but after that, it was all gravy, $25.00 a pop, all cash, which got them exactly three minutes of happy time on his nitrous gas tanks. And sometimes Margo gave them a little rubdown for a little extra, but that was an extra he let her keep.

Bear glanced at his watch; it was already 2:30 PM. and his appointment with Buster was set for 3:00. There was time for one more. Unlocking his left bank of desk drawers, Bear removed his new passport, dropped it on his desk, and then fixed himself with a short snort. A wave of heat rose to the top of his head and then he saw a series of quick bursts of pink and blue sheet-lightning. From a far off distance he could hear a chorus chanting his mantra: *I am the King, the flow goes through me! I am the King.* Were they taunting him? Bear listened carefully, but the voices faded away. He soothed his nose by inhaling deeply of the mentholated Benzedrine and when he was finished, he simply dropped the tube on the floor. Good Margo. She would be more than happy to pick it up.

Obtaining his new passport had been much easier than he'd anticipated; it had been issued to him in his birth name: "Mark Clarichevik," the same as his father's—he had simply omitted the *Jr.*, an omission the passport agency hadn't picked up. He thought he should keep it close by, just in case he needed to leave in a hurry. But so far, everything had been moving along, quite smoothly in fact, which was proof enough that he'd chosen the right path. "The easy way is the right way." He'd learned that in The Wei, and selling drugs had proved to be a whole lot easier on him than trying to please a bunch of whiny patients who would buck around in their chairs like frightened trout whenever he approached with his drill. Giving them a snort or a couple of pills was the easiest way to get them to appreciate his dentistry. Very profitable, too.

And what could they do after he'd made them his "special patients"? What could they prove, especially if it meant embarrassing themselves? Margo and her Polaroid camera always saw to that. Yes, he was safe. And he couldn't forget about Mr. Malone, the one with the large gold fixed partial. He had been keeping an eye on it ever since the old gent's last appointment when he had nicked the two stationary teeth that were holding it fast. They ought to be rotten by now and the gold partial should be ready to harvest. The time had come to tell the old gent that what he really needed was a full mouth denture.

Bear next considered his money. The $820,000 sitting in the Montreal bank was everything he and Ma had saved, and knowing that it was now beyond easy reach made him feel more secure. Some of it was the clean money which also included the money he's received from Ma's profits, but at least half was the skim he'd been blending in over the years. Quite a tidy sum, this $820,000. He had ten days to invest it, which he was going to do as soon as he heard from his contacts. And he had plenty of cash on hand if he wanted to purchase more gold.

Gold was the real reason he'd set up his own dental lab, which allowed him to slip through a loophole in the Gold Reserve Act which otherwise forbade private ownership of the metal, but a dentist with a dental laboratory could buy all he wanted without catching flak from the federales. And he'd increased his store of the precious metal as soon as he heard Ma mention that the Gold Reserve Act might be rescinded—this could happen this year was what she had said. And he knew that when the restrictions were lifted, everyone hoarding gold would be worth a fortune, because everybody else would be buying in and the spot price would soar. And that was exactly when he intended to sell out and make himself another fortune.

He'd already taken physical possession of large amounts of the metal. But what a headache! Always having to worry about getting ripped off. Then he'd learned that it would be far easier to just purchase commodity contracts, then the bank could worry about storage. He'd been making some real smart moves along these lines. For instance, on his last trip to Cayman he had accomplished a lot and Ma hadn't been any the wiser. However, just to keep her from being suspicious, he'd set up a piffling family trust for a few hundred bucks at the bank where she took her clients' business. But later that afternoon, when she thought he was up in his room taking care of his foot, he had visited the bank across the road from their hotel and had arranged to do something so monumental that Ma would never dream he was capable of operating on such a grand scale. She thought she was the only one who knew how to play the tax haven game? Ha! He could show her a thing or two.

Bear leaned back in his chair and scratched his belly with both hands, exulting at how much richer he'd soon be just by trading on some information that Ma was either too honest or too dumb to exploit! He glanced at his Rolex—it was time to head out. He ran a rag across the tips of his new black boots to bring up a shine, then slipping on his new Vuarnets and grabbing his brown leather briefcase, he headed out for his meeting with his new lawyer, Buster Hosterman.

◆❖◆

Buster Hosterman, thirty years older than Dr. Clare, now had three of the town's most significant clients: the Highridge Country Club, the police department, and now Dr. Clare, which explained his unusual effusiveness when he greeted his client. Placing his hand between Dr. Clare's shoulder blades, he genially but firmly piloted the dentist through his brown and green plaid-decorated reception area and into his private office.

Legal counsel to the police department going on thirty-two years, Buster had all this time watched Sommers, his junior, work his way up through the ranks to become Highridge Chief of Police. Never one of "his boys," Sommers' rise to power had simply galled him no end, which he counteracted by always sporting a pair of spit-shined macho-black officer's boots not only to proclaim the seniority of his affiliations to the department but coincidentally, to remind that upstart Sommers of his powerful position as an elder in Highridge political circles. The exciting black boots also served him well in court because, whenever those shiny blunt boot tips peeked out from underneath his brown pin-striped trousers, they sent just the right sort of message to judge and opposing counsel alike, which was simply that he, Buster T. Hosterman, was tightly wired into the system. As a matter of fact, when *he* entered the courtroom, he simply buzzed in like a kamikaze to blow his opponents the hell out of the water, which was why his colleagues called his sort a "bomber." And just like any airborne aircraft, Buster had never turned a square corner, ever.

It was whispered that Buster had certain peculiarities. Something having to do with his connections to the force; nobody spoke these rumors in too loud a voice, but Buster was said to have ended up just as fond of his boys as he was of his boots, and it was also sometimes said that this was how he could get his boys to give him the unlisted phone numbers of opposing counsel, which he'd pass on to the unlicensed P.I. who handled his wiretaps. Or so it was said.

Buster had attained his current high position in the local bar association through apprenticing himself to another good ol' boy from Missouri who just happened to be a judge; the judge had let him slave for him in exchange for three hots and a cot, but this had been more than worthwhile because his apprenticeship allowed him to be admitted to the Bar merely on the basis of passing an examination—which the judge's former law partner had conveniently graded. And so, thanks to the vagaries of California law pertaining to lawyers, he had become one without ever having to set foot in law school. But this wasn't what made him a legend. No—the event that bestowed his reputation as a *bomber* was the way he had handled his own divorce. He had shucked his first wife after she had given him twenty years of her best—along with four squalling brats—and had replaced her with a small mail-order bride from the back side of the Philippines. The new wife, he bragged, was a timid woman who was more than happy to scrub and clean and not give him a lick of trouble.

To dodge alimony, Buster had to show that his old lady was "at fault," so he'd dragged the hapless woman through five years of hellish litigation on a trumped up charge of adultery, which he embellished with further hints of her bestial practices with the family pet. Having spent many a tender moment down on the farm with his daddy's chickens, his tales had been colorful and convincing. And then he got the local judge, who just happened to be his golfing buddy, to issue a writ declaring the ex-Mrs. Hosterman an unfit mother and so Buster succeeded in barring his former wife from seeing her own children. When the impoverished and by then hysterical lady died of an overdose of sleeping pills, Buster was prompted to crow that it "just proved how right he was to have dumped her." This, however, had all happened long before "No-fault Divorce."

But then, as he was himself fond of saying, "The divorce laws might've been changed, but so what? The game's still the same." And although the new no-fault laws hadn't put a dent in his style it certainly had put a crimp in his income. He still had confidence, however, that he could turn things around—he just needed to find a deep pocket in somebody else's pants.

And so what do you know? In through his door walks this dentist Mark Clare, and he, Buster T. Hosterman, gets this big chance to prove that he still had it in him to spin the old wheel a new way.

While guiding Bear toward the chair next to his desk, Buster patted the dentist gently on his back, letting his hand drop lower with every thump. Buster wheezed sympathetically, then said, "Hi buddy, so what's cooking today? Just you come on in here and take a load off." To conceal the urge to grab Clare and push him down in his chair, Buster rubbed both hands on his jutting paunch. Doc Clare had already paid him a $5000 retainer, all cash, up front—the biggest wad of bills he'd ever seen in his entire career—and right now his instincts were telling him if he played it right Doc Clare would be good for maybe another twenty grand altogether. Buster's voice was honey. "Now tell me, son, what's this thing you've got going with the IRS? Hmmmm? Did you clear 'em out of your office like I told you to?"

Waving a curled hand dejectedly, Bear eased himself into the chair with a mournful sigh. "Buster?" He whispered softly in a sad, low voice. "It's not the IRS that's got me worried. It's Ma, I mean, you know, L.C., my wife. I'm sure she's cheating on me. Home late every night. For a year. It's been killing me . . . and I just can't take it another minute." Bear sighed again and hunched earnestly toward Buster, elbows on knees, with his hands hanging curled between his legs.

"So L.C. is cheating on you? So tell me, what's new?" Buster crowed with indignation. "Just give 'em a chance and that's *exactly* what broads like her do. I'll tell you how it is: Good guys—decent guys like *you*—kill yourselves workin' so *they* can go jetting around the world and spending your money. And then they have the nerve to start whining and carryin' on about how you don't meet their needs, whatever the hell *that's* supposed to mean!"

"Yeah. You sure got that one right, but I've got to make sure about a few things first. I've got an informant on Cayman and he's gonna be getting back to me soon." Bear removed his dark glasses, slowly, seductively, like a stripper removing the final scarf and then he gazed up into Buster's face and blinked his big gray eyes as if he were on the verge of weeping, "But, it just tears me up to think she'd do something like that to me after all I've done for her."

◆❖◆

Bear kept his attention on Buster's hand. That old country lawyer shtick hadn't fooled *him* a bit. And he'd been right about wearing the boots. He could tell they turned Buster on—the old auntie probably enjoyed a hard smack of wet leather, too. Bear thought about delivering him one as he licked his lips, and then letting them part ever so slightly, allowed Buster search his wide-open gray eyes; when he saw the hungry expression flitting across Buster's face, he knew his plan had worked: the old AC-DC shyster was already dying to lay hands on him. But there was nothing to fear—he could tell it had been a long, long time since Buster's gun had held any bullets. Yes, Bear reassured himself, the most Buster could expect to get out of him would be a little cash and a few hot looks, and these he had plenty to spare.

He was here, not so much as a result of being audited, but because of the decision he'd made while attending his self-empowerment sessions at The Wei. That was when he'd realized for a fact that his mistake about letting Ma go to law school didn't have to mean that he had to go on punishing himself for the rest of his life. Three years of her being a lawyer was more than enough and now he was going to do something about it. And just because she'd sworn never to leave him didn't mean that he couldn't leave her. She hadn't thought about that. Yes, he had her coming and going, so, come his birthday, next month, he was planning to give her a big surprise: an ultimatum—she could either give up that law practice of hers and stay home, or else take a hike. Stay or leave—either way it would have to be on his terms. And if she wanted to stick around, she *had* to close her office and resign from the bar because now that he'd decided to change his life, the last thing he'd be needing was a straight-arrow lawyer hanging around his neck.

He'd laid some big plans. With all his new connections and the cash he'd just transferred to Canada, he was going to get in on the ground floor of the fast-growing Colombian drug trade. To hell with weed and to hell with speed—cocaine was going to be the future. Hadn't the Surgeon General just described it as non-addictive? Well, at least not like heroin—that's what the Surgeon General had said, and that's why he was going to be the one to run the entire distribution system for all of Northern California.

So this business about Ma being unfaithful was just his slick way of handling Buster. And he needed to handle Buster because he sure as hell didn't want the greedy old queen to discover that his real reasons for wanting to dump his Ma had something to do with the new way he was going to be making his living. If Buster should ever get wind of the truth, well, he might get some funny ideas about wanting to jump aboard and be his partner, and he sure as hell didn't need any more partners. Margo was more than enough. Besides, he knew that if he ever had a need to make Ma out as some kind of amoral slut, then all the Highridge judges would be willing to hump for him—he'd heard they all hated women lawyers. And with all his connections to the police, the press, and the local courts, Buster was just the sort of lawyer who could pull it all off.

Buster's cigar wheeze interrupted his thoughts.

"Hey Doc . . . I feel for you, man. So let's get a few things started for you right away, today. But I have to be up front with you buddy, it makes no difference if she's cheating or not, we're not supposed to argue that sort of stuff anymore, at least not in court, because of this new no-fault law." Buster, whose face had been somber, now winked and grinned wolfishly. "Course you can trust me to mention what she's been up to when I see the judge. He belongs to the club, same as me, and when it comes to no-fault he's the same as all the rest of the judges in this here town. See? They're not going to be turning on any dime just 'cause the law's been changed. Trust me, they'll know who's to blame for busting up your happy home just as soon as they see your old lady's face in the court room. Don't you worry 'bout *that.*"

"That sure makes me feel better to hear you say that. You know, now that I feel more comfortable with you . . . why don't you just call me Bear? All my friends do." Bear batted his eyes at Buster with lamb-like innocence.

Buster squeezed Bear's shoulder. "Well Bear, you have to realize that this no-fault business is a whole new ball game, so L.C. now has the right to claim half the community property no matter how bad she's been cheating on you—assuming she can discover what and where it is, if you get my drift. But she might end up with the house because of the kid. Did you know that?"

"No, I didn't know that." Bear dropped his head to conceal his surprise. Until now, he thought he'd had a pretty good grip on all these new laws. He forced himself to sit still and slowly rubbed a tight fist in the palm of his hand.

Buster marched officiously back to his desk and sat down to face his new client. "Now, how 'bout your son, Benjy? You want him?"

Bear shook his head. He'd forgotten all about Benjy. "No, I think I'll let Ma keep him. And if I have to pay child support, well, I guess I'll pay—if the court orders me to, but not a penny extra, you understand."

"I think the court will order you to pay maybe $200 a month—and that's max—unless you're going to show that you're making some money. If you do, you're going to get stuck for more. You get what I mean? You gotta make it look like you're barely scraping by. On the other hand, you might want to think about starting a custody battle—this might get her to soften up when it comes to divvying up the property. Well, just think about it . . . no need to decide right now. And since you've incorporated that dental practice of yours, you can expect L.C. will probably want to subpoena your corporate tax returns and your books and records. You get the drift?"

Oh yes, thought Bear. He understood perfectly. He already knew how to avoid being subpoenaed—he'd have Buster voluntarily provide her with uncertified copies of his corporate tax returns under the pretext of saving her the costs of discovery; that way he and Buster would avoid being held in contempt for supplying her with fake records. He needn't mention something like that to a guy like Buster. With a bomber, *that* was a given. So, Ma would be too broke to put up a fight, and her being a lawyer would be rammed down her throat in Family Court. All Buster had to do was to let on that she was one of those "libbers" and the judge would let Buster paper her to death.

As if Buster had just read his mind, Bear heard him declaring that he'd smother L.C. with depositions, interrogatories, and motions, and that she wouldn't see daylight for years once he got started on her.

"Now when do you want her served? And where?" Buster asked.

Bear looked up in time to catch the sly look on Buster's face. "Well," Bear shook his head, "that's going to depend on my, uh, informant. He's on the island right now, keeping an eye on her. If she's doing what I think she's been doing, then I'm thinking it would be kinda nice to surprise her on my birthday, at dinner—after she gives me my birthday gift. Got the idea for that from a book I read—it said a guy should take them out for a big meal in a fancy restaurant where they'll feel too embarrassed to throw a fit. But, of course, I have to think strategy here, because how I go about setting things up still depends a whole lot on the IRS. I just might have to use her for a while, especially if I can't find myself another tax attorney. She's a real good tax attorney, you know." Looking at Buster like an innocent, Bear fluttered his lashes. "So you gotta understand—I can't make any firm plans just yet, I have to wait and see what's going to happen with my audit." He didn't want to commit to any fixed timetable, and besides, all he wanted to do right now was to get his ducks lined up and then he'd be able to sit back and see just how Ma would react to his birthday surprise.

"Well, Doc, I think I've got the picture. You just take your sweet time." Buster's voice sounded subdued. "I've gotta put in a call to another client who's been waiting on me. It's one of my boys—the wife's charged him with brandishing a weapon. Just take a minute. So why don't you go make yourself comfy out there?" Buster motioned to a hard wooden chair in his bleak reception area, "And I'll have your divorce petition out to you right away. Look it over and let me know. And don't *worry.*"

Bear sat stiffly on the wooden chair in Buster's anteroom and pondered his options. He'd made contingency plans galore. He'd figured out all of his moves depending upon what Ma might do. For instance, if she ever wised up to him, then he'd had it all planned to keep her in line by stealing her passport so Buster could whip it out in court to show the judge how many trips she'd been making to tax havens, then he'd have Buster do this big song and dance about her laundering money for the mob. Faced with this, she'd crumble; she'd back down and stay in her place and then if he felt like it, he could dump her and make himself look like a victim. He'd been laying the groundwork for this particular scenario for months and months, buying sympathy for himself with all those stories about her—he'd spread them all over the club—about how she had left her poor husband sitting all alone at home just so she could jet off to those crazy tax havens of hers.

On the other hand, ever since he'd begun to tell lies about her he'd also begun to wonder whether he might be on to something. Just because he could count on her to keep her word and never leave him, this didn't mean that she'd never cheat. What if she really were cheating on him? Would she dare? The thought made him sick to his stomach. She wouldn't dare! Would she? He would never admit this to anyone, but he wasn't sure. And that's why he'd asked Harold Dolphe to keep an eye on her.

Scratching his arms, Bear fidgeted in his chair while he thought about what would be the best thing to do. If he needed a divorce, should he proceed at once and get it over with? Or would it be better for him to wait until *after* he'd gotten Ma involved in his audit so that if the IRS closed in on him, she would still be around for him to blame? The hair on his neck suddenly rose. How could he blame Ma if she'd never signed any of his dental corporation tax returns? Ah, good thing he was a fast thinker—he could turn this to his advantage by claiming that she hadn't signed them because she'd planned it this way, just to make him look bad. After all, he was merely a dumb, kind-hearted dentist and she was this brilliant, hard-as-nails tax attorney. And Rizzo was exactly the kind of guy who would buy into that. Sure he was. He could tell he was, just from the way Rizzo had laughed at his joke.

Well, no matter what happened, it was time for him to collect all his secret records and stash them in a safe place. They held all the secrets of his cash collections and the drugs he'd sold and the kick-backs between him and Manny the pharmacist. They also listed all the names of his special patients and what they paid and these were essential for keeping a handle on Margo. He knew she was dipping her beak, but so far her forays had been confined to small raids on the change drawer. It couldn't be helped, but she was getting pretty darn slick on his new computer system so he needed to keep the records in his possession to prevent her from getting any ideas that she could get away with pulling a fast one on him.

When Buster appeared with the documents, things finally fell into place: He would get Ma involved in his audit, and then, if she refused to fold her law office and stay home, he'd dump her.

Buster handed the documents to Bear, who tucked them in his briefcase without looking at them.

"I think you forgot something," Bear said.

"I haven't forgotten *anything* son," Buster's voice was paternalistic. You mean the audit. The agents. I told you I had a plan. You told the agents about L.C. and her tax haven shenanigans, right?"

"Of course."

Buster jabbed the air with his finger to emphasize his point. "This is something you should know—a very simple technique, but it always works: You be sure to keep to the same story about how she's this jet-setting, tax haven lawyer and you're just a molar mechanic. You just remember to stick to your story like a snail sticks to a blade of grass and you're gonna win hands down. Tell it over and over—that she's responsible for *everything*. You tell 'em she's *brilliant* and that's why *she's* the lawyer in the family."

Great minds think alike, Bear observed to himself, but to Buster he said, "I already told them all that."

"Good! Very good. If the IRS tries to nail you, then *she*'s the one who'*s* gonna end up swinging in the wind. See? Nobody's gonna believe that this brilliant-tax-attorney-wife of yours is *not* to blame for your tax problems. By the way, son, just what *is* the problem?" Buster was again standing behind his back and Bear expected to feel his hand on his shoulder.

"It's nothing. Really. I dunno." Bear suddenly felt tongue-tied. He did not want to get into such things with Buster.

"C'mon Bear, you have to tell me everything. I'm your *lawyer*, son. Your ol' dad has all the responsibility here. You retained me to protect your interests and that means we're in everything together." Buster suddenly tuned his voice to a whine. "I *can't* do my job unless you level with me, son. And I can't have a client who doesn't." This time Buster's fingers beat a tattoo on Bear's shoulder blade.

What the hell, I'll tell him. He's my lawyer, and besides, I can tell he's hot for me. "Just a little bit of skimming, Buster. Not much, really. Just a *little*," Bear said sheepishly.

"Well. Is *that* all it is? That's *nothing.*" Lotsa doctors, they do it all the time. This won't change a thing," Buster soothed. "Things might get rough, son, but I want you to know something: any client of Buster T. Hosterman can count on his good buddy to *make* things come out right."

Bear instantly felt a great sense of relief—as if a wide band of leather strapped tightly around his chest had suddenly been released. He had a true friend in Buster Hosterman.

◆❖◆

Buster Hosterman had somehow managed to contain himself until Bear stepped out the door. Now he exploded with joy. "A little bit of skimming!" he squealed. "Oh shit, what a glorious day! Skimming's *always* good for at *least* another 10K of billings and *this* case is going to be a mother-lode! I just knew it!" Buster danced a little jig around his desk and then sat down, panting with excitement.

CAYMAN **Tuesday evening - February 26, 1974**

Linnell jumped from Billy's cab and raced through the lobby. She imagined she looked like a wildcat on a hot-wired fence, probably smelled like one, too. Her legs appeared charred, but they were only oily and covered with sand, and her hair was filthy, matted with oil and crusted with salt. Linnell clutched the hotel bathrobe up around her ears and hoped that no one would see her as she bypassed the elevator and slipped up the stairs to the second floor. She would die if she didn't shower, and she was ready to kill for another candy bar. Although there was no need, she slunk toward her room.

The lights in the hallway on the second floor had been turned higher so that she could now see the powdery trails of sand that ran the length of the carpeted corridors, every now and then curving in toward a door. A careful inspection revealed the faint trail that lead toward hers. No surprise about that. She'd been expecting an agent to visit her room. When she opened her door, she called out in a lilting accent as if she were the maid. This would give the spook a chance to escape by way of the balcony if he were still in there. These courtesies existed between hunter and hunted.

She was greeted by welcome silence.

Then she flipped the light switch and stepped out of her sandals so her tracks wouldn't meld with those left by her visitor. She could just make out the faint smudge of sand on the threshold where he'd wiped his feet. Then she looked for her briefcase and breathed a sigh of relief to see it still sitting on the table. Her hunger now forgotten, Linnell examined her luggage which she had deliberately set up as an open invitation on her bed. At first glance it appeared undisturbed, but she could tell that someone had made a thorough search of her personal effects because she found the pocket of her navy-blue warm-up jacket turned inside-out, and there now were two narrow slits—just large enough to admit a flashlight—in the lining of her suitcase.

She opened her wallet and counted her bills—nothing had been stolen. Had to be an agent, then. She next turned to the table to inspect her briefcase. She had left it latched but unlocked so the spook would not be tempted to remove it from her room. She put her hand under the latch as she popped it open and was not surprised—the little red bead was gone. Crouching down, she explored the floor and finally found it on the carpet, next to the table leg. Linnell stood up and reached for the curtains—all of the pins were now stuck in the fabric. Her rudder! Linnell dashed to the closet. She'd hidden it inside the Kotex box next to the blankets on the top shelf. She had assumed that the spook would be a male, that he would observe that she hadn't unpacked, and thus he would give the closet nothing more than a cursory glance.

Linnell pulled the box off the shelf. What a relief! Her precious rudder was still packed tightly between the pads. She pried it out and saw that the clear tape which she'd pressed over its tiny lock hadn't been torn. She would leave it here for the duration, she decided. Linnell inspected her briefcase. All of her files and trust documents were still there; they seemed undisturbed. It would make no difference if an agent saw the trusts, she reminded herself. They would be reported, as required, to the IRS Office of International Operations upon her return. Her note pads and coded client memorandums were still on the bottom, underneath all the files containing the trusts. And then, at the bottom of her briefcase she found a slim, unmarked manila folder.

"I completely forgot about *this*," Linnell exclaimed aloud. She flipped it open and found a copy of a page from the Physician's Pharmaceutical Reference Book:

"PERCODAN *Oxycodone Hydrochloride. Habit forming: semi-synthetic narcotic analgesic with multiple actions similar to those of morphine the most prominent of these affect the central nervous system and regions composed of smooth muscle. The principle action of therapeutic value of the oxycodone are analgesic and sedative.* **WARNING**: *Oxycodone can produce drug dependency of the Morphine type and therefore has the potential of being abused.* Addiction. **ADVERSE REACTION**: *Euphoria, constipation."*

Karen had scrawled a note at the bottom of the page, next to a photograph of the pills: *"If this is what Bear is taking, then I thought you might want to know, since the copier doesn't reproduce colors, that the yellow pills are the highest dosage."*

Linnell crumpled the sheet of paper and dragged herself over to the bed to sit down and think. But she couldn't—the very idea of Bear being addicted to narcotics was too awful to contemplate. She stood up, smoothed and folded the paper—as if that would make its message disappear—and placed it back in the file folder and then she raced for the shower. She shivered until the warm water made her relax and then she began to scold herself for over-reacting.

She had to keep an open mind about this . . . she had to think positive. After all, she had seen Margo's name on all of those vials in his bathroom. It could be that *Margo* was a drug addict and that Bear was, for some reason, trying to help her. Yes. Sort of like the way he'd felt compelled to help his friend

Davie. Little Davie Merino—the whirlwind. She hadn't thought about him for such a long time. Linnell thought about him now while she stood in the steamy shower and laundered first her bathing suit and then herself.

She tried to convince herself that all she needed, really, was a little food in her stomach and that when she did, she'd be able to make more favorable sense of things. Linnell tried even harder to think positive thoughts. But it wasn't working. She'd seen Bear taking those yellow pills. The question was, how many and for how long? She'd better try to call him now, before going downstairs to dinner. It would only take a few minutes.

Linnell put the call through to California and again listened to the busy signal at Bear's office. She immediately had the operator put a call through to her house. A few words with Helene might yield some useful information, but her first concern was for Benjy. He should be home from school by now.

The phone rang six times then Helene finally answered, out of breath.

"Helene, it's me! How's things?" Linnell managed to flatten the edginess out of her voice.

"L.C., how're you doing? Your voice sounds funny. You okay? We're fine. We were outside, in the garden. Here's Benjy, say something to him first, then we can talk."

Benjy reported that he had been showing Helene how to play pirate and dig for treasure, and then, only after she was sure he was fine, she asked him to tell her about Bear. Benjy paused for a second. His voice turned quiet. "Well Ma, like usual, I guess. He doesn't say much to me. He came home past my bedtime last night, but Helene let me stay up. I wish he would play with me, but he just sort of makes these funny noises when I try to talk to him. So I went to bed. You coming home soon?"

Linnell swallowed her uneasiness and told him not to worry and that she'd be coming home soon. Benjy, sounding more cheerful, said his good-byes then passed the telephone back to Helene. Linnell chose her words with care, being well aware of the rumors that all telephone communications between the states and tax havens were being monitored by U.S. agencies, so she didn't want to risk saying anything about Bear taking drugs. What if she were wrong? What if all he'd done was maybe take a few leftover pills that he'd been prescribing for Margo? Worse yet, what if he should somehow figure out what she was thinking about him? He would never forgive her. Never.

"Helene, listen." Linnell forced herself to speak as matter-of-factly as she could. "Something might be going on with Bear, actually, I don't know what, but I want you to do me a favor. If anything seems the least bit peculiar about his behavior, then I want you to take Benjy to your house and keep him near you. If you do, then tell Karen and let her know where you are. Her husband's name is Ray. Her number's in my address book, next to the phone. I want you to call her right away, she can fill you in on some details—tell her I just found her note and read her message—and then I think you'll know what I'm getting at here. Tell her I just called you and that I'll get in touch with her soon."

"Okay, I found the number for Karen's house." Helene's voice sounded guarded. "Now listen, L.C., I can only guess what you're getting at here, but I've got my eyes open, and I know how to handle things, so don't you worry."

"Have you talked to Bear lately? I've been trying to reach him for days, but his line's been constantly tied up."

"Well, he just called here a few minutes ago and he sounded fine to me, so stop your worrying. He says he's leaving the office early today and having dinner at the country club. He's staying there, you know. "

"That's good . . . I guess. Well, if he calls again, say hello for me and tell him all's fine over here, and If you'll hold for a sec, I'll give you the call routing info and the telephone number for the hotel and my room number so you can by-pass the desk clerk and call me directly if anything comes up."

Linnell provided Helene with the call-routing information, then said good-bye. Feeling less agitated now that she had touched home base, Linnell dressed quickly and hurried down to the dining room. The dinner hour was over, so the room was nearly empty; the lights had been lowered, and most of the guests were outside at the beach bar, waiting for the discotheque to open. Snatches of music burst from the cocktail lounge where the band was rehearsing for the evening show—a limbo contest—to be followed by disco.

The air was too festive for her mood, so Linnell retreated to a far corner of the dining room and chose a table with clean linen. Pulling the large rattan chair away from the table, she sat facing the wall to avoid being disturbed. She needed to think. The waiter appeared instantly and offered her a cocktail, compliments of the management as thanks for her having done such a good job. Linnell declined and hastily ordered her meal, a turtle steak, Creole style—turtles were now being raised at Mariculture, the huge turtle farm at Boatswains Bay—and some key lime pie for dessert and a pot of Colombian coffee. The waiter, sensing her desperation, handed her a plate with one fluffy roll and a pat of fresh butter. As soon as he turned his back, Linnell tore it in half, stuffed it into her mouth, and felt an immediate wave of relief.

When she traveled, she made it a point to have at least one meal a day where she was served. It felt wonderful to just sit back and have everything handed to her—no wonder Bear enjoyed it so much. Not that she was complaining about serving him dinner. It was just that cooking was her job and Bear liked to remind her of this, especially at the table.

He would joke about this, and then sometimes he would reach out with his fork and spear the best morsel from her plate—the one she'd been saving for last—and then he would always say the same thing: "You see?" he would say, "It's like this: Men don't have to ask. Look at *me* for example—I don't have to ask for permission to have what *I* want. Because all a *man* has to do is to just help himself." Her tidbit would then disappear in his mouth. "You know why?" he would ask, chewing and grinning at her with satisfaction. And then he would deliver the same old punch-line: "*I'll* tell you why: Because this is a *man's* world, sweetheart." But he was just joking—he had to be—because shortly afterwards he would usually go out of his way to give her a little trinket. Or sometimes even more—like the hundred dollar bills she'd just found in the card.

But she would always think, *Oh sure. A man helps himself. That has two meanings, and he only knows one.* That's what *she* always said. But only to herself because there was no point in fighting with him at the table and besides, as the wife, it was her duty to be the peace maker, just as her mother had been.

Nonetheless, Bear's shenanigans often gave her a chilly feeling toward the opposite sex, which was, she suspected, exactly what he intended. He had apparently formed the crazy idea that getting her to see all other men as the enemy was a good way to bind her closer to himself. Silly Bear! But now that she thought about it, maybe this explained why the more she did for him, the less he seemed to appreciate her. This had become her very own Catch-22: On the one hand, he would treat her as if she were less important than him because she needed him for protection—and she did; she needed to know that she had a good, solid husband at her back so she could go out there, practice law, take on the whole damn world. But then on the other hand, should ever another man dare pay *any* kind of attention to her, Bear would be right there at her elbow, demanding proof that she needed only him. And she had to keep him happy, because without his approval she'd have to close her law office. Either that, or get a divorce--and that was now out of the question.

Linnell returned to the matter of Karen's note. Could Bear possibly be addicted to Percodan? And if so, what did this mean? For him, and for his dental practice? And what about her? After all, if it weren't for her, he wouldn't have any kind of dental practice at all.

This was so, because after finishing his first semester, he had shocked her with his confession that he had exhausted his small inheritance and couldn't afford to stay in dental school. She had been a good soldier about this unanticipated turn of events, which had prompted gusts of admiration from him. They next decided that she should quit the low-paying job she liked and take a higher-paying job, but one with no future. She hadn't felt like a martyr about any of this—lots of women worked to "Put Hubby Through" with the understanding that for the rest of their lives, they would together reap the benefits. Except nowadays, with no-fault divorce, most of these arrangements were being stood on their heads. Since this had not happened to her, she was regarded as one of the lucky ones. In any event, "putting hubby through" had quickly taught her what many women before her had already learned: that it was going to take a whole lot of hard work on her part if her husband was ever to become one of those "self-made" men.

He was largely oblivious of what she did to support him because he spent most of his time cramming for exams with his three dental school buddies, Davie and Rudy and Arnold. Fortunately, the guys paid her to shop and to cook their dinners, which in turn led Davie to announce that since she with them so much, she really ought to be known simply as "L.C." just so it would be clear to everybody that she was "one of the boys," since in those days guys who were buddies addressed each other by their initials. In fact, at that time she hadn't cared *what* they called her because she was so obsessed with making it through.

After passing the dental boards, the four guys went their separate ways but they still competed with each other to see who would be the first to pay off their dental school debts. They all slaved and saved like mad, but for some reason Davie always came out ahead. Not only was he the first out of debt, but in very short order he had a magnificent home—with a large swimming pool and a tennis court and a garage filled with those fancy red sports cars—and a stunning model for a wife. It was absolutely miraculous. How could he do all this and still have enough time to play golf twice a week? This really ate Bear up. He redoubled his efforts but he could never surpass Davie no matter how hard he worked and she had been afraid he was going to kill himself trying. Finally—and it was a godsend to her way of thinking—the secret to Davie's amazing success was revealed the night he was busted for dealing drugs.

After a long and humiliating trial, Davie was convicted for peddling the cocaine he'd been purchasing through his practice for use as a topical anesthetic. Davie had been selling to the street, so to speak, and one of his buyers was an undercover agent. That's all it took: one honest agent, and Davie lost everything, including his beautiful wife, and he ended up having to trade in his pelf for a five year stint as a guest of the government.

Linnell had hoped that Davie's conviction would be a lesson for Bear and that he'd finally learn how to relax and enjoy himself with his family. But when he refused to listen to her, or to spend any time with them, Linnell, exasperated, finally made up her mind to do something for herself. And even though she had a baby, she'd also had Helene to help her, so on a whim she decided to go to law school. She was determined; she'd dug in her heels; it was either law school or else she would break all the rules and simply leave him. What was the point in being married if she was, in effect, still living alone?

They'd had a great battle over this—Bear had tried every which way to break her down. And then she'd played her ace: She'd threatened a divorce, so finally, in the end, he caved in, but only after he got her to swear on her knees that she'd never leave him if he allowed her attend. She had sworn. She had given him her solemn word, and he had cried salty tears of gratitude in her lap, which was the first—and last—time she had ever seen him display any raw emotion.

Once in law school she was so overwhelmed she could scarcely keep track of much else. However, at mid-term, when she finally came up for some air, she had been shocked to discover that Bear had taken over Davie's practice. He was "just holding things together for Davie," he'd said, "until Davie was released from San Quentin." In fact, to this day, Bear still visited Davie at least once a month—which meant he was spending more time with his good pal Davie than he was with his son.

Yes, her husband, the esteemed Dr. Clare, had been regarded as a saint for standing by his good buddy this way, but she had felt miserable because she knew he would be working even longer hours than before in order to handle the additional patient load. It looked like nothing was going to change. But this time, when she griped about how little time this left for them to spend together, Bear would brush her aside, saying, "Hey! Everything I do, I'm doing for *you*. You should *know* that."

Linnell's fingers suddenly gripped the edge of the table. She now realized why Karen's note had led her to thinking about Davie. Wasn't it just short of amazing how they had so suddenly become so incredibly affluent? So affluent that Bear could simply skip out and buy a big spread in *the* most expensive section of town? And very soon after that, in fact too soon after that, had come the expensive cars, the country club, and all the rest of the goodies. Yes, the good times certainly had begun to roll—but only *after* Bear had arranged to step into Davie's practice. And Davie had been making it by peddling drugs. Linnell closed her eyes and saw Bear's face. It was bloated with evil and his baleful gray eyes held an icy light.

She suddenly felt herself losing her balance, overcome by the sort of dizzy feeling you get when the ground slips away from beneath your feet. For a second she could actually see her world crumbling. Was this all in her imagination? For the first time in her life, Linnell didn't care. If he was dealing in narcotics, they were *all* in jeopardy. They could lose everything: Bear, his freedom; and her, the life for which she had sacrificed.

Then Linnell caught herself. Oh, for Godsake! she thought. He'd never do something like that. Not stodgy, routine-driven Bear. Besides, he'd seen what happened to Davie. So he wouldn't dare. Would he?

"The wise thing to do would be to take a few steps to protect myself," thought Linnell. Then and there, she made a decision: there would be no big birthday surprise for her husband this year. At least not until he set her mind to rest. And she would protect the SUP corporation and its profits by holding onto the shares until she got to the bottom of things. But she really shouldn't do anything more than just that, at least not until she'd gathered more facts.

But, what if something should happen to her before she could get to the bottom of things? And she *had* to get to the bottom of things because any uncertainty about something like this would simply eat her alive. Temporary measures were in order: She had to draft another Cayman trust—a testamentary trust for Benjy's benefit—the sort that would take effect only on her death. And she would immediately draft a Holographic Will, a handwritten document which would pass all of the SUP shares to her testamentary trust should she meet with accident—this way she could be sure that Benjy would inherit her property and Bear would not have any easy time of it if he wanted to fight his own son for her Cayman corporation because he'd have to come here, to Cayman, her territory, to do battle over the shares—that is, if he ever discovered them . . .

The waiter appeared with her dinner and Linnell dove in. Now that a few things were settled, she could at last indulge her truly incredible appetite. The tender turtle steak, enrobed in a rich sauce of exotic spices and festooned with fresh spinach, was tender and deliciously aromatic; on the spectrum of flavors, it was halfway between pot roast and the dark meat of chicken and with the first forkful, she forgot about Bear. The waiter kept filling her cup with freshly brewed coffee and replenishing the warm bread and butter. Linnell inhaled the meal and then she mopped her plate clean with a morsel of bread. Basking in comfort, she leaned back in her chair.

After such a splendid dinner, she felt a bit calmer. But tired. Very tired. At least she was now able to put a more positive spin on things: Maybe Bear wasn't dealing drugs. No, most likely he wasn't. It was more likely he'd gotten into Percodan for his headaches. Prescribing it in Margo's name, obviously, to cover things up perhaps because he was so ashamed. Well, if it was only this, they could always do something, and no one would have to know. But she would have to get him to a doctor. She could get him to do that, she thought.

See? It's always *some*thing! Like being bitten to death by ducks, thought Linnell. Well, there was nothing she could do from here. She would just have to be patient and wait until she returned home before getting into the thick of things. Right now, however, what *she* needed was a vacation. And by God! She was going to have a good one. Linnell stood up, stepped back into the shadows to stretch, and yawned. Looking toward the beach through the arches, she scanned the crowd outside and spotted a familiar face with a head of reddish-brown hair. The turned-up nose was now pointing eagerly toward two scantily-clad termites—young ones who weren't trying very hard to conceal their profession. The Hyena was on the prowl tonight and just the sight of him hungrily scouring the grounds for fresh meat was enough to send her flying up to her room. She was looking forward to a good night's sleep anyway, so if there really were any problems, they would just have to wait.

The light was shining directly in his face, so Harold Dolphe momentarily lost sight of L.C. when she stepped back into the shadows of the dining room. Nervous at the thought of losing her, he edged closer to the trees that surrounded the beach bar until he could see her again. He stood quietly and eyed her legs as she climbed the stairs to the second floor—she really did have great legs—and then he waited until he saw the lights going on in her room. Dolphe flapped his shirt to cool his sunburn and fidgeted with his trunks. The sand had dried inside his shorts, furthermore, he felt miserable and put upon because he'd had to sit around on the beach the entire afternoon, a towel on his head and his oiled ass in the sand, just so he could keep an eye on L.C. while she cavorted with the Cayman divers like some teenage groupie. He itched. He couldn't stand it anymore, and as he walked back to the beach bar, he slid a hand inside his pants and scratched like mad.

His hand froze and then he jerked it out when he saw that the cutest chick was finally giving him the big eye. He grinned broadly at her. He'd been keeping an eye on her too—she'd been circling him, pretending not to see him, for the last half-hour. Now she seemed to be heading for a bar stool and leaning forward—definitely to get a better look at him, resting her big boobs on top of the bar and pressing down to make them bulge out of her bikini top—and all *this,* just for him! It looked like she'd finally made up her mind. And now she was smiling at him and rubbing a long brown leg ever so slowly up and down the wooden leg of her bar stool. Dolphe puckered wet lips and nodded his happy approval. The girl fluttered her eyelashes, then lowered them, and then turned to giggle behind long slim fingers with her sidekick.

Then Dolphe sighed as if the weight of the world had just landed on his shoulders. The chicks would just have to wait—he had to get back to the matter of earning a living. But no problem, he knew that once they made up their minds, they were the kind who'd stick around. To guarantee this, he pulled out a fat wallet, laid it on the bar and then giving the pretty one the high sign, he pointed to himself and mouthed, "I'll be back." As soon as the cute one rewarded him with a flash of white teeth and another wink, he grabbed his wallet and slipped away.

Dolphe strolled toward the bushes to ditch his beer bottle—a pretext for grabbing the camera he'd hidden there—and then headed up the outside stairs to the second floor to stake out L.C.'s door. Maybe he could sneak another photo of her. Perhaps this time she would be entertaining a visitor in her room. But he'd better watch his step; he didn't much care if she knew he was here, but he sure wasn't interested in finding out what she'd do to him if she should happen to catch him spying on her. She'd almost had him this morning. That miserable hell-hole of a broom closet—he knew she was standing outside the door—and then, when he'd finally caught up with her, he found her hitting on yet *another* guy. Right out in the open, at the beach bar, which again forced him to duck—this time into the dining room—so he could take some more photos. What a shitty day! There had better be something in it for him. He was a lawyer for crissakes, a member of the California State Bar and not just Ivener's gopher. Yet Ivener *still* treated him like one, even though he had been made a *senior* associate of the Ivener firm.

This time Ivener had sent him offshore—all expenses paid—to do two fairly simple things: To rent some space for the firm's biggest client, and to get a line on what L.C. was doing here in Cayman. A fancy assignment, all things considered. But Ivener wouldn't be exactly thrilled to hear about what he'd found: five trusts in her briefcase this morning. Five! And furthermore, she was undercutting their fees—doing the same work for less than half what they'd charge, which translated into a loss of $20,000 in billings for the Ivener firm just this month alone. But, worse than that, even though he had searched everywhere, he couldn't find her rudder—which was what Ivener wanted the most. And so did he. It had been his plan to make a copy of it for himself before turning it over to the boss.

Dolphe thought about his future as he slowly climbed the stairs to the second floor. After his fright over the indictment had subsided, he'd wondered what effect staying with Ivener might have on his career. Then, when he'd seen that Ivener wasn't worried about it—in fact, Ivener had laughed—he'd decided to stay put, just keep his head down and stick around. This way he could draw his perks and his salary while he worked on the other deal he had cooking, a deal which sounded like it had a whole lot more potential than practicing law.

Harold Dolphe slid through the door on the top landing—making sure that it didn't slam—and then crept back to his hiding place around the corner from L.C.'s room. He could tell from the slashes of light at the bottom of the doors that almost half of the rooms on L.C.'s corridor were now occupied.

The deal he was working on now had materialized because of The Wei, where he had been making some extra money on weekends by serving as a Wei-trainer. He was known there only as "Harold," because just like at the office, Wei-farers were supposed to use only their first names. As a trainer, however, he got to see the roster of enrollees, and that was how he'd managed to spot the name—Dr. Mark Clare. He'd guessed it was L.C.'s old man. After sparring with her for over a year, he was curious about what sort of guy she had married, so he'd assigned the unsuspecting initiate to his training group. He wanted to study him, because if there was any kind of chink in her old man's armor, he was going to find some way to use it.

Before they were allowed in, the prospective Wei-farers had to first sign a contract which spelled out their duties and obligations—which included keeping everything secret—and then they were assembled in groups of 200 and lead into a hall where they were locked up and subjected to a barrage of psychobabble for an entire weekend during which time they were deprived of all nourishment and facilities. He could see how profitable it was from the standpoint of The Wei—you didn't have to feed or take care of them. And he had also learned, without having to suffer it himself, that hunger and discomfort were a remarkably efficient tool when it came to cutting everyone down to an easily processable size. He had also seen more than one big shot peeing down his pants leg, and with great satisfaction he'd learned that those preppy little cheer leader types—the ones who had always blown him off before—would now do almost anything for a little taste of his candy bar.

Talk about encountering the human condition! Thanks be to The Wei, he'd smelled enough of it to last him a lifetime. By the end of the weekend, however, the initiates would be broken and they'd be ready to follow orders and do just about anything they were told.

That was when the most important part of his job began. That was when he would tell them to *share*. Yes, either share or be denied membership and waste that last 48 hours of suffering. His job was to see to it that they all "put out." So, "put out" they all did, and the so-called Encounter Sessions would begin late that evening, last all night, and then pick up again the following weekend.

The new initiates, bonded together through their common and self-imposed misery, would then sit cross-legged on the floor in one big circle in order to *Replay the Tapes of their Past,* which was nothing more than a mass confession. The trainers were instructed to bounce anybody out of the group who tried not to share their most intimate secrets—unless Harold stepped in. He had the last word in these matters, and it was his important responsibility to make sure that no one with money was ever kicked out. And so it was Harold Dolphe who ended up being the only one who actually *Got It* since it was also his job to compile a dossier on anyone who had the potential to be of some use.

Everyone in his training group shared, all except Dr. Mark Clare. Dr. Clare would attend his encounter sessions and just sit there as unmoved as a loaf of white bread. Harold had him pegged as being a cut above the rest of the lettuce-heads. And strangely enough, no one suggested that Dr. Clare—everyone was now calling him "Doc"—be tossed out. He also saw how Doc never missed a chance to pass out his business cards. So, Doc Clare was an enterprising kind of guy. He liked guys like that, and he was curious about what Doc was promoting. That's why one night he decided to throw a little parking-lot party after a sharing session—to see if he could get Doc to let his hair down. They ended up sharing a joint, and when Doc finally loosened up, the two of them hit it off.

It wasn't too long before they were meeting like this on a regular basis, thus he wasn't the least bit surprised when Doc finally told him that he had been experimenting with some other very fine mind-altering substances which he could get through his practice. Harold had wanted to sample some too, so in order to accumulate more points with the dentist, he had begun to assure Doc that Doc was a born leader, a *king* among men. Harold always made it a point to treat the dentist with the utmost respect—always calling him *Doc*, or *doctor*—he even suggested to the other Wei-farers that they come up with a special mantra so Doc could celebrate the "Essence of his Being" and the obedient souls concocted this ridiculous chant about Doc being a "king." And then, to his utter surprise, he saw that Doc was taking all of this seriously.

After that, he knew Doc wasn't as smart as he'd first thought and that it was safe to let Doc know that he, Harold Dolphe, was actually a lawyer—"a professional, just like Doc"—at the Ivener law firm.

"What a strange and wonderful coincidence the way life brings certain people together," Doc had said, repeatedly. After that, Doc confided in him on a regular basis. In fact, Doc had revealed something of utmost importance: That he was going to sell his practice and get into a more lucrative line of work, and that he had an important position set up for his good pal Harold Dolphe and that all of these things would come together just as soon as he "got things sorted out with his wife."

Harold had picked up on that, so late one evening, to get the ball rolling a little faster, Dolphe decided it was time for him to do a little sharing of his own: After he and Doc rolled a joint and they had gotten good and mellow, he whipped up a couple of whoppers for Doc about how L.C. had "carried on" at the Ivener firm. He didn't come right out and actually say anything, he just laid out a few hints—all nonsense, of course—but it seemed to be exactly what Doc needed to hear, because Doc immediately confessed to his own tale of woe: That he was having some trouble "getting it up."

Although he was sure that Doc's problem came from sampling too many narcotics, he saw this as his chance to convince Doc that his impotence was due to his having such a ball-busting wife. From then on they were allies, and Dolphe, emboldened, planted yet another seed in Doc's mind which had grown into this present mixed blessing which had him crouched on all fours in this half-lit hallway, keeping an eye on Mrs. Clare's door. Dolphe could remember the exact words he'd used to prompt Doc into sending him on his present mission: "A woman as lucky as L.C. really has *no* business working and traveling and leaving a man like *you* all alone by himself. Unless . . unless, you know, she has a . . . ," and then, instead of saying, "a lover," he had pointedly coughed. Doc had immediately changed the subject by offering to give him a baggie of pure, uncut snow if he would keep an eye on L.C. come her next trip. Photos would be nice. And a full report.

He certainly had earned it, Dolphe thought. And he had an earful to give him tonight.

As for Willy Ivener, that was an entirely different story. Ivener wasn't that easy to read. For example, when he told Ivener that L.C.'s husband had enrolled in The Wei, his only comment had been, "Yes, I know. You might as well get the usual profile on him, and her too, if you can."

Harold knew Ivener well enough to understand that he was telling him to spy on the Clares. And he was certain that Ivener had been wondering just how much L.C. was cutting into their business. As soon as he reported that L.C. was going to Cayman, Ivener sent him off on this trip, not only to take care of some things for their biggest client, The Wei, but also to report on L.C.'s activities and to bring back her rudder. But he had a gut feeling that Ivener wasn't telling him everything, which made him all the more curious about what the man really was up to this time. Ivener was secretive about so many things—for instance, The Wei and all of the money it collected.

The Wei and its money. Now *that* was important. Where did it all go? And most important—who got to spend it?

In several daring daylight forays, he'd tried to find out by sneaking into Ivener's office through his remarkable closets. He'd begun to methodically search through the files hidden in Ivener's desk. And so, bit by bit, he had learned that all of the California units of The Wei—there were now well over 200—were transferring enormous royalties to some mysterious foreign foundations in the Bahamas. This meant that millions upon millions of untaxed dollars were flowing offshore *every month.* The foundations had been carefully named to make them seem related to such well-known charities as the Red Cross and the Cancer Society. And there was no end to their enormous investments: securities, T-Bills and certificates of deposit, not to mention countless real estate partnerships. All tucked away at brokerage houses and banks scattered throughout the United States.

With nothing more than some simple arithmetic, Dolphe had arrived at the dizzying figure of half a billion dollars as the approximate amount that had already been shunted tax free to the Bahamas. And this was just from California! Aroused by the thought of being so close to such vast sums, he'd become even more curious. If Ivener was legal counsel, then who owned The Wei? He became bolder, his forays continued, and all the clues seemed to lead to one and only one conclusion: That the slender, pale-faced Willy Ivener was far more than just legal counsel to The Wei. In fact, Harold, after risking his neck in order to gather this information, would bet his life on the proposition that Ivener owned the entire operation and that the foreign foundations were now being used as fronts.

Harold remained seated on the carpet in the darkened hall, trying to imagine what it would be like to dive into such a huge pile of money. If he could get his hands on even a small part of it, he'd certainly spend it better than Willy Ivener ever could. He would have a grand home on a huge estate, not in a little suburb like Highridge, but farther down the peninsula, in Hillsborough perhaps. *His* mansion would be filled with beautiful women who would do whatever he said, a cook to fry him up some mouth-watering meals, there'd be a full staff of servants, and yes, even a yacht . . . or a jet. Anything was possible. He just had to find some way to make it happen.

And just maybe, he had.

He had recently learned, through Doc, that L.C. had been secretly writing a tell-all article about foreign foundations—something to do with how they might be subjected to taxation by the federal government—and that it was going to be published in the Universal Tax Journal in a couple of months. His initial reaction had been to envy L.C. for the publicity she'd get and the fame and profits that were sure to follow—there wasn't a tax attorney in the United States who wouldn't give both eye teeth and a couple of molars to have his work presented in such a prestigious forum. And then the significance of Doc's revelation had finally hit home: *Tax* foreign foundations? Tax *foreign* foundations? Ivener would certainly want to know about something like that!

He could still recall the way Ivener had tried to conceal his reaction when he'd told him the news—although Ivener had looked plenty disgusted, he had merely replied, "That's very nice." And then, when Harold threw in the part about L.C.'s tax research being published in the Universal Tax Journal—and Ivener had responded by suddenly swiveling his chair to face the wall . . . well, *that* said it all. Now he was sure he had stumbled onto something that was very important.

Harold rocked to-and-fro on his haunches. Surely there had to be *some* way for him to pull all of this information together and get it to working for him.

The light disappeared from under Linnell's door. It looked like she was going to be turning in early. Harold Dolphe looked at his watch. It was exactly 10:35 p.m., which made it 7:35 p.m. in California, time for him to trudge back to his hotel and call in his reports.

HIGHRIDGE **Tuesday Evening - February 26, 1974**

Bear checked into the club and took only a light snack for dinner and then hauled his briefcase and an armload of files up to his second floor suite. From this high vantage point he could peek out the window and see if anyone was trying to watch or sneak up on him. He felt he couldn't be too careful, so he had already arranged to take his important calls at the club in order to avoid Helene's sharp eyes—and the sharper ears of Benjy, who might be curious about what he was doing.

It was now exactly 10:30 p.m. in Cayman, and the call he'd been expecting would be coming in soon. To kill time while he waited, he examined the papers from Buster's office. A "Petition for Dissolution of Marriage" and a "Financial Declaration" that would have to be included with his papers when he filed for divorce. He was interested only in the latter because the court would rely on it for determining how much he would have to pay for child support. He wanted to work on it now so that everything would be ready to go just as soon as he knew which way he was headed. He had decided to use the information provided by the Code Two computer print-outs to complete his Financial Declaration, because they disclosed only half of his gross receipts. The court would deduct his expenses from these figures to assess what was left, and then an almost minuscule percentage of this sum would be available for child support. He already knew he could get away with puffing up his expenses—what would a bored and petulant judge know about running a dental practice? He felt bad about Ma getting the house. He didn't like that. He would have to put some more thought into that one.

Bear set the Financial Declaration aside and began to examine his patient files. Well, thanks to Margo, at least his office was under control; she had done her usual good job of filling the blue and yellow tabbed files with the phony X-rays, so now all he had to do was to count how many there were in order to justify the prescriptions he'd be writing for narcotics. He did this every quarter, just in case he'd be called on to explain why he was purchasing such a large quantity of them. Not that the Drug Control Act was ever enforced; it seldom was when it came to dentists. But there was no point in getting sloppy and ending up like Davie Merino. Of course, it was a good thing he'd hung onto Davie, because the man had become a great source of information and new connections—San Quentin was a finishing school when it came to distributing drugs—and he'd have an even better use for Davie when he was released. Davie would do an excellent job when it came to keeping a handle on Harold Dolphe.

As for his patients, they were no problem because they never saw their charts. Besides, between his cryptic notes and near illegible handwriting they would never understand how he was using them to order narcotics. Now all he had to do was divide the charts into two groups—he would order cocaine for "numbing gums and oral tissues" for the first batch, and for the second group—the less fortunate because he would be scheduling them for extractions—he would prescribe Percodan, ostensibly for post-surgical pain relief. Now all he had left to do was estimate the number of sniffers he'd be seeing this week so he could order the nitrous gas tanks from his new supply house in Oakland. And should anyone happen to ask why he was ordering so much gas, he had a simple explanation: "He hadn't realized . . . but his tank valves must have been leaking for months." He'd already stashed a couple of defective valve sets in his laboratory to be used, if necessary, for this very purpose.

Bear scratched his neck while he thought about how good it was to have Margo handling the less significant tasks, such as ordering the supplies and taking care of such piffling stuff as the linen invoices and the injection sets. That was part of their deal—she would attend to these minor details so he could handle the more important matters.

The phone rang and Bear carefully noted that it was 7:45 p.m., which meant it would be 10:45 p.m. in Cayman. He let it ring four more times and when he finally lifted the receiver he heard the overseas operator announcing that he had a long distance call from the British West Indies.

"Hi bro." Harold spoke rapidly. "I'm real sorry to have to tell you this, but you're right . . . I think you get my meaning? She's been trotting around in nothin' but this lavender bikini—and no wedding ring. I took photos for ya. First thing, though, she goes to the bank, spends less than an hour on her clients and this gives her plenty of time for the beach. Okay—I'm gonna tell it to you straight: She was hanging out with this young guy down at the beach bar. First she sucks up a big jar of booze and then she hits on him big time—but he's no dummy. He takes off on her, so then she starts fooling around with, get *this,* at least twenty locals out in the water. Looks like she's got the hots for the island dive master. He's got this old heap and he's been hauling her all over the island. They ended up at his warehouse tonight and I caught them smooching around in there after everyone left. Big party. Booze all over the place. Used a flash with my telephoto lens. Oh yeah, one more thing—he's a big black dude . . ." Harold paused.

"Go on," Bear said, his voice flat and unresponsive.

"So then I followed her, and when he was through with her she looked like she'd taken his best shot. She was a mess. Then she takes her sweet time, gets all dolled up for dinner and then the waiter falls all over her, too. I'm *really* sorry to have to tell you this, Doc . . ."

For the longest time there was nothing but the sound of static crackling between them. Bear finally spoke. "You sure you got photos of all this stuff?"

"Yeah. Sure do . . ."

" Okay . . . then, just keep it up . . . I'll talk to you tomorrow."

"Well, I want you to know," Harold's voice now brimmed with unctuous sympathy, "you're not going to pass through this dark valley all by yourself. The Wei is with you."

Bear replied dully, "Sure, bro. Yeah. Thanks a lot."

Bear dropped the receiver onto its cradle and reached for his bottle of tablets. Downing four Quaaludes, he fell into bed and waited for them to hit. The thought of his Ma screwing around on him—and in front of the whole goddam world, no less!—caused his heart to leap noisily under his ribs. He couldn't rest. He would never sleep. Hell, he could scarcely *breathe.*

Through a slowly descending curtain of blood, Bear could see the future unfolding. Pressing his eyes closed with his small-fingered hands, he could see it all . . . her eyes bulging, her tongue shooting out from her mouth as his hands closed slowly, slowly, slowly around her neck. And then, just as he was about to cast off into the darkness, an idea, a brilliant idea flashed before his eyes. He had to remember it in the morning. With a mighty effort, he fought off a great wave of drowsiness and reached for his pen and on the telephone note pad, in a barely legible hand, he managed to scribble what looked like one word: "Willkills."

HIGHRIDGE **Tuesday evening - February 26, 1974**

I bid him look into the lives of men as though into a mirror,
and from others to take an example for himself.
Adelphi—Terence [Publius Terentius Afer]

Her starkly glamorous apparel and a near imperceptible air of nervousness proclaimed that she was waiting for a gentleman to join her for dinner. A work of art, ageless in her beauty, she presented a ravishing vision of bright white skin and black satin against the blood-red velour of the cushions. And much like the beauty coiled upon the banquette, this sparkling, flower-laden bistro, tucked behind a dark hedge of carefully trimmed shrubbery, was one of those sub rosa fantasies that sprang to life only at nightfall.

Tufted red velvet banquettes ran the length of the softly glittering room and on the opposite wall, intricately beveled mirrors reflected the candlelit bowers of pale pink camellias and lilacs that embellished each table. The ceiling was draped with a pink silky-looking fabric which hinted at the boudoir and served to dampen the sound. Between the flowers and the lush folds of silk, guests were given the feeling that they would not have to worry too much about being overheard or too closely observed.

Every now and then the candlelit enchantress would lean forward and turn blue-green eyes toward the foyer. Having already received an appreciative stare from the maitre' de, she tested the room by slowly lifting an unblemished white arm to adjust the veil that ballooned from her tiny black cocktail hat, carefully noting how this simple gesture—which just happened to accentuate the opulent curves of her high-necked but sleeveless black-satin top—caused every man to stop breathing. A black fur-trimmed wrap, draped carelessly over the cushions behind one bare shoulder, matched the glamour of her long black silk skirt; silk thongs of black satin fastened spike-heels around her slender ankles. She rested a satin-gloved hand on her furs, crossed her ankles to one side and forced herself to sit motionless, moving only her eyes. The scene was playing itself out exactly the way she imagined it should. But if he knew what was best for him, he'd better arrive soon! She didn't appreciate being kept waiting. So where was he?

She leaned behind the lavish barrier of flowers that sat at the front edge of her table and stole another glance at herself in the mirror. No one dressed like this. Not anymore. Nowadays everybody wanted to look like a druggie rocker, but as far as she was concerned, the disco scene was passé—it had too soon become a vastly ridiculous sea of macramé tunics and unisex bell-bottoms—a mess of gold chains nestling on bristled chests bursting from their too-tight pastel polyester leisure suits, bared midriffs, and three-inch platform shoes. And all of it thrashing and flailing away as far as the eye could see. To her way of thinking, such absurd costumes—albeit a great improvement over the waist-cinchers, foundations, padded bras and seamed hosiery that had loomed in her future when she was a little girl—had already become just another uniform. Not for her all this marching in lock step. She was different, she was unique. And she would prove it tonight by giving the good folks of this bistro a new and different show. So—ta da! Eat your heart out, Highridge, because here she was—a retro-Lana sans underwear, a decadent Marlena, sleeping her way to the top. Or so they would think.

Confident that no one in Highridge would ever guess who she was, she didn't give a damn about the identity of the rest of the patrons of this particular restaurant—favored as it was by local merchants for outing their mistresses. But still, it was best not to push things too far. So where was the damn man? she wondered again, this time with genuine concern. He had promised to meet her here, in this back corner booth. No doubt because he needed to be absolutely secure in his conversations with her. Well, in his line of work, he needed to be careful, she understood that.

Her thoughts were interrupted by a discreet cough. She looked up, startled, but managed to greet her tardy dinner companion with the starriest of smiles. Willy Ivener stared at her for a long time, then ignoring the padded chair set opposite her at their table, slid into the velvet booth and inched his way along the banquette until he reached her side.

"Deborah, you're looking so splendid, you almost had me fooled." Willy spoke with a toothy smile, but Deborah could see that his eyes were the same as always. No matter what pleasant thing he might try to do with his face, the look in his eyes never wavered. It was a watchful look. Alert to the movement of prey. Deborah next took in Willy's pallid complexion—were those bruises on the sides of his forehead?—and thought about vampires and the uses of Max Factor Pancake makeup. There was a new look about him that made her think of a Death's-head moth. Well, thought Deborah, if she had just been indicted, she probably wouldn't look so red-hot herself. Deborah acknowledged Willy's compliment by flirtatiously lifting the dark cloud of her dotted veil with elegant gestures—but only high enough to leave uncovered her glossed and darkly glistening lips. She followed Willy's eyes while she reinserted a long jeweled hat pin at the back of her hat.

"You like my hat?" Deborah spoke coquettishly.

"My dear, you look gorgeous. But take care, you don't want to hurt yourself—that's a wicked-looking pin."

"Oh, that. Don't worry, Uncle Willy, I won't hurt myself. It's part of the costume. I imagine women once really knew how to use them—they needed them for protection when they dressed like this." Deborah gave the hat pin a twist and smiled wickedly, knowing that she had succeeded in making him nervous. She knew just how to annoy him with what he described as her "rake-hell ovarian-attitude." He was so quaint.

"So," Deborah continued, "I'm glad you think I look good, because I have a question for you, darlin' Willy. You must tell me something, or else it's *all* over." Deborah fell silent when she saw the elderly waiter approaching, carrying two stems of the superb house champagne. Slowly pulling off one of her long satin gloves, Deborah studied the awestruck expression on the older man's face while he informed them with a slow bow that this was a tribute to the Lady from *l'auberge*. She watched him back away, as if she were royalty. Sitting proudly erect, she acknowledged this tribute with a regal smile and then she slowly fluttered her lashes and lowered her eyes, not looking up until she was sure he was gone.

Then she grinned, showing small perfect teeth. It didn't seem possible, but only an hour before she had been appearing on quite a different stage, starring in the role of a ground-up loser, fresh from the Highridge County divorce mill, who was in turn playing the part of Dr. Clare's new sex toy. It had taken her only a half hour to change—a smidge of blood-red lipstick here, a dab of blusher there, the hair, the nails and the gown, and presto! Now she looked so wicked!

Pleased with herself, Deborah shot a mischievous look at her Uncle Willy through her veil.

◆❖◆

Willy took stock of his delicious godchild over the top of the large, handwritten menu. He had to admit, she was getting very good at her game and he knew that she was intent on trying to test him. She was now on his short list of favorite subjects; but that hadn't always been the case. In fact, not too long ago he had even found her most annoying, quite wild and freakish, almost out of control. But then, people can and do change, he reminded himself, and it was really quite gratifying to see her ripening into such an alluring woman.

Deborah had asked for this meeting and he had offered his true-enough fear of surveillance as a reason for meeting her here, for dinner, instead of at his office. However, surveillance or no, he would have had to meet with her here, simply because he could not risk having her waltzing around at the firm and discovering that he kept a picture of her on his desk. A photograph upon which he'd written a message which was intended to lead people into thinking that he had, if not a wife, then at the very least, a mistress. And if he were to suddenly ditch her photo, his staff would notice, and then questions would be asked and all sorts of new rumors might fly. The charade about having a woman was important, not only because it portrayed him as enjoying an enviable private life, but, even more important, because it saved him from having to waste any more of his precious time keeping the rest of the she-demons at bay.

As a matter of fact, no woman could possibly interest him, nor for that matter, could any man. His pilgrim's progress had taken him far beyond such pedestrian gratifications, so much so that he had coined the flip phrase: "Been there, done that," to express his ennui. This had not always been the case, of course. In the not too distant past every manner of priapic pleasure had been his for the asking. His sexual sojourns had taken him from the back alleys of Tangiers to the best houses of London and Paris and West Los Angeles—and he had indulged in them so extensively that not only the acts but also the performers were now but a dim recollection.

Now he could scarcely remember any of it—except perhaps for that one occasion when he, apparently intoxicated, had tried to avenge Leda with one of the swans in Kew Gardens. Yes, he'd already had more than his fill of such things, and although he had lived for them once, they no longer offered him much of a challenge. However, there remained one game that still gave him an adrenaline rush. It was an end-game because, in the end only one of the players would survive. And that was why, at the age of sixty-five, he had decided to dedicate the rest of his life to playing the heroic David to the mighty gap-toothed Goliath of the IRS. As for Deborah, well, too bad for her if she didn't like it, but she was now playing a significant role in his secret game.

People no longer seemed to recall, but he had known Deborah from the day she was born, being that she was the only child of the couple who had once been his closest friends. He had even courted Deborah's mother—a woman much younger than he—that is, he had done so until she met and promptly eloped with Deborah's father. After recovering from this impossible turn of events, he had decided to clasp the happy young couple to his bosom. Thus it came as no surprise to anyone that it should be he, the lawyer, who would be called upon to serve as Deborah's guardian upon the sad occasion of her parents' death. A terrible sad death that had come by way of an automobile accident—alas, the brakes had mysteriously failed—over the Christmas holidays when Deborah was only six. Thereafter, "Uncle Willy" had taken it upon himself to manage the petite heiress' minuscule estate, and he had applied her funds so that she could be raised by a housekeeper on her own ever-diminishing ranchette. Why, he'd even seen to it, after the homestead was finally parceled and sold, that there would be just enough money left after paying his costs and fees, to send Deborah off to a decent boarding school. He had eventually enrolled her at Stanford at his own expense. But then, in her final semester, she'd simply skipped off to New York to hang out with one little theater group or another. He had been disgusted to see that she had a tramp's instincts, just like her mother. However, after she'd had her first taste of the raw rejection this sort of business brings, Deborah had returned to California to sit at his knee. It took only one look at the lovely bud to convince him that a mutuality of uses yet remained—she being, naturally, of greater use to him than he would ever be to her.

Sitting close to Deborah like this, he could appraise her pearlescent beauty, which by far surpassed that of her mother. But still, a touch of plastic surgery here and there would do her some good. He had even explored this matter with Deborah and she had surprised him by quickly agreeing. She was ambitious, all right. All she really needed was to lose a few pounds, perhaps undergo a slight paring at the tip of the nose and the addition of a little touch of fullness to those already lovely lips and she'd be incomparable, more ravishing than her mother had ever been.

The waiter stood patiently, waiting for Mr. Ivener to order. With a nod of approval from Deborah, he ordered for both. Knowing that Deborah adored veal, he requested it prepared with a reduction of white wine and sherried butter, dressed with fresh lemons and capers, and accompanied by thin spears of sautéed baby asparagus lightly kissed with curried creme. He sat motionless for a moment, as if he were giving the matter deep thought, but really just to see if Deborah was impressed, then requested a dab of champagne sorbet to follow the entrée, "To clear milady's palate." For himself, it would be a simple piece of white fish, poached, no fats, no oils, and steamed broccoli without any salt. Willy waited until the waiter departed and then he picked up the thread of their conversation.

"You have to ask me something or *what's* all over?"

Taking a small sip of champagne and then wrinkling her nose, this time Deborah spoke quietly, in a sober voice. "Yes, Uncle Willy. I *need* a few answers. For instance, why did you plant me in Doc Clare's office? Isn't his wife the one you're really after? And just what *is* it you want from her, anyway?"

He knew Deborah was shooting randomly, trying to flush him out. She had this ability to sense his moods and sometimes even to guess his thoughts. He didn't like this.

Willy raised the flute of champagne to his lips as if to give it a kiss and then turned to Deborah and fixed her with a disapproving look. "My goodness! After her? You astonish me. What kind of talk is that? Let's just say I've got an *interest* in the Clares. Perhaps I can *help* them. You mustn't concern yourself about them, my dear. You merely have to obtain the records I want. I'll take it from there." Willy drew back from Deborah to let her know he'd be offended by any more questions along these lines.

He had a lot riding on the young woman, more than he ever wanted her to know—more than he wanted *anyone* to know—and he didn't need another curious cat hanging about his premises. Best for him to clip her whiskers immediately; besides, Deborah was merely an asset, a pawn—albeit the most attractive one in his portfolio—whom he intended to use for the extraction of additional mileage from his connections in the entertainment industry. And as Deborah well knew, this was to her benefit, since it was he who had acquired, through serving as tax counsel to the high mucky-mucks at the studios, the juice to launch her career from the top, thus sparing her years of clawing and struggling. But first, before he was willing to do this for her, there was this little acting job she had to complete for him.

His present arrangement had him paying her a generous $1000 up front and another $1000 when she finished her assignment. It was a fairly large sum for a girl her age, but still, not so large that it would allow her to escape his control.

Ivener gently stroked the dark fur of Deborah's wrap and then leaning back into the cushions, examined his godchild with a practiced eye. In his considered opinion, she had the look. Even without him, he knew that she'd make it—but this was the last thing he wanted her to realize. Even though she was only twenty-three, she was streetwise—unlike L.C., who was merely intelligent—and he had to remind himself every now and then that the creamy white mask that Deborah kept turned toward the world concealed a remarkably busy set of wheels.

Deborah interrupted. "Willy, that doesn't answer my question. What makes you think you can control L.C. through her husband? And why be so indirect? Even if I do get something on *him,* what makes you think she'd even give a damn? I wouldn't if I were her."

This time two waiters materialized, and Deborah paused until their dinners were served.

Willy made no attempt to answer, instead, he waited politely until Deborah attacked her asparagus and then he picked at his fish in silence. Deborah chewed daintily, and then seeing that he apparently intended to ignore her, she picked up a salad fork and twisted it in his direction in a small show of force. Raising her voice, she repeated her question.

Willy felt his heart race and then bump irregularly. He quickly delivered a series of sharp thumps to his chest, coughed, and then decided it would be best to throw her a few tidbits of information. "Harold Dolphe keeps me informed. The IRS is auditing the Clares and Dr. Clare ought to be worried, assuming, of course, that Dolphe's got his facts straight. You see, the Clares file joint tax returns and if the IRS goes after him, this would be devastating for her because she's a tax attorney. You were there when the two agents showed up, remember? And didn't you tell me you heard Clare say that his wife handles his paperwork? Sounds to me like her license is in jeopardy, not his. You see, when two or more agents show up unannounced, it's always a prelude to a criminal investigation. As I've already explained, I'm sure the good doctor's been skimming."

"Well, if Doc's already done the dirty deed, what can you possibly do for him after the fact?"

"Oh, there are plenty of things I could do for him. For example—I could shift the blame."

"You mean, to his wife? You can *do* that? How?"

"You're quick on the uptake, m'dear. Of course I could. How hard do you think it is to create a paper trail? If I wanted, I could create an incriminating file that would be more than enough to get her indicted. Whip up a few back-dated memos, that sort of thing. And I'll take bets that our Dr. Clare would help me, too. And don't forget about Margo—she'd do anything Clare told her to do—and *she* can testify against Mrs. Clare. This would get him off the hook with only a fine and leave poor Mrs. Clare totally vulnerable."

"What makes you think Clare would do something like that to *her* . . . his *wife*?"

Willy thought it was time to fog. "Listen, I was merely speaking hypothetically to give you an idea of what I could do. I'm not saying I *would* do this, in fact, I can assure you that I would do *none* of those things. However, I just want you to understand that should it get down to the machinations of marriage—and especially the Clare marriage—it could be a very changeable proposition. In any event, you needn't get involved in any of this. Just do your little job and then you can move on to larger matters."

He had thought about burglarizing L.C.'s law office, but after learning that it was wired, he'd changed his mind—furthermore, he couldn't risk having his own little Watergate added to his current load of tribulations. He had also considered offering L.C. a bribe by way of paying her a huge consultation fee in exchange for a bit of legal research—and then he'd realized this would serve only to further pique her curiosity. So he'd dropped this plan, because the last thing he needed was for her to catch on to what really was worrying him. Besides, Ms. Crusader Rabbit wasn't the sort who'd succumb to a bribe. That's why he'd hired the damn woman in the first place: to be his window dressing lawyer. Even if she didn't realize it, she certainly had the looks, and he had intended to use her for the same reason airlines featured female flight attendants: to convince the clientele they were in for a safe and glamorous ride. But, things hadn't turned out quite the way he'd hoped because L.C. just couldn't stop reading the law and questioning his way of doing things. Yes, the trouble with L.C. was that she thought she was going to be the pilot. He hadn't bargained on that.

Willy stared into space. He had to get his hands on L.C.'s tattle-tale tax article, and that damned secret rudder of hers, too.

He was brought back by Deborah, whose voice had developed an obsidian-sharp edge.

"I'm here to tell you something important." Deborah spoke firmly. "You're going to have to pay me another 5K up front . . . *and* an additional 10K for the entire job or else . . . or else I'm quitting!"

Willy could see that she meant it—her face was dead white and her eyes darkly serious.

"What do you mean, *quit*? You? Ending your career before it's even begun? Don't play games." Willy laughed, but raised a pale hand to his mouth.

"Uncle Willie, what I *mean* is just this: I fully intend to walk this job if you don't pay me extra for hazard-duty. You never said one *word* to me about Dr. Clare being a coke-head! And he certainly has some weird ideas of *fun*. I've seen him up close and personal and there's something about him that's absolutely unreal, like he's about to trip out—or explode in a rage. You never warned me about any of this! So, what do you expect?"

Willy, feeling cornered, cleared his throat. "Well, I expect you to do whatever it takes."

Deborah considered him for a moment, then in a softer voice said, "That's what I thought. Well, that's not going to come cheap. Do you know what I mean? Need I tell you more? The man's crazy. A pig. How'd *you* like to be trapped in the same room with a disgusting animal like that?"

"Well, as a matter of fact . . . if I were a bit younger I'd probably like it."

"Uncle Willy! How can you talk like that! This is no joking matter!"

As a matter of fact, Willy knew exactly what Deborah was talking about. He had studied Dr. Clare's dossier and had concluded that although the man appeared to have everything one could desire: looks, money, material success; close beneath that prosperous and glossy veneer was a greedy, shriveled soul with a troubled marriage, a drug habit, and furthermore and best of all—he seemed headed straight for a nervous breakdown. So, no. No he *didn't* want to hear anything more about the Clares. He just wanted results—hard evidence of tax fraud to dangle like a sword of Damocles over their heads. Especially Dr. Clare's; he wasn't about to forget that sick look he'd seen on his face the night before—part fear, part envy.

Willy Ivener picked up his napkin and pressed it hard to his mouth. "Deborah?" he said, pausing dramatically, watching her trying so awfully hard to read his face. "You're getting *tough*!" He chuckled softly just to put her at ease. "But I *like* you, and I trust you to do a good job for me. Let's say this—you'll receive an extra *three* thousand dollars because I want you to succeed in your long-range plans and because I get a great and genuine pleasure from that. But *please*—don't be so tough with your poor Uncle Willy."

"Uncle Willy! You're not listening. *Five*. Five thousand or I walk."

Willy decided it would be unwise to adopt a take-it-or-leave-it attitude at this stage of the game, besides, he would get more than his money's worth if he kept her a happy team player. Besides, he'd soon be managing her income, and this would allow him to recoup a hundred times over whatever she wangled out of him now. Besides, how far could she go on a few thousand more?

"Okay. All right. Five thousand it is. But that's *total*."

"Plus my contract with the studio?"

"Of course your contract with the studio—that goes without saying!"

Willy felt a sense of relief when he saw her leaning toward him to peck an appreciative kiss on his cheek .

Deborah hastily made ready to leave, as if she were sure he would change his mind if she stayed. "Oh Uncle Willy! I love you! I promise—you won't be disappointed." Pulling her wrap tightly around her voluptuous figure, but leaving one round white shoulder exposed, Deborah slid away from him. Her eyes twinkled back at him vivaciously, then she picked up her gloves as she stood up, waved them at him and then bent over the table and whispered: "I'll be seeing you in a couple of days . . . and since it's only $5000 please *do* make it cash."

Willy twinkled back at her and then watched her duck out the rear exit. *Five thousand dollars,* he told himself. *A bargain, because when I'm through, I'll have all of them out of my hair: Dr. Clare will frame L.C. for tax fraud, she'll lose her license, then I'll blackmail the shit out of him. He'll end up doing whatever I say. Right now, however—he's going get me that damn foreign foundation tax article . . . and keep that big mouth of his zipped, too.*

◆❖◆

Willy Ivener always bet on himself; a virtue he'd quickly acquired as a youth when he first began running numbers for the local fathers. Even then he had known the score: There were only two basic tenets in life: *How much?* and *Who gets?* He'd spent the rest of his life answering those two questions. And since he was not so much a gambler as an investor engaged in the business of gaming, he knew that the key to winning any game was keeping to the side with the most favorable odds—so the first thing he'd mastered was stacking the deck. Not boldly, but subtly, insidiously. And thanks to the careful way he'd made book all through law school, by the time he passed the bar exam the nut he'd accumulated had grown so large he was able to afford his own law office without having to do any time at a major law firm. He had applied the same philosophy to his practice and thus he had never raised any of his associates to partner—he bonded them with luxurious perks and a pleasurable environment not found at other firms—which had afforded him the even greater luxury of keeping both the source and the amount of his income a mystery throughout his entire career.

Ivener thought about this as he sat hunched over his simple dish of poached pears, and then for some reason he thought about his mother and recalled her advice. She had always said that taking in only the big picture would never be enough to guarantee one's success. *"One must also attend to the smallest details of any plan, so don't you ever forget . . . it's the smallest of them that might lead to your death"* was what she had warned. But why was he remembering this now? To his mind her warning must have had something to do with women—they were the sort of details a man had to tend to, every now and then.. For instance, take L.C.—now here was a detail that required some attention!

He'd taken her into his firm because he could tell she was one of those Good Girls—not at all like Deborah—carefully wounded while raised so that she would end up with a Good Girl's need to prove that she was one, which in turn meant she could always be counted on to make herself useful. Every bit as bright, if not brighter, than Harold Dolphe, L. C. possessed two additional qualities that had made her especially attractive to him as an associate: She was both tender-hearted and inexperienced, which had led him to assume—perhaps a trifle mistakenly—that she would be far more malleable than that obsequious toad, Dolphe. So, on a whim, he had added this youthful woman lawyer to his roster. And he'd also relished the idea of her serving him instead of that fool she had married. Then, after a month of observing her, he had come to realize that she was starved for appreciation, which meant he could turn her cheaply—with praise—while paying her half the salary he was paying Dolphe. Yes, if only she had stayed on—she would have provided terrific window-dressing for his firm.

She had been useful to him for almost a year . . . and then she had quit! He had not been pleased. And now she was competing with him. Ferociously, too, which came as quite a surprise. But no matter, she'd soon be fixed to his liking. And he had learned his lesson: He would not make the same mistake by letting the leash go slack on Deborah. Ivener dabbed at his lips as if to punctuate his thoughts. He had larger matters to attend to than these women, and by far the most important of them was the state of his health.

Slim to begin with, he had been steadily losing weight and feeling wrung out, but so far his physicians couldn't find what, if anything, was wrong with him. This had been going on now for almost six months, long before his indictment for tax fraud, and it annoyed him no end to have to listen to them prattling on as to how his symptoms were due to stress. It wasn't stress. Stress he could handle. He could tell it was something else.

Willy Ivener lifted his spoon and his immaculate cuff slid down to reveal the same strange splotches of color—the color of eggplant—at the side of his wrist as he now had concealed under the theatrical makeup at his temples. He observed the new stains only long enough to idly wonder why he hadn't noticed them before and then his thoughts slid back to his usual obsession: The Wei.

Truly his baby, The Wei; he was determined to protect it.

His idea for the scheme had sprung from his youthful LSD-laced foragings into Buddhist and Hindu philosophies, from which he had skimmed a few arcane bromides in order to fashion its hip mumbo-jumbo. At first he had wanted to call his new enterprise *The Willow*—the meaning behind his first name—but then he had astutely reasoned that the American public would be more entranced by something more exotic sounding, something that would call up the perceived mysteries of the India or the Far East. So L.C. was right—he had fashioned an acronym from his initials, William Edgar Ivener, and had come up with *The Wei*. The name sounded great and it had been a most happy coincidence that it also spelled out a Chinese word which, loosely translated, meant *The Path*.

The Wei promised the Wei-farers who "Got It"—If you had to ask *Get what?* then you still didn't "Get It"—a road to success by way of "Getting Your Life to Working for You." And to gain entrance to this fabulous garden of bliss you needed only to come up with a few hundred bucks. Such a deal! Who would be able to resist?

Actually, it was a bit more complicated than that, what with all the clever contracts he'd contrived to intimidate and entrap the dumb mooches. The Wei-farer's quest for self-empowerment began at a mere $350, and for those who were hooked, it quickly escalated to $700, which the sheep were more than willing to pay to get into his "Advanced Training Courses." And for *only* another few thou, a Wei-farer could be allowed to enjoy a private lodge on the Nevada side of Lake Tahoe and partake in a wide range of highly personalized body-work courses in a jurisdiction where self-indulgence was not seen as a crime.

Had it worked? Well, it had certainly Gotten Life Working for *him*.

The millions that had come rolling in over the past ten years stood as a testament to his brilliant and farsighted planning. In California alone, hundreds of thousands of people had forked over their hard-earned dollars so they could join up with his New Age self-empowerment movement where they could get their warm fuzzies by surrendering their sense to its spoon-fed group-think. And for *only* $25.00 more, there was even a flag that a Wei-farer could hang on his wall at home! In fact, at this very minute, his new offshore division was shipping thousands of coffee mugs and T-shirts and banners from Taiwan to be merchandised to the Wei-farers at a tidy tax-free profit throughout the United States. Willy chuckled, bemused. California was such a glory-hole for all these self-empowerment movements and The Wei was the slickest and the tightest run of them all; quite simply, it was the best idea he'd ever had.

The Wei had become an invincible movement. Its tentacles now extended into the highest echelons of the state's procurement offices. It had even spread into the prison system so that the inmates could enjoy the search for self-realization and enlightenment at taxpayer expense. If things kept rolling along in this fashion, he'd soon have a nation of obedient dead-heads who would jiggle and dance to any tune he played. But he had lost his interest in this side of politics; all he cared about now was making sure that his final killing would be large enough to allow him to fold everything and slip away. The time had come—albeit sooner than he had anticipated—for him to give this alternative some serious thought.

There had been some new and unforeseen developments.

Until recently, most people had never heard of tax havens and few had any reason to think about them. But this was changing fast because the media had begun to editorialize about the "fat-cats who were using tax loopholes to send their money offshore where it couldn't be taxed." A big noise had suddenly arisen in Congress, and the Treasury Department—and specifically the Ways and Means Committee—wished to put a stop to all such activities, which meant there was little time left to waste. In fact it was perfectly obvious that his well-publicized indictment was an important part of the government's overall scheme to scare taxpayers away from offshore tax-dabbling. And this time it was different, because this time the government needed a conviction so that he would serve as an object lesson to all the others who wanted to swim in his school. Well, he would just have to show the Treasury Department all over again that it just couldn't win.

He'd quickly set his snoops to work in the Capital, and they had just given him some splendid news: although practically everything pertaining to tax havens was going to be shut down, so far the tax laws relating to foreign foundations were going to be left alone—at least, for now. This was wonderful, because foreign foundations were the key to his entire operation. So now he had only to focus on two main objectives, but these were of crucial importance: First, he had to ensure that the House Committee on Ways and Means would not stick its big nose into the realm of foreign foundations, and second, he had to keep his indictment from enveloping The Wei. Fortunately, the IRS still thought The Wei was just another one of his clients, which allowed him to hide behind the privileged information defense—but if it should ever get wind of the fact that he and The Wei were one and the same, this defense would be lost and the whole scheme would unravel. And should the IRS ever get its hands on the archives which showed that The Wei was merely a small cog in what was now a gigantic international profit-making combine—and therefore not the least bit exempt from taxation—the agency would search for The Wei's assets and seize them.

That was why he was having all these documents moved—it was his humble opinion that it no longer was prudent to store them in the Bahamas. The government there was unstable—as were some of its bureaucrats, who were becoming bolder about extracting a little mordito for their own selves, and he was afraid that blackmailing a wealthy white U.S. citizen might soon be seen as the most profitable way for them to go. When it came to lining their own pockets, these politicians weren't stupid.

As for the foreign foundations, they had been set up many years ago in the Bahamas by an elderly client who had never quite grasped the significance of what he had been advised to do. After he passed on, absolutely no one had ever thought to inquire as to who would be managing them in the future. As a matter of fact, there would be no change; from the beginning, Ivener had always operated them himself. Just as soon as he saw that The Wei was about to become a gigantic cash cow, he'd promptly transferred "The Wei Program Format" to his offshore foundations. Then, after a couple of years, he'd had these same foundations license the format back to a large number of seemingly unrelated United States charitable corporations—at an *enormously* stepped-up basis. This scheme allowed huge sums—disguised as "royalties and licensing fees"—to be extracted and shunted offshore. Once offshore, the money could then be recycled, again tax-free, through his corporations in the Bahamas.

Even more incredible—all of this had been going on for years and years without the least bit of scrutiny or governmental interference from anyone on either side of the equation. Thus, through an additional twist in the skein of his laundering operations, he had reinvested substantial amounts, tax-free, in the United States. The U.S. was a tax haven in and of itself—but only for foreign capital—which was what his now laundered money appeared to be. Meanwhile, new money continued to pour in. He had millions parked in the U.S. via domestic trusts and holding companies and partnerships controlled by his dummy trustees and fake directors. And no matter how fantastically complicated these operations might appear to an outsider, it had really been quite simple for someone like him. Thus, when Dolphe told him about L.C. and her illuminating article about foreign foundations, he had wondered what on earth she was up to. What did she plan to do? Show the IRS how to reach out and pluck him?

The possibility of such a calamitous turn of events had startled him into action. He put his new crop of law clerks to work on researching the law and they had found a glimmer of light at the end of the tunnel: So far, nothing had ever been published on the subject of taxing foreign foundations. L.C.'s article would be the first. Thus, until it was, he could still marshal an argument that the tax laws were so incomprehensible that it was anyone's guess as to what they actually meant—this would give him the ambiguity defense. Perfect. And he needed things to stay this way. Close to a billion dollars was at stake here. All he needed was just a little more time—another year at the most—so that he could purchase an island, establish his own government and then he'd have a tax haven of his own. Then he could skip the country and thumb his nose at the lot of them. For the time being, however, he had to stay put and make sure that his schemes weren't prematurely exposed.

Thus, should L.C.'s article be published right now, while Congress was in an uproar, it could be used as a key to opening up The Wei to public scrutiny and then the Ways and Means Committee would be after him, tooth and claw. This couldn't be allowed to happen. And now that he thought about it, there was another question: What had set L.C.'s mind to this peculiar task? Had she found her way into his secret files? This was why he had to get into her rudder—he had to see if it held any clues as to what she was thinking and who she was seeing. What if all this time she had been a spy? Working hand in glove with some of those new agents in the IRS Special Services Division? Come to think of it, why else would she have been so curious about whether his initials had some connection to The Wei?

CAYMAN Tuesday evening - February 26, 1974

Pleased that he had succeeded in stirring up the Bear, Dolphe returned to his hotel, where he unpacked his phone scrambler, attached it to the phone jack, then plugged it in and requested the hotel operator to connect him to a long distance line. Dolphe flipped on the switch, dialed the code to Ivener's office and as soon as Ivener's code registered on his scrambler, Dolphe pressed his mouth to the receiver and spoke without any salutation: "Five trusts this trip. Could *not* find rudder. Took photos of her. Facilities are ready." Dolphe rang off without speaking, knowing that Ivener would never reply. He packed up his scrambler, and then he began to think about L.C. while he rummaged around in his laundry, trying to find some clean underwear.

"What if she were set up to look like a snitch!" Dolphe exclaimed. What a brilliant idea. She'd be black-balled forever. Then Ivener would have an easy defense—he could argue for a dismissal on the grounds that the charges against him were based on privileged information that L.C. had leaked to the IRS! The fall-out would be stupendous. L.C.'s practice would dry up tighter than a nun's pussy once the word got out that she was a government informant! Ivener would be rid of his competition, and *he,* Harold Dolphe, would be Saturday's hero. Then Ivener would make him a partner and then he would be able to root around like a gopher in all those juicy offshore accounts.

Great plan, but how could he make it all happen? Unless he had proof, some kind of hard evidence to pin on L.C., the scheme could very well backfire on him because Ivener might think *he* was a snitch if it looked like he was trying too hard to slime her. Even so, the concept *was* brilliant, it just needed more work.

When Dolphe stood up to dress, he saw that the very idea of screwing his nemesis had made a very nice crotch-bird fly up in his tent. Which reminded him . . . there were two girls waiting for him at the beach bar. Happily, the night was still young, and he had just enough energy left to have a little fun of his own. Dolphe whistled while he dashed some cologne under his arms. Then he patted a fistful of bath powder on his belly. First a thick gold chain around his neck, then a clean polyester Hawaiian shirt, and he was *ready*! Harold Dolphe grabbed his dive-bag—the one that was crammed with his overnight gear—he had this feeling that he was going to get lucky tonight.

CAYMAN—Seven Mile Beach Wednesday - February 27, 1974

For what seemed like the first time in years, Linnell awoke with a sense of joy. She was free! She rolled over and looked at her watch on the bedside table. Wonderful news—she had slept for almost twelve hours. She yawned and stretched lazily. Stiff from sleeping so hard, she rolled out of bed and hobbled slowly over to the door to the balcony where she leaned for a moment to restore her balance, then she cranked it open so that she could listen to the sound of the waves and inhale the warm air. Translucent ultramarine greeted her eyes, with air and sea heading off to a magnetic infinity with no discernible break at the bleached-white horizon.

She was amazed by the quality of blue nearest shore—a luminescent sapphire that she'd seen nowhere else in the world—and the length of the opaline rollers slapping languorously over the crest of Seven Mile Beach. Still in her pajamas, Linnell stepped out onto her balcony to look down the beach, and saw three couples holding hands, carefully spaced and slowly strolling inside their bubbles of love toward the next hotel. Honeymooners, she guessed; she watched them with a touch of envy until they disappeared behind the trees.

For a moment there was absolute silence. No birds crying into the wind and no voices floating up from the beach bar. Closing her eyes and tipping up her face to receive the sun, Linnell abandoned herself to the bliss of not thinking. Perhaps there really were Loas who rose at dawn to exhale perfumed blessings into the wind. Linnell tossed her hair over her shoulders and stepped closer to the balcony rail and began her Tai Chi regimen of slow movements and ritualized poses. With her hands held high overhead, Linnell began to slowly bend from side to side and then she was surprised to feel a cool breath of wind blowing across her chest. She stopped, looked down, and found that her top had come entirely unbuttoned. Glancing around, Linnell was relieved to see that—thank goodness!—the other balconies were empty. She laughed aloud at her silly mishap and hastily buttoned up before stepping back into her room. Today was the day she'd been waiting for and now it was all hers.

"Gotcha!" Dolphe whispered to himself. He placed the black cap over the expensive telephoto lens to keep the light from reflecting off the lens and tipping L.C. to his presence. This would more than make up for the lonely night he'd just spent passed out in the bushes in front of the hotel.

He'd shot his entire wad buying drinks for the chicks until he was sure they would float away on their very own tide—which they eventually did, at 3 a.m.—without taking him with them. Infuriated, he'd grabbed a mat from one of the chairs in front of the hotel and had retreated with it to sulk in the bushes. Waking up in an evil mood, he had focused his camera on L.C.'s balcony just in case he could catch her fooling around with another man. No luck with that, but this last shot was super! And he'd caught her flashing a whole lot more than that famous smile of hers, too. Along with the terrific photos from the day before, he now had more than enough evidence to corroborate the story he'd soon be telling "The King."

Talk about irreconcilable differences! Dolphe stroked his camera. It would take only one look at these photos to get Doc to want to dump L.C. flat on her ass. And the beauty of it, thanks to "no-fault," was that he could dump her without having to give her so much as an explanation, and he, Harold Dolphe, would see to it that Doc never did because—knowing L.C. and her curiosity about what made everything tick—this would just drive her nuts!

Dolphe, now satisfied that his mission was complete, unscrewed his telephoto lens and shoved his equipment back into his satchel. At last, he was free to finish the day any way he chose. He would take a cab over to the warehouse to give it a final check, then he'd have a big lunch, and then he'd be free to spend the rest of the day on the South End just loafing and fishing.

RISK

Linnell checked her telephone—the light wasn't blinking. Good! This had to mean that everything was fine at home. That being the case, the first thing on her agenda today would be calling Colin's office and leaving the code-words that signaled "transaction complete," then all that money in the escrow account would be hers alone. She'd always imagined herself feeling elated at this point, but now that her dream was realized, she actually felt rather flat and matter-of-fact. In fact, a bit empty now. There was only one more thing she felt she had left to do—and that was drafting a testamentary trust for herself and Benjy. She had decided this would be necessary after all. Bear would never have to know about it, in fact, nobody except Colin would ever know—unless she died, and then who cares? She wouldn't be here to face the music.

Linnell completed this task in fifteen minutes flat and then—she couldn't explain why, perhaps it was instinct—she set up her briefcase exactly the same as the day before, making sure that the little red bead was fast in the clasp. After tying on her lavender bikini and sliding into her sandals, she wrapped a towel around her hips, pinned her room key inside her suit, and hurried down to the lobby to buy a large straw hat and another bottle of sun screen.

With her new hat in one hand and her sandals in the other, Linnell sprinted over the burning sand toward the water. She dropped her sandals at the log and draped the towel over her sunburned back while she slathered herself with sun screen. Great day. Perfect weather. After tucking her hair under her broad-rimmed hat, she chose her direction. North? North it would be. To the next small hotel for the excellent lunch it served at water's edge. She would have a large mid-day meal, take a nap, and then hitch a ride back to her hotel for a swim in front of the hotel, where, thanks to her successful enterprise, no sea urchins lurked to jab at her feet.

Linnell jogged along the edge of the water and sang: *Free! I am free! Free from sorting socks and folding towels. Free from angry looks and daily snarls.* And what was she free for? she asked herself. *For Life!* she answered joyfully. When she reached the line of breadfruit trees in front of the small hotel, she fell silent. Pretending she was an agent on a top secret assignment, she dodged from tree to tree as if she were on a reconnaissance mission.

"*Yo*! L.C.! *I* see you sneaking 'round. What you doin' baby?"

"Oh! Hi, Henry. I'm fine. Just sneakin' up on you, is all. Good to see you, again." Linnell blushed. She hoped Henry wouldn't guess that she had been playing Let's Pretend. "And so what's for lunch today?" She tried to speak with the offhanded nonchalance of one who was accustomed to eating lunch there every day, but a squeak of laughter gave her away.

Henry grinned as if he were on to her and handed her a menu. She draped her towel over a bar stool and sat down to order. She was surprised to find the place almost deserted. Dead. Then she realized that although this was her day off, everybody else she knew would be working. As for the bankers—they were most likely downing their first drink of the day. Probably what Colin was doing right about now, especially if his secretary had just given him the news about the speedy completion of her project.

Linnell ordered lunch and told Henry to put it on her tab. What she really liked about this side of the island was the way hotels allowed regular visitors to run a tab at any watering hole on Seven Mile Beach. She only had to leave her name and where she was staying and her charges would appear on her hotel bill. It was a great arrangement, because this way she could spend the entire day on the beach without having to worry about carrying money.

A spicy aroma announced the arrival of lunch. Henry set down a loaded tray and disappeared to take a nap, leaving her all alone with a platter of shrimp gumbo, fragrant with Jamaican spices and embellished with spears of fresh papaya. A sweating pitcher of iced tea, sliced lemons resting on a plate of brown sugar, and a crusty fresh-baked roll balanced the meal, but there were no utensils and only one cotton napkin. Well then, she would eat with her fingers and guzzle straight from the pitcher! Linnell carried her feast to the large flat rock that stuck up in the middle of the tide pool in front of the small pelapa. She planned to sit down on the rock so she could watch the fat orange-tailed fish, tame as dogs, roiling the water as they fought for her scraps.

Linnell savored every bite and when she was finished, she rinsed her hands in the tide pool, then wadding up her towel to serve as her pillow, she found a breadfruit tree, lay down in its shade, and fell asleep in the sand.

She did not know how long she'd slept, but when she awoke, it was as if to a world before man, and like earlier that morning, there was no sound except for the muffled thump of the waves. The air, heavy with a quietude bordering on the ominous, possessed a new quality which made the sunlight seem thick. Still sleepy, Linnell waded slowly into the water and out to the edge of the shallows and stood like the tiniest of golden spikes, a singularity amidst the grand emptiness. To the west there was only a vast expanse of jittery water, a vibrating arc beneath the charged blue sky. The glare was all encompassing, as if the glacial whiteness had crystallized, suspending her inside, and whenever she turned her head, even slightly, tight twists of heat devils shimmered at the corners of her eyes, signaling those spots where the wind was down. Linnell shaded her eyes with both hands, then froze, captured by the sight of the majestic wave that was mounting off shore. A sharp crack, followed by a resonant boom, heralded its near arrival.

Her eyes widened in shock.

Linnell was sure of it. It was Her. The great Efik Ba-Abaloah, rising up from the deep. The wave, a visible manifestation of Her awesome power. Rising, then curling into a translucent tube of staggering length, it expanded to blot out the horizon and Her breath fluted through its gigantic morning glory throat as the wave mounted higher and higher, tons of water into the sun, until the blue wall collapsed with thunder into millions of foam-rimmed trapezoids that roared toward the shore.

A torrent surged over Linnell's shoulders. As if caught in a dream, she felt the sand slipping away from beneath her feet. Still slow from her nap, Linnell gasped for air and tried desperately to tread water as she felt herself being lifted and turned upside-down. Clamping her eyes shut, she clenched her teeth against the onslaught, but salt water drove deep into her sinuses and her shoulders burned as she was dragged, helpless, across the stirred sandy floor.

Linnell was still aware, she knew she was being tugged out to sea. Toward the abyss where her body would never be found. She struggled with all her might against the tide but was held firmly in its grip. *It's all over*, she thought. *I'm fish-food* . . . Her throat burned with the fires of exhaustion. Her thoughts blurred. And just then, Linnell felt herself rising up from the deep. She opened her eyes and through turbid water glimpsed silvery daylight above her head. An invisible hand again flipped her head-over-heels and this time sent her flying toward shore.

The water sank down and a stunned Linnell found herself planted, amazed and upright, on the beach, her journey complete. Salt water streamed from her hair, nose and mouth. Awestruck and trembling, she watched Ba-Abaloah drawing Her power back into Her skirts, then with frightening majesty, roll slowly up the coast, flinging Her cape into the silence that followed like a meek courtier at Her heels. A final glaze of warm water was sent skimming across the white pan to end with a hiss at Linnell's sun-browned feet.

"I'm still here." Linnell howled into the wind. "I'm alive!" A plume of water became discrete beads of silver in the distance. She could see each one loft high into the sun, transformed into mist. Watching them sparkling in the breeze, for a split-second Linnell could feel the wheel of the great white-sailed ship as it careened through the heart of the universe. Just as suddenly, the mist evaporated, the breeze disappeared, and the sea flattened itself into a checkered apron of flickering wavelets.

It was over.

Linnell felt as if she had been sucked into a different dimension, then spit back to earth. Yes, it was a miracle . . . the Loa had found her, they had pulled her away from death's cape. Her knees were still wobbly, but after only a few steps, the trembling stopped. She stepped out of the water just as lush guitar chords poured from the grove behind the pelapa.

Very much back to reality now, Linnell found the melody familiar. It was one of the musicians from her hotel, hiding out up here to rehearse. When the rhythm finally settled into a steady Bossa Nova beat, Linnell grabbed her hat and her towel and walked with measured composure across the sand toward the road in front of the hotel. In the distance, she saw a long black Lincoln. After what she'd just been through, somehow she was not at all surprised.

◆❖◆

Linnell sat very soberly in the air-conditioned car. Right away Mama N'dobah had understood that something important had just happened to Linnell and so after they exchanged greetings, Mama allowed Linnell to remain at her side without any small talk.

Linnell had at first tried to explain the wave, and had asked Mama to tell her more about the Loa, but Mama N'dobah replied that Linnell should accept, and at the right time, she would understand. With that advice, Mama fell silent.

Linnell fell silent too. She had been saved. Snatched from the deep. By the whim of the Loa? Were there really such miracles? Or a reason? She looked down, deep in thought, wondering who, if not Mama, could answer these questions. "I have my life," she said finally, not realizing she was speaking aloud.

"You say Life? What for you talkin' 'bout life, woman?" Mama asked.

"Life? Is that what I was saying?"

"Sure did, honey. Well, you wanna know 'bout life? I can tell you somethin' about *that*."

"Oh, please do. I can always use some help," replied Linnell.

"It's like this . . . There's some that jus' wanna know. And there's others who don't wanna know, they jus' wanna do. And then you got some who jus' don' givva shit. So all *you* gotta do is jus' sort 'em out and then life is simple. And dearie?"

"Yes?" At the same time that Linnell wanted to believe what Mamma said—or, more accurately put, that Mama believed what she was saying—Linnell sometimes wondered if the woman might be putting her on.

"Heads up for people who do only one." Mama chuckled.

"Yes. I think you're really on to something there. And which are you? What do you do?"

"Little bitta all. See? I be well-rounded." Mama grinned at her.

Linnell laughed. She felt better. And then Linnell really thought about it. Maybe that was why, as Bear said, sometimes she just didn't get it. Maybe she'd be much better off if she not only tried harder to broaden her thinking—but learned how to think in an entirely new way. Just what this new way was, however, she didn't yet know. She'd have to think about it.

"You still be with the animal?" Mama asked.

"You mean my husband, Bear. Yeah. I still am. But, I dunno. Sometimes it feels too much like I'm on a forced march. The way things are now, I don't know how much longer I'm going to last. But when I go home, I'm going to try making some changes . . . although I've got Benjy to think of, you know."

"Don't you go and get all hung up on your child. You happy? He be happy too. You use the think-needles like I taught you to?" asked Mama, abruptly changing the subject.

"Well, yes and no. I'm practicing. Just not on Bear. At least, not yet. How will I know it's working?" Linnell asked.

"When it's right. You'll know." Mama laughed her mysterious laugh, then nodded her head.

◆❖◆

Although she didn't quite know why Mama N'dobah had taken a liking to her, Linnell was grateful it was a liking and not something else. After telling Mama N'dobah that she hoped they'd meet again real soon, she thanked her for the ride and then stepped from the air-conditioned car into a wall of searing heat. The salt that had dried on her face made it feel like a mask, and now her nose, drying instantly, began to itch; Linnell drew a sandy finger across her forehead to lift her hair from her forehead so she could scan the ocean through the arches of the hotel lobby. A few long clouds hung low on the horizon. It promised to be a sultry evening. She could see that she wasn't the only one to be knocked out by the heat. A group of recently arrived guests stood in the shade of the hotel's entry portico, while the doorman, fanning himself with a folded Wall Street Journal, directed the sweating porters who were sorting luggage and air tanks and diving gear. It had to be the last flight from Houston. She put on her hat so she could study them from under its brim.

It was actually the lone traveler who had her attention. Linnell automatically took in his confident stance, and then, when he turned, her heart gave a startled thump. Oh-my-god! thought Linnell. This is some face! From brow to chin, his features were symmetrical and sensual without tending in any way toward the feminine. By what trick has nature made this possible? She wanted to study him longer, to pinpoint the secret of his face, but he turned away the instant he caught her stare. Had she made him feel self-conscious? she wondered. Oh, surely not. A man with his looks would certainly be long accustomed to stares. She quickly took measure of the depth of his chest and the width of his shoulders and then let her eyes lock on his back.

Oh, *fabulous*! thought Linnell, giving thanks for the way his torso tapered without indenting too much at the waist. He was a perfect specimen. Glossy with good health. Much better than that ideal man she had been so methodically fashioning in her head. And best of all, he was not too tall. In fact, he was exactly the right height when measured against her legs. And yes! It was almost too much to ask for, but there they were: small round buns in perfectly fitted khakis. He kept them turned in her direction and her eyes lingered on them for a moment more and then slowly rose to again take in his broad-shouldered back. He was bulked to perfection; *meaty,* she thought. And she was a wolf and here was a feast! She stared at him hungrily, waiting for him to move, and when he did she could feel her teeth sinking into the delicious triangle of muscle that swelled between his shoulders and neck. Chew him down to the bone, she thought. Deliberately slowing her feet, she skirted the group with a racing heart, hoping for another look at his sphinx-perfect face. She sent a thought-wave in his direction and willed him to turn around. To point that perfect nose at her just one more time!

But he didn't.

Disappointed, she sighed audibly, almost comically, and with a quick flick of her wrist, snapped her beach towel around her hips and stepped lightly through the arches into the hotel lobby.

She was happy; so happy to be alive, and so lucky to witness such marvelous things. Linnell floated through the hotel and all the way down the path to the beach. Tossing her hat and her towel on the log, Linnell sprinted across the burning sand and then dove without fear, straight as an arrow, through the curling top of a warm breaking wave. Still, the stranger's face remained in her mind, and by the time her feet finally found the sandy floor, she was already reminding herself that she'd been done in by another handsome face once before—the face of Mark Clare.

◆❖◆

Robert Jordan spotted his subject immediately. He instinctively turned in the direction of the set of perfect ankles and golden thighs that emerged from the car. He didn't know why, but he'd had a feeling this might be her, and when he caught a glimpse of her face, he knew he was right. Now it would take all of his might to keep from turning around to stare at her as she walked behind his back. Wow! Was he dreaming, or what? He'd seen bathing suits like hers—ring bikinis, with the strategically placed top and scanty bottom held together at the navel by a large ring—but never in his life had he ever been so close to one that was so perfectly packed. He could tell she was only a few feet away. He hadn't expected anything like this. She was a knock-out! That small head-shot of her in the IRS file didn't come near to doing her justice. Damn! What a wonderful assignment!

Then he slammed on the brakes. Better get a grip! Jordan told himself. He forced himself to turn slowly on his heels, making sure that his back would be turned in her direction when she passed. He didn't want her to see his face. But he could tell she was staring at him because he could feel a burning sensation between his shoulder blades. The mavens were very clever, very perceptive, he reminded himself. Could she be on to him so soon?

He glanced at his watch: He'd won the bet.

He had arrived forty-five minutes ago, on the afternoon flight from Houston, and everyone in his party had been left to roast in the stifling Cayman Islands customs house until a taxi could be found to take his group to this side of the island. Now he was thirsty and stunned by the heat. He decided he'd better not stop for a drink because he didn't want to risk losing her. Jordan's shirt was already half-unbuttoned and his tie hung loose around his neck—he pulled it off and stuffed it in his jacket pocket, then looping his jacket over his thumb, he tossed it casually over his shoulder and discreetly stalked his subject through the hotel. When he reached the small parapet that separated the dining room from the courtyard, he sprang easily to the top of the low broad wall so that he could look between the shaded columns. He finally spotted her out in the water, bodysurfing in the curl of a breaking wave. He watched, fascinated, studying the way she moved.

Like he'd seen Rizzo do it, Robert Jordan unbuttoned his shirt with one hand and then he became aware of the perspiration trickling down the small of his back. He stiffened—there also were eyes on the back of his head. He wheeled around as he stepped off the wall and caught the beady stare of this poor slob whose raw meat red face seemed frozen in a look of pure envy. Jordan couldn't understand the why of such an intense expression, but the guy really had a serious sunburn and the weirdest reddish-brown hair he'd ever seen. Jordan acknowledged the red-nosed young man with a friendly nod and immediately turned back to his subject.

"Amphitrite into the waves . . . like a flash of lavender light," Jordan said to himself. He next chose a few words to describe her body: "High curves, long limbs, a golden water-goddess, beautiful of face and full of grace." Useful words—he would save them for later. He was not surprised by his having automatically composed a few lines of poetry for her—this had proven to be a highly profitable habit, the outcome of a course he'd taken at Michigan State University. Before opting for a more practical major of business and accounting, he'd had one semester of *Ancient Civilizations* at MSU. The class, even though outside his field, had served him well because it had led him to invent some really good lines. Not that he had to chase women all that much. They usually chased him, which was just fine with him since this tended to broaden his experience. In any event, he'd learned that all women—even the frostiest—loved it when he likened them to a goddess, especially when he could tell them which one. And this one was Amphitrite—Goddess of the Sea—long-limbed, top-heavy, obviously lively and athletic. With an enchanting, yet somehow slightly intimidating face. He looked forward to studying it more closely. Jordan rehearsed in his mind what he would say should he happen to bump into her later that evening. Maybe she would be in the hotel bar tonight? He caught himself short. Hold on here! he told himself. This is supposed to be strictly a working trip, and he'd better not forget it.

Pleasurable though they were, Robert Jordan knew better than to get lost in his dreams. He'd better stick fast to reality—and reality, for him, for the next several months required him to keep a steady foot on the first rung of the ladder that stood before him now. It was going to be a long climb, but he was determined to reach the top plateau of a major accounting firm, hopefully in the international division. Right now he was just doing his time at the IRS because he needed the money so he could afford to go on boning up for his CPA. exam. And so did his folks—his dad had recently been felled by a stroke, and after twenty years, his mom was now back to work, trying to hold things together by slaving part-time at some crummy job that only paid her two bucks an hour before taxes! His folks were the self-reliant sort who would never ask anybody for anything, so he was determined to help them. His plan was to put in a year at the IRS and then move on.

He was here now as a matter of stubborn persistence: He'd heard that Edgardo, the agent who'd been assigned to Cayman for the past several months, had been assigned to a case on the opposite side of the island, which had given Jordan a chance to beg for an offshore assignment. He'd always yearned to visit the Caribbean and this was the only way he could afford it. He'd finally persuaded Rizzo to send him instead of a Miami-based agent by pointing out that he already knew the case history better than anyone else and that it wouldn't take him any two days to locate Mrs. Clare. Having reviewed the tapes of her telephone calls, he knew exactly where to find her—from her conversation with her housekeeper. In fact, he had bet Rizzo twenty bucks that he would find the subject within one hour of his arrival. Rizzo, who was quick to appreciate that time was money, finally agreed—albeit reluctantly, since Jordan had been with the IRS for only six months.

Rizzo had kept him in suspense until the very last minute, which meant that he'd had only a half hour to pack and get to SFO in order to make the flight to Houston where he had to change planes and catch the afternoon flight on Cayman Airways. Because of the fog at SFO, all flights had been delayed, so he'd managed to make his connections by the skin of his teeth. Then there had been that delay after they'd landed at Owen Roberts Airport; but despite everything, he had nevertheless made himself an easy twenty bucks. And now he would have plenty of time to spend on the beach because his meeting with Edgardo wasn't scheduled until 10 this evening.

His assignment seemed simple enough: He was to keep the subject under surveillance so that he could determine whether she was socking Dr. Clare's skim into a secret bank account. Jordan had been hastily briefed and from reading between the lines, he knew there were no limits on what he might do. With one exception, however, and he could now see it was going to be a big one: Rizzo had warned: "Just be sure to make things look right—so you'd better not get *involved*, if you know what I mean." Jordan knew what that meant. Rizzo wasn't easy, so if he wanted to get around him he'd have to play it cool. Rizzo had said that Linnell was now 35, and her dossier stated that she had been married for fourteen years. This surprised him because the head-shot of her in his file—with bangs and a pony tail—made her look like a teenager. He'd also learned that she had a seven-year-old named Benjy, and he could remember thinking, when he saw this, that when he was twenty-one, his subject had already been married for nearly eight years.

Jordan returned to the lobby and found the pay phone, called the Miami office, and with a few coded words, alerted them to the fact that he'd locked onto his subject. They would relay this information to Rizzo. Now that the line was gone, Jordan approached the front desk. The secretary for the Special Services group had booked him into a beach-side room next to Mrs. Clare's, and as soon as the desk clerk handed Jordan his key, he told the clerk to skip the maid service—he didn't want to be disturbed at all during his stay—and headed up to the second floor.

Jordan liked his room. It was bright, clean, and comfortable, but not fancy, with a balcony overlooking the beach. And it had a big king-sized bed, Jordan was pleased to observe. Tossing his duffel bag down on the bed, he tore off his clothes and pulled on his old khaki shorts. His next discovery was that he'd forgotten his flip-flops. Well, he would have to go barefoot until he could buy a pair. In this half-dressed state, Jordan let himself into the subject's room with a standard matrix master-key. He planted the bugs the way he'd been taught: First, he inserted a powerful, miniaturized model—new technology—under the plastic cover of the telephone wall outlet and then he taped the other one—an older model, the size of a pack of cards, perfectly functional but more or less a decoy—to the backside of the night-stand at the side of her bed. Very clever, he thought, because the subject might stumble upon the transmitter behind the night-stand, destroy it, and then speak even more freely than before.

Jordan laughed when he saw how Mrs. Clare had set up her briefcase. He spotted the pins and had to wonder what he would find of value if she was so sure that her briefcase was going to be searched. When he popped it open, he saw the red bead dropping out of the catch and he slapped his hand on it before it could fall and be lost in the carpet. Look at *this*, thought Jordan, she *knows* this trick. Of course she would, she's a *maven*, he reminded himself. Mavens were always prepared for head-trips and games. Jordan set the bead on the table so he'd remember to put it back and then looked out the window. Now that he knew where to look, he quickly located the flash of lavender bobbing up and down in the waves; his heart quickened; the contrast of colors was stunning. Jordan proceeded to carefully remove the contents of the briefcase. There were five trust files. When he saw that each had a form 3520 to be filed with the Office of International Operations, he did not examine them further because he could tell there was nothing illegal as far as they were concerned. He set them aside and explored further and found note pads, pens and pencils, a Cayman Islands turtle decal, a BNA journal on foreign trusts, and an unmarked folder containing a handwritten letter of wishes and her draft of a testamentary trust for the benefit of . . . *only her son.* It seemed strange that she hadn't mentioned her husband and there was nothing to indicate what—if anything—she wanted to transfer to the trust. Fortunately, he knew enough about testamentary trusts to know that if she were hiding money, she certainly wouldn't be using a trust like this since it would not come into being unless she died. Since it was handwritten, Jordan guessed that she had drafted it only recently, probably during this trip, which made him wonder what was going on in her mind. Then he recalled what Mrs. Clare had said to her housekeeper about her husband possibly being . . . sick?

Underneath all the papers in the unmarked file, he found two items that confirmed his suspicions: a file that contained only a crumpled page that had been folded in half, and a heavy gold ring. It looked like the page had been first discarded and then retrieved. Jordan unfolded it and observed that it was a copy of a page from the Physicians Pharmaceutical Reference Book. He studied it closely and then read Karen's note. This might explain two things, he thought: what Agent Rizzo was hinting at when they left Dr. Clare's office, and why the subject was not wearing her ring—he'd spotted that right away.

Standing next to the window, behind the curtains, Robert Jordan peeked out and saw his subject stepping out of the water. He'd better speed things up. He examined the briefcase, looking for secret compartments and the slits in the lining where documents could be slipped. He found plenty of hiding places, but they were all empty. He looked for scraps of paper bearing numbers or codes, but he found nothing that even suggested the existence of bank accounts—secret or otherwise. Not even so much as a matchbook cover. Satisfied that he'd done a thorough search, he replaced the contents of the briefcase, stuck the red bead in the clasp when he closed it, and then checked the pins to make sure they were still intact. He looked for a radio—which would have the potential for interfering with the bugs—but there was none, which saved him the trouble of having to disable it.

Jordan looked at his watch to pace himself. He began with his subject's purse, carefully examining every compartment and looking for cuts in the lining, then the wallet, where he found only Cayman bills—he quickly computed that his subject had exchanged $200 U.S. into Cayman currency. He next inspected the linens and the mattress and all the drawer bottoms to see if she'd taped anything to their undersides and then he looked in the pockets of Linnell's clothes which were still in her suitcase and, finally, he checked under the lining of all her shoes. After glancing at the closet, which was still empty, he proceeded to the bathroom where he searched every nook and cranny, removing the toilet tank lid to see if his quarry had taped anything to its underside. He found nothing. Before diving into Linnell's cosmetic kit, he found her perfume, which he uncorked and sniffed. Finding a bottle of sun tan lotion, he quickly opened it so that he could sneak a dab to rub on his face and chest. He put an extra dab on the end of his nose and then carefully replaced the bottle, making sure it appeared undisturbed. Then he read the label.

Oh God! It's that self-tanning stuff. Got to get it off, or I'm gonna look like a clown!

Jordan had just enough time to check the rest of the contents of the kit and then he quietly crept out, remembering just in time to lock the door. He jumped into his shower without bothering to undress and soaped himself down. He grabbed a towel to dry off and then to save time, wrapped it around him while he changed the lock-set in his door. After securing his room, he installed his recording paraphernalia and the receivers which were meant to pick up the transmissions from the bugs in the adjoining room and then he tested his sound-activated recorder. Jordan looked at his watch: he'd performed all his tasks in 12.5 minutes flat. Pretty good, he thought.

"I'm ready for the beach now," he said aloud and saw the spool of the recorder slowly turning in response to the sound of his voice. Satisfied that his equipment was functioning, he tossed his towel aside, grabbed his large beach towel and his sunglasses, made sure he had the right key for his door, and headed down to the beach to keep an eye on Mrs. Clare. He bought himself a paperback book, some inexpensive flip-flops and a large bottle of tanning lotion, then he headed out to the beach bar, where he picked up a vodka and orange. He was ready to begin his surveillance. He chose a shaded vantage point under a tree where he could watch his subject from behind his book.

He'd covered a lot of ground, and it was only 5:00 p.m., island time. Just then Jordan looked up and spotted the young sunburned fellow who had been staring at him earlier. Yes, that's the same guy, Jordan observed to himself. *Wonder why he's wearing all those clothes out here in this heat? Oh yes, his sun burn. He appears to be watching my subject. That's no surprise, who wouldn't?* Jordan took pains to note, for his own satisfaction, that this was his first *official* observation of his subject. Making himself comfortable behind his book, Jordan had a sip of his drink and then sat back to congratulate himself on having snagged such a terrific assignment.

Linnell arched her back and floated on top of the waves, lazily backstroking every now and then to keep herself aligned with the hotel. Flipping over, she dove to the bottom to scoop up a handful of soft-as-flour sand so she could squeeze it until it oozed through her fingers, then she watched the sand sparkle as it drifted in the current, first to the side and then back to the ocean floor. Needing another breath, she imagined herself a dolphin and with her legs pressed together, kicked her feet as she imagined a dolphin would do and propelled herself up to the surface. A long swell lifted her high in the air, giving her a clear view of the entire shoreline and then it widened into a trough and she sank down again. It was heaven—the water was now warmer than the air. She guessed she was 40 feet from shore and that the depth of the water at rest was probably a few inches shy of six feet. Very comfortable, very safe, she concluded, and if there should be another one of those giant waves, this time she was wide awake and well-positioned to ride it in.

Content to just float in her tepid bath, she couldn't keep from admiring the contrast of colors between her lavender bikini, her glistening brown legs, and the vivid ultramarine of the water. It was so soul-satisfying to be saturated in color, especially after the long Bay Area winter of muted greens and gray fog. She was already acclimated to the sting of salt, so she focused her unblinking eyes on the white floor beneath her feet and saw that a few long-spined sea urchins remained on the rippled sea bottom. She first examined the patterns they made and then ducking her head completely beneath the surface, she dove and swam farther out and when she opened her eyes, she caught sight of a ghostly fish gliding stately across her path. There were indentations on either side of its bony skull and it paused to give her a steely eye before a flick of its tail sent it darting into the darker blue of deeper water.

Linnell felt a shock of recognition—just when she thought she was safe—here was Willy Ivener. Yes, it had looked just like him. Willy Ivener the barracuda. Indicted for tax fraud. Linnell shivered suddenly, though the water was warm. No matter that she pretended otherwise, she had to face up to it: She disliked the man. She had lost all respect for him. In her opinion he was not a brilliant genius so much as a fast-thinking, smooth-talking con who had never been the least bit concerned about IRS rules or regulations or his clients' interests. If he felt like ignoring them, he would do just that; it was all just a game to him. And he'd treat her carefully crafted memorandums the same way—he tossed them aside. The damn man didn't give two hoots about whether he was exposing his clients to ruin. Why? Because he was a pirate through and through. A slick, cocky, rich one, who played at the tax game just for kicks, and despite all of his fine talk and fancy tastes, he was just as cruel.

She, on the other hand, was a privateer—an entirely different creature. She couldn't help it, it was simply her nature and no matter how loose the flag or absurd the statute, she knew she would always haul in her booty within the law. So long as there was a legal loophole, she would find her way through, otherwise no. To her mind, privateering was to piracy as lawful tax avoidance was to illegal tax evasion—and a privateer played by the rules. But a pirate disrespected all flags and when it came to the rules, a pirate thought they should apply, but only to others.

So, given that Ivener was a ruthless pirate and she was merely a small-time privateer—shouldn't she be just a little bit concerned about how far he might go to get even with her? After all, she had been making some inroads into a field he'd always regarded as belonging entirely to him. Linnell recalled one of her first assignments at Ivener's firm: She had been ordered to flood a large San

Francisco law firm—a firm which had been setting up foreign trusts— with requests for appointments for what she later learned were nonexistent "clients." Petty stuff—meant to annoy—but so typical of what Ivener could do if he felt like harassing the competition. Then it dawned: Could it be that all those annoying cat-calls were coming from Ivener's office? The Hyena perhaps? Why certainly! Of course! Why hadn't she thought of this before?

Now that she had that one figured out, Linnell paddled in circles and watched the fish that were circling her. It reminded her of her own law firm, and how small it was as compared to Ivener's. In fact, Linnell reasoned, she was such a small fish that he would doubtless find it beneath him to get lathered up over a law firm as small as hers. And surely, if he had any concerns about what she was doing, they would all disappear once her article on foreign foundations was published. When that happened, Ivener would be able to see for himself, once and for all, that she intended to expand her practice into an area entirely different from his. Yes, thought Linnell—once her article was published, and her new specialty established, Ivener would most likely never give her another thought.

Her own thoughts ended abruptly when she caught sight of the cloud of tiny lemon-colored fish that were ballooning around her dangling feet. Taking care not to blink, she quickly ducked her head underwater and wiggled her toes and saw thousands of bright spots simultaneously flick like gold coins and then shoot off as one body into paint-box blue waters, leaving only their incandescent contrails to shimmer and then fade away. Finding a cool current, Linnell luxuriated in it until she felt slightly chilled and then she rolled over and slowly backstroked toward shore. Refreshed by her swim, Linnell grabbed her hat and strolled in the direction of the beach bar. She was surprised to find the beach nearly deserted, except for a man—great legs, however—who appeared to have fallen asleep under his towel. Only a few die-hards lingered at the bar, the rest were at dinner. She wasn't that hungry. A snack would do fine. Linnell veered suddenly toward the kitchen to see if the cook would be willing to make her a sandwich to take up to her room.

◆❖◆

Jordan, still watching his subject intently, began to feel uneasy because it looked like she was heading up the beach straight toward him. This time he was sure his cover was blown. Had he stared too hard and given himself away? What to do now? Jordan grabbed his beach towel and tossed it over his head, leaving only his legs exposed. He would pretend he was sleeping, count to twelve—she would have passed him by then—and then have a look to see where she was heading.

Jordan counted slowly, whipped the towel off his head, and was surprised to find himself all alone on the beach. How could she disappear so fast? Now what to do? He didn't quite know. He brushed off the sand, finished his drink while he thought about what to do next, and then returned to his room, where he found that his tape recorder had produced yet another disappointment: It hadn't picked up any voices in his subject's room; the only sounds it had recorded so far were those of her telephone repeatedly ringing.

What he really needed, he thought, was a long cool shower. The drink, the rhythmic clap of the waves, and having to sit for so long in the sun had left him feeling very relaxed. Yawning uncontrollably while he stripped, he looked at his bed. A nap would feel good. Then he decided against it, he might sleep through his meeting with Edgardo. Probably the best thing for him to do would be nothing, just wait here in his room until his subject returned. After all, she was wearing only that bikini, and she would need to return to her room to dress for dinner. Turning off his air conditioning to eliminate all extraneous background sounds, Jordan entered his bathroom, sat down on the edge of the tub, felt how cool it was to the touch, and then got the idea that it might feel good to sit in it while he worked the kinks out of his legs. He climbed in, leaned back, and rested his neck on the cool edge. He wasn't used to sitting around all day. He sure felt sleepy, and the bathroom itself was pleasantly cool. His face felt so warm . . . he yawned, and then yawned again . . .

Seven Mile Beach **Wednesday Evening-February 27, 1974**

Linnell skipped up the outside stairs to the second floor and glancing down the hall, she saw light shining from under the door of the room next to hers. It looked like she had a new neighbor. Opening her door very quietly, Linnell entered, flipped on the light switch, and looked at her briefcase. It appeared undisturbed. She held her breath as she approached the table. Preparing herself for the worst, she held her hand under the briefcase latch, popped it open, and then breathed a sigh of relief when the little red bead dropped into her palm.

It looked like she was at last free of surveillance and this made her feel more relaxed—it was tiresome to have to be so on guard. Just as she'd expected, the contents of her briefcase, spooked the day before, had no doubt served to convince the agent that she wasn't up to any monkey business. She examined the pins on the back of the briefcase and was immediately reassured when she saw that they were still intact. And then, when she turned her head, she saw that the red message-light was blinking on her telephone.

When Jordan awoke, he was shocked to discover the state he was in—stark naked, looking up at the underside of the sink, and covered with perspiration because he'd forgotten to turn on the air conditioning. He climbed stiffly out of the bath tub and shuffled in pain to his bedside table to check the time—he'd been asleep for almost two hours! Catching sight of the state of his recording equipment, he was somewhat mollified. It had been busily recording things while he was asleep. It sounded like he would have to wait until later to check it out, however, because at the moment the spool was turning as it recorded the new sounds now being produced in his subject's room. He sat close to the microphone to listen: there were a few thumps and then the wail of her voice: *"Oh . . . where did I put it, where is it? Oh here it is . . . throw the damn ring in the ocean!"*

He could tell she was infuriated. Hoping to hear more, Jordan placed the microphone almost inside his ear and then jumped when he heard the amplified sound of the door being slammed. He could hear the receding sounds of her footsteps in the hall. And now he couldn't follow her because he wasn't dressed! Twice! He had lost his subject twice in one day. Well, at least now he could run through the tape and see what had been going on while he was asleep. Jordan punched the rewind button and then let it play from the beginning. This time he was rewarded. The transmitter had picked up the sounds of Linnell returning to her room and her call to the hotel operator to pick up her messages. The overseas operator had apparently called Mrs. Clare's room three times and then there was another call to her from the desk clerk who told her that her secretary had called twice and that a party named Nancy had left a message for "L.C. to call back ASAP and to be sure to call her only at home." Jordan sank to his knees and listened very carefully to the recording of his subject's return call to the woman named Nancy:

"Nancy, that you? It's me, L.C. Something up? How'd you track me down?"

"L.C.! I stayed at the bank this afternoon just to get this info for you. Listen, you keep this a secret. I can get fired for telling you this."

Jordan was excited, this might be it! The stuff that would nail the Clares. He moved closer to the tape recorder and turned up the volume.

"Nancy, don't worry. What is it?"

"I called your house, tracked you through Helene. Listen, I called you because I was wondering . . . did you know your husband closed all your bank accounts? All of them, except for the dental corporation. That one's still here, but it only has a few thousand dollars.

"What? I don't believe it! When did this happen?" Linnell's surprise sounded genuine enough to Jordan.

"The day you were at the club . . . This past Monday. I just learned about it today. I only had a few seconds to read the boss's desk . . . Bear apparently told him to wire all the funds to some Canadian bank in Montreal. Listen . . . Bear ordered a code for the Montreal bank account. The instruction was to hold all the funds there for ten days . . . and no access to them without the code number. That's all I could catch without getting caught."

"Good lord! Are you sure?"

"I'm sure! I double-checked the records for all the Clare accounts this afternoon, and except for the small amounts left in your office accounts . . . the big ones have all been closed. The chief handled it personally, he stamped all of the account cards himself. No mistake."

"Can you get the access code?"

"Not a chance. You know that's impossible."

"What bank in Montreal?"

"I don't know."

"Oh God!

"I guessed right . . . you didn't know about this."

"Nancy. I'm almost afraid to ask. How much? Bear's never told me."

"You've got to be joking! It was $820,000."

"What? I could die! I had no idea we had that much!"

"L. C.! Oh dear! All this time . . . I thought you knew."

The recording equipment was so sensitive that Jordan could hear a man's voice calling Nancy away from the phone. He listened to Nancy's hasty farewell and then he rolled the tape to see if anything more had been recorded. He next heard the recorded sounds of Linnell moving a chair, and other rustling noises in her room and then her voice saying:

"What am I going to do? What?. . ." He listened once again to the part where there were thumping noises and her saying, *"Oh . . . where did I put it, where is it? Oh here it is . . . throw the damn ring in the ocean!"*

Jordan removed and dated the tape cassette and installed a new one. Dressing quickly, he checked his room to make sure it was secure and then, keeping an eye out for his subject, he went downstairs to grab a quick snack before entering the lounge for his meeting with Edgardo.

HIGHRIDGE **Wednesday evening - February 27, 1974**

Bear was bushed, today had been his biggest day ever. He'd kept Margo running her tail off and he'd sent Debbie on countless trips to the back laboratory to clean dental trays and run the autoclave so he could grope her when she passed him in the hall. She didn't say much, but from the look in her eyes, he could tell she wanted him bad. He planned to do something about it real soon. Debbie hadn't said one word to Margo about her training the other day. That was another good sign.

Right now, though, he felt as if he were coming unglued. Maybe it was the Percodan, but then he knew from his experiments over the last several months that he could always count on the white lady to give him a lift. It had taken him that long to find the right sequence. And sometimes, when he hit it just right, when the soothing morphine blanket was pierced at its fuzzy center by the exhilarating upward thrust of the cocaine—he would be carried to a peaceful island where everything was wrapped in a soft golden glow. He'd found the sequence that seemed to work best: Percodan in the morning—mostly for the pain and to placate the voices; Dexies around 10 for a steady rev. Then he would save the best for last: cocaine. Cocaine to top off the afternoon.. In the evening he usually took 'ludes if he was home and he had to sit still and watch television.

Bear leaned back on a pile of pillows while he sorted his cash; pretty good for one day: $2500 from the nitrous, and $1200 from the Percodan. He hadn't sold any more cocaine because he'd decided to keep it for himself. And he hated Ma. Hated her! Hated her! Did she take him for a fool? He relished the thought of wringing her neck. Slowly crushing her; dropping her, limp, at his feet. The ring of the telephone interrupted his thoughts. It was exactly 8:45. This has to be Harold . . . good man, thought Bear. He let the phone ring one more time before picking it up.

"Yup." Bear mumbled to Harold in a foggy voice to convince him that he had just been awakened from a deep sleep and thus spoke spontaneously, without premeditation..

"Hey bro! I wake you? Sorry. Hey listen, I got more bad news. I hate to tell you this, but today it's been more of the same. It's kinda hard to believe . . . and if I didn't have all these photos, well, I wouldn't believe it myself."

Bear breathed heavily into the mouthpiece but said nothing.

"Hey, Doc? You there? Take it easy man. Anyway, I'm leaving early tomorrow. I'll see you as soon as I get in."

"Okay," Bear mumbled, yawning audibly. "Hey, before you hang up, you might want to think about this: I had a visit. The IRS, couple days ago. I've been meaning to tell you, but it slipped my mind 'cause I've been so shook up." Bear yawned again, then continued more brightly. "They tried to get me to confirm what my wife told them about Willy Ivener. They said it would be to my advantage—these were their exact words—to cor-ro-bor-ate," he stumbled on the word, as if he didn't know exactly what it meant, "what she told them. Course I turned 'em down, but it seems Ma, I mean, you know, my wife . . . it seems she's planning to testify against Willy. She's gonna be the government's star witness." Bear now could hear Harold breathing heavily on the other end of the line.

"The IRS! L.C.! You get any names?"

"Yeah. Chief Agent Rizzo and some younger guy, Gordon or Jordan, I can't recall . . ." Bear had to stop and stifle a snigger—Harold was so hot to buy into this stuff, it was laughable.

It took Harold only a second to reply. "You know something? Maybe it would be a good idea for you and Willy to get together. What do *you* think?"

Bear smiled. "Yeah, well, if *you* think so, then it sounds okay to me, too. Why don't you set something up?"

"Hey bro. Just leave it to me. Gotta go." For the first time ever, Harold was the one to cut off the call.

He knew exactly why Harold had hung up so fast. Just like Margo, he was so totally predictable. Bear grinned broadly and leaned back on his pillow and recounted his cash; he could change it for $100 bills in the morning. A sudden flash of light streaked across his vision. Sometimes it felt as if he were looking into the sun, except it didn't burn like the real sun did. Maybe this was a sign. Yes, that's what it was. Now he was certain: He had been chosen. Others could tell. That's why they all called him the King.

Bear dropped the bills and closed his eyes while he mulled things over. Ma had really messed things up for him. Just last week he'd had everything arranged so he'd have a handle on her, and now look what she'd done! She had ruined everything by going and humiliating him! He couldn't, he *wouldn't* let her get away with this. Divorce was too good for her. Besides, if he divorced her, she and the kid would end up in the house.

Bear rubbed his forehead, then snickered. He was nobody's fool. He reached an unsteady arm towards the telephone, dialed for the overseas operator and when he reached the hotel desk clerk he told her not to disturb his wife. He just wanted to leave her a little message, he said. Then he dictated a few words to the desk clerk and swiftly cut off the call.

Now Bear knew for a fact that he'd upset the voices because now they were filling his ears with spluttering sounds. The hiss. The hum. The steady flatness of the noises and then static—he couldn't stand it anymore. This happened when he got too excited; the voices would then take advantage, they would creep out of their hiding places behind the crackling and tease him, just like little Stevie once did. Sometimes the noises merged into rhythms and they would join together and thump like drums . . . and sometimes they would chant, soft and slow, giving him messages he couldn't understand . . . over and over.

Over and over and over again: *Orrrrrrry gory bloooody-cutty.*

Bear pressed a pillow to his face. "Stop! Please, no more. Can't you hear me? I'm begging. Please stop!" They would have to obey because the King had said *please*.

It was important to keep the hummers under control, because if he didn't, then people might give him these funny looks, which was what happened the week before, when for a few seconds he'd let them escape. A few 'ludes should do it, he told himself. Bear stumbled out of bed, took three capsules, then rolled over on his back and then helpless to stop, began counting the dots in the acoustical ceiling.

CAYMAN **Wednesday evening - February 27, 1974**

Edgardo Cortina, an accountant who had left his country long before the Batista regime had been felled by the Cuban revolution, had shown his gratitude to his new country by seeking a position with the IRS, where his bilingual skills and even temperament had quickly lifted him into the highest echelons of the Special Services Intelligence Division. He was now assigned to the Caribbean unit which had been recently enlarged as a result of the hearings in Washington about money laundering and tax evasion.

Now that diplomacy had failed and negotiations to defeat the bank secrecy laws of Mexico and the Caribbean had collapsed, the Treasury Department had decided to take an alternative route and put a dent in offshore money-laundering through a more vigorous enforcement of the nation's tax laws. Posing as an ornithologist, Edgardo toured the Antilles with his load of cameras and telephoto lenses so that he could keep track of his human flock while ostensibly searching for rare birds throughout the Caribbean.

This evening, after a long day spent photographing grackles—which had coincidentally enough allowed him to take some really splendid pictures of the warehouse district—he sat at the end of the bar, sorting out the familiar faces from those of the tourists. It would be easy enough to spot Jordan, he thought—his sunburn and short haircut would give him away.

He'd been on this rock for the last several months, studying the nesting habits of the Cayman nightingale and the Greater Antillian Grackle, on a tip that the Ivener office was about to move some of its offshore companies from the Bahamas to Cayman. But his favorite subject was Ye Olde Banke. He'd been gathering some embarrassing information about several well-known U.S. pols who were using the bank as a stashing place for their "excess campaign contributions" and then illegally purchasing bullion contracts. No doubt it was his most recent summary of this matter which had led to his hasty reassignment to the other side of the island where he had been directed to keep an eye on the lawyer from the Ivener firm. A hint, he supposed, that he ought to know better than to name any sensitive names when he filed his reports about Ye Olde Banke. But he didn't mind his reassignment in the least, because having to keep Harold Dolphe under surveillance had led him back to his favorite haunts on Seven Mile Beach. He had also, like so many others, purchased a $1000 bullion participation certificate at Ye Olde Banke in order to make himself look like a regular. But at the same time, at a different bank, one with respectable European affiliations, he had also purchased two $5000 contracts on margin. He was looking at a possible profit that could possibly fetch as much as $60,000 if the market were to shoot up as high as he anticipated, once the U.S. restrictions on owning gold were lifted.

Edgardo listened to the band and watched all the people swarming into the lounge, then he felt, rather than saw, a presence at his elbow. Without turning his head, Edgardo spoke. "Hey, Jordan . . . how 'bout a beer?" Out of the corner of his eye, he saw the man's head turning in his direction.

"Well, let me guess, it's Bob Jordan. No?"

"Edgardo?" Jordan felt his face turning red, he had fallen for the oldest trick in the world.

"Right. Hey, it's okay, amigo. You're still learning." Edgardo clapped Jordan on the back and yelled for a couple of long necks. Although nobody seemed to be paying any attention to them, they pretended to be college classmates and spoke openly, as if they had nothing to hide, before wandering over to sit in a booth directly opposite the dance floor.

They traded stories about their cases. Edgardo described how he'd been pulled off his case and assigned to the surveillance of a young California lawyer who was an associate at the Ivener law firm. In turn, Jordan told Edgardo about his case, which involved a dentist named Clare and the surveillance of his wife, a tax attorney. Jordan told Edgardo that he hadn't discovered any evidence against her—no doubt because she had anticipated a search of her personal effects. Edgardo immediately pointed out that she probably was a member of the clique known as the Haven Mavens, a clique that loved to play head-games with the Intelligence Division.

Edgardo advised Jordan that all of the haven mavens were so accustomed to surreptitious visits from the I.D. agents that the fact that she had been prepared for his visit actually meant very little, one way or the other.

"So why do I bother?" Jordan asked.

"You never know what you might find and besides, it's a nice trip. No?"

"Sure is," Jordan agreed.

"Then don't complain." Edgardo remained quiet for a moment, thinking. "Wait a minute, didn't you just say *Clare*? A woman lawyer by that name once worked for the Ivener outfit. She goes by the name of L.C. Clare."

"Yes. That's the one. I'm staying next door to her now. Bugged her room this afternoon."

"Well, amigo . . . I have some news for you. Happened yesterday. My subject, Harold Dolphe has been spending a lot of time hanging around here just to follow Mrs. Clare. She almost caught him yesterday when he first tried to slip into her room—and I know it's her room, 'cause I checked. He managed to dodge her, so when she finally went down to the beach—where, by the way, she spent the whole day—he finally got in there. He has a master key to this joint so I hope you remembered to change your lock. Anyway, Dolphe was in there nearly half an hour, but he left empty-handed. He spent the rest of the day on the beach, watching her while she swam with the sea-urchin divers. Then he followed her, and I followed him, out to this old warehouse where the diving crew threw this big shindig over their successful haul."

"Where's he staying?" Jordan asked.

"He's bunked in at that small hotel south of here, it's just down the road a few steps. He's been running in circles up and down the beach. I got so sick of shagging him that I checked the flight schedules just to see when he's taking off. He's leaving for Houston first thing tomorrow morning."

"You're *sure* he didn't remove anything from her room?"

"Yeah, positive. I searched his room and that warehouse as well, but I didn't find anything except a camera and a phone scrambler—so he's not up to his usual tricks this trip."

"Mrs. Clare's files look okay," Jordan assured him, "she's just doing trusts. By the way, was Mr. Ivener the only one named in the indictment?"

"Yeah, he's the only one, so far," Edgardo replied.

"So, what's this Dolphe guy look like?" Jordan asked.

"Sorta rusty-red hair . . . he's one odd-looking dude." Edgardo put his wallet back in his pocket to signal that he had to get back to work.

"Not sure 'bout this—but maybe I saw him, earlier, when I arrived."

The two agents ended their meeting with a loud discussion of football scores and then Edgardo took off into the night, leaving Jordan alone to finish his beer.

CAYMAN **Wednesday evening - February 27, 1974**

Linnell sat in the sand on the beach, trying to figure things out. In the first place, why had he kept so much money a secret, especially from her? Their life's savings. $820,000! And how had he managed to save so *much*? And now all that money was hidden in a bank somewhere in Montreal. Her instincts told her to hop the next plane—go home and have it out with him once and for all—while her logical side kept reminding her to stay cool and think like a lawyer. Yes, think like a lawyer. That's what all her law profs liked to say—probably just to be annoying, she'd always supposed. Be logical, apply deductive reasoning, that's what they meant. So, why couldn't they stuff the gibberish and just come right out and say it?

The moon emerged from behind a cloud. She focused on the waves, listening to the soft popping sounds as the water sank into the sand. *Could this have something to do with the IRS? The audit? Sure it could—the IRS probably called Bear the same day they called me. And that would've been sometime last Monday, the day I left town, which is when he bank wired the funds. Most likely the IRS got a bit heavy-handed and he panicked. Yes, this makes sense.*

But Linnell's gut instincts still nagged at her, warning her that there might be a lot more going on than she had so far imagined. There was something here that just didn't add up. But what? Linnell wandered toward the edge of the water and looked out to sea and this time saw only the flickering path of chilly moonlight snaking off to a dark horizon. And then she remembered: The escrow account! The $480,000 that only she could touch! Getting it had been her sole preoccupation for over a year. $480,000! More money than she'd ever dreamt of having. How could something so monumental simply slip her mind? As if the getting of it was all that mattered, to be forgotten once gotten. Fool! What she was forgetting was that the getting of it was just the beginning. Now the larger lessons loomed: Learning how best to use it. Linnell opened her hand and stared at her gold wedding band. She had wanted to pitch it far out to sea. Thank goodness she'd given herself a chance to cool down.

Looking up at the moon, Linnell wondered if Bear was looking at it too. What if through some magical means he could see what she'd almost done? Her marriage, if not exactly satisfying, was at least solid. Wasn't that part of the problem . . . that it was as stolid and unmoving as a rock? Linnell Clare squeezed the ring with all her might to see if she could bend it out of shape. If she could, then it would be a sign that she was wrong.

Solid and heavy, the ring remained intact and Linnell finally slid it back on her finger. She was used to it, so she might as well wear it, she thought, then she trudged through the sand up the path to her hotel. Brushing off sand at the door, Linnell slipped into the lounge and sat down behind a small group of locals whose eyes were fixed on the new color television set in the corner of the room. They were whispering. Curious, Linnell moved closer and heard them talking about the earthquake. It had happened mid-afternoon—they were saying things about it being large enough to kick up a tsunami—and they said they were still pretending to know nothing about it since they didn't want to tell the tourists and get them upset. Nothing big; just a tremor from somewhere at the bottom of the ocean, miles away, they were saying. And then the locals fell silent and went back to watching the program—a re-run of The Man from U.N.C.L.E. involving some hyperactive spies switching briefcases and smuggling documents.

So! The giant wave was the result of an earthquake! And it had been sheer luck and not the divine hand of providence, not a miracle, not the hand of a caring Loa that had saved her from drowning this afternoon. Not that she was complaining, mind you, but she felt just a tiny bit let down—she had rather liked the idea of being considered somehow special, special enough to be saved by the spirits of the deep. Linnell sat quietly, sobered by reality, and then she couldn't stand it any longer . . . she had to know. She had to call home and find out what was really happening.

She jumped up and headed toward the telephone in the lobby and spied the young telephone operator sitting all alone behind the counter. The girl's dejected expression spoke volumes about how it felt to be left out of the fun. The operator saw her and suddenly brightened. Grinning broadly, the girl grabbed a pink telephone message slip, waved it in the air, and called across the lobby: "Hey Ms. L.C.! Your lover-boy called!"

Linnell, startled, rushed over to the desk, picked up the message, and read: "Hi Ma it's me Love Your Bear."

He'd actually called to leave her his usual message! Linnell stared at the telephone slip and felt all her anxieties melting away. It was just so comforting to see these same old familiar words and even if he was still calling her "Ma" she didn't care, it was such a relief to hear from him! Then she felt a pang of guilt over the hissy-fit she'd just thrown.

Yes, a mind can certainly do a lot of funny things, thought Linnell—and she'd almost let hers come *this* close to ruining the most fabulous day. Linnell read Bear's message one more time. God! Did she ever feel better!

Relieved of tension, Linnell yawned and realized how utterly exhausted she really was. In fact, her head simply reeled from all the things that had happened to her over the past two days. Linnell listened to the music coming from the lounge and thought about dancing, tired though she was. Then she yawned again. It would be much better for her to go to bed. So, there would be no dancing and prancing around for her, tonight. She would return Bear's call first thing in the morning, and then, surely, everything would get sorted out.

Just before falling asleep, a thought came to her out of the blue, and she felt she had better set it down in her rudder. Creeping into her bathroom with her ball-point pen gripped in her teeth like a pirate's blade, Linnell reached up and retrieved her rudder, carefully peeled off the tape, laid it flat on top of the bathroom counter and wrote the date and then the following words: *A miracle is simply physics unexplained.*

CAYMAN **Thursday morning - February 28, 1974**

Her first thought on waking was that she had to call Bear. Why all this pussy-footing around? Why not simply ask him to explain to her why he'd done what he did? He must have some very sound reasons for sending their money up to Canada—she would no doubt approve—and then she could stop ruining her vacation with all this needless anxiety.

Filled with a new sense of confidence, Linnell rolled over and reached for the telephone; she was just about to ask for a long distance connection, when she happened to glance at the time: It was already 8:00 a.m. here in Cayman, but it would be only 5:00 a.m. in California. No; bad idea, she thought. Waking Bear so early might put him in too bad a mood and then she'd get nowhere with him. It would be much better to wait until after he'd had his first cup of coffee. Yes, she would wait; meanwhile, she could go into Georgetown and visit Colin, maybe even do a little shopping. Linnell asked the desk clerk to call Sonny, the dive master's youngest son, and have him pick her up for a ride into Georgetown, and then she asked for room service.

By the time room service arrived with her coffee, she was thinking more clearly. She couldn't very well light into Bear about closing their bank accounts without costing Nancy her job. The situation called for a different approach. She'd back off—maybe just thank him for the flowers and then sort of look for an opening to attack the matter indirectly. Linnell reassured herself that being kind and considerate was not at all the same thing as waffling.

When Linnell finally climbed out of bed the temperature was already in the high 80s and she wondered if she could find a way to wear her bathing suit to the bank. If she could, it would save her the time of coming back here to change. She already knew that no matter how much money she had on deposit, it would not exempt her from the bank's dress code—they'd arrest Lord Rothschild himself if he appeared in a bathing suit. *All* visitors were required to comply, and the "no bathing suits" rule was strictly enforced.

Linnell decided to wear her bathing suit under her clothes. First she cooled herself down with a splash of cold water to her face, and then she quickly tied on her bikini and slipped into the jacket of her navy-blue warm-ups—she could leave it open part way and still meet the dress code. After stepping into her cotton skirt and her flip-flops, she was ready to go. Linnell picked up her briefcase and headed toward the stairs that lead down to the lobby. She hadn't really paid all that much attention to it, but after passing the room next to hers, she thought she'd heard the door closing quietly.

Or was she simply imagining things? She looked behind her and saw nothing irregular. Then she ran toward the elevator. For some reason, she wanted to get off the second floor.

While they were puttering south toward Church Street in Sonny's jalopy, Linnell looked at the building on the other side of the road across from her hotel. Ye Olde Bank made all the rest of the banks on the island look like disaster areas—its lovely lawns, a scarce nicety on the island, had been groomed to a velvety green and thick clumps of red and yellow ginger had been planted along both sides of the path to its entrance; the spotless glass entry door sported a neat white sign at its very center, and each and every gleaming window held a slatted blind that had been tipped evenly, just so.

"Crime pays," Linnell grumbled.

Sonny, chattering away as they drove, glanced at her in his rear-view mirror and caught her disapproving expression. He grinned back at her in the mirror. "You buy any gold, Ms. L.C.?"

"Stop teasing. You know I can't. I'm a US. citizen. We're restricted, you know."

"I pay my bills, but I have some little money left. I think I do that, buy gold, double my money."

"Well, not at that place, I hope," Linnell said dourly, "they don't look like they need any more business."

"Oh, now Ms. L.C. you sure be cranky this morning. *Everybody*, they go there to buy the gold." That said, Sonny concentrated his full attention on avoiding the construction trucks that were now bumping along with them on either side. They arrived at her bank at exactly 8:30 a.m., and Sonny told Linnell that he would stick around so he could drive her around when she was through working.

Linnell proceeded directly to Colin's private office.

Colin stood up and spoke graciously, in the presence of his secretary, as soon as she entered the room: "I, for one, am not the least bit surprised by your remarkable success. That was brilliant, both in concept and execution. We congratulate you."

Colin dismissed his secretary. A tray of shortbread biscuits sat on his desk and now he passed them to her. Then he asked her if she wanted cream in the coffee that had been prepared just for her. Linnell couldn't help noticing how attentive he'd become to her every wish. Obviously, he'd picked up the scent of big money here, and no doubt he was already counting how much she'd be bringing in the following year. That was certainly worth a biscuit or two. Linnell reached out and helped herself to another. Her purpose in meeting with Colin, however, was not to crow over her success but to tell him her plans for her SUP Ltd. shares: For the time being, and until she reached her final decision, she would keep them under the bank's custodianship—not transfer them either to Bear or their Cayman trust.

Colin leaned back in his chair and smiled at her carefully.

Linnell could tell from his face that Colin was delighted to hear that she'd be leaving the $480,000 on deposit, which would allow the bank to continue to enjoy the spread—at least for a while—until she decided how she wanted it invested. And she was pleased, too—from now on the bank would pretty much do whatever she asked. Now that she had made some money of her own, she could tell that it no longer made any difference whether she was married or not. Her money was here, it was under her sole control, and that was power. She crunched her biscuit with satisfaction. Yes. With money, even stale biscuits like these tasted better. Linnell smiled graciously to conclude their meeting and then signed her testamentary trust and passed it to Colin with instructions that it be placed in his files, again pointing out that this particular trust was meant to take effect only upon her death. That done, she now had plenty of time to think about how best to handle the matter of the SUP Ltd. shares. It was just as Colin said—there was no need to rush.

"Well Linnell, that's sensible enough. Shall do as you say," Colin replied, nodding sagely. "Anything tip the scales here?"

Linnell took in his body language. She could tell he was tickled by her success because his elbows rested with elaborate casualness on the arms of his chair and his fingers, braided into what she called "the Kissinger position," were secretly wiggling with satisfaction inside his palms.

She wondered what Colin would have to say about Bear's recent behavior and shortly found herself telling him what Bear had just done with their savings. "And what do you make of that?" she asked.

Colin suddenly sat up straight, then propping his elbows on his green desk blotter, he stared at her gravely over his knuckles. He remained silent like this for several long seconds, then suddenly reached down and with a soft grunt, lifted up a telephone directory and slapped it on top of his desk. He shuffled through the pages, then stopped. "Here, you take this." Colin spoke grimly; then tore out several pages and passed them to her.

She examined what he had just handed her: a list of all the banks in Montreal.

"I can only say this," Colin added, "the banks in this city usually have access codes of eight digits. I suggest you concentrate on that."

Linnell's face felt warm against the air-conditioned room. There was no avoiding it—Colin was sure she had serious marital problems. And eight digits, no less; a number of that magnitude would be impossible to guess. Linnell Clare struggled to contain her dismay. Now she was sure something was wrong; she'd had a sense that something was rotten the day she'd left home, but she'd put it down as nothing more than a figment of her imagination.

Linnell frowned. Although the thought was sickening, it was still rather fascinating to imagine that at some future date she would be able to look back and pinpoint the exact moment in time when that first fatal crack opened up in her life. To know precisely when everything she'd ever known first began to shatter and fall apart. *"Hey there! Now you just wait a minute!* scolded her practical alter ego. *"You're not sure about any of this, are you? You're not! So stuff this theatrical nonsense!"* Linnell willed her face a blank. Making ready to leave, she closed her briefcase and just as she rose from her chair, the telephone rang.

Colin lifted the receiver and covered his free ear in order to listen more carefully, then smiling, signaled for her to wait. Carefully setting the receiver down in its cradle, Colin shot his cuffs to indicate his satisfaction and then laid his hands, palm down, on the top of his desk; he finally looked up at her with dancing blue eyes. "Now, *here's* some good news."

"What's that?" Linnell, now feeling quite sober and depressed, was in no mood for games.

"Well, I think you must see for yourself. When you return to your hotel, I think you're going to be finding quite a crowd around that bank over there."

Linnell was surprised that Colin would allow anyone to see him so excited. "Oh, just tell me, *please,*" she begged. But she could see it was useless. Colin had a look on his face that told her he was determined to be a tease.

"No I shan't do that, you must see for yourself. *Quite* edifying." Colin's eyes were glowing and his cheeks bloomed pink with obvious pleasure.

"Colin, *you* are edifying." Linnell bared her teeth at him in a mirthless grin.

He grinned back at her wickedly. "Enjoy!" Colin waved good-bye and immediately picked up the phone to place a call.

Linnell grabbed her briefcase, ran downstairs, and jumped into Sonny's death-trap. They rattled through the dusty streets and onto the highway toward Ye Olde Banke and when they arrived on the scene, they found what looked to be every vehicle on the island. Bicycles, mopeds, trucks, not to mention hundreds of cars, now flowed from the parking lot and filled both sides of the road. People were milling around the doors and some of them clawed at the windows, but most stood in clusters on the lawn in front of the building.

"Sonny, stop! We've got to see what's going on here."

Linnell and Sonny joined the crowd. They were struck by how quiet it was for such a large group—too quiet—except for the rush of sound that seemed to come from the area in front of the main entrance. Linnell pushed her way forward and finally saw what everyone was examining. It was the small sign on the door, the same one she'd spotted earlier that morning from the road. It was actually a sheet of the bank's gold-embossed stationery, taped to the inside surface of the glass. A short message had been carefully typed in the middle of the page:

Esteemed Patrons and Friends: Ye Olde Banke Has closed.
We sincerely regret this Inconvenience.

Inconvenience? Nice touch that, Linnell thought. The bank had failed. And its management had bailed. A wave of ashen faces pushed up to the door to read the notice, then turned and politely stepped back to make room for another wave. Linnell could see for herself that the crowd was still dizzy with incredulity, collectively holding its breath. But a low-pitched rumble was beginning to build on one side of the group, reminding her of all the stories she'd heard about how the Loa of the Underworld, who, if disturbed, would search for a weak spot in the earth's crust where they could vent their displeasure. A bank failure! She'd never seen anything like it before, and the troubling spectacle of such a loss, now unfolding before her very eyes, wiped away all thoughts of Bear.

"Sonny, where are you?" Linnell whirled around and saw him standing in the middle of the lawn. The crowd seemed to be moving faster now; she inched her way back to him and grabbed his hand. "Let's get *out* of here before this place explodes!"

Sonny appeared drained of life. "The diving crew . . . they put all their savings here!"

"I hope you haven't invested anything with this outfit."

"No! My family, they be safe! But my boys, this be their bank. They *all* come here."

Then it dawned on her: Good news! The diving crew was saved. She had paid them with drafts from her bank, which meant it would be a week before they would be presented for payment. She still had time to ask Colin to issue a blanket stop-payment and issue new checks to her crew. She tried to explain this to Sonny. She yelled in his ear. But he was too dazed to listen. Linnell finally patted his hand and then left him standing on the trampled lawn.

Like everyone else, Linnell was stunned by the news. Without wasting any more time, she sprinted back to her hotel and used the front desk phone to call her bank and order a stop on the bank drafts—she'd have Billy tell the crew—and then she ran up to her room to ditch her briefcase and then flew downstairs to join the crowd. There was no laughter today, only nervous chatter and the clink of glasses. Linnell finally found a place for herself at the beach bar. Fifteen minutes later, hundreds joined them and it was bedlam.

Every now and then there would be a lull in the roar and Linnell could hear a faint echo of yelps from across the road. She closed her eyes while she listened to the voices rising and falling all around her and when she opened them she found herself staring straight into the heart-jolting face of the man she had first seen the day before. He was standing alone on the other side of the bar.

What was it about him that drew her? she wondered. He was a hunk, all right, but it was something more than just his good looks. Well, whatever it was, he had it. And there were others who thought so too, she observed. The termites, half-clad and circling behind his back, were giggling and making ready to pounce. Linnell knew he must have been looking at her for quite a while because the termites, who had been keeping an eye on him, were now staring at her too. Linnell caught her breath as she watched him turn around and push his way past the girls and then stand behind them at the back of the crowd. He seemed to be thinking things through—maybe thinking about how to approach her? Then she saw him push his sunglasses down over his eyes before turning to face her again. She flashed him her most beckoning Grace Kelly smile because she wanted him to know it would be okay for him to come over and get acquainted. His face softened as if to thank her for her nice smile, but otherwise he didn't budge. She raised her ringless right hand and watched him through her fingers as he glanced at her repeatedly; but again he made no attempt to move in her direction.

What kind of game is this? she wondered.

Well, no loss. And who cares anyway? she told herself. Guys like him were usually so stuck on themselves, they weren't worth the trouble. Besides, he was much too cleaned-up, much too crisply well-groomed, which had to mean that somebody was ironing his shirts and running his clothes to the cleaners. She concluded that he had to be married, or else there was some woman in his life taking care of him. Having settled on this explanation, Linnell found it easier to observe him with a bit more detachment. She could tell, even from this distance, that he had a comfortable, self-confident attitude. His age? He had to be somewhere in his very early thirties. She had never before thought about dating a younger man and now she found herself wondering why not. Maybe somebody here knew his name. Not that it made any difference, she told herself. She didn't really care; she was merely curious about interesting-looking people, was all.

Linnell made a determined effort to ignore him by forcing herself to concentrate on the numerous stories about the bank failure. Everybody was beginning to grasp just how they'd been taken: The bank had never had any gold; it had merely sold what traders referred to as "naked contracts." Nicely engraved certificates—in, short, worthless paper—kept afloat by nothing more than the bank's own hot air.

As the day wore on, it became increasingly clear that all of its depositors had been, as they said: *Screwed, blued, and tattooed*—there was no such thing as depositor's insurance for this bank or any other on the island. The word was out that the bank manager must have vanished shortly after midnight because lights had been seen in the bank until then; somebody else announced that all the Lear jets had left the airfield, which triggered a new rumor that the birds had flown out around 4 a.m., which suggested to others that the culprits must have hopped through the Antilles and off to the Middle East. Some said they'd heard a cruiser speed into the harbor and that it had whisked the scoundrels away; while others opined that some favored depositors had swooped in like pirates in the middle of the night to do some looting. Before she knew it, the day had passed; but she continued to visit and collect stories from everybody until she finally realized it was 3. a.m. Friday morning. Linnell dragged herself up to her room. It was only then that she remembered the calls she had wanted to make, and especially to Bear. She had plenty of news for him now. And a perfect pretext to question him about what he'd done with their bank accounts.

HIGHRIDGE **Friday morning - March 1, 1974**

Something called out to him in his sleep and shortly before dawn. When he awoke, Bear was startled to find himself staring up at the ceiling and for a moment he was immobilized. In the half-light, the symmetrically pitted ceiling tiles made him feel he was trapped on the wrong side of the grids of a stereo amplifier. To escape, he opened his clenched fist and reached out for his Ma. Good Ma. It always made him feel safe to know that he always had such a good woman, there at his side. He raised his hand to tap her three times for good luck like he always did, but today his hand fell into empty space where her hip should have been.

He was flustered. Confused. And then he realized where he was—and it all came back to him: His Ma—she had betrayed him! And the whole world knew and was in on it, too. Falling out of bed and stumbling into his dark bathroom, Bear groped in his kit bag and found his bottle of pills. This time he left the four Percodans in his hand and picked them up with his tongue. He tried to drink from the faucet like he did at home, but it was impossible because this one was knobby. He had to be careful not to chip a tooth. Fumbling angrily in the dark, his hand finally found a Styrofoam cup which he filled from the tap. Gulping greedily, he turned on the lights in the bathroom and gasped at the sight of the face in the mirror. It had to be the fluorescent lights—they made him look baggy and green, as if he'd aged ten years overnight. A spasm of nausea clutched at the back of his throat and for a moment he thought he was going to vomit. He dressed hurriedly and ran to his car.

By the time he reached the coffee shop, he was feeling light-headed. Even the voices had failed to emerge. But they were still in there somewhere. He could tell. Just recently they had begun to warn him by hissing and spitting in his ears. They were beginning. Faintly, faintly—they were growing somewhere in the back of his head, filling all those damp places where it was still deathly cold and dark because his sunshine nuggets were taking so long to get to work.

He had ordered his usual breakfast and it sat in front of him now, getting cold, while the waitresses kept urging him to take *one-itty-bitty-bite* as if he were some overgrown child. Ordinarily he'd be pleased to be the center of so much attention, but food didn't taste so good to him anymore, and he had this terrible ache in the pit of his stomach when he thought about his Ma. Ma, who'd made a fool of him in front of everybody on the island!

While crockery clanked and the ungodly racket of human voices buzzed all around him, Bear leaned on his briefcase; then he opened it and tucked the note he'd made to himself deep into one of its slotted pockets. Ivener would soon call him, he was sure of it; so he'd better tell Margo that he was expecting a very important call today. Bear forced himself to eat a few bites and then felt glad for it. What a relief to know that even without the click, his sunshine nuggets could still kill the pain—he had been right to increase the dose. Except now his entire leg tingled and he couldn't feel his toes, but other than that, he was already beginning to feel better by the minute.

When he was finished with breakfast, he called Margo's apartment from the restaurant to give her his orders: She should prepare his private office and instruct Debbie a bit more thoroughly this time because he intended to repeat her test. He also remembered to tell Margo that he was expecting a very important call, so important that no matter when it came in, she should put it through to him without any delay.

CAYMAN **Friday - Noon - March 1, 1974**

The sun was brightly overhead when Linnell awoke. She was glued to the sheets and the room was stifling because she had forgotten to turn on the air conditioner the night before. And she had overslept. Linnell looked at her watch: it was already half past the noon hour—which made her feel even more sluggish—but it was now exactly 9:30 a.m. in California. Perfect! Bear probably was at this very moment taking his first coffee break. She called the front desk and instructed the operator to call Dr. Clare in California but told her not to identify her or the source of the call. Linnell was on to Margo, and she didn't want to give the mean old bat an excuse to set up her usual road blocks.

HIGHRIDGE **Friday morning - March 1, 1974**

When Bear arrived at his office, Margo first took him aside to show him all the files she had prepared and then he slipped her a ten to show her his appreciation. And when he walked into his private office he found an even more spectacular tableau—Debbie—good girl!—was there in her proper position, obviously eager and ready for him to begin. Bear studied her avidly while he opened his desk drawer to fetch his paraphernalia for his morning boost. Trouble was, lady snow would still give him the needed boost, but then, as he'd come to fear, she would also stir up the voices. He'd better hurry before they began. There was no time for floating. No time for any warm glow. Bear popped open his briefcase, grabbed Mr. Wattaman and slid him out of his flannel bag.

Today would be a special day. The day for the settling of many scores. And she was going to pay. That's what she was here for. And her legs were the same as Ma's. They were all the same. Evil, crazy, disobedient, just like his Ma. Let her keep on thinking she could tempt him. He'd show her who was boss! Bear whacked Mr. Wattaman across the palm of his hand. Then he stopped, struck by the image of the woman in the mirror. Blindfolded. So eager. So obedient. But he was on to her now; he knew she was only doing this to fool him. Make a fool of him so the whole world could laugh. He lowered his voice until it resonated with just the right amount of sly humor.

"Are you prepared?" Bear unzipped his pants to mislead her with the sound.

"Yes, yes, yes," Bear heard the panting and watched his slave closely for any signs of rebellion and then, when he saw the buttocks quivering he brought this infraction to a halt by administering a series of sharp little slaps to the bouncing cheeks. In a rough voice, he ordered her to hold still and correct her presentation. He saw the white moons rising swiftly to pleasure him. She wanted it bad.

"And what do you say?" Bear demanded.

"Yes." Deborah replied.

"Yes, *what*!"

"Yes, *Dr. Clare.*"

Bear retrieved Mr. Wattaman and said, "That's right. Now continue from here . . . Are you prepared?"

"Oh *yes*, Dr. Clare."

◆❖◆

Deborah recognized her cue and this time she was careful to follow the script that Margo had drilled into her. Steadying herself on the sink with one arm, she thrust the other one between her perfumed legs, then by bending her elbow like Margo had shown her, she managed to hook her little finger into the backside of her panties. It made no difference to her if he was kinky or just plain sick, she just wanted him to hurry things up; just get it off so she could get back to her real business here. She could hear him, he was breathing hard, and despite herself, this excited her. She finally got a grip on the gossamer fabric and pulled down on it until the waistband of her panties slid over her high round hillocks, then she slowly pulled them down until her moist mound was . . .

BBZZZZZZZZZZZZZZZZ! Bear's private office was suddenly filled with a fiercesome blast! The intercom!

Deborah flinched.

And Bear jumped clear off the carpet, sending poor Mr. Wattaman on his first aerial flight. Furious, his face engorged, Bear spied Mr. Wattaman's pale rubber tip poking out from under the drapes; he savagely kicked him under his desk and grabbed the receiver. "What'n hell's *wrong* with you Margo! What kinda goddam emergency is happenin' NOW!"

"Long distance call for you, Dr. Clare. You *told* me you were expecting an important call." Margo's voice twanged over the loudspeaker and her tone was defiantly calm.

"Get off the damn intercom!" Bear was livid.

Margo switched to the phone, then said with saccharine sarcasm: "Doc, you *told* me you were expecting an important call."

"Tell 'em to hold! Tell 'em I'm with a patient and I'll-be-there-inna-minute!" Bear managed to calm himself and then zipped up his pants. "Margo, when I'm through with this call, you 'n me, we're gonna have ourselves a little talk!"

Gripping the phone in his white-knuckled hand, Bear said curtly: "Debbie. Out!"

CAYMAN **Friday - Noon - March 1, 1974**

Linnell heard Margo tell the overseas operator that "Doc" was with a patient and that he'd be on the line in a minute. As soon as she heard his voice saying hello, she took a deep breath and rushed in: "Hi Bear. The flowers were gorgeous and I just got your message. I tried to reach you but your line is always—"

Bear interrupted. "Yeah, Ma. And I'm kinda *busy* right now, got a patient waiting, my little *sweet*heart."

Linnell heard her blood pounding in her ears. "But . . . but . . ."

"But, *what*!" Bear now sounded angry.

"Then I'll make it *quick*," she heard herself assuring him. Linnell was now furious with herself; she always lost her nerve when he used this tone of voice on her. "You know that bank? The one across the road from the hotel? It failed. I mean right before my eyes. You should've seen this place yesterday. All the customers were locked out." Now she was stammering like a frightened child. He had the power to do this to her and he knew it. "I mean there are no customers anymore, because the bank's *gone.* I mean, it's folded . . . it's *failed.*" Bear said nothing in reply and Linnell was concerned that he'd been cut off. "Bear? Bear are you there? Can you *hear* me?"

Finally he spoke. Feebly this time. "Yes. I'm here. What's that you said? Did I hear you right?. . ."

Linnell interrupted. "Bear, I mean . . . I guess you can understand, but I have to ask . . . our money, is it safe? I mean, have you called our bank lately to see if all our money is still *there*?"

There was another long silence and then Bear's voice suddenly switched, it was high-pitched, angry. "Whatsa *matter* with you? You know better than to ask me about that! Sure our money is safe! It's sitting right here, at the Highridge Bank, just where it's been for the last seven years. *You* know *that!*"

"You're positive . . . you know for sure that *all* of our money is *still* at the bank?"

"Well, Ma, there must be something wrong with you—didn't you just hear me? Now *listen*! It's *all* here. At the Highridge Bank. Every penny. Now, I'm *busy*, so don't waste any more of my time with this stuff. You goin' crazy? Or what!"

Linnell, shocked by his tone, remained silent.

"Anything *else* happening?" Bear asked meanly. "I mean, what have *you* been doing?"

"I've just been working, like usual, and then I went to the beach." Linnell's voice automatically turned apologetic. "Oh . . . I almost forgot to mention—the island must be crawling with agents. They've already searched my room. By any chance, have you ever heard anything from the IRS?"

Here was her last hope. If he said yes, it might explain a few things.

"Yeah! How'd you know that?"

Ignoring his question, Linnell asked, "When, exactly, did you *first* hear from the IRS?"

"Just this morning. I just got an IRS notice. For an audit. We can talk about it when you get back here. Gotta go! Love ya! Bah!" Bear slammed his phone down hard.

Bah? What kind of talk was that? And how dare he hang up on her like that! Furious, Linnell slammed the receiver down so hard that an object fell from her bedside table and crashed to the floor. Linnell crouched down to see what it was and then suddenly felt sick to her stomach. She held her breath and stared at the transmitting device lying next to her foot, its small antenna now twisted. A bug! *The* bug. The IRS. She should've known.

Linnell sat on the floor next to the surveillance device and studied it in deafening silence. Trying her best not to make any noise, she carefully removed everything from the small table and then she picked it up and carefully turned it around so that she could examine how the transmitter had been attached. With duct tape. With the air conditioner off, the tape had softened in the heat. She tiptoed into the bathroom to get a towel to muffle the bug, and then picking it up as if it were a live grenade, she replaced it, pressing the duct tape firmly so that it wouldn't come loose again.

From now on she knew exactly what she would have to do. The receiving device could be anywhere within a 100 yards. Closing her eyes, she tried to visualize herself at the center of a circle having the radius of a football field; everyone within this range would be suspect. Then she tried to recall her telephone conversations—had she said anything that could be misconstrued? She began to perspire, wondering what she might have said, and then she was overwhelmed with a sense of relief—thank heavens she'd always used a code for her Sea Urchin Project . . . and that she'd never left any documents lying around!

This bug had to have something to do with Willy's indictment and the tax haven investigation. The IRS knew she was a maven, and they probably thought she still had some connection with him. What else could it be? Linnell picked up the telephone and asked the operator for a long distance line. She had to get word to Karen about the tap. They had already established code words just for situations like this.

HIGHRIDGE **Friday morning - March 1, 1974**

Sick to his stomach, Bear remained slumped in his chair.

I feel like a pail of worms. I've been screwed out of my gold! $200,000 down the toilet! That fucking bank! And Ma! That bitch! I'm gonna fix her, too! Bear unlocked the desk and looked at his supplies. There was plenty left for another snort. When he was through, he angrily swept his paraphernalia back to its hiding place and locked it up. Then yanking open his door, he yelled at Margo: "You! Margo! You get out here, *now*!"

Margo rushed into the reception area with a finger over her lips. "Shuush Doc. You have a patient in here!" Margo jabbed her thumb in the direction of one of the operatories.

Bear grabbed Margo by her fleshy arm and hauled her down the hall toward the dental lab.

Deborah shot out of the back bathroom in time to hear Bear thundering: "Don't you ever shush ME! Dammit! I ordered you to block the calls when I'm training!" Frightened by his sudden tantrum, Deborah peeked around the corner and watched Dr. Clare dragging a weepy Margo out the back door and around the building, and they were both yelling so loudly that she could hear their voices through the wall.

"Okay! Here's my chance. This is it!" Deborah sprinted to the front desk, seized Margo's purse, removed the keys and replaced them with the phony set she had made out of keys she had filched from the hardware store. Marking time under her breath, Deborah entered Dr. Clare's private office and attacked the drawers of his huge mahogany desk. Margo's keys didn't fit the locks on the left side of the desk, but they did open those on the right. Deborah pulled the drawer open and spied the tape recorder and saw how the capstan rolled and switched off, recording the sound of her movements.

"Sound activated!" Deborah exclaimed. The recorder's capstan spun as she spoke. "That *crazy* pervert! He records himself getting it off!" Deborah yanked the cassette from the machine, slipped it into her pocket, then replaced it with one of the cassettes lying loose in the drawer. Then she saw all the files in

Dr. Clare's open briefcase. She was just about to examine them when she looked down and saw the enormous condom-wrapped dildo under the desk.

The hair suddenly rose on the back of her neck.

"Oh my God! He really *is* crazy!" Deborah felt her skin crawl.

But there was no time for fear. She flew to Margo's desk behind the reception counter and tried the keys in the drawer locks. The first drawer contained only cash—looked like less than a hundred, mostly ones and fives, she hurriedly closed and locked it again—then she found what she was looking for in the adjacent drawer: A pile of floppy disks for Margo's computer, with days and months carefully written on their jackets. Deborah pawed frantically through the disks, looking for a disk labeled "Code 2." Her ears hadn't deceived her! Now nervous and afraid of being caught, she grabbed the disk on the top of the pile—even though it was marked "Code 1"—and then closed and locked Margo's desk drawer. She raced back to the bathroom and hid the keys and the disk in her coat pocket.

She had the presence of mind to flush the toilet a couple of times and when she stepped back into the hall, she saw that the two crazies had just entered through the front door. They could see her standing there at the end of the hallway so she wiped her hands on her skirt to let them think she'd been in the bathroom all this time. Margo's face looked pouty and sullen and Bear was now patting her on the arm. Then the phone rang and Deborah saw Margo motioning to Dr. Clare to take the call in his private office. Deborah waited until his door was closed and then slipping into her coat, she headed for Margo. Leaning over the reception counter, she whispered that she needed to go to the store to buy her own special supplies because she'd been surprised by her period.

"Okay, sweetie. Take an hour." Margo smiled at her indulgently.

Deborah rushed to her car, her heart rattling hard in her chest. She had to stay calm because she still had so much to do. With that cheerless thought, she nervously ditched her purloined goods under her car seat as she pulled into the street from the parking lot. She headed straight for the new computer store, in a small strip-mall on the edge of town. As soon as she found it, she retrieved the disk and casually sauntered in. There were few customers, all of them computer nerds, and none of them looked at her. She ordered a duplicate of the disk and a print-out of the data on the floppy and told the clerk she'd be back after work to pick it up. The keys! She'd better not forget the keys! Her plan was to take Margo to lunch—and she'd better remember to volunteer to drive so that Margo wouldn't reach for the fake set of keys she'd slipped into her purse. She could kick over their purses and make the switch—they always placed them under the table when they ate, so that would probably work.

When Deborah returned to the office, she looked carefully at Margo to read her face and the set of her shoulders—if they were hunched, she was out of here and to hell with Willy. To her great relief, Deborah saw that the old cow was her usual self-satisfied self. She immediately asked Margo if she'd like to join her for lunch. Her treat and she would drive. Margo agreed the instant she heard Deborah say she was springing for lunch.

CAYMAN **Friday - March 1, 1974**

Jordan yearned for some time for himself. Shadowing Mrs. Clare for the last 48 hours had certainly taught him how quickly surveillance work could lose its glitz and as much as he enjoyed the sight of his subject, he couldn't get used to the feeling of always having to be so tethered to another person. Take right now for example, instead of going downstairs and grabbing a bite to eat—he was hungry and he'd forgotten to bring any snacks up to his room—he had to sit in his room. But he felt he'd better stay put because on the hunch his subject was about to make some important telephone calls. Jordan yawned, bored—he sure hoped she'd be getting to it soon—then he saw his recorder beginning to roll.

At last! Some action! Jordan stood next to his microphone and listened to Linnell's conversation with her husband about the bank and quickly grasped what his subject was doing: she was cleverly using the bank failure as a pretext to finesse some information from Dr. Clare about what he had done with their money. Jordan pressed the microphone next to his ear so he would catch every word and next heard Dr. Clare telling lie after lie about the whereabouts of their money and concluding with another lie about receiving notice of the IRS audit only that very morning.

Jordan thought about Dr. Clare's comment about the audit notice. Then it dawned—this proved that what Dr. Clare had earlier told Rizzo about Linnell being already involved in handling the dental office audit was a bald-faced lie! And whoa! Now Dr. Clare was telling his wife she was crazy! He was hanging up on her! Jordan held the microphone away from his ear to avoid the amplified noise of the slamming receivers. He next heard a crash coming from the adjacent room. Linnell had to be furious—he could tell from the sounds coming through the wall—she must have kicked something. Like maybe her chair? A long silence followed. She was probably sulking, he guessed. Jordan saw his tape stop and all he could do was sit there, patiently, wondering what his subject was doing. Finally there were some muffled sounds he couldn't make out. The tape rolled, then picked up speed and Jordan listened to his subject's unsuccessful attempts to reach her secretary. What would she do next? he wondered. When he thought she was making ready to leave, Jordan set the microphone down. This time he was prepared to follow her.

Robert Jordan lagged a comfortable distance behind his subject, appreciating her ring-bikini and the way it rode her hips. Actually, this part of the shag wasn't bad at all. In fact, it was pretty damned wonderful. Everybody wore bikinis, but hers was the best. Jordan sighed, frustrated, then watched Linnell unselfconsciously toss her hair and he immediately began to think of ways to get around Rizzo's orders. That knock-out smile! That firm small chin with it's hint of a dimple! No photograph could perfectly capture her beauty because so much of it lay in her moves and the unexpected way her expressions could change—her face was one of those rare faces that compelled you to watch just to see what it was going to do next.

How to meet her? How could he get her to speak to him? Maybe he'd get his chance, right now, because it looked like she was maybe going to settle down on a nearby chaise and maybe do some writing. Jordan watched his subject purchasing some postcards and saw her tucking them between the pages of her yellow legal pad. Then he had a terrible sinking feeling; she was passing the chaise longues and all the tables in the courtyard; now it looked like she was heading out for the beach! Grabbing his sunglasses out of his pocket, he slipped them on and sat down at a table and watched his subject settling down all by herself in the middle of the beach. He couldn't follow her out there; too obvious.

After spreading his towel in the powdery sand beneath a tree just outside the courtyard area, Jordan stretched out; his eyes automatically fastened on his subject, who now lay on her stomach, trying to write. He stared at her cleavage while adding things up. Well, so far he hadn't found anything much. She hadn't said anything that sounded even remotely suspicious, and she hadn't tried to call or get inside the bank that had failed. He'd hailed a cab to follow her to make sure, and he knew she'd just glanced at it on her way to Georgetown and then on her way back, she'd merely joined the crowd to read the sign on the door, just like everybody else. Then she'd returned to the hotel to sit at the beach bar and get in on the excitement. Nothing shady about that.

But she had to be very upset about her husband, he thought. Closing their bank accounts and sending all their money up north. Maybe she was working on some plan to get it back But then, maybe not. How would she know the real score? He had to wonder--was she even aware of her husband's business at Ye Olde Banke? It now seemed clear enough, at least to him, that she had absolutely no idea what her husband was up to—or that he had been purchasing gold there—or else she would have found some clever way to broach the subject when talking to him about the bank failure. But all this paled when compared to the larger questions about Dr. Clare himself: Why the big con? And what was *she* doing with a jerk like him? Was it the money? The kid? Could it be that she actually *loved* him?

He sure hoped not, because so far the best part of all this was something he couldn't report—her face when she first looked at him: part frank appraisal, part come-hither shocked stare. And again, her face, at the beach bar. He'd caught her watching him. As closely as he was watching her. It wasn't entirely hopeless. Beautiful women—so like swans in a shallow pond, pretending to be oblivious to the moiré images of hope they left in their wake. Except this swan seemed genuinely oblivious to the effect her beauty. And he had dreamed about her. He had never dreamt of any woman before. He had to explain this to himself.

Was it her? Or just the effect of this time and place? A promise-filled aura, an energy concentrated by the heat hovered over the island. He'd felt it as soon as he stepped from the plane. And it seemed to affect everyone here the same way. All was possible. Jordan closed his eyes and heard her voice teasing him, saw her face hovering over his. He could feel her hair spilling onto his shoulders, then her body with her large cool breasts pressing hard into his chest. The two of them, lying face to face on a smooth cotton sheet from the bed in his room. Where? Yes, here. Here, where it was so soft in the sand, with nothing over them but a warm breeze and a midnight-blue sky. Jordan saw his hand stroking the curve of her back and rearranging her legs. He would take her by surprise, roll her over and press her into the soft sand so she could reach her arms around him and pulling him down, take him deeper inside.

Slightly dazed by the onset of a hard erection, Jordan rolled over and opened his eyes and saw that his subject, innocent of the designs of his imagination, was still writing industriously. Satisfied that she wasn't going anywhere, Jordan stretched out in the dappled shade of the tree and closed his eyes to finish his daydream.

◆❖◆

Linnell lay with one elbow propped in the sand, writing a list of what she had to do: First—she had to call Karen as soon as possible to let her know that their office lines might be tapped; second—find out why she had called; third—ask her if she'd received "the contract." Linnell dropped her pen. Now she was angry. Never mind how delayed her reaction—IRS or no, Bear had behaved atrociously. Slamming the phone in her ear like that! He might be right about a whole lot of things, but that was so rude! Linnell sat up suddenly; her shoulders were already burning and she'd left her sun screen lotion up in her room. She jumped up, grabbed her papers and towel and raced over the burning sand toward the stairs to the second floor. She could finish writing her postcards on her balcony and then maybe later, go for a swim.

Robert Jordan turned his head toward the spot where he'd last seen his subject before opening his eyes—his heart stopped—she was nowhere in sight. *Now* where'd she go? Why did she always have to disappear like that? And what should he do? It was too hot to think. He couldn't stand it anymore—he had to cool off. Kicking off his flip-flops, Jordan sprinted down to the water and threw himself into a cresting wave. Refreshed, Jordan walked, dripping, to a chaise, now full in the sun. He didn't have to worry about sun burn. His skin went straight to a golden bronze. Stretching out on the chaise, he picked up his book to shade his eyes and fixed them on Linnell's balcony.

Linnell returned to her room and stepped into the shower to cool off. As soon as she was finished with drying her hair, she looked outside. Perfect weather, again. Then she slid into her brown tank suit, wrapped her beach towel around her and stepped onto her balcony. Moving her chair so she could keep an eye on the beach, she sat down at her table and began writing her postcards to the "Cs". She glanced down to the beach. And there he was—stretched out on a chaise with a book in his hand, and this time he was staring up at her. She smiled, waved, and then dropped her head to hide inside her hair. Okay. Classic opening move. Next move would be his. Linnell counted to three and slipped on her sunglasses so he couldn't tell she was waiting for him to give her a sign.

Jordan was overcome with a sense of relief. Yes, there she was. And she was definitely looking at him now. She was waving! He recovered in time to grin and wave back, then he stretched. He thought about Rizzo's warning. Well, Rizzo be damned. He was going to do something about this while he still had the chance.

◆❖◆

The sight of him made her feel like a dancing wolf. Here was a man at home in his skin. And, better still, there was only a tight pair of navy-blue racer's trunks between it and the world. Oh, *yes!* There was more! Much more. The curve of ribs cloaked in muscle. And the perfectly turned legs—thick hard thighs, tight walnut knees, solid round calves—were enough to set her heart to howling. Linnell picked up a postcard to fan herself, set it down, snapped her pen closed, opened it—but didn't drop it—then tried to present a show of composure by scribbling on the cards she'd bought to send home to the "Cs". But she couldn't tear her eyes from him. Now he was crossing his ankles and stretching, expanding an evenly tanned golden chest until it was big as a dance floor. Linnell quickly shifted her eyes to the cards she'd just signed. There were the usual missing-you-messages but on her card to Nancy she saw that she'd signed it "With legs 'n bulges," instead of "With love 'n hugs." She tore up the postcard and froze, panic-stricken that she was about to do something even more foolish.

She could feel his eyes. Lifting a curtain of hair from her face, she turned her head slightly to peek at him out of the corner of her eye. He was staring up at her and his face held such a look!—part hunger, part yearning—that she suddenly felt dizzy. She sprang from her chair and raced from the balcony into her room. She did not stumble or trip, nor did she break a nail or bark her shins. She was strangely calm. With a certain hand, she ran a comb through her hair and touched perfume to the hollows at the base of her neck. There was not a second left to waste. She knew what she wanted. She was thirty-five and this was an island floating in time. Why should she be denied?

Then he smiled to himself, his expression a sensual combination of yearning and anticipation; crossing his ankles, he laced his fingers together and raised his arms over his head and watched her as she sat on her balcony, a Juliet, writing. And then he saw her take one look at him and fly into her room. Oh, no! *Now* what? This time Jordan jumped up and headed toward the stairs to the second floor. Then, to his great relief, he saw the door opening on the landing above him and there she was, looking down at him, with a towel over her shoulder and a book in her hand. And wearing a different bathing suit, too. The lavender one had been amazing, but this one was jaw-dropping. Exactly the same color as her tawny skin, with fluorescent stuff on its edges—the only cue that she wasn't stark naked. And now she was heading straight toward him. Jordan froze. She looked like she was about to pass him without speaking.

"Hi there," he croaked. He felt like an idiot.

"Hmmm. You sure don't move around much." Linnell's voice held a challenge. She stopped and stood close to him.

Jordan inhaled, recognizing the perfume. "I see you're here on your own," he managed.

Linnell tipped her head back and looked up at him boldly. "Let me remove all the guess-work for you—I'm alone. I'm going for a swim, and then I'm going for a walk on the beach. Okay?"

While Jordan was recovering, she stepped lightly around him and headed off in the direction of the water without turning around. He called out: "I just have to make a phone call—I'll be down in a minute!" Jordan took a few steps before looking back at her over his shoulder. Then stepping behind the stairwell where she couldn't see him, he watched her long tanned legs scissoring over the blinding white sand. As soon as he saw her spinning out her beach towel, he took the stairs three at a time.

Jordan checked the tape in his recording equipment—just background noise, nothing decipherable. As for Rizzo? Forget it. He'd touch base with him later. He quickly brushed his teeth, ran a comb through his hair and then slammed out of his room and sprang down the stairs. Hooking his towel on his thumb, he tossed it over his shoulder and even though the soles of his feet were on fire, he strolled unhurriedly over the burning sand. Cool. That's how he'd play it. He located the spot where Linnell had been sitting. Her sandals and book lay on her towel, which meant that she was somewhere out in the water. Squinting into the sun, he finally found her floating just beyond the breakers, her arms and legs glistening gold in the aquamarine swells. Was this just a dream?

Jordan charged into the water and swam to find out.

Treading water, Linnell turned to watch solid arms methodically pin-wheeling in her direction, then lazily rolled over to float on her back. The angle of the sun signaled the approach of her favorite hour—when the breeze would turn soft and steady and the water would lay easy as an opal. A good time for scuba diving at Spanish Cove, a great time to hide under a tree with a book and a bottle of wine, and the best time of all for a long nap with someone you really love. And she had never done any of this. She had always been too busy. Always working, or taking care of something for somebody else. And if *she* wasn't busy, then Bear was. They had always been too busy working for tomorrow to spend any time together in the here and now. And thirty-five was the middle of a life. Perhaps the filet. Trouble was, there was no way to know—until it was over and it was too late.

Jordan lifted his head to look around. There she was. He was at most only twenty feet from her now. Taking a deep breath, he closed his eyes and plunged forward, increasing his speed. When he thought he had reached her, he came up for air to look around. She was nowhere in sight. Jordan swallowed salty water and slowly turned in a half-circle to search for her and was blinded by sunlight ricocheting from millions of dappling waves. Treading water, he reached up to rub his eyes and felt something clamp hard around his ankles. He gasped and was immediately pulled underwater before he could kick himself free.

Like otters, they popped up to the surface together, face to face, and when Linnell saw his astonished expression, she laughed. "There! *That* should teach you."

Jordan coughed water. "Hey! It's *you*! You just scared the hell out of me!" This was not at all what he wanted to say. Then he took another look at her and almost choked. *Did she know he could see clear through her suit? That the water had turned it nearly transparent?*

Linnell backed away and taunted him with a cat-like grin. "You've been asking for it. I saw you staring at me—you've been staring at me ever since you arrived. You had me wondering if you were a spook and if you are, you're going to get something far worse than just *that* . . . I'll bet you already know my name."

Robert Jordan was completely taken aback. Was she joking, or had she found him out? Somehow, in the face of all this, he managed to remain cool. He decided to tough it out. "Well, yeah. Sure I do. Uh . . . I asked. You're L.C. Clare. I'm Robert . . . uh, Robert!"

"What's this? Do I hear an echo?" Linnell taunted him with a mischievous smile, then backstroked as if she were expecting a retaliatory dunking.

"No. No. I'm Robert *Roberts*," Jordan was surprised at how well he was doing. "Just don't try to drown me. Have dinner with me. Tonight!"

Linnell, back to adulthood, shot him a mock-skeptical look and paddled away.

With one powerful stroke, Jordan was abreast of her. Treading water in front of her, Jordan managed to gasp, "What was that? Was that a yes? Don't say no . . . I've been looking for you."

"*Looking* for me?"

" . . . All my life . . ."

◆❖◆

Linnell looked at him, greatly amused. She was about to laugh, then she caught the expression on his face. He had the desperate look of a man who meant every word. If this is a line, he's got it nailed to perfection, thought Linnell. And he was a bit younger than she'd first thought—somewhere in his mid-twenties. Linnell ducked her head underwater and cut her arms into the shallow waves and the two of them stroked side by side toward shore.

They took turns examining each other as they dried themselves off. He looked older now. More sure of himself. She didn't want to stare at him too long. Were his eyes blue? He was squinting into the sun so she couldn't tell. Studying his profile from under her salt-encrusted lashes, she took in the smooth curve of his sunburned cheek and the small scar on his chin, then leisurely worked her way down to his neck and shoulders. It was at this point of her eye's downward journey that she saw a vision of golden honey, slowly trickling down through a dry heap of bleached bones. Why, this was herself! she realized with a start. This was what she had become after fourteen years. Fourteen years, she now realized, of living in an arid desert of cut and dried routine. Should she lie to herself and pretend that she didn't know what was happening here? Linnell inhaled. The air seemed perfumed; the colors had suddenly become more intense. When she shook out her towel, she noticed that his towel lay in a heap next to her sandals, as if it were intended as a sign of surrender. And she loved that, too.

Jordan broke the silence. "May I ask you something?"

Linnell nodded.

"What's L.C. stand for? Those your initials?"

"Yes, my initials. It's a nickname. "L.C." I got it before I went to law school . . . I don't really care for it, but it's useful because it makes it easier for me to deal with the good ol' boys. I'm still the only woman lawyer in my town, and I learned early on that when I use my initials on documents I get less static from the good ol' boys because this way they can't tell, that is, they can't tell I'm a woman until they meet me and by then it's too late to change things. But I prefer Linnell." This was her special litmus test; it was already understood that her marriage was not going to make any difference here—he'd seen her ring—but still, she wanted to be fair to herself as well—so this would give him a chance to cut and run if he couldn't handle the fact that she was a lawyer. Best to get this part over with now, she thought. Before she could be hurt.

There was no reaction from him—none whatsoever—so she relaxed and allowed herself to study him more carefully. *He's shorter than Bear but taller than me, and his hips are narrower than Bear's.* The wolf inside her suddenly sprang to life and she imagined what it would be like to nip at his ankles and bring him down in the sand so she could straddle him and lick his face. At her touch he would become a wolf too, and then there would be plenty of growling and sharp white teeth and the tearing off of clothes and joyful tail-wagging chases up and down the beach. Linnell tried not to laugh at the spectacle she saw in her mind, but her thoughts finally broke through into one gleeful hoot.

Linnell felt herself blushing from forehead to chin.

"Why are you laughing?" Jordan looked genuinely puzzled.

"Oh, I was just thinking about a joke. No. That's not really true. I guess I'm laughing . . . because I am happy." Linnell looked away from him because this was the absolute truth. "You see . . . It's so odd." Linnell kept her eyes hidden as she spoke. "This sort of thing seems to have happened to everybody else I know, but till now, never to me—but for some reason, I feel as if we've met before and that we already know each other, and I can't explain why. Has this ever happened to you?"

"Well, yes . . . sort of." Jordan quickly changed the subject. "Hey, I rented a car. It's at the hotel. How 'bout we go for a ride and you show me the sights?"

"Well . . . let's first go for a walk."

Linnell immediately turned and walked north and he followed her up the beach. When he caught up with her, he walked at her side, next to the water. A gentle breeze ruffled the ragged leaves of the dune vines far to their right, and Linnell Clare suddenly stopped to gaze at the expanse of empty white beach. Overwhelmed by the billions of winking crystals, she squinted to save her eyes from the blinding calcium light while she willed her heart to stop pumping so hard. She forced herself to think about turtles. There had once been hundreds of thousands of them and this was the beach where they laid their eggs. Eggs, she thought. Sperm. Pulsing. Life.

"You okay?" Jordan's voice expressed some concern.

"Fine. I'm just fine. I was just thinking about the turtle farm, that's all. It's north of here. I was just wondering if you'd like to see it."

"Sure!" Jordan couldn't help staring at Linnell's tanned, silky legs. Marvelous, the way they exactly matched her brown tank suit. Not so marvelous, however, the way the wind was drying it out and making it lose its transparency. All those delicious cracks and crevices were fast disappearing before his eyes. He caught his breath. She was wearing her ring. God! He hoped she hadn't caught his look of disappointment. "Hey! I'd love to," he added. She was beyond arm's reach, yet he could feel her smooth shoulder as if it were under his hand. Then he was afraid he'd sounded too eager. Considering what he'd just been thinking right now, he'd better be more careful about how he was coming across. He paused for a moment and then changed the subject. "I understand there were lots of pirates around here. That true?"

"Yes. Blackbeard. Henry Morgan. The island was crawling with pirates. Now all we've got here are spooks."

"Spooks?"

"Sure, spooks. The island's always being visited by them."

"Oh yeah. Of course. The IRS. That tax haven stuff."

Jordan suddenly realized that he was playing the game, and rather well, too. Which reminded him—perhaps he'd better get down to some business. He paused for a moment, then asked, "Linnell, do you like being a lawyer?" Maybe he could get her to discuss her law practice, which in turn might lead to her revealing whether she'd ever been involved in her husband's shenanigans. This was something he had to know—and now was the time to find out, before he got himself in here too deep.

"Fine stream of consciousness you've got there," Linnell replied. "If you're asking me if I'm a pirate, the answer is no. *I'm* a privateer, there's a big difference, I want you to know." Linnell began to describe what it was.

Jordan interrupted her with a laugh. "No, that's not the question. I just want to know if you like what you *do*. You know, being a lawyer . . ."

"I certainly do! It sure beats cleaning toilets."

Jordan's tan face suddenly split into a mischievous grin. He could tell she was feeling more comfortable with him. "So, let's have dinner. We can go in my car. Okay?" He patted his pocket, making sure he still had his keys.

"That sounds fine," Linnell replied. Then she suddenly remembered the spooks and gave him another look. She wasn't sure about *this* one—he could be an agent, though it was rather hard to believe. Best to err on the side of caution, she reminded herself, and behave accordingly. But God! His face was sublime. He lifted a hand to shade his eyes and for the first time she saw that his eyes weren't blue. They were actually brown, like hers; she must have been given the impression of blue from the pale wash of color that rimmed his eyes. He looked like he could use a good night's sleep, she thought, and she found herself wondering what he'd been doing the night before.

"How long you going to be here?" Linnell asked.

"Oh, couple more days, maybe a week. Depends on business. And you?"

"I don't know for sure." Linnell was equally vague. She suddenly fell silent. So much had happened it was hard to believe that she had been away from home for only five days. It felt a lot longer—a lifetime, in fact. And now, here she was, with this gorgeous hunk who was following her around like a lovesick puppy. It was nice, *very* nice, and she wished this moment would last forever, at the same time she knew that she'd better take care.

When they were midway between the two hotels, Linnell stopped. She needed to sort out her thoughts. What did she really want? She had to decide. Linnell draped her towel over one of the logs that separated the breadfruit trees from the beach. "My feet are on fire and I can't walk another step. Why don't you go get your car? I'll wait for you here."

He looked at her hard, as if he were trying to read her thoughts.

"I'll be here," Linnell reassured him and abruptly sat down. He gave her another piercing, serious look, turned around, and immediately loped away. Linnell Clare, fixing her eyes on his heavily muscled back, watched the golden triangle of flesh growing steadily smaller and smaller while her thoughts flew back to the day she'd left home. She had the sensation of peering down the wrong end of a telescope because home suddenly seemed so far, far away and here there were so many new paths to explore. What should it be? Yes? Or no?

Linnell sat very still, scarcely breathing.

Then she sighed. Such conflict! If only she were home—just for a second; just to see for herself what was really happening there; it wasn't her imagination. Bear had changed. There was something quite different about him now. He had given her the evil eye. And he had hung up on her rudely. Did this make it okay for her to do as she pleased? Did it really matter? Linnell Clare closed her eyes to the sun and in the redness behind her lids she could see the Cayman Trench stretching for hundreds of miles on either side. And just as clearly, as if she were submerged five miles beneath the sunny azure of the Caribbean, she could see the cold earth slowly yawning open beneath her feet. And this man, this man who was no stranger, this man who was rain on her desert . . . what would it be? Yes or no?

SEVEN MILE BEACH **Friday-March 1, 1974 - 3 PM**

Linnell looked up; she had made her decision, and now that she had, there was no time left to waste. It felt as if hours had passed since Robert Roberts had left for his car, yet from the sun she could tell he'd been gone for, at most, only twenty minutes or so. But wasn't that more than enough time for him to get his car and drive back here? Linnell squirmed on the log.

She might as well get herself prepared for disappointment. He'd probably decided no—and probably the very instant she had decided yes. He could see she was married. And she'd made it perfectly plain that she was a lawyer. No doubt that had done it. She'd played it all wrong. Linnell twisted around on the log, pretending to stretch, all the while hoping to spot him on the road. She hadn't asked him what kind of car he was driving so she didn't know what to look for. Shrugging her shoulders, Linnell brushed the sand from her legs and jumped up. He'd stood her up; she would have to walk back to her hotel, alone, and from now on she'd dread seeing him. Linnell tossed her towel over her shoulders and turned to walk south.

She had taken only two steps when she heard a horn honking wildly from the road. Seconds later, the man she knew only as Robert Roberts came bounding toward her through the scrub. He now wore faded jeans and a white cotton shirt and he carried a large plastic bag—she recognized the logo of the hotel gift shop.

"I'm sorry I took so long. I had to change, and then I thought I ought to pick up a few things for you, too. It might cool down when we have dinner."

Linnell revived instantly. "Fat chance of that!"

"You mean you don't want to go?"

He looked so crestfallen, his face so openly disappointed, that Linnell was both thrilled and amazed. "I mean—it's not likely to cool down."

"Oh. For a second there I was afraid you were saying you'd changed your mind." Jordan held out the bag. "Here. Hope you like it."

Jordan, now going by the name of Robert Roberts, had at first been aghast at the ridiculous name he'd chosen. Robert Roberts—hell, it was better suited to a bible belt preacher. But then when he remembered how he'd given his real name to Linnell's secretary, he felt better. He hadn't screwed up entirely. It seemed that despite his blunders, he was acquiring a better feel for the game. And—thank God—she had waited for him. All this time he'd been worried about whether she would, or if she was just trying to ditch him.

His confidence fully restored, Jordan studied Linnell's face as she opened the bag and he could tell she was puzzled by what he'd bought—a large cloud of silky fabric, blazing with scarlet and fuchsia and flame-red swirls. He enjoyed her wonderment as she pulled it out and then her amazement when she saw it was a sarong, and he was pleased beyond measure that Linnell made no attempt to conceal her delight when she wrapped it over her bathing suit.

"This is . . . this is *beautiful,*" Linnell exclaimed, tying the tail of the fabric tightly around her waist.

"Thought you'd like it," Jordan said in an offhanded manner. But his eyes feasted on her with undisguised admiration. "There's something more in there, but they're already yours."

Linnell looked in the bag and found her sandals, wrapped in tissue paper so they wouldn't soil her new evening gown.

"I found them on the beach. Thought you might need them. Okay? Let's go." Jordan took her by the hand to steady her.

Linnell felt a subtle shock of electricity at the touch of his hand and covered it up by making a show of stepping into her sandals. Her hand felt so right in his that she let him hold it as he lead her toward his car.

Though she was in a state of near melt-down, she still had the presence of mind to wonder if he was playing a game. If so, he certainly was going to great lengths. Was he married? —she'd wondered about this before, while watching him at the beach bar. Linnell looked carefully at his hands, especially the ring finger. He had wonderful hands, terrific hands, and she was relieved to see no sign of the tell-tale band of white skin that spoke of a recently removed wedding band. Perhaps he wasn't married after all. For some reason this was important to her, his being unmarried.

Jordan had draped her towel over his shoulder, and when they reached his car he spread it across the hot vinyl seat. They climbed in and there was that moment of silence as both wondered how close to sit. Jordan joked about how he'd gotten the hang of driving on the left side of the road, and Linnell, pretending to keep her eyes fixed on the blue water beyond him, moved slightly farther away from him so she could better study his face. She liked the set of his jaw—firm but not stubbornly set and with none of the pursiness that so often flickered about Bear's lips. Bear actually had a small mouth, given the size of his head. But it could open like a chasm. This man had a mouth that was sculpted, a sensual mouth that did not look overused, with a full lower lip. From his decisive movements and his assured hand on the wheel, she could tell he was very coordinated. An athlete. And from the size of his shoulders she guessed that he had, unlike Bear, really played football in college.

They headed north and arrived at the turtle farm just in time to watch the turtles being fed. The turtles were kept in the huge water-filled tanks that spread across the farm's level grounds, offering their bright unblinking eyes to the sun. Linnell and Jordan stood closer to each other, leaning over the vast vats to catch their reflections and they both gasped with surprise at the sudden eruptions of snapping beaks and thrashing stumps that greeted them whenever they got too close to the surface. The caretakers lugged huge burlap bags of turtle food that bore a suspicious resemblance to ordinary dog kibble and then slit them open over the tanks. The voracious reptiles—some already three feet wide—stretched their necks and gobbled eagerly. They were amazing—in only five minutes the water was sucked clean of all traces of kibble and again became darkly undisturbed mirrors staring up to the sky.

Robert Jordan took her hand, squeezed it gently, then let it go. Linnell was overwhelmed by a sense of rightness and shocked at this, gave him a quick, open smile. It shocked her to feel how at home her hand felt in his. And it shocked her that more and more it was beginning to feel as if Bear didn't exist and never had been. Jordan stood close, yet he was careful not to touch her as they returned to his car.

This time they headed down the coastal road until they found a small restaurant at the edge of the water at Southwest Sound, an ideal site for cocktails at sunset. They chose a small table at water's edge, underneath a netted tent in the sand, and after ordering frosty, salt-rimmed margaritas, they decided on their dinner. They chose ecrevisse—sautéed crayfish—and while waiting for this delicacy to be served, Jordan pulled his chair next to hers. Their drinks quickly disappeared and they ordered another round. Jordan moved closer so that his leg pressed lightly against her knees and wrapped his arm around the back of her chair. She studied his face, vaguely listening to him telling her about a boy's life on a ranch in Montana. They both knew the game. And they played it ever so slowly; skillfully allowing the tension to mount and then deliberately destroying it so they could build it again.

Licking the salt from the rim of her glass, Linnell slowly sipped the tequila and engaged in small talk, scarcely paying attention to her own words as she recounted what she liked most about the island and how different it was from the regimentation of her daily life in Highridge. She absentmindedly related funny anecdotes about the scandals at the Highridge Country Club—describing her friends, the games they played, their affairs—and managed to avoid his eyes by gazing, instead, at his untroubled forehead. Actually, she didn't want to talk at all, what she really wanted was to sit in his lap and hug him to her while tracing his thick sun-bleached eyebrows with the tip of her tongue. The perfect opacity of his skin. Oh God! He was hot. And was she ever getting smashed!

She quickly changed the subject and asked him if he'd played football and he told her no, that he'd been too busy working on his father's ranch during high school and all through college and that he'd had no time to take it up because he returned home to work the ranch every chance he got. He'd graduated Michigan U, he said and Linnell was enchanted that he wasn't one of those spoiled football heroes after all. That his perfect physique had come from hard physical labor made him all the more precious in her eyes. And that same look in his eyes, the one she'd first seen long ago when she'd first met her husband. He had it too, and for a moment she felt scared until she realized that he was a different man altogether. They were both surprised to discover the interests they shared despite their vastly different beginnings. They both wondered how things worked, what made them tick, and he had read almost all the same books as she —better still, gaining different insights. He loved Schezuan and cooked Italian, lived for water sports and had learned how to sail on Lake Michigan, where he'd crewed for a year. She didn't have to ask him how he made his living because he volunteered that he was in banking—some midwestern outfit she'd never heard of before—but what he did next was something she knew she'd remember for the rest of her life.

They talked easily and moved carefully, cautious as Tesla coils inside their separate fragile globes, both aware of the electrical storm that crackled between them whenever they touched. Still avoiding his eyes, she studied his face as he quizzed her about her marriage. Again, the mouth; the seductive angles of his chiseled nose; the even texture of his skin. And the scent of him—almonds, musk, the salty waters of concentrated lust—was driving her so mad that by the time she was finished with her second margarita she had already slipped out of herself and become a great starship unmoored. Floating free in a golden universe. Her bones crystalline antennae, alert to the invisible signals that came at her in great pulsing waves in search of her docking station. Linnell turned her head and this time gazed deep into the golden windows of Intergalactic Space Traveler Roberts. He was leaning toward her from outer space and then she froze when she saw him suddenly reach out with his fork—to spear the largest of the succulent ecrevisse that lay glistening on his plate. And then, without either of them missing a beat of their conversation, she watched him set it carefully, tenderly, on her plate.

It was too late. She couldn't save herself. He had pierced her armor and shot her straight through the heart. No longer a spaceship, her tongue ached with desire and a silvery torrent suddenly welled at the base of her jaws.

With that, Linnell swallowed and sat ramrod straight and lifted an ice-filled glass to her burning cheek. Oh God! Just look at her! Here she was—an international tax attorney, licensed to practice in all the federal courts of the United States, a poor woof in the warp of Highridge's social fabric—getting smashed in public and carrying on like a panting eighteen-year-old on her first heavy date. Surely others could see what was happening here! Linnell tried to peer through the folds of the mosquito netting to see if anyone was looking at them and the pink haze filling her head lifted just enough for her to wonder if the agent who'd bugged her room was here and watching her every move. Then she had an even more sobering realization: It no longer mattered.

Linnell relaxed, set her drink down, and leaned back into the crook of his thick warm arm.

◆❖◆

Jordan, having steered the conversation around to marriage in general, hoped to get her to talk about hers in particular. Instead, she told him how much she loved her son, and spoke of loyalty to family. His heart sank. And then with a faraway look in her eyes, she corrected herself and explained that she was loyal to the idea of family. His heart rose. That was different. But still, as much as he admired her for valuing loyalty, he was at the same time afraid it might lead her to harm's way. She wouldn't realize—how could she know with a sneak like her husband?—just how vulnerable she was to Bear's cunning ways.

Linnell pulled away from him just then and he was surprised. Had she sensed what he was thinking? Here he had just gotten comfortable and now she was getting nervous again. What could he do? He couldn't help it—he had this intense urge to hug her and hold her tight until she stopped struggling. And that wasn't a line—he really had been looking for her all his life. It also felt like any second now he was going to drag her under the table.

But instead, Jordan removed his fork from Linnell's plate, set it down, and shifted his weight to give her a little more room. He signaled the waiter to remove their plates and with a supreme effort at self-control, steered the conversation back to her marriage. He asked her how long she and Bear had been married and the quick flick of pain that creased her forehead when she replied fourteen years told him everything he wanted to know: If she had ever been in love with Bear, it was all over now.

Then she looked straight into his eyes and her face began to glow as if lit from within and he caught himself just in time—he'd almost slipped—he'd almost told her that she looked too young to have a seven year old son. Jordan suddenly saw visions of himself lobbing the little guy tennis balls.

And then she surprised him. She leaned into his arm, and for the first time in his entire life he had the sensation that this time he really had it all.

HIGHRIDGE **Friday - March 1, 1974**

Friday afternoon, after lunch, Deborah locked herself in the back bathroom. Dropping the cover down so she had a place to rest, she leaned against the cold porcelain toilet tank and propped her feet against the door to make sure it stayed closed. Dr. Clare had just tried to grab her again. And this time right in front of Margo, no less! Such goddam nerve that man had, especially after this morning's shocking near-miss. It was hard to fathom. He had to be crazy. Deborah wondered how much Dr. Clare was sharing with Margo about what was going on. Bourgeois voyeurs, that's what they were. Disgusting. The man reminded her of a caged animal who was about to break loose. And those scary gray eyes, with those tight pinpoint pupils.

Pinpoint pupils!

It suddenly struck her—he had to be hooked on something a lot worse than cocaine! She'd better visit the library tonight and see what she could find about the signs of drug abuse, and then she would go the store and pick up some more stuff for the weekend. Fruit especially. She needed another pineapple, and she really ought to get some more oranges. And plenty of coffee; because she had lots to do over this coming weekend.

Deborah tried to imagine Doc's wife. Willy had described her in terms of her looks: tall, long legs, an extremely attractive blonde. The woman sounded normal enough and Willy had said she was very smart, so what was she doing with a freak like Clare? For the money? Probably. Perhaps for that fantastic house of theirs. But still, it was hard to understand. If only she could meet her, see what she really was like. She could tell Margo was jealous of her; hated her, actually, because whenever she mentioned Mrs. Clare, Margo would practically turn green and spit up. And then she'd begin to brag—blah, blah, blah—about how Doc wouldn't dare keep any pictures of "the wife" in his office.

Deborah shivered when she thought about what she was doing with these crazy perverts. All of them were crazy, Willy included. A little acting job for her Uncle Willy? "It's not going to be so bad," he'd said. "Nothing a little soap and water can't later clean up." What a lousy thing to say. And he had to have known *exactly* what he was getting her into—and he hadn't said one single word to warn her or clue her in to the danger she faced. She'd remember that.

Well, Uncle Willy would get the Code 1 disk all right, but not until she had her hands on every penny of that money he'd promised. One thing was clear: She must be doing something awfully important for him or else he wouldn't have caved in like that. She could probably guess why. He was going to do a little bit of blackmail, that's what she thought. She wouldn't put something like that past her dear Uncle Willy. She'd had a print-out run of the data on Disk 1 and it revealed the names of all of the patients Dr. Clare had been "treating" for the last four quarters—she'd recognized several prominent businessmen; there were also some judges and quite a few local lawyers. Yes, given Uncle Willy's yen to control the whole town, this operation must have something to do with extortion. And from what she had seen so far, Willy was right—Doc Clare had a tax problem. A biggie.

Getting the files had been easy: She had seen Margo carrying a large number of them out of the office late Monday afternoon, the same day the two special agents had visited Dr. Clare. Margo had let her leave early, but she had stayed to watch the office, and Margo had been too preoccupied to see her hunched down behind the wheel of her car. Then on Wednesday she had loitered in the front office while Margo was refiling them; at lunch time she'd snagged an armload of files while Margo was at the bank and Doc was engrossed with a patient. She'd smuggled them out of the office by hiding them in a garbage bag which she'd ditched outside the back door of the dental lab, then she'd picked it up after the office was closed.

After spending her lunch hour comparing the patient files with the computer print-out, she now knew that the colored tabs affixed to the outside edges of each file were significant: The blue or yellow tabs indicated that these were the "special" patients that she had heard Margo discussing with Dr. Clare. The "specials" had little or no dental work and their files contained only X-rays, but the print-out of the Code 1 disk for these same patients revealed that these patients were paying cash for nitrous and other "medications" such as Percodan and amphetamines and other drugs. Furthermore, each and every one of the "specials" had numerous prescriptions for "topical anesthetic," and the topical anesthetic was pure cocaine. It now seemed clear enough to her that the other colored tabs—like the green and red ones—were being used only for camouflage so that the significance of the yellow and blue tabs would not be so apparent.

And there was another level of subterfuge; she had seen Margo collecting wads of cash from Doc's patients—the print-out of the Code 1 disk had also proved to be a list of everybody who paid cash—but the payment records kept in the patient files did not reflect any cash payments at all. Now she tried to recall exactly what Doc had said at her first "training session." With her ear for dialogue, she was sure he'd said something about "Code 2" and even though she hadn't found anything marked Code 2 the first time she'd searched Margo's desk drawer, her instincts told her that this Code-2-whatever-it-was had to be something very important. So, most likely there was another disk called Code 2. And if there really was such a disk, then it probably was still in the computer, which would explain why she hadn't found it in the drawer. Come Monday, she'd find it, find out what it really meant, and then her job here would be over.

HIGHRIDGE **Friday evening - March 1, 1974**

Late Friday afternoon, when he was all alone in his office, Bear stood in his private bathroom scrubbing his hands. Spreading his fingers, he lathered and scrubbed, lathered and scrubbed—making sure that his nails were spotless. Applying lotion and then fussily rubbing his hands together, he leaned closer to the mirror to see if the drops had worked: They had—the pinpoint pupils had dilated to a more natural state and all traces of redness had vanished. Patting his jaw line, Bear dimpled coldly while he examined his face. Then he touched the outside of his jacket pocket to make sure the bag of cocaine didn't bulge. He'd worn his rubber dental gloves while packing it into the plastic bags, one inside another, to make sure that he wouldn't leave any finger prints. Finally, he pulled on his shirt cuff and inspected the microphone in his right sleeve, making sure that the wire was still jacked into the mini-recorder hidden in his shirt pocket under his jacket.

He was sure it was Ivener who'd been trying to reach him—Helene had called Margo to tell her that she had received an early-morning call for Dr. Clare from a man who said he was "a friend at The Wei" and then, as if to prove him right, Harold had called just before lunch with the cryptic message that Ivener had agreed to meet with him early this evening. Such prompt attention from the Ivener camp was very encouraging. Harold had said that he'd be driving, taking great pains to explain that it wouldn't be any trouble for him, "Because he wanted to give him the photos and they wouldn't be ready until late this afternoon." Bullshit! Harold just needed an excuse to tag along, and he wanted to tag along because he was curious, which had to mean that Ivener wasn't telling him everything. Their meeting was set for dusk, in the parking lot of the restaurant near Ivener's office.

Bear locked up his office and fifteen minutes later he pulled into the parking lot and saw Harold's car parked on the windowless side of the building and no sooner had he set his brakes than Harold was sliding out and rushing over to greet him. Bear observed that Harold exuded a new air of officiousness, as new as the suit he was wearing. An expensive suit, too. And his nose and forehead were almost cranberry red from sun poisoning. Bear lowered the window on the passenger's side and suddenly noticed that his hand was clenched into a white-knuckled fist. "Easy does it," he thought, forcing his fingers to unfold and letting his hand hang limp.

Harold poked his head through the open window. "We thought it would be better if we sat in my car. That okay?"

"How 'bout in here? Mine's larger and far more comfortable." Bear waited for Harold to turn around and the moment he did, Bear reached under his jacket and switched on his recorder. Harold offered no argument. He swung open the back door of the Cadillac and motioned for Ivener to join them. Bear observed Ivener's gait; the man appeared thinner. It was also obvious that Ivener didn't much care that his employees were dressing better than him, which made him wonder if Ivener was losing his grip. The indictment has to be taking its toll, thought Bear.

A deferential Harold Dolphe remained standing until Ivener had made himself comfortable in the back seat, and then he slid into the front seat and introduced Dr. Clare to his boss. Bear rested his right arm on the top of the car seat and then, barely turning, presented his left hand, palm down, to give Ivener a Hollywood handshake. "You can call me Bear," he said, offering Ivener the grim smile he'd been practicing earlier. "My wife's told me a lot about you, so I feel like I know you already. I gotta apologize for her volunteering to testify against you. You did a lot for her, so it really makes me sick to think she'd want to turn on you like that."

Ivener's reply was confined to a sudden, soft glance. When he spoke, however, it was with a voice that belied his apparent frailty. "Well, Dr. Clare . . . *Bear* . . . I'm glad to meet you at last, although I'm *not* yet quite sure what prompted you to make this appointment. Please, why don't you call me Willy."

Ivener's narrow face was unmoved, but when he fixed his large pale brown eyes on Bear's face, they glowed with a feverish benevolence. Bear was surprised to find himself once again staring at Ivener in semi-darkness, but this time the man did not seem the least bit threatening or sinister. In fact, seen up close like this, Ivener's face was almost beautiful in its fragility.

Ivener remained silent. Then, reaching out, he patted Bear's shoulder and praised him for the skillful way he had handled himself at The Wei programs.

An awkward silence hung heavy in the air.

Harold, who had been sitting in the front seat of the Cadillac, taking everything in, suddenly interjected: "Here, these are for you." He passed a manila envelope to Bear.

Bear could feel that it contained photographs.

"I suppose I should take a look at them," Bear mumbled. He knew what he'd find, but he was actually curious. Switching on the dashboard lights to give himself more light, he examined the photographs. He saw a scantily clad Linnell sitting with a large black man in an old dusty car; another shot of her smiling at this same man on the beach; and then—just like Dolphe said—here she was with her tits falling out of her bikini, living it up with some young dude at the beach bar; then again, in the water with all of the rest of the hard bodied, brown-skinned divers; and then at the warehouse . . . where Ma—her robe now hanging open over the same skimpy bathing suit—stood in the arms of the same large black man, this time smiling up at him, and finally, on her balcony . . . Bear blinked at the sight of his wife's large firm breasts, inhaled sharply, and quickly searched the envelope for the negatives. They were missing.

Harold sat waiting for Bear to do something. He had left his hand on the seat, palm up, with his fingers wiggling so Bear would know he could slip him a baggie and Ivener wouldn't be any the wiser.

Bear looked at Harold's waving fingers. His voice turned hard. "The negatives. *Now*."

Harold shrugged and grinned sheepishly, but quickly reached in his pocket and handed Bear a narrow yellow packet. Bear held one of the negatives up to the light. Satisfied, he slipped them into his jacket, and then mumbling that he'd take care of Harold later, leaned back to enjoy the look of frustration that crossed Harold's face.

Harold, peeved, made a whining sound in the back of his throat. Ivener gave Harold one stern look and Harold quickly gave Bear's shoulder a heavy pat and said, "See you *later*, bro."

Bear and Ivener sat looking at each other in silence.

"Well, I know what *your* problem is," Bear finally announced. "And it looks like she's been keeping a lot of secrets from *me,* too." Bear patted the envelope. "If those agents hadn't dropped by my place I would never have known what she was up to."

"So. The IRS visited you just to see if you'd be willing to cooperate with them? No other reason?"

"You got that one right. Well, I've got to tell you, she's got a helluva lot of nerve, doing this to you. In fact, I have to admit, I can't figure her out."

Ivener replied, "*Your* problem seems to be all over Cayman these days. It seems to me that a woman like L.C. would want to be faithful to a man like you, that she'd be grateful. And I am sincerely sorry to hear that she's betrayed you like this, but I am also quite flattered and touched that you've asked to see me in order to air your thoughts."

Bear got the feeling that there was something artful in the way Ivener was choosing his words, so this time he didn't reply.

Ivener suddenly gazed more intently at Bear. "You're a man of great accomplishment. You're a great credit to The Wei, and you *should* have some pride. That's only normal. However, if I understand you correctly, the natural flow of things makes me wonder if you're casting about for an appropriate—let's say it this way—a *proper* way to deal with your situation. Is that so?"

Bear thought: Here it comes. "Yes. Yes that's true, and that's why I'm glad *you're* here to help me. It never hurts to have a little help with *things*." He held his breath while he waited, hoping that Ivener's double-talk was actually leading somewhere.

"The Wei teaches that the *best* way is the *easy* way," Ivener declared. "Now I ask you, can you tell me what could be more difficult than a divorce? I mean, it's become nothing more than a cold-blooded hassle over property and I find this new no-fault system quite troubling because it fails to provide any catharsis. That's what bothers you most, isn't it? And that's why The Wei is here to provide you with some relief. Perhaps only a man, a man such as yourself, would be willing to cut the knot . . . perhaps . . . in a more permanent way? If you're thinking along those lines, then I think we ought to explore the matter more. Let's talk about it."

"You mentioned something about giving me a little help with . . . uh, *things.* Are you suggesting that you can *arrange* something for me?" Bear was now sweating, he wanted to stop this fencing around and get to the point.

To his great relief, he heard Ivener continue: "I have a problem. Perhaps you can help me solve it. By the way, this is a very comfortable car, but let's just step outside for a minute? I need some air."

Ivener opened the door and slid out of the Cadillac. Bear followed.

Ivener spoke first. "It's quite simple, really. I'd like you to get me a copy of her research. Specifically, her research on taxing foreign foundations. I understand you know all about this, so I presume you can do this for me?"

Bear was stunned, utterly flabbergasted by the modesty of Ivener's request. Finally, he found his tongue. "Is that all? Sure. I can do that. I can get it for you tonight. I was planning to check out her office anyway, so that'll be easy."

Ivener suddenly reached into his jacket and Bear froze, then relaxed when he saw that Ivener was only removing a small pad of paper; Ivener jotted a message and held it up in front of Bear.

Bear read what it said: *Say yes if you want her out of your hair. This time, for good.*

Bear was more surprised by Ivener writing a note than he was by the message. He looked at Ivener in wonderment and saw that the man's eyes were now boring into him—it was as if the man really was a magician who could read his mind. He would take the leap. Bear nodded his head, then waited to see what Ivener would do next.

Ivener stood with his head tipped back slightly and his eyes locked on Bear's. He was waiting for a reply.

Bear saw no harm in saying one word. He leaned down toward the thinning hair, down toward the bony skull with the eyes that bored into him, and said one word: "Yes."

Ivener placed the first note in his pocket and then scribbled rapidly on a new sheet of paper. Bear stood before him, as if in a trance, until Ivener held out the note for him to read:

Your wish is granted.

Don't worry—Harold knows nothing. Use him as a courier. Do not call me. I will not call you. You will select the date by giving Harold a check to pay for your enrollment in The Wei Advanced Training Program. The date on the check will be the target date. Tell Harold to deliver the check to me along with an itinerary of the target's scheduled activities.

Not wishing to leave any prints, Bear studied the note without touching it. The word, *target,* underlined in a heavy hand, made him stare. He tried to imagine Ma as a target—it all sounded so businesslike, so sterile. He nodded again. He very desperately wanted to tell Ivener to be sure to make her death look like a suicide, but he was afraid to say anything more aloud.

They shook hands again and this time Bear noticed the sharp bones in Ivener's thin, cold hand. The meeting concluded just as abruptly as it had begun. Ivener stepped into the shadows and Bear climbed back into his car and sat in the darkness while he thought about the best way to alter his recording so that if it ever were necessary, he could frame the lousy lawyer. As soon as he saw Ivener turning the corner and he knew the man was safely out of sight, Bear reached inside his jacket and switched off his recorder.

Willy Ivener slowly climbed all the stairs to the restaurant before doing the same to his.

◆❖◆

Bear headed straight for Linnell's office. He glanced at the time and thought: *Karen should be out of there by now.* He knew Karen's schedule, he'd called her enough to know her comings and goings. *Night-lights are on . . . she's locked up and gone home.*

These days his lips moved with his thoughts because he'd found this would help him get the voices to stop interfering. They had come back with a vengeance and he could feel them humming madly, buzzing like flies, banging against the walls of the black box in his head. He had the keys to Ma's office—Ma always left them at home when she traveled—and now, when he shook them, the sharp metallic sound combated the sound of the voices buzzing in his ears, making it easier for him to think.

Bear entered through the back door and proceeded directly to the utility panel where he keyed off the burglar alarm. Another thing that Ma didn't know—she was so dumb, so slow—was that the guy who'd keyed the house and his office had done her office too. One of his special patients. Bear nervously hummed his mantra while he prowled through the office.

"I'll just take a look at her mail," he announced aloud. He jerked to a stop. He'd better put on his dental gloves. No point in leaving his prints all over the place. Bear pulled them on and then pawed through Linnell's mail bucket, looking for letters from the Cayman Islands—there were two envelopes from the island. He counted on his fingers—the postmarks were two weeks old—then he ripped them open to see who had sent them. One letter was from the bank where he'd set up the family trust the year before—it merely confirmed Ma's appointment. The other was from the Cayman Chamber of Commerce.

"Nothing! Just junk," he complained loudly. Disappointed, he stuffed the ripped envelopes into the wastebasket and moved over to Karen's desk. Then he lost his balance and lurched into her chair, sending it careening into the metal filing cabinet. He moaned, then cursed and kicked the chair and it crashed into the desk the very instant the telephone rang. Startled, Bear listened to it for almost a minute, his head throbbing with white flashes of light each time it chimed, and just as he reached over to yank it out of the wall, it stopped. He cursed it and continued to forage.

"Her fuckin' desk is *locked!*" Bear was somehow amazed by this. He tried all the drawers until he found one that opened. "Nothing but lipstick and hand lotion . . . shit!" Finding the light switch on the wall, he flipped on the overhead lights and just then a sudden numbness in his leg made him stumble sideways toward the metal filing cabinets.

"Ohhhweee . . . Bitch left her keys!" Bear squealed delightedly. He turned the key and pulled the drawer out until it hit the stops.

What he was looking for was right under his nose: a file captioned: *Taxing the Foreign Foundation.* This was it, and it looked like it had just been typed. Hands trembling with excitement, he pulled the manuscript out of its folder and carried it to the copy machine. It took him only ten minutes to copy the entire manuscript and then he jammed the original back into its folder and shoved it into the file drawer. He stood thinking for a moment, as if he were trying to remember something, and then he slammed the file drawer closed and opened the one just beneath it. And now—time for his real mission: He reached into his pocket and carefully withdrew the bag of cocaine and tore open the outside bag. Holding the innermost bag by a corner, he dropped it behind the last file, poking it down with one finger to make sure it wasn't visible. He had planned to leave it in Ma's desk, but this way was fine because it would fix both of them.

"Fixem-fixem . . . fixem both." Bear crooned aloud. He knocked the drawer closed with his elbow and turned the key; then carefully shoved the empty plastic bag deep into his pocket. He was a very bad boy. Very bad. On his way to the door, he spotted the roses sitting on Linnell's desk, hanging from their twisted limp stems like dark clusters of rotting mice. He wanted to swat them across the room. Smash them against the walls of her office. Grind them like he would grind her. "No! No! I don't want to get stupid here," he moaned loudly. He thought about searching her desk, took one step into Linnell's private office, changed his mind and bumped into the door frame as he turned to leave.

The telephone began to ring and ring and ring. Where did his head stop and the world begin? Sometimes he couldn't tell when the sounds were so loud.

He had to escape the confusion. Feeling dizzy and slightly nauseated, Bear hurriedly turned off the overhead lights and re-armed the burglar alarm, then cursing, stepped outside and pulled the door closed. He had what he needed to set Ivener in motion. It was going to be so easy. Should this bother him? If only he could kill her himself. With his own bare hands. Then he remembered the words of The Wei: *The best way is always the easy way.* Let Ivener do it, thought Bear. It's easier that way. "Poor little Markie," he cried aloud.

Bear drove his car around the corner and stopped. He had to decide: the yellow pill now? He still had one on him. He fished it out of his wallet and swallowed it without water, then chased it down with a square of chocolate Ex-lax. Then he remembered all the gold he'd lost and sniffled, on the edge of tears. He was afraid he was going to cry. His last hope—that Ma was mistaken about Ye Olde Banke—had been dashed. When he tried to get through to the bank, the overseas operator had connected him with the island telephone exchange and they'd confirmed that all telephone lines to the bank were disconnected. He hated Ma. *Hated* her. She was to blame for everything.

He decided he'd better keep Buster working on the divorce; it would only have to be for a little while longer and besides, Buster might think something was fishy if he called off the divorce just before Ma winds up dead. Buster was just the sort of gossipy bastard who could get to joking about how Bear would do almost anything to avoid paying legal fees. Well, one thing was certain: As soon as Ma was whacked, the divorce would be moot, so what he had to do now was to make absolutely sure that nobody else got wind of his plans to dump her—if word ever got around that they were actually on the outs, this would make him look like the suspect.

He knew his rights: Buster had to keep everything secret—he'd learned that from Ma. So, bottom line, he'd let Buster spin his wheels until Ma was gone. Meanwhile, he would see to it that Buster had a warrant ready so Ma's files could be searched the instant she returned. No. He'd better *first* get Ma involved in his audit—and *then* have her office searched. That way everything would appear to be tied together, and best of all, there'd be no fingers pointing at him. Blinking and yawning, but still wide awake, Bear gradually became aware that one eye was slowly shifting in and out of focus.

CAYMAN **Friday evening - March 1, 1974**

They drove slowly up the coast toward the hotel. Earlier that evening, Linnell had playfully called him "Roberto," and he'd told her he liked it a whole lot better than Robert Roberts. Still slightly buzzed from the margaritas, she nestled close to him until he pulled up to the hotel, then she pulled away, explaining that she'd better be careful because she might be under surveillance.

Jordan didn't know what to say. Her explanation had puzzled him at first and then he recalled, with no little shock, that she would necessarily be referring to what he was supposed to be doing. He kept forgetting about that. Why? Because *this* was real, and all that other stuff—the sneaking, the bugging, the lying and spying—it all seemed like so much crazy, unreal nonsense.

Remembering that as a married woman she needed to be discreet, he let Linnell out of his car in the parking lot and then just in case anyone was watching, he slowly followed her and stood outside the entrance while she headed through the darkened lobby toward the outside stairs that led up to the second floor. Before following her, he looked through the arches toward the beach bar. It appeared deserted. All the customers were apparently in the main lounge.

As soon as she was about to step outside, he decided he'd better not wait any longer. He quickly skirted the room as she opened the door. She stepped outside, and before the door could close, he slipped through it, grabbed her by the wrist and pulled her toward him, away from the light.

"I wish . . . " he said. He wanted to find something in her eyes. Linnell's face seemed expressionless in the shadows, but her eyes lit up for a second before she drew back. That flash in her eyes was all that he needed. Wrapping an arm around her shoulders, he whirled her around until she was under the second floor landing. And then she surprised him by adding an extra turn and he found himself pressed up against the wall underneath the stairwell next to the bushes. Linnell stood on her tiptoes and pressed herself against him and then jumped away and Jordan could see her eyes spark with excitement. He looked away as if pretending not to see her, just long enough to make her drop her guard, and then he grabbed her and wrapping one arm around her waist and the other about her shoulders, he turned his cheek into her hair like a cat making ready to mount. Then he kissed her fiercely and he felt her leaning into him and cool lips parting and a hot tongue teasing and then he saw a billion stars blaze in the darkness behind his lids.

◆❖◆

The kiss sent her flying down through soft petals toward a vanishing point at the center of a perfect pink rose. His shirt fell open and there was skin like cool satin that quickly burned hot against her chest and arms. Wrapping her arms around his expanded back, she leaned into him as he peeled off one strap of her bathing suit top and then his hand tore open her sarong and he pushed his leg between hers and she felt his hand and tried not to bite when her mouth found his neck. He picked her up and she heard him moan with pleasure when he set her down on his hardness and then the cold earth cracked open and fiery lava sizzled up to meet the hand that firmly held her breast. Oh. Oh! He was *there*. She caught her breath and held on, savoring the pulsating thickness of him and then, quite unexpectedly, their boundaries disappeared and the arms of the universe began their slow spiral as they embarked on their first journey through starlit space. *Oh thank God . . . yes . . . she had found him at last . . . her astronaut of inner space . . .* Linnell felt herself disappearing into a new dimension.

She had almost disappeared entirely when she heard an earsplitting crash. The building shook and her eyes flew open in time to see a shaft of bright light piercing the stair risers to cut across their faces. The door to the second floor landing had been slammed open, hard against the wall. Then came a boisterous shriek. Jordan's head jerked up. Linnell leaped from his arms. Panting, enraged, she wanted to howl and tear into the interlopers, bite them into small pieces; but instead, she faded quietly into the bushes and struggled to pull on her clothes.

Loud squeals and the faint sounds of scuffling floated down from the second floor landing. A man whined, "Aw, c'mon babeeee." A woman's voice bleated: "You-better-let-go-of-me! Oh! Hey! Henry? Oh *gawd.* You see what I see? There's someone down there. *Lordy! They're* getting it on in the *bushes*!" The woman shrieked, then giggled hysterically, loud and drunk.

Linnell's mouth turned dry. Had she been spotted? She must be crazy; the island was literally crawling with spooks and here she was, half-naked, making out like a weasel in heat, under a stairwell next to the most heavily trafficked lobby on the entire island! She hastily tied her sarong and looked up at Jordan. His face was creased with pain and he was holding his breath. Linnell pressed a finger first to her lips and then to his and then they both stopped breathing and held onto each other while the loud, drunken couple staggered toward them down the stairs—their heads craning in their direction—and then the two drunks veered away, yelling and laughing, across the sand toward the beach bar.

The spell had been broken.

"I must be crazy . . . this is crazy," Linnell finally whispered. " No. No, I don't mean that! Roberto, you're not a mistake. And I want you. It's just that I *can't* right now."

"Don't go," Jordan implored.

"Roberto, I know this sounds like a cop-out, but I *can't* . . . Not until I get things sorted out. Got to do that *first*."

Jordan leaned on the wall while he tucked in his shirt.

"Thank you, Roberto . . . for the most beautiful day I've ever had in my life." Linnell spoke softly. She hesitated, waiting for him to speak, and when he didn't, she stepped out from the shadows and onto the landing. "I have to go now. So . . . you know . . . I have to go."

"Can I see you tomorrow?"

Linnell nodded her head. "Tomorrow," she said, but her voice sounded flat, as if she were having a difficult time controlling her emotions. She looked serious for a moment and then she tried to smile but all she could manage was a terrible grimace. She fled up the stairs to her room.

Jordan thought he'd seen tears sparkling in her eyes and he felt comforted—at least she felt as miserable as he. He watched Linnell step rapidly up the stairs and when he heard the door slam, he walked out to the beach and waited until he saw the lights going on in her room.

Robert Jordan, feeling as if he'd just been kicked into limbo, limped into the cocktail lounge. He wasn't in any kind of a drinking mood and he'd be damned if he was going to go up to his room and listen to any damn microphone on a Friday night. He'd watch the dancers, maybe have a few dances, himself. Then he shook his head. No. He didn't want to touch anyone or have anyone touch him. He would see her again. Tomorrow. And Rizzo be damned, he was going to warn her about her husband. He was positive she didn't know anything about his double life. He had to do something. He couldn't just leave her to go it alone with that crazy sonnavabitch.

◆❖◆

Linnell looked at the time. Ten minutes had passed and she was still shaking. Oh lord, had she ever wanted him. She still did. But she'd told him the truth—she was a privateer and that meant she had to play by the rules. Was that really the truth? Maybe not. Probably not. Maybe she was just afraid of getting caught. She didn't know any more. Right now, however, what she wanted the most was to hear the sound of Roberto's voice. If only he'd call. But still . . . she *did* owe something to Bear—how could she betray him like that? After all, Bear was still her husband, and she still had a duty to show some respect for the office even though there was little left for the man. Linnell grimaced at how close this sounded to what some people were now saying about the president.

Linnell reached for the telephone.

As soon as she touched it, it rang. It had to be him! Roberto! Linnell lowered her voice to what she hoped was a sultry purr and to her great disappointment, found herself purring hello to the overseas operator. It was an emergency call—would she accept charges? "It's from your secretary," said the operator. There was a crackle of static and then Linnell heard the fright in Karen's voice.

"L.C., *where* have you been! I've been trying to reach you! I'm at work, but right now I'm in your private office and I don't want to turn on the light. I've been under your desk for what seems like forever!"

"Under my desk? What happened, an earthquake? Are you okay? What's going on!"

"I couldn't get to the phone! Something awful just happened. Not an earthquake. Bear. He was in here tonight! Ray dropped me off here this evening and I was just about ready to get to work when I heard somebody coming in the back door . . . the alarm didn't sound. He has your keys! At first I didn't know it was him, I thought it was a burglar, so I grabbed my purse and ran . . . hid under your desk."

"*Who* came in? Bear? Did you see him? Are you sure it was him?"

"Yeah! Bear! It was him all right. I don't have to see him. I know his voice. He was ranting and raving and I couldn't hear everything but what I did hear sure tells me he's crazy."

"What was he doing? Could you tell?"

"He was searching the office and cursing and kicking things around. He got into the filing cabinet because I had no time to think about grabbing the keys. He tried to get into my desk. He used the copy machine a long time. I could hear him slam a couple of file cabinet drawers. Oh yeah, he went through your mail."

"Karen, listen. Retrace his steps. Tell me everything you can."

"The mail—I heard him tearing some open. He kicked my desk chair. He must have gotten his hands on your foreign foundations article 'cause it was in the drawer I was opening when he bust in. He got into another drawer too, I could hear him opening and closing two drawers. And he almost found me, he stepped into your office, but then must've changed his mind. Brrrr. He scares me, he really does."

"Karen, stop! Think. He got into only that one filing cabinet, the others have different keys, remember? I want you to open all the drawers in that file cabinet and search each one, see what's been disturbed. Or, maybe he's left some kind of calling card. Anything's possible. Go look! I'll hold." Linnell flopped down on the bed and waited for Karen to return while she listened to the rise and fall of the static on the long distance connection.

"L.C.! I found something. In the second file drawer, behind a folder—it looks like a bag of powdered sugar. I have a bad feeling about what it is."

"Sugar?! Put the bag down carefully. I think it's cocaine. Do you think it weighs more than an ounce?"

"Oh sure—it's way more than that." Then there was silence.

"What are you doing?" Linnell asked.

Karen replied, "I just took a chance, I put a tiny bit of it on my lip, now it's numb. It's coke all right. What should I do with it?"

"It's the pure stuff he uses as topical anesthetic. There's something about this that's really fishy, it makes me think about Bear's pal, that dentist—the one who was convicted for peddling cocaine and sent to San Quentin. Davie Merino. Bear took over his practice when Davie was sentenced. I feel there's some kind of connection here. So, you'd better flush it! I can't tell you why he'd do this—it's just like a bad B-movie. Maybe he's crazy—or maybe he's trying to set us up. I can only guess. But get *rid* of it and for godsake, hurry! I'll hold."

Linnell spoke carefully, mindful of the transmitter taped to her bedside table.

After a full two minutes, Karen returned and picked up the phone. "Okay. Done. I flushed it. What next? Oh God! I almost forgot to tell you—this might be really important, considering what's just happened. The publisher told me to give you this message: He said he has to edit out all that stuff you wrote about how the government uses foreign foundations. He said you're getting too deep into CIA territory. That's why I tried to reach you the other day. So, Bear got his hands on the manuscript before I had a chance to tell you, so all this CIA business is in the stuff he copied—and I know this is what he copied 'cause he left the pages in reverse order. I just checked the file."

Linnell did not feel as calm as she sounded. "We can deal with that when I return. You get what I sent you? The contract. Has it arrived? Did Bear take it?"

"No, I know it hasn't been delivered yet, and I expect you'll be back here before it arrives."

"Well, that's some good news. I'm going to cut my trip short. Don't tell anyone. I want Helene to get Benjy out of the picture, maybe take him to Disneyland for a couple of days. You'd better lock up now, and get the locks changed first thing tomorrow. Get a different security company. Then stay home. I'll call you."

"Do you want me to call Helene?"

"No. I'll call her. And save all the newspapers, I have to read about Project Haven Mavens. Your time is what? Eight p.m.?"

"Right."

"Okay. Don't stick around to play detective. Say hello to Ray, and have him come pick you up right away. See you."

After Karen hung up, Linnell lay on her bed, realizing that she'd forgotten to warn Karen about the telephone tap. Hell! A bug was nothing compared to what she faced now. Bear was obviously up to his neck in something illegal and trying to make it look like she was involved too. So it served him right—the agency that was spying on her would now most certainly turn its attention to him.

Linnell called home and spoke tersely with Helene about taking Benjy home with her and to call his school so he wouldn't be reported as missing, and then she spoke briefly with Benjy and told him to have a good time. Helene took the phone back. "L.C., I think you should know—your husband's been staying at the club and he's only called once, to see if he had any messages, so I don't think he'll even notice if we're not here. By the way, I received a call for him early this morning. Someone from that Wei Program. A man. Said he was a friend. Wouldn't give his name. Said he knew where to reach Dr. Clare if he wasn't home."

"You're sure it was a guy?"

"Positive. If you ask me, I think that Wei outfit is responsible for your husband's strange behavior. He's probably having what those people call a 'mid-life crisis'. Well, don't you worry. I'll take good care of Benjy. Maybe you should try to get Bear some professional help. You know, you two have been together so long . . . so, just think about it."

Linnell turned off the light and sat at the open window, thinking. Helene meant well—but it was clear she didn't know how serious the situation really was. Now that it was clear that Bear was up to no good, she had to decide what to do.

The weather was warmer than usual because the breeze had kicked up and was changing direction. Unusual for Cayman, because this time of year the wind usually blew from the northeast. The humid gusts had sucked the mosquitoes up from the salt marshes and driven them toward the hotel and she could hear the soft thumps of the mosquito abatement pumps between the cracking sounds of the rising breakers. Linnell carefully removed her love-stained sarong—the only tangible souvenir of her adventures with Roberto—and pressed it to the damp heat between her legs; then she rolled it up and stuffed it in a corner of her luggage. And then she was overcome. Oh where was he? *Roberto,* she wailed. She had pushed him away. Pressing a pillow to her face, Linnell sobbed wildly for an entire minute before finally managing to get herself under control. Just being with him made her feel so alive—thirty-five going on eighteen.

Moving like an automaton, Linnell methodically sprayed a thick mist of mosquito repellent on her legs and pulled on her navy blue warm-up jacket, then locked her room and crept down the hall. She hadn't seen Harold Dolphe for a while and the half-lit corridor gave her a spooky feeling that he was waiting to leap at her from the shadows. She looked all around her and saw nothing suspicious, only a quiet, empty corridor. A lump rose in her throat when she descended the stairs. It was all so incredible, how fast things could change. And to think that less than an hour ago she had been *this* close to heaven at the very same spot she was staring down at now!

As if to scold her for letting it all slip away, a ground wind sent powdery sand, soft as ashes, swirling hard around her ankles when she stepped onto the concrete landing at the bottom of the stairs. The two drunks who had ruined everything were long gone, and now she was all alone, becalmed on the dead sea of her mid-life crisis. The ache in her loins contracted and died and then she felt leaden, as bottom-heavy as a Russian nesting doll. Linnell took a deep breath. The air was heavy with moisture. A storm, rare for March, was blowing south of the island and a half-moon glowed briefly before it was masked by low scudding clouds.

She trudged through the sand toward the water, thinking about how being a lawyer had changed her. Three years as a lawyer was enough to turn anyone into a cynic, but she had fought this by constantly reminding herself that everybody had problems, that everybody always thought theirs were the worst in the world, and that she was doing good by helping them. But now it was time for her to help herself, and she had to face up to the fact that Bear *was* hooked on drugs and that she had to decide what to do—not for Bear's sake, but for herself, and for Benjy, too.

She'd better face up to it now: She'd been so enamored of parading her scruples—so proud of herself for being *such* a good girl—that she had driven off the one man in the world that she really wanted . . . and all for the sake of the man that she didn't. Linnell thought about Roberto and tried not to feel stupid as she sat, staring glumly, in the direction of where she'd last seen the moon. She stared blindly at first, and then as her sadness diminished, she began to envision the lands beyond the watery horizon: Mexico—the Yucatan Peninsula, Chichen Itza, Uxmal—an ancient lost world which just like lost love, lay bittersweet, far beyond reach.

"Funny, that's how Bear makes me feel about him," thought Linnell, "that some truth about him lies just over the horizon. And the trouble is, no matter how hard I try, I'm unable to see what it is because I can't seem to get the right angle on him. I think I now understand why—because I've always been looking at him from the wrong perspective, because I've always tried to understand him through the eyes I'm supposed to have as a good wife.

"Now, why have I made this mistake, do you suppose? Because of religion? Yes. I've been handicapped, not so much by spirituality as by religion. See? The Church speaks of God as if God were a male, and it maintains, quite literally, that men were created in *His* image. And patriarchal priests—they teach us that males are the norm and that females are somehow lesser, an unnatural, wayward force which men are obliged to contain. And we've still got plenty of sanctimonious men in high places who maintain that political authority ought to reside—as a matter of genetic disposition, no less!—only in the hands of the husband. And it's men—who first anoint and then appoint themselves the mouths of God—who preach that men have a God-given right to insist that a *good* woman would no more question a man's authority than would a good man question God's. This is exactly how I ended up like a trained seal, how I was taught to believe that I have to prove—over and over again—that I'm up to snuff."

Completely taken by her new train of thought, Linnell dropped to her knees in the sand. "Where is it written that God has a cock?" she exclaimed. "Why not a well-rounded Ba-Abaloah, with the music of the universe pounding to the rhythms of *Her* mystery places? Male, female—who says God has to be one and not the other? See? It's nothing more than a matter of politics, and politics always turns about your perspective. Religion, politics—they're just another name for the struggle over "Who's gonna get," and "Who's gonna get to tell who what to do." "

And that's when it hit her.

"Think! Dammit! Think! Monday, the very same day he tries to freeze-dry you with his eyes, he sends you a cheap bunch of roses and a measly two hundred bucks . . . and then sends our fortune up to Canada. I fly south and our money flies north. Jesus! Why didn't I see what this meant? If all he wanted to do was to hide our money from the IRS, then he would have sent it *here*, to Cayman, with *me*. Why did it take me so long to see what he was up to?"

Well, the answer was simple. While he was hiding their money from *her*, she was trying so hard to be such a good-girl wife that she had refused to let herself think such awful things about him. But now that she had given herself permission, she could see Bear's modus operandi: The look that was meant to kill, followed by a token gift of flowers and a dab of money. His insincere endearments, followed only 12 hours later by his arrogant lies. And then tonight! Salting her law office with drugs! And calling her "Ma"—that was no doubt his clever way of encouraging her to make excuses for him—as if he were not a knowing adult, but an innocent child. Linnell suddenly thought about her car—that had been a very large gift. She was now sure that something huge and horrible was headed her way—it just hadn't reached her yet.

Linnell leaped to her feet. What should she do? She needed a plan, something to flush him out in the open so she could take a straight shot at him without shooting herself in the foot.

◆❖◆

Jordan sat at the bar in the cocktail lounge, listening to the music and noticing that he'd already seen these faces the day before—pretty young women in halters and shorts, making no bones about staking their territory—which made him feel all the more lonely.

Frustrated, disappointed, and now very bored, Jordan picked up his drink and carried it to the house telephone. He would call her room. See if she was okay. What if the real reason she'd pushed him aside was because she had somebody else lined up for the night? No. Now, that was really dumb. He ought to know better than to think such thoughts. But still, he had to know what she was doing. Maybe he could talk her into coming downstairs and joining him for a nightcap?

Jordan dialed Linnell's room and was surprised that she didn't pick up the phone. Curious, he returned to the second floor, only to find her missing again. At first he was upset, but then, after reviewing his tape of her telephone calls, he had a sense of foreboding. Now he was sure that Dr. Clare was very dangerous—and after listening to Linnell's sobs—she'd even called for "Roberto"—he was certain she was out on the beach, brooding, alone in the dark. Then he froze—he was supposed to have touched base with Rizzo this evening. He'd better get this out of the way, then he'd go out and hunt for her. Jordan called the overseas operator and asked for a direct connection to Rizzo's private line.

The phone only had to ring once and Jordan heard Rizzo's voice.

"Rizzo here. So, it's *you*. Enjoying your vacation?"

"I can think of a few ways it could be better," Jordan replied. "I thought you'd like to know—she's clean. The subject came here just to set up some trusts. But her old man is an entirely different story. She doesn't know about him. You're right about him doing drugs. Mrs. Clare's secretary just called a minute ago to warn her that Dr. Clare just salted her law office with coke. Mrs. Clare warned her secretary about him taking over the practice of a guy who was busted for dealing. Davie Merino—he's in San Quentin. Anyway, Mrs. Clare ordered her secretary to flush the coke and now she's cutting her trip short."

"So, he's got a drug problem? No surprise there. But, uh . . . did you find anything about matters within *our* jurisdiction?"

"Well, yes sir. I think maybe so. Mrs. Clare didn't know about anything about this when it happened, but her husband closed all their accounts at the Highridge Bank and bank-wired the funds to a bank in Montreal. He stashed the funds in a numbered account and Mrs. Clare has no idea where the money is now. He apparently did this the day we paid him a visit."

"Jordan, what took you so long to report this? This is crucial info."

"I just heard about it. A bank employee, Mrs. Clare's friend, just called to tell her about it—so that's why I'm calling you now." Jordan hoped this would wash. He remembered Rizzo saying that they'd be tapping *all* of the Clare's lines . . . but Nancy, the operation officer's assistant, had called this past Wednesday from her *house*. Thank God for that—it meant there would be no way for Rizzo to learn that he hadn't understood the significance of Bear's actions to the IRS. He'd been thinking only about how it would affect Linnell. Just another sign, he supposed, that he wasn't cut out for this line of work.

"Good work! Well, we'll be moving in on Clare first thing Monday morning. As for you? You can stay for the weekend. Now go live it up! But you'd better have your ass back here by Monday morning. Later."

Jordan was relieved. The surveillance was over! He couldn't wait to pack it in; he immediately disconnected his recorder and after tuning out all the lights he stepped out on his balcony to check out Linnell's room. It was still dark. With a pounding heart, he quickly entered her room and then clicking on his flashlight, removed all the bugs and gave everything another quick search. Finding nothing new, he ducked out the door and returned to his room without anyone spotting him dodging around in the hall.

◆❖◆

Linnell remained on the beach, still thinking about what to do next. As if cautioning her to stay alert, the ocean sent a large wave crashing up the gentle incline, forcing her to jump up and step smartly to avoid a good dousing. She decided that she had better go home. Immediately.

She used the telephone in the hotel gift shop to call the airline and was informed that the next day's flights were fully booked but that there just might be a seat on the eye-opener to Miami. They would let her know first thing in the morning. Assuming she was still under surveillance, Linnell decided not to visit the cocktail lounge, being that it was the IRS' favorite hang out. It might be best to call it a day, she thought. And besides, she ought to get everything packed, just in case she got lucky. She took one more look out to sea, and despite the lingering warmth, actually shivered.

◆❖◆

Robert Jordan had just finished replacing the locks in his door when he heard the hall door slam—the same door that had ruined everything earlier that evening. He froze and listened to the familiar pit-pat of sandals on the carpet. Then he relaxed—from the sound of the approaching footsteps he could tell it was her and that she was alone. What a relief! This had to mean she would be turning in early. Jordan remembered the way her eyes had burned gold when she'd looked at him and suppressed the urge to call her. She must have been under enormous pressure tonight—wondering about her husband and all the money he'd hidden—yet she'd still had the grace to cover this up. He wondered if he would have been capable of doing the same thing.

Jordan's hand remained on the telephone, then he picked up the receiver and called the airline to see if they had recently reserved a seat for a woman named Clare. When the reservations clerk said no and that all seats were taken, he was greatly relieved. Good! She would be here at least for another day, so he'd have plenty of time to tell her everything. Jordan thought about their unfinished business under the stairs and was again sorely tempted to knock on her door. Then he thought the better of it. No. He'd better wait til tomorrow. After what she'd just learned, she probably needed more time to herself. And he could use a little shut-eye himself.

Jordan called the front desk and ordered two picnic lunches for the following day, then kicking off his flip-flops, he tore off the rest of his clothes, climbed into bed and sat amongst his pillows inside his mosquito-net tent. Jordan reached out and switched on his bedside table lamp; he would read for a while.

He leaned back into the big white pillows and made plans for the following day. Tomorrow was going to be one of those perfect days and he knew exactly what he was going to do. Satisfied, Jordan yawned and a few seconds later was hard asleep.

CAYMAN **11:30 p.m. - Friday, March 1, 1974**

Linnell returned to the second floor. The slashes of light at the bottoms of the doors provided some comfort—it looked like most of the second floor rooms were now occupied, which meant she was not all alone. There was even light coming from the room next to hers, she observed.

Oh! What a day this had been! Such highs. Such lows. She was drained. Linnell forced herself to pack and by the time she climbed into bed, her stomach had tightened into a knot—one more night and she'd be lying next to Bear. Intolerable! she thought. She could *not* let that happen again. No more meat loaf. Not at any price. Now she was sure—she wanted Roberto and only Roberto.

So why not try to find him?

Lifting the receiver, Linnell rang the front desk and in a quiet, small voice asked the operator to put her through to the room of Mr. Robert Roberts.

"You sure he be staying *here*, dearie?" chirped the young clerk.

"That's what he said," Linnell whispered. She had an ominous feeling.

"We be *so* sorry. There be no Robert Roberts staying here."

It was the final blow.

Linnell hung up without speaking. *Dammit* all anyway. She should have known! What had happened to her instincts? Disuse atrophy—that's what. Her instincts were shot—they had simply withered away, leaving her *this* close to making an absolute fool of herself. How could he fake something like that? She should have known he was too good to be true. Too perfect. Too darling. Linnell threw herself down on her bed, put her face in her pillow, and tried not to cry. Tears escaped, nonetheless.

Well, I'm only human, thought Linnell, blowing her nose. Forcing herself not to think, she grabbed another pillow, placed it over her head and, exhausted, quickly passed out.

CAYMAN **Saturday morning - March 2, 1974**

The telephone must have rung at least ten times before Linnell heard it and woke. She grabbed it as she looked at her watch. It was 6:30 a.m. and it was Cayman Airways on the line, calling to advise her that there was one seat available and that she could have it. The flight was scheduled to depart at 7:00 a.m. Springing out of bed, Linnell called the front desk to tell them to get her a taxi and that she'd be paying her bill on the fly.

Linnell took her last look through the window. This morning the ocean was offering itself in long swatches of indigo florescence to a blazing orange ball of a rising sun. The air was still, and the water simply humped lazily up to slide over the crest of Seven Mile Beach before splaying into immense golden fans in the creamy sand. Linnell mourned as she listened to the syncopated slap of the waves. It was going to be another perfect day in the Caribbean and *she* was about to return to the fog and the dripping and the cold Bay Area grays.

Linnell retreated to her bathroom, swept her cosmetics into her case, slammed her luggage closed and turned into the bedside table and smashed her toe. For a second the pain was so excruciating she had to sit down on the edge of her bed. Holding her foot and rocking to and fro, she looked around the room, and then she remembered: the bug! Should she take it? She'd always wanted to take one apart. No. She should've thought of this sooner, now there wasn't enough time. Well, best to leave it alone—then the spooks would never know she'd been on to them. Linnell hopped back to the bathroom and pulled on her lavender bathing suit, shimmied into her jeans, stepped into her sandals and tossed on her navy blue warm-up jacket. Grabbing the box of sanitary napkins, she pitched it into her suitcase—she would retrieve her rudder later—she would carry her bags to make sure they wouldn't go astray.

In five minutes flat it looked as if she'd never been there. She took a moment to look at her empty room and was suddenly overwhelmed by a wealth of bittersweet emotions. What an adventure! And now it was over. She reached in her wallet, placed ten Cayman dollars on the table for the maid, and then grabbing her bags, limped out of the room, leaving behind only an unlocked door. Linnell paid her bill, said her good-byes to the sleepy desk clerk and limped to the taxi. She dared the driver to get her to the airfield in five minutes for an extra five. Her toe had stopped throbbing and was now turning purple.

"Why is it always *something?*" Linnell sat in the back seat of the cab, massaging her foot, and thought about how this sort of painful accident always seemed to happen to her only when she was home. Now, just thinking about home seemed to bring on the curse of these small calamities. *It's always something—a fingernail torn to the quick, a nasty paper cut, or a kick to the shins. Every single day it's always one thing or another, except when I'm here on the island.*

A klutz. That's what he'd called her. Well! He was no one to talk. Something was going to be done about him; just what, however, she didn't yet know. Waiting in line to board, she had another unsettling thought: What if she never came back? Linnell felt a wave of anxiety, as if she were already home. Why was she thinking such thoughts? Linnell made a deliberate effort to shake off the gloom, then taking a final breath of island air—a languid combination of sea tang and steaming foliage—she limped up the stairs and through the small door to the darkened cabin. Her nose immediately detected the top-note of mildew that identified the sturdy aircraft that flew the Caribbean routes. The flight was packed with ordinary Caymanians heading off to shop in Miami as well as the usual contingent of US bankers and accountants who would soon be spending the rest of the weekend playing catch-up, back home in New York. But this time she wasn't interested in their stories about the bank failure. She needed to focus her thoughts and come up with a plan.

She found herself sitting next to a pale-faced accountant who pressed his engraved card into her hand as proof that he was a maven and in the loop. When she saw that he was a partner in a major international accounting firm, she handed him her card. Apparently satisfied that she wasn't with the IRS, he immediately began to brag about how he had transferred a million dollar pension plan to a Cayman administrator, letting on that his client was a foreign subsidiary of a major oil drilling company. He was exceedingly proud of his clever new ideas and gave her a few tips about holding companies that she had never thought of before. Immediately back to the game, Linnell pretended that this was old news and then excused herself so she could go hide in the lavatory and copy his advice into her rudder.

When she returned, the businessman's breakfast was already being served: an omelet, coffee, and raisin-filled sticky-buns. She ate slowly, suspecting that this might very well be her last pleasure for months to come. Five minutes before landing, the cabin fell silent. They were strangers again, and the cabin was filled with the sound of shuffling papers and clicking briefcases as the aircraft gently turned and dropped into its final approach to Miami International Airport. She thought of Roberto. She now realized that she had been so taken up with the moment that she had entirely neglected to find out exactly where he worked—there was only this vague recollection of his mention of a bank. Somewhere in the Midwest. She must have been *bombed.*

And how could he talk about so many things without even once mentioning where he lived? Yes, she knew what that meant—it had to be just as she'd first suspected: He was married. A married man "Who had been looking for her all his life!" Thank heavens she'd laughed.

MIAMI, FLORIDA **March 2, 1974**

A bored Miami Airport customs agent poked at her luggage and asked her where she had been and what she'd been doing and how long she'd been out of the country. She replied, "Cayman, lawyer, about a week," and he waved her through without bothering to open her bags and then tossed her bags onto the conveyor belt. Picking them up at the end of the long, low counter, she sped to the ladies room, pawed through her luggage, and found her pumps. She had an idea . . . she would cut out the sides and toes and turn them into strappy-looking heels and this would help take the pressure off her poor banged-up toe. Using her pen knife, Linnell fixed her shoes. Feeling more comfortable, she click-clacked out of the ladies room and down the length of the echoing terminal toward the pay phone at the gate of her connecting flight. Linnell read the departures board with dismay. The flight from Miami to SFO had been diverted to Chicago where it was scheduled to lay over for four additional hours because of the bad weather on the west coast. SFO was blanketed with impenetrable fog and the flights that were supposed to turn around at O'Hare were still on the ground. Linnell shivered at the thought of being trapped in Chicago; it was a good thing she hadn't checked her bags through to SFO.

HIGHRIDGE **Saturday - March 2, 1974**

Willy Ivener found an empty manila envelope and absent-mindedly packed it with $100 bills while he thought about his forthcoming trial. He was calculating the odds. He knew that after spending all those millions just to indict him, the prosecution was after something more substantial than their usual offer to settle for a price. This time there would be no settlement, Willy thought. This time the prosecutor wanted his head on a pike so he could have bragging rights about being the big-shot who'd finally put Willy Ivener away. He knew the type.

But he also knew how to play the game far better than that numb-nut of a prosecutor ever could—or ever would. He had assembled a highly skilled defense team for himself and they were already geared up for a fight. And now that one of his major problems was about to be eliminated—thanks to Dr. Clare—there no longer was any reason for him to delay the proceedings.

And this was because of his health. It was failing and nobody knew why. His doctors had repeatedly warned him to start taking it easy. He'd pooh-poohed them even though he knew there was something seriously wrong with him. The night sweats were increasing. He'd been tested for TB, several times in fact, yet the lab reports always came back negative. It was a mystery to all of them, and although he always managed to look sharp and lively, he now felt tired all the time. His baffled physicians, once they had heard the sound of his cough, had even penciled him in for a week at the Mayo Clinic. But he'd had to duck out because he needed to keep a close eye on *his* lawyers to make sure they wouldn't screw up and get into the myriad operations of The Wei.

So, here he was—caught between the IRS and his own doctors and lawyers. Everybody was investigating everybody else, and he needed to get this ridiculous predicament behind him, and quickly, before anyone had a chance to stumble onto the truth. He had to get this trial behind him, and then he'd have all the time in the world for his health and his final coup: establishing a tax haven empire. Just for himself. And The Wei was the most important component of this plan because it was the fountainhead of all his wealth.

Ivener considered his options. If by some strange twist of fate his trial took a turn for the worse, he could always skip. He'd always planned for this, but he'd kept this alternative hidden, especially from his staff. If they thought he was willing to cut and run, they might want to jump ship prematurely and this might make it look like they knew he was guilty. His two senior law associates—named as unindicted co-conspirators in the current proceedings—had been quietly retired to Mexico where they couldn't be reached. They were in their late seventies—too old and too tired to fight—but they would never dare rat him out because they had forged the signatures on all those dummy corporations his firm had been using in his tax shelter schemes. He'd seen to it that they would have a comfortable retirement providing they stayed put in Mexico. As for the rest of his staff? The law clerks and associates and secretaries? They were still loyal, especially Harold Dolphe. Dolphe had done him a service, not only for getting a handle on L.C., but also for leasing a warehouse instead of a more obvious and easily found building in Georgetown proper. Yes, Dolphe would soon be a partner. Ivener laughed at the thought. He'd be a partner all right, but only a pack-horse partner—good only for carrying the load and sharing the blame.

As for the Clares—he planned to attend to L.C. as soon as she returned from her trip. The prosecution hadn't disclosed its witness list yet, so he had to dispatch her immediately, before it became known that she was a government witness. Or, to put it more accurately, before it became known that he knew she was going to testify against him. Pretty woman, L.C. Too bad she had to be wasted. That husband of hers would be far easier to handle and much less of a loss. Ivener made a mental note to start some rumors about Dr. Bear Clare and his unpleasant relationship with his beautiful wife. But, enough about Bear—he had far more interesting matters to attend to at the moment. Having finished with counting and stacking the bills, Ivener shoved them down inside the envelope, sealed it, then tapped it against the edge of his desk.

◆❖◆

Today, Deborah was covered with pale makeup and wore over-sized glasses and a turban. They met at the same bistro as before, and after exchanging air-kisses over their salads, she got straight to the point. Had her dear Uncle Willy brought her the money? Deborah set a large package next to her on the table.

"Well done, my dear. And I must say I love your new look. I hardly recognized you. And I see you have a large package for me. Splendid! And now I want you to know that I have one for you too. Have you ever seen so much money?" Willy passed the manila envelope to Deborah underneath the table. Deborah grabbed it and ripped it open under the table cloth and quickly counted out 40 crisp 100 dollar bills. The serious expression on Deborah's pale face made Willy smile. Really, underneath all that stage grease was such a naive child.

"And this is what *you* want, Uncle Willy." Deborah handed Willy a computer disk labeled "Disk 1" and the package which contained the 50 page print-out. "It's what you've been looking for. Just as you thought, they're skimming. I'll be going in there again next Monday and I expect to get some air-tight proof that they're keeping a double set of books."

Willy had already explained to her that unlike past years, the IRS no longer could pass out copies of a taxpayer's tax returns, thanks to the newly enacted Privacy Statutes of 1974. This meant there no longer would be any easy way for them to discover whether the Clare income tax returns were fraudulent. So, if they wanted to prove Doc was cheating, Deborah would have to obtain some hard evidence that he was cheating, and the best proof of this would be, as was usually the case, the maintenance of two sets of books. Uncorroborated testimony—for instance, Margo's, and assuming she could be made to squeal—wouldn't be enough to support a charge of criminal tax evasion, nor for that matter could it support the more interesting practices of extortion, which Willy also had in mind.

"Does this help you get a handle on L.C.?"

"Deborah, as I've told you before, L.C. is of no concern to me whatsoever." Now Ivener was annoyed. "I have nothing but praise for your performance, my dear, but you must stop worrying about matters that don't concern you. Just finish up. It'll be just another few days, at most, a week, and then you'll be out of there. Think of that! And think about how much more you'll be making in the future. You're going to forget all about this as soon as you're settled in Hollywood, and believe me, so will I. I guarantee it."

"Hollywood! You've got that arranged already? When do I leave?"

"Next week, if you're successful. I want you to look at these contracts I've prepared for you." Willy handed her a manila folder and patted her hand, observing how incredibly beautiful her eyes were when she was getting her way. He could have told her that he no longer really needed her services because he already had what he wanted—this morning, only an hour before, a special delivery package had arrived containing the first half of L.C.'s article on foreign foundations and a typewritten note:

The rest to follow. Will advise through your Wei-trainer H. Dolphe the exact day I want to take the Advanced Wei Program."

But he had decided not to let Deborah get off so easily. She had muscled him for an extra $3000 and now she would have to stick around and earn it. Of course, he couldn't blame her for trying to get more. He would have done much the same thing. Willy reached out and retrieved the contracts that Deborah was examining. "Now . . . I want you to hold out your hand."

Deborah gave him an uncertain smile in reply as she placed her hand on his. He lifted her hand and turned it over and then unfurling his fingers, dropped a small blue velvet box in her upturned palm.

"Go ahead. Open it." Willy ordered.

Deborah lifted the cover and a pin—a small five-pointed gold star with small but perfect blue-white diamonds set at each tip—sparkled back at her. Truly surprised, she gasped with delight.

"That's better," said Willy. "Your Uncle Willy loves to see you looking happy. Just think, in a few years you'll have your own star on Hollywood Boulevard."

"Oh Uncle *Willy.* It's beautiful! You've got such good taste. If I could have a *real* uncle, I'd want him to be just like you."

After their pleasant meeting, Willy watched Deborah as she drove away. He actually felt rather sad that Hollywood wouldn't be seeing her any too soon. He would have to first send her on a small detour—keep her busy in one of those little New York drama groups for a couple of years so that she'd be far away from Highridge and any reminder of those wretched Clares.

Willy returned to the more important matter of what he had planned for the Clares.

Bear had certainly worked fast. And if today's package was any kind of a sign, he would soon be receiving L.C.'s itinerary and this would allow him to select the best place for her to be kidnapped. He had hired experts for this, professionals—Tonton Macoutes—who had honed their skills under the Duvalier regime. With his usual prescience, he had contacted them the day before his predictably fruitful meeting with Bear. They had already disembarked and he was expecting them to arrive very shortly at the port of New Orleans. The point-man, the deceptively fragile-looking, slim and articulate Claude Claudine, would be accompanied by the huge stevedore Grande Charlus, who was built for heavy lifting. They were Creoles who had returned to the Caribbean when they were young boys, and if for some reason they couldn't exit through New Orleans, or if there was any kind of a slip-up and it looked like they might get caught, then they could easily disguise themselves as husband and wife and return to Haiti through the Bahamas.

HIGHRIDGE **Saturday - March 2, 1974**

Buster Hosterman had given Bear a special appointment for Saturday, a favor extended only to his most important clients.

"Come on in good buddy." Buster let his face fall into a look of doleful commiseration and jammed his hands in the pockets of his brown pin-striped trousers.

"Just a short meeting today," Bear sighed. "I've got a few things I need you to do. Here, I brought something for you to give to your process server. It'll make things easier when the time comes to serve her. It's kinda messy so why don't you get your secretary to type this up? And you can make a copy for me, too." Bear handed Buster Hosterman one of his finely engraved cream-colored envelopes. The face of the envelope offered no clue as to its contents, but it contained the information that Buster had been longing to see: The itinerary of Linnell's daily movements—her telephone numbers and her office address, the location of the club and the hours she spent there with her friends, the routes she took to and from her office, the grocery store where she liked to shop, and a description of her new car—he could never remember the license plate number—and a photo, just a head-shot of her; he'd even included a brief description of Benjy and the hours he spent at school.

Bear watched Buster as he studied the handwritten itinerary. "I even included the address and unlisted telephone number for my home," he added.

"This'll help me a lot. When do you want her served?"

Bear scratched his head while he did some rapid calculations: He was expecting Ma home on Wednesday, so he needed a day to get her involved in his audit, so it would probably be best if he had her "targeted" for the end of the week. But even though she would most likely be dead by next weekend, he'd better allow some extra time just in case something went wrong. Right now, and for the time being, it would be best to keep Buster thinking that he expected Ma to be served with his divorce papers two weeks from now, even though Ma would most certainly be done in by then. Then, after Ma was dead, he wouldn't have to say anything to Buster about calling things off. In fact, he wouldn't have to say anything at all. As far as others were concerned, they would see him as a grief-stricken husband, and Buster—and his secretary, too—would have to keep a lid on things because of the lawyer-client privilege. He could remember the exact way Ma liked to put it: *A lawyer must preserve a client's confidences at every peril to him or herself*—so he could rest assured that no one outside of the Hosterman law office would ever know that he'd been planning a divorce. Meanwhile, Buster could still be of use to him.

"How about having her served two weeks from now." Bear replied. "I've changed my mind about having her served at my birthday dinner. I don't want to have to sit down and have dinner with her! You want to know why? Take a look at *these!*" Bear slapped the photographs of Linnell on Buster's desk.

Buster whistled. "You sure got the goods on her. Do you mind if I hold onto these? I think the judge would like to take a little peek. I'll be seeing him at the club in a couple of days."

"I don't want you to show them to anyone until *after* you have her served," Bear replied firmly.

"I guess you're right."

"There's more to this than you can see in these photos," Bear added. "I heard from my informant on Cayman. My investigator saw her running all over the island, carrying on with that guy. *Him.*" Bear held up the photograph of the Cayman dive master and then flipped it down on Buster's desk.

"See? The scoop is that she's in deep with the mob—I had my guy check into *that,* too. She's been laundering money—that's how she could afford that pricey new car—and now she's going to mule for 'em, too. She, and that

Karen in her office—they're in it *way* over their heads! I'll bet she's even been stashing narcotics in her file drawers. You can be *sure* that's where she's been hiding the stuff. It has nothing to do with the divorce, but still, it wouldn't hurt anything to have her file drawers searched, let's say—early next week? Why don't *you* pick the day?"

Bear observed Buster studying his face and allowed him to see a quick smirk Buster would finally be seeing him in a brand new light; in fact, he could tell, just from the way Buster was looking at him now that Buster was finally getting the idea that his client already knew how to play hardball. Now for the juiciest tidbit; he'd saved it for last so Buster would remember it best:

"You know what else I just heard? I'm going to let you in on it, but if you ever say you heard it from me, I'll swear under oath you're a liar. Well, I got this dope straight from the IRS: My wife's going to testify against that guy she used to work for, Willy Ivener. That's the *real* reason why I was so shook up when I called you last Monday—she's going to be the government's *star* witness. That's what the agents told *me*." Bear saw that Buster's pupils were dilating with excitement. Good. He was counting on Buster to spread it around, and it sure looked like Buster would be doing just that. It wouldn't be long before every lawyer in town would be hating Ma's guts for being a dirty snitch and better yet, after Ma turned up dead, everybody would be putting two and two together and saying that Ivener had a motive for getting rid of her.

Suddenly, in the midst of all this, Bear felt his guts give a rumble and he was almost bent double with pain. It felt as if his bowels were alive and his stomach seething with wriggling worms. He looked at his watch; he was into the danger zone—he hadn't had anything for almost an hour and the voices had already begun to whistle nastily in his ears.

"Hey Buster. Where's your can?" Bear was half-way out of his chair as soon as Buster pointed the way. He hid behind Buster's bathroom door while he gave himself an injection—he was now carrying an "emergency kit." He'd learned that injections worked faster and weren't as messy as snorting, and then for insurance, he swallowed two of his yellow pills. Waiting a few seconds after feeling the bloom, Bear flushed the toilet and bounded into Buster's private office.

Buster's secretary returned with the papers, which she had neatly captioned: *L.C. Activity Schedule.* All the information Bear needed to give to Ivener was now neatly typed on one page. Buster handed a copy to Bear, placed a copy in his file, and returned Bear's handwritten notes. Bear was pleased to see that Buster's efficient secretary had even included a Xerox copy of Ma's photo on each set. He examined the one that had been given to him—It was a little fuzzy, but it was good enough. And so it was with no small measure of appreciation that Bear handed Buster the Petition for the Dissolution of the Marriage of Clare.

"I signed it," Bear announced proudly. "But . . . you've got to promise me something."

"What's that?"

"You've got to promise to keep everything under your hat. You know—don't jump the gun. You can't have her served for another two weeks because I'm gonna need her to handle my audit. And besides, I already know you have to keep all my business confidential. Right?"

"That goes without saying." Buster stood up again, this time beaming with pleasure, and walked around his desk to give Bear's hand a shake. "Now, just you let me handle things. Okay?"

"Yes, and thanks, Buster." Bear squared his shoulders, side-stepped Buster's attempt to pat his butt, and made his escape. He had managed to solve another problem: Ma's activity schedule had been prepared on a typewriter that couldn't be traced back to him.

◆❖◆

Bear dropped into his favorite coffee shop and told the waitresses that he'd just heard the bad news about his wife volunteering to testify as the government's witness against William Ivener. Basking in their sympathy, Bear curled his hands and rolled his eyes as if he were in pain, then lowering his voice to force them to lean closer, he whispered dramatically, "I hear this Ivener guy has some really *strange* connections, you know what I mean? And now I'm kinda *worried* for her. You know . . .?"

When Bear returned to the club, he knew he'd read Buster right—it was working, a couple of members approached him to ask if L.C. was really going to be the "key government witness against Willy Ivener." They were lapping it up! Feigning surprise, he drew a few members close to him and again whispered his concerns about his wife . . . "Now that she's enraged such a *powerful* man, I'm kinda worried." Bear hunched his shoulders and rolled his eyes and with his body language flavoring his every word, he let everyone know two important things: that he was helpless to control his "strong-willed wife," and how profoundly concerned he was for her safety.

That evening, Bear met Harold in the club parking lot.

"I *knew* you'd come through," Harold enthused, quickly slipping the powder-filled baggie into his pocket. "And if there's anything else I can do for you, just let me know."

Bear clasped Harold's hand. "I've got some big plans for you, Harold, but right now all I want you to do is to give this to Willy. It's important. Tell him it's my check for the Advanced training course."

Bear handed Harold a stapled and taped envelope containing the L.C. Daily Activity Schedule prepared by the Hosterman office, and his check, drawn on the dental corporation's checking account, which he had dated for the following Friday, March 8, 1974.

Harold grinned. "I'll drop this off first thing Monday morning. And thanks, bro. You've done more for me than you'll ever know!" Harold winked, patted his pocket, and left Bear standing all by himself in the parking lot.

MIAMI **Saturday - March, 2, 1974**

Karen was home when Linnell called her from Florida, and since it was Saturday, and Karen had already been to the office to pick up the mail, they decided to meet there the following day. They spoke only briefly because it was long distance, but Karen did have some good news: The Sea Urchin Project contract had arrived earlier that morning and she'd taken it home for safekeeping. But when Linnell told Karen that she'd be going straight home from SFO that evening, Karen protested.

"But, L.C., he's so unstable, he could be dangerous. You can't predict what he might do," Karen warned.

"Don't worry. He can't be worse than he was when I left him last week. And if he looks even the least bit dangerous, I'll cut and run."

Linnell thought about their conversation when she boarded the plane for Chicago, and by the time she had settled down in her seat, she was in need of some reassurance herself. How should she go about things? What was her plan? Should she confront Bear directly? What if he turned violent, as Karen feared? She placed her briefcase and purse on the adjacent seat because she needed to concentrate without being disturbed. While the aircraft ascended, she set her watch back an hour to Central Standard Time and then she closed her eyes and tried to imagine what would happen that evening. *Think like a lawyer*, Linnell kept telling herself.

Hours passed while she looked out the window. Linnell could make out dense bright patches of white as they hurtled down through the towering clouds. Her problems were abruptly cleared from her mind when she heard the changing pitch of the engines and realized they were about to land. The windows dropped beneath the ground-hugging fog, the wheels touched down, and for a bad moment or two it felt as if the aircraft was sliding on black ice. The tires finally caught with a high-pitched squeal and then the aircraft began to lumber and drone down the runway toward the terminal. The stewardess again informed the passengers that because of the dense fog blanketing the West Coast, all incoming flights from the coast to O'Hare were delayed and since there would be a shortage of aircraft for all outbound flights, the passengers would have to disembark and change planes. "Please keep your eye on the departures board and listen for announcements," the harried stewardess importuned.

Having nothing to do for hours, Linnell put herself into what she called "The Airport Trance." She nibbled at a tasteless lunch and mindlessly flipped through a magazine, hoping for inspiration. On a whim, since she had so much time, she decided to shampoo the salt out of her hair. Linnell found the ladies lounge and undressed—revealing her lavender bathing suit top and plenty of sun tan—and scrubbed and rinsed her hair. The second application of shampoo resulted in a billowing tower of white lather that wobbled atop her head. Linnell had just finished sculpting it into a tall, sudsy headdress when she heard a deep voice.

"Way to *go*, baby. You looking *fine*."

For a moment, Linnell felt as if she'd never left the island. She turned around slowly to avoid upsetting her towering headdress, expecting to see a familiar face. She saw, instead, a tall, heavyset black woman who was standing in the shadows behind her back. Her hair stood proud in a black-is-beautiful Afro and she wore a striped garment—red, black and green—fashioned out of a soft knit fabric with vertical stripes that were stretched to their widest across her huge breasts. Gold chains swathed her thick neck and her large feet appeared solidly anchored to the marble floor. One of her fat hands gripped a plain wooden pole that she had apparently commandeered to use as a staff.

"Chile. You look jus' like that *queen*. The one that got the powah. An' you looks like you got *lots* of it, baby."

"Beg pardon?"

"That Egypt-shun gal. She who be stacked jus' like you, an' has a stick big as *this*." The black empress pounded her staff for emphasis.

The vibrations from the tile-whomping blows convinced Linnell this was no apparition and now she wondered if it would be safe to ignore her; then she took a good look in the mirror and saw what the woman was talking about: What with her shampoo, now a stiff meringue smoothed into a turban atop her head, her face a deeply tanned mask, and her mascara now smudged to accentuate the tilt of her eyes—she indeed appeared to be somewhere half-way between Nefertiti and Theda Bara. But despite this slightly comic aspect, she still looked fascinating, exotic, nothing at all like her ordinary self. Linnell smiled, and she was secretly pleased at the way her tan set off the whites of her eyes and her teeth; then she laughed, partly embarrassed and partly surprised by the woman's easy familiarity.

"Well, thank you. I guess."

"Now, you use it or you gonna lose it."

"What, may I ask, is this thing you say I should use?"

"The powah, chile. Like I jus' tole you."

"Powah?"

As if to say that Linnell was too dense for words, the woman first rolled her eyes and then with slow dignity, turned away and rolled out through the swinging doors.

Linnell looked at herself in the mirror again. Who were they? These women who were so willing to shower her with their pearls of wisdom? First Mama N'dobah with her advice about life, and now this one, with advice that she couldn't quite understand . . . A complete stranger has just paid her what seemed to be something akin to a compliment and then orders her to . . . *now* she got it! Boy was *she* slow. The *power*. She should use the *power*. Linnell closed her eyes and saw a plume of water sparkling high in the air and for an instant she thought she was back on the beach in Cayman. Then it came to her instantly—and she knew exactly what she was going to do about Bear.

◆❖◆

Departure times blared over the PA system: The flight to San Francisco would be boarding in ten minutes and she had only ten minutes to set things in motion!

Linnell hoisted her suitcase up onto the counter and tore through it while thinking about what had just clicked. It was as if she had spent her entire life stumbling around with her head in a bag and then suddenly the bag is lifted and she could finally see. In this sudden new light she could finally see what she'd always been missing: that she'd always had power—she'd simply failed to realize it before because she had bought into the drill that she owed it to others to be a "good girl" and that she was obliged to please others, and never mind about herself. Now she knew that smart girls knew better—she also knew why anything she did to please Bear would never be enough and that this was *not* because there was anything wrong with *her*.

No. It was simply that Bear needed a crowd's-worth of applause and she was only one person—and no single person, no matter how devoted or loyal or good, could possibly compete with a herd when it came to feeding his impoverished ego. Bear's true mistress was his peanut gallery and he lived for its love; he felt he was nothing without it. So it was important for her to understand—which at long last she did—that Bear lived in fear that someday his cherished audience might see through his Superman armor and discover the weakness hidden inside. Now she understood why he always tried to persuade her to dislike other men. Not to bind her closer to him as she had first supposed, but to ensure that she wouldn't get any funny ideas about attracting another man, a man who might want to compete with and expose him. This explained why he liked to see her looking so plain, and why he wouldn't tell her he thought she was precious or beautiful or—heaven forbid!—sexy. He simply didn't want her to know that she had the power to make trouble for him. Yes, he was a worrier all right, just only about himself. In fact, after all these years, he didn't know or even care who she was, he just needed her to stick around and make herself useful, and on necessary occasion, serve as proof that he was a real man.

Well, she was going to hit Bear right where he lived: First, she would fix herself up so he could get an idea of what was coming his way; then she'd show him she had what it took to make him the laughingstock of Highridge. She'd let him think that she would soon be strutting her stuff in front of his peanut gallery, inviting every man there to show the world that any one of them had what it took to beat his time. He'd be horrified! He would come unglued trying to imagine what people would be saying about him. And what could he do? Kick her out into the street? No! He couldn't do that, because No-fault Divorce was a whole new era, and furthermore, she, better than anyone else, knew exactly how to drive home the fact that no matter how much she humiliated him, their property would *still* have to be divided equally because the law had been changed—there would be no more of this old-fashioned business of threatening to cut her out of her share of their community property in order to punish her for stepping out of line. Yes, thought Linnell, she was going to show him indeed that "No-fault Divorce" was a double-edged sword.

In fact, she'd probably have to do little more than just hint at what she could do and odds were he'd do anything she said to keep this from happening. But if he wanted her to back off, then he'd first have to fork over her half of all that money he'd hidden. And then, just as soon as she got her hands on it, she would dump him.

Right now, however, all she wanted to do was to give him a little show, just a little clue as to what might be coming his way. And she would *not* say one word about the cocaine he'd planted in her office. That way she could play with his head exactly the same way he'd been playing with hers. And by next Monday she'd also know exactly what she was going to do next.

Linnell quickly set to work on herself. She needed a glamorous outfit to show him how much she had changed. She needn't do too much because she looked better now than she ever had in her life. She radiated confidence and her complexion had improved remarkably because she'd finally had enough sleep. Linnell quickly dried her hair and then instead of skinning it into pony-tail, she combed it out until it fell in smooth golden curves around her face. A sweep of mascara—to call attention to her sparkling eyes; a touch of powder and a gloss of lipstick and then she was ready to dress. Stripping off her jeans, Linnell shimmied into a tight skirt that drew attention to her legs, then she tossed on a blouse, leaving it half unbuttoned, and tightened her belt to draw attention to her narrow waist and her small round buns. Linnell stepped back into her heels—and voila!—there was no more Ma. And there would be no reverting back to her old not-so-heroic habit of doing whatever it took to buy the peace. Linnell tossed her hair over her shoulders and took one last look at herself in the mirror. He had never seen her looking like this—in fact, neither had she. It would drive him crazy. Linnell was now so pleased with herself that she made a vow: No matter *what* she looked like, she would never, *ever* again give anyone the power to make her feel there was something lacking in her either as a woman or because she was one.

Feeling much happier than when she'd walked in, Linnell grabbed her gear and with her head held high and a new lilt to her walk, dragged her luggage behind her by the strap down the center of the terminal. Out of the corner of her eye, she could see the effect she was having: Men were openly staring at her with new appreciation. Some smiled at her and others tipped their hats and a gentleman stepped forward to carry her bag when she boarded the flight to San Francisco. Yes indeed, thought Linnell, confidence is the most powerful pheromone of them all.

◆❖◆

She should have known it would turn out like this. Although the aircraft had immediately pulled away from the gate, it soon became part of a long line of aircraft waiting to be cleared for take-off. After sitting on the runway for at least forty minutes, the pilot finally estimated that because of a head wind, they would be arriving at SFO around 6:45 p.m. Linnell immediately reset her watch to Pacific Standard Time, pulled a blanket over her head and fell asleep.

She was awakened by the landing, and when she stepped off the plane, it was as if into spring. Quixotic California spring weather—there was no sign of the fog that had blanketed the state earlier that day. A warm dry breeze gusted across the runways. Spring had arrived in California on a desert wind. Linnell found Charles, and then drove him through a car-wash to remove the dust from the parking garage and then hit the freeway for Highridge. While she drove, she tried to recall what Helene had said about Bear being at the club. Was he staying there overnight? she wondered. Or just staying there for dinner? Well, it made no difference, she reasoned, because soon enough she'd find out.

The temperature plummeted and it was completely dark by the time she finally pulled up the driveway. With the engine still running, Linnell pressed the button on the remote control, the garage door rose, and then, as her first act of defiance, she backed Charles into his stall. Weary from her long journey, she decided to leave her bag and her briefcase in the trunk. She also decided to leave her garage door open when she saw that Bear's garage door was closed—his Cadillac no doubt was in there already—just in case Bear should give her a reason to flee.

Linnell slipped out of her garage and looked around. Yes, from the flickering light she saw in the living room, it looked like he was already home. It had to be the television, she concluded, and he was probably already flaked out on the couch, with his eyes glued to the set. Linnell wanted to hurry and get it all over with, but now she was sorry she'd worn her pumps because gravel was coming in through the cut-out sections, which forced her to tip-toe over the gravel in order to keep her ankles from turning. And her purse, now swinging from side to side, made her feel even more awkward.

Awkward was not what she wanted to feel right now. By the time she reached the more solid path that led up to the entrance, she was walking faster, near to a run. The was something in the air: A chill, an unbearable tension so heavy she could actually feel it in her sinuses. Perhaps it was the bushes on the other side of the path. They seemed thicker somehow; they must have really grown while she was gone, because now they loomed like a threatening presence in the dark. Remembering the blackjack that Karen had fashioned, Linnell stepped behind the potted palm at the entrance and pulled the coin-filled sock from her handbag. Holding the end of it in her teeth, she fumbled for her house keys—she'd been on such a long journey, they were strange to her now—and finally managed to insert the correct one in the lock. She hoped Bear wouldn't hear her and come to the door; she wasn't quite ready to set eyes on him yet. With the coin-filled sock still dangling from her mouth, Linnell quickly turned the key and let herself in, then closed the door quietly, fully expecting to hear the sound of the television. But there was nothing. Dead silence. Out of habit, Linnell opened the alarm box, hit the button that disarmed the front door and punched in the code before stepping forward. Just as she was about to turn the corner from the entry to the living room, the light in the living room began to flicker again.

She stopped in her tracks. She even stopped breathing. Why was it so quiet? Puzzled, Linnell crept around the corner and immediately saw the sharp-toothed, machete-like shadow swoop up the wall and swing wildly across the ceiling over her head.

The force of the scream that followed slammed her up against the wall, and it wasn't until after she'd slid all the way to the floor that she realized that this heart-stopping shriek had come from deep inside *her*. Coins wobbled and whirred across the marble entry but she didn't care because her eyes were fixed on what was producing this horror show: A spider. This one looked to be the size of a Chihuahua. Christ! Linnell gagged. A tarantula. Crawling slowly down the brilliant path of light produced by the blinding security-light that sat on the floor next to the leaded glass French doors at the other side of the room.

The gigantic was now creeping toward her across the carpet, pausing only to lift a tentative leg into the blue-white shaft of light and sending its serrated shadow streaking across the white walls like an assassin's ax.

Panting furiously and cringing against the wall, Linnell pulled herself up from the floor, keeping her eyes fixed on the monster. This one looked like a mutant from outer space; not striped like the usual tarantula, but coal black and dragging a swollen belly. Christ Almighty! What to do! She couldn't just leave it to wander around the house. What if it was searching for a place to lay its eggs? Or did the small ones come into the world running? What if it should climb onto Benjy while he was sleeping? Linnell stared at the alien creature's curved mandibles. It was too large to smash, besides, just imagining the sound it would make should she dare to crush it made her sick to her stomach. Linnell gagged again and almost lost what was left of her lunch.

Swallowing bile, Linnell forced herself to walk. Face flushed, hands dripping sweat, she turned on the lights in the kitchen while her eyes searched the room. They swiftly found what she needed—drying her hands on her skirt, she armed herself with a broom and the kitchen wastebasket and sped back to the living room. She told herself that if she could do this, that it would be proof enough that she really had changed. Holding her breath, she set the plastic basket on it side, and with one mighty swipe, she knocked the spider a hole-in-one before it could jump. Barricading the mouth of the basket with the broom, she grabbed a small silk pillow from the living room couch and stuffed it down into the basket and then trembling with nausea she carried it toward the French doors that led to the patio—her skin crawling at the sound of the creature scrabbling wildly inside its thin-walled prison. Linnell shot open the door latch, turned the handle, and pushed.

The ear-splitting of the burglar alarm was accompanied by the brilliant flash of the exterior security lights that flared on the instant the door flew open. Startled, Linnell screamed as she pitched the wastebasket clear through the circle of light and into the darkness and then, leaping backwards, felt her right heel spiking deep into the carpet. The heel, already weakened, gave way. Crumpling, Linnell flailed for the door, missed, and fell backwards into the living room. It all happened in less than a second, but still, between the furious bleeps of the siren, Linnell thought she'd heard an almost simultaneous loud *thnmmk.* Stunned into silence, she could see a metal object throwing off light as it spun across the patio tiles.

"Damn!" thought Linnell. She must have broken the door handle. But this time, instead of scolding herself, which she usually did when she broke something, Linnell merely felt amazed. So she'd had a little accident! So what! Linnell Clare pushed her hair out of her eyes and with shaking hands and a churning stomach, she jumped up, quickly latched the leaded glass doors and then, without bothering to turn off either the alarm or the lights, she ripped off her shoes, grabbed her purse, and slammed out the front door. Heedless of her bruised toe or the gravel under her feet, Linnell ran wildly down the path, dove in her car, and for the first time in her life got her key in the ignition without fumbling.

Linnell tore down the driveway and was half-way off the hill before she realized she was driving without her lights. She switched them on—just in time to keep from ramming her beautiful Charles into a chrome-stripped old jalopy parked halfway into the foliage at the side of the road. Linnell congratulated herself. Things were going to be fine. She had handled things okay. And yes, she could tell, something inside her had really changed. And to hell with Bear—wherever he was—she was going to spend the night at a motel.

Claude-Claudine, he of the narrow, strong hands, had been waiting for her to return. He had been instructed to come early and familiarize himself with her surroundings. He had been checking the list of telephone numbers too, and calling and calling, even driving by her office just in case she should return earlier than planned. He knew where to look for her because all of her favorite places were on the list, and he had especially enjoyed waiting for her here because this was a beautiful house with nice views all around.

But now he was truly amazed. He had missed.

It was incredible that he should miss. And with two knives, yet. He had lined up the young American white woman and had timed his swing so that he could get her in the neck as she emerged from her garage. But then she kept swinging the purse, and swaying to and fro like the snake—already a bad omen—and then she had slipped into the house too soon for him to throw a clean line. He'd had to leave the slower-moving Grande Charlus with his rope in the shadows behind the dark bushes so that he could more quickly run to the back of the house to a place where he knew he could watch his yellow-haired target.

There he had studied her, fascinated by her strange ritual with the spider-demon. And he had watched her from the darkness at the edge of the patio, with his wiry arm arched like a scorpion's tail to let the knife fly. She had opened the door. He had expected that. But then came the lights—a great surprise. And the sirens—they had startled him, ruining his timing. And then the brave foolish woman, she falls back inside and this makes him miss. But not by that much. It was good that Grande Charlus had not been here to see him fail. Claude-Claudine cupped his hands over his ears to block the mocking wail of the sirens. They must leave this house. It was not a good place.

Claude-Claudine slipped into the bushes and watched the yellow-haired, long-legged woman with the golden skin. She could run, but she couldn't escape. No one escaped. Claude-Claudine pulled on his black leather gloves and crouched low as he crept at the edge of the circle of light, keeping a wary eye on the ground. He did not want to meet the large angry spider tonight. Kneeling down in the flower bed near the door, Claude Claudine sensed he'd crushed something beneath his knee. It felt damp. He reached down into the darkness and felt something clinging stubbornly between his gloved fingers. A hooked twiggy thing that wouldn't let go. He slapped his hand against his wet knee and it began to prickle as if stuck by a hairy burr. He had to wipe his gloved hand under the arm of his black woolen pea jacket to get rid of it.

Crossing the patio on all fours, he reached the shelter of the wall and stood up to collect the second knife he'd let fly, and with so much force it had closed the door. The other knife—the one he'd thrown first—would take longer to find because after hitting the door hinge it had spun across the bricks and into the flower bed on the far side of the bright circle of light.

HIGHRIDGE **Sunday afternoon - March 3, 1974**

"You're home early, but still, you sure got yourself a *great* tan. Can't wait to hear."

"Yes. I'm back. But this time it doesn't feel so good to be home."

Karen and Linnell had met in the parking lot of Linnell's office. Karen unlocked and opened the door and then handed Linnell her new set of keys. Side by side, the two women crowded into the office, both of them wondering if changing the locks had done any good. They stood back to back and warily looked around.

"Where's Bear?" Karen whispered nervously.

"Hell if *I* know. He wasn't home last night. And I must have cleared out before he got there."

"When I last spoke with Helene, she said something about him taking a room at the club."

"Well, goody for him. Now, let's get to work. The mail—I need to see the stuff from the IRS—let's get it over with so we can be ready for tomorrow. I know just what I'm going to do and I need you and Ray to help me." Linnell swept the shriveled roses off her desk and dumped them in her wastebasket.

Karen sorted the mail. She carefully slit the envelopes and sorted out the copies of the dental corporation tax returns that had been sent to Linnell by the IRS—easy to find because the form number, "*1120,*" stood out in bold print at the upper left hand corners—and fanned them across the top of Linnell's desk. She placed the rest of the mail in a pile on the floor. "How'd you get the IRS to send them to you?" Karen asked.

"Just my charm, I guess. By the way, you get any more of those cat-calls while I was gone?"

"Nope. Not a one. In fact, the last ones were that morning, the day you left. So now we know for sure that the caller is on your case, not mine."

"Aha! I'll bet Harold Dolphe has something to do with them. He's just the type. He was on the island. I saw him hanging around my hotel. That would explain why there were no more calls."

The telephone rang and Karen looked at Linnell. Her face said it all: Who would be calling the law office on a Sunday afternoon? Who would know she was back?

Linnell reached for the telephone. What if this was Roberto? It could be. He would know where to find her. Her heart thumped with excitement. "Hello?" Linnell spoke softly, her mind's eye focused on the image of his face. There was a silence on the other end of the line so profound that Linnell knew her caller was holding a hand over the mouthpiece.

"Hel-LO!" Linnell concentrated her voice into the mouthpiece. Was this a long distance call? Perhaps the operator was still trying to connect her to the calling party. Oh Roberto, she thought. Be there. *Be* there. Linnell heard a strange sound: An expulsion of breath that ended in a wheeze, as if the caller were laying a curse by expelling a lung full of hatred into the mouthpiece. This was followed by a dead silence. Linnell held the line open until she heard the click of the call being cut off.

"Who knows I'm back?" Linnell asked.

"Besides me?" Karen's face turned thoughtful. "Only Helene. I didn't tell Ray. No one else I can think of. Another hang up call?"

"Yes."

"I'll log it," Karen announced. She pulled out the cat-call Calendar, where she had been listing the hang-up calls over the last few months. Linnell looked over her shoulder and saw that it was just as Karen had said: The cat-calls had stopped the same day she'd left, and this was the first one since.

Karen held out the calendar. "What do you make of it?"

"It's hard to say. Seems like the pest is trying awfully hard to make me feel paranoid. It's most likely the Hyena. He's the type who'd play this sort of game. But we've got to ignore it, at least for now. Let's do our work and get out of here."

Linnell wanted to work fast, so she stood over her desk in order to see everything at once. She intended to get a court order to force Bear to pay the maximum amount possible for child support. She expected he'd fight this, so she had to do a thorough job and the information she needed to pull together was required to be included in her divorce papers. On a whim, Linnell asked Karen to dig out the copies of the Clare joint tax returns she kept in her files—the 1040s—for the same three years as the 1120s and to fan them out on her desk, next to the 1120s. This would allow her to get a quick picture of their total income and to double-check it against the salary that Bear was pulling from his dental practice and reporting on his dental corporation tax returns.

Karen laid out the copies as directed and Linnell first examined the tax returns for the dental corporation, beginning with the oldest and working her way to the present. The only pattern she could detect was a large increase in Bear's operating expenses. Nevertheless, she could see that he had been taking home a comfortable salary over the last three years—nothing hugely spectacular by any means, considering the time he spent in his office, but still, nice enough. She was thinking about telling Karen to remove everything, when she happened to glance at the copies of the Clare 1040s that she had asked Karen to get from her files—the joint tax returns—and for the first time she saw something that literally took her breath away. She looked at all of the tax returns once again to make sure she wasn't imagining things.

"Karen! Come here! Take a look at this!"

"What's wrong?"

"I'll show you in a minute. Just get into that pile on the floor and sort out the copies of the Clare joint tax returns, the 1040s, and staple them to the IRS envelopes so they won't get mixed up with this stuff on my desk. Just set them aside—we'll look at them in a minute. Those are supposed to be the same as the 1040s I've just laid out on my desk—I ordered them from the clerk the same day I asked the IRS to send me the dental corporation tax returns."

Linnell waited until Karen was finished and then drew Karen toward her until they were standing side to side.

"Now, what do you make of this?" Linnell pointed to the documents laid out on her desk and told her to first examine the corporate tax returns first—the 1120s—and then to compare them with the Clare personal tax returns, the 1040s. "For each one of these three years Bear reports a larger salary on his corporate return than is shown on our copies of the 1040s—that is, on the copies that he's been giving to me. Look at *this.*" Linnell handed Karen a copy of the most recent Clare joint tax return that showed Bear's salary of $118,000. "We are looking at the 1040 that you just got from my files. And now, compare that tax return with this." Linnell handed Karen an IRS copy of the dental corporation tax return. "See? This is the dental corporation tax return that I just got from the IRS and Bear is reporting that he took a salary of $168,000 *for the very same year!*"

"A fifty-*thousand* dollar difference?" Karen now had a worried look on her face.

They proceeded to compare the tax returns year by year, and found the same discrepancy for each: All of the dental corporation tax returns showed Bear taking a salary that ranged from $20,000 to $50,000 higher than what he was reporting on the 1040s—the Claire personal tax returns which had been stored in her files. They both saw that the spread was the largest for the most recent year.

"Do you think this is why he's being audited? I mean, it's such an incredibly asinine thing to do. Why would Bear's accountant do something so stupid?" Karen sounded amazed.

"No. I just can't believe our accountant would ever do anything quite so foolish as this. But still, all the copies we've examined show that he'd signed and stamped every damn one of these things, and that Bear and I signed them too."

The two of them sat in worried silence.

Linnell spoke first. "Karen, I just thought of something. I passed the bar a little over three years ago. Maybe that's when he first began doing this stuff."

"Are you saying he's been cheating the IRS to get even with you for being a lawyer? That doesn't make much sense."

"Well, you're right. It seems senseless. But, listen . . . let's just suppose that he did want to get even with me. For working. For being a lawyer. I want you to get something for me. Just for the heck of it, I want you to find the cover letter Bear's accountant prepared when he sent us our 1973 tax returns."

While Karen searched her files, Linnell remained deep in thought. She wondered if she'd just discovered the reason why Bear hadn't demanded anything of her when he'd given her Charles. Considering the money he'd stolen, he could buy her ten Jaguars and still have money to spare. It was even possible that he'd purchased Charles with the money she'd earned and given to him to invest.

Karen handed her the accountant's letter—and Linnell saw that it was not a copy, but the original.

"This looks like the usual thing he sends to Bear along with our joint tax returns—the 1040s." Linnell stared at the letter, deep in thought. She finally spoke. "See? The accountant's letter is addressed to Bear. Bear files our tax returns and then he hands the accountant's letter and the 1040s over to me so I can keep them in my files. He always says it's more private this way, but I think the real reason he's been doing this is to convince me that everything's on the up and up."

The two of them examined the accountant's letter, which merely stated that he was sending the Clare tax returns to Bear at his office; and then, at the very same moment, apparently having thought the same thought, they yelled simultaneously and reached for the wastebasket. Karen lifted out the roses and Linnell retrieved the card that had come with them.

"See? Just as I thought. Look at this!" exclaimed Linnell. "The typing on this card shows that Bear and his accountant have the very same kind of typewriter—one of those IBM models with a platen-ball that can be switched to any style and size of type." Linnell handed Bear's card to Karen. "See? The typeface matches the accountant's, exactly. It's 10 point—the typeface used by accountants because it fits into the small lines of a tax return. Now remember, all we've ever had, as far as the Clare joint tax returns are concerned, are only the . . ." A sharp pain hit Linnell under her ribs; she had seen, in an instant, the awful significance of her discovery.

"*Copies* . . . Xerox copies!" Karen finished Linnell's sentence. "Yes!" Karen hissed, "all he's ever sent us are *copies* of the tax returns. I think I know exactly what you're getting at here!"

Linnell picked up the accountant's cover letter and showed it to Karen. It was dated *April 15, 1973*. They examined it closely and then, for the first time, Linnell saw that the numeral *5* had been typed over a tiny dab of white-out; she next looked at the copies of the Clare tax returns that lay on her desk.

Linnell spoke quietly now. "All Bear has to do is to white-out a few numbers on the originals prepared by the accountant and then type in whatever he wants—this is easy enough for him to do, since he has the very same kind of typewriter as his accountant. So here's what I think he's been doing, and why: The accountant prepares our tax returns, then Bear alters them and brings them home on April 15—the last day for filing—with the phony story about how the accountant always waits until the very last second to get around to doing our taxes. Bear does this so I won't have any time to study the tax return before I sign it. And then, in order to conceal that he's stealing from me, all he has to do is to change a few numbers again, after I sign it. See? Since we're already at the eleventh hour, even if I should happen to notice the changes he's made, I would have no way of attaching any significance to them.

"This happens a lot—people often see things without attaching any significance to them. As a matter of fact, even though I'm a tax attorney, I actually do little more than glance at our tax return before I sign it. Why? Because what I *do* see is that the tax return has already been signed and stamped by our accountant—so naturally, I think everything's legit. Then Bear leaves the house, telling me that he's taking the tax return straight to the post office so that it will be post-marked before midnight. But instead, he goes to his office and alters our personal tax return once again so that it will once again conform to the 1120, the dental corporation tax return. And then a month or so later—when he knows I've gone on to other things—he gives me the accountant's letter. He covers up his lie about the accountant being tardy by changing the date on the accountant's cover letter to make it look like the accountant had sent him our tax return on April 15—and then he gives me the Xerox *copies* he's made of what I've signed, so, of course, I just file everything and forget about them. Furthermore, he makes sure that I never get to see his dental corporation tax returns. Do you see what I'm getting at here?"

"Yes. I sure do! *After* you sign the *altered* originals of your 1040s, which he's altered so you'll think he took a smaller salary than he really did, he makes a set of copies for *you*—then he changes the originals back again in order to conform them to the corporate tax returns he's filing with the IRS—but which *you* never get to see. Then, like you said, he mails everything to the IRS at the very last minute. Sure, that makes sense. But I have to tell you, a week ago, I'd never have believed it. But now, yes—I can see him doing something like that."

"Okay, now here's the proof." Linnell pointed to the IRS envelopes on her chair. "Look at them, I'll bet every single one of them shows a salary that conforms to what he's been reporting on the dental corporation tax returns."

Karen examined each copy of the Clare joint tax returns that the IRS had mailed to Linnell's office. "Sure enough, the salary he reports on these 1040s is the same as the salary he shows on the dental corporation tax returns. And here, like you said, is the proof."

And even though they were only copies of the filed originals, both Linnell and Karen could now see and understand the significance of the faint smudges that had been left on the pages where the numbers had been typed, whited-out and retyped. Bear, pressed for time, had done a sloppy job of whiting-out and retyping his last-minute revisions.

Linnell reached for her calendar for 1973. "Ha! more proof—April 15 fell on a Sunday last year! Any accountant, especially those who really do wait until the last minute, would know that taxpayers have until midnight of the next business day to file their returns should the filing date fall on a weekend. So in '73, we had until midnight on the 16th to file." Linnell picked at the fleck of white-out until it came off. "When Bear was changing the date on the accountant's letter, he didn't realize this—so he types in a 5 instead of a 6. See? Look at this." Karen looked at the letter and saw that once the white-out was removed, the original date typed by the accountant had been April 10. "Do you realize that discovering this is simply a fluke? A matter of luck? If I hadn't looked in my files, I would have looked only at the stuff I got from the IRS and then I would *never* have discovered that Bear has been lying to me about his income."

Karen pulled up a chair to sit down and then leaned against Linnell's desk. "Pretty slick, huh?"

Linnell closed her eyes. The true meaning of her discovery had just struck her. "You know something? Bear's IRS audit has nothing to do with any of this stuff."

"What! How's that?"

"From the perspective of the IRS, there's no discrepancy between our personal tax returns and the dental corporation tax returns—at least as far as Bear's salary is concerned—therefore the discrepancy I just discovered here today can't be why he's being audited. The IRS is definitely on the trail of something else. Something really serious. And I'll bet you can guess what."

Karen sat straight in her chair. "I know where you're going here. What you mean is that the IRS suspects Bear is under-reporting his income. That he's skimming cash, right off the top. Right? And just guess who is going to be made the scapegoat here!"

Linnell's laugh was bitter. "Right! The *brilliant* international tax attorney. *I* am the one who's going to be blamed. You can bet he thought of this angle right off the bat." Linnell looked at the accountant's letter again; Bear had indeed found an ingenious way to cheat both her *and* the IRS. And worse still, since she was his wife *and* a tax attorney, the IRS would of course assume that she was the one who had dreamed it all up.

"Your license!" Karen exclaimed.

"Yes. *My* license. I'd be stripped of my license to practice law if I were found guilty of tax evasion. Bear planned it this way. That skum-bag's dead meat as far as I am concerned."

"Dead meat?"

"He's not going to get away with any of this." Linnell spoke with quiet determination. There was only one thing she had to remember: This was war, not a game for good girls who played by the rules. She had all along planned to take Bear by surprise by coming home early. Well, that part of her game would remain the same, but now she was going to add one more twist. "Okay," she declared, "this is war, but now I know exactly what I'm going to do. But first, one more question. Since Bear was in here to steal my article and plant drugs in my files, why do you suppose he didn't take our tax files?"

"That's easy. He probably forgot about them, same as you almost did. He was too busy setting you up to give them a thought. And besides, you can't think of everything when you're high. And he was high as a kite! Now *I* have a question: Why did he steal your tax article about foreign foundations?"

"I simply can't imagine. But for now, we've got to get cracking—get the form book and type me up a petition for the dissolution of the marriage of Clare. We're going to be in a race for the court house—but I'm going to win because he's not expecting me home until Wednesday. We can discuss what I have in mind as soon as you're through. By the way, don't tell anyone, except Ray, that I'm back, and we're not going to discuss *any* of this on the telephone. It could be that all of our lines are tapped. I'm going back to the motel where I stayed last night. If we need to talk, you can reach me there."

CHANCE

HIGHRIDGE **Monday - March 4, 1974**

Deborah glanced away from the mirror and stared through the window of her small apartment. Oppressed by the gloom outside, she was sure that another week at the Clare office would do her in. She went back to staring at herself in the mirror. A little artwork would be necessary today, but still, the sight of the dour expression on her chalky face made her wonder if the lines would set in permanently. Deborah leaned closer to the mirror and painted a few zits on her chin. Satisfied with her handwork, she dabbed a little Vaseline the length of her nose. "Ugh!" Deborah said, turning away from her reflection. She looked at her watch. There was just enough time for her to complete her mysterious toilette.

Deborah next spread newspapers on the floor all around her and then she reached up and removed her wig and ran a hand over the lengthening stubble. It had broken her heart at first—to have to destroy her shiny long hair, but this had been necessary because it allowed her to more comfortably wear all the wigs required for her many roles. Now Deborah lathered her scalp and skillfully ran the straight edge razor up the back of her neck and over her crown, paying special attention to her hairline. When she was through, she picked up all the newspapers, folded them carefully to avoid dropping any hairs on the carpet, and then stuffed them into the paper bag that contained all the hair she'd cut and shaved off before. She wiped the razor clean with a paper towel, rubbed her head, and placed everything in the same bag of debris. She was almost ready to put on her frizzy blonde wig which she'd fluffed into an even larger cloud. She was now ready for her biggest performance.

Deborah thought about her difficult situation: *The beast has been coming in early just to feel me up and it's getting harder and harder to conceal my revulsion. Margo told me they just liked to play these little sex games. But I know he's got a lot more than games on his mind. The man's got more than a few screws loose, too. And that Margo! She's dangerous because she'd do anything to cover up for him.* Deborah looked at herself in the mirror again and this time she felt like crying. But instead of weeping or feeling sorry for herself, she pretended that she was a whole lot tougher than she really felt.

She next examined her apartment to make sure that everything was perfectly clean: all debris had been packed into plastic garbage bags—even the vacuum cleaner bags—and the place was spotless. This time, before leaving, she hid her duplicates of Margo's keys in a handkerchief to keep them from rattling and then she placed a copy of the Code 1 disk inside the lining of her purse. From now on, she was going to have to play everything by ear. Deborah picked up all the plastic garbage bags and carried them to the refuse bin. She tore them open, and mixed everything into the trash, which she knew would be picked up late Monday evening.

Deborah made coffee as soon as she arrived at the office and she had just handed Margo her cup when she saw Dr. Clare driving into the parking lot. Margo took the cup from Deborah's hands and after taking a sip, she looked at Deborah coquettishly over the rim and announced that Doc had decided to continue her training that afternoon. Deborah barely managed to flutter her lashes by way of reply. And to think that she'd once found Doc attractive. In fact, to be perfectly honest, she had to admit that in the beginning she'd found him extremely handsome and this whole situation rather titillating. Now she knew better.

"Doc thinks you should be ready for him by now." Margo leered archly to make her point clear. Just as she spoke, Dr. Clare swept in, with his briefcase swinging and his jacket a-flap.

Deborah turned her back to the two of them, but managed to hover just close enough so that she could pick up their conversation. Dr. Clare was instructing Margo to go to the bank as soon as it opened—telling her that Tuesday would be the big day. Deborah knew what that meant: the nitrous sniffers would be swarming all over the place. And then she overheard him saying: "Sixty patients, that's a lot."

Pretending to be busy sorting tray set-ups, Deborah listened very carefully and caught Margo telling Doc that he'd better watch his step because the wife would be returning on Wednesday. Dr. Clare walked in front of Deborah to get her attention and in a mean voice ordered her to find someplace else to keep busy because he wanted to use the laboratory. Margo gave Deborah a look that said, "You'd better hop to it, he's in a bad mood!"

Deborah scuttled off to hide in one of the operatories.

"Debbie's such a *good* girl. So helpful." Margo addressed her comments to Doc's hunched-up back.

When Doc reappeared, Deborah could easily detect that he had become a different man: Doc's eyes now blazed and his dimples twinkled, and it was with a near manic glee that he summoned them up to the reception counter to tell them the latest jokes he'd heard at breakfast. He actually giggled; he howled; he got all teary-eyed from laughing at his own jokes, actually clapping his hands together as if he were a little boy.

He's really wound up, thought Deborah. And if she didn't know better, she would've found him entertaining—in a wild-eyed sort of way. She also noticed that Margo simply took Doc's transformation in stride, which meant she was accustomed to these dramatic mood-swings. This knowledge provided little comfort to her however, because it was just this sort of volatility that scared her the most. Deborah was very careful to laugh loudly at his jokes, but she refused to make eye contact with him. However, when she returned to the laboratory a few minutes later, she soon discovered the reason for his dramatic mood-swing. It sat at the bottom of the waste basket: a fresh syringe with its needle intact; a few drops of clear liquid remained in the glass barrel. Deborah picked it up to examine it and a drop of the liquid fell on a finger. A few seconds later, when she reached up to push her frizzy hair from her eyes, she accidentally touched her hand to her lips and they began to tingle and then turn numb. She caught her breath.

He was *injecting* cocaine.

Deborah looked all around the laboratory and observed that one of the upper cupboards had fingerprints around its handle, then she listened to the noises in the office—fortunately, Dr. Clare was already at work on a patient and the whir of his drill would obscure any sounds she might make. She dragged a chair to the counter, climbed up and opened the cupboard—this was exactly where a tall man like Dr. Clare would be storing his cache. She found what she was looking for behind some large cans of plaster-of-paris: rubber tourniquets, syringes of all sizes, pill bottles, capsule holders, numerous packets of drugs—and many bottles of an odorous solvent that smelled like chloroform. She examined the packet labels—which described their contents as 100% pharmaceutical grade cocaine. The bottles of pink pills were labeled

"Dextroamphetamine" and there were dozens of small plastic vials filled with thick yellow tablets that bore labels marked "Percodan." She took samples of everything. Then she stepped down, hid her spoils in a garbage bag, and ditched it outside the back door of the lab. Before she could do anything more, she was interrupted by Margo, who was calling for her to hurry up front. Deborah grabbed her purse, and carrying it low by her side, she rushed out to see what Margo wanted.

"Debbie, It'll only be five minutes, sweetie. I gotta go to the bank. Don't panic, just take the calls for a coupla minutes. The computer's still on, so don't you dare touch the keyboard. Doc's with a patient now and I'll be right back."

Deborah waited until Margo was out the front door before grabbing for her purse. Keeping one eye on Doc, she pulled out the keys. She had to be careful not to attract his attention—if he turned his head he would see her face, but he wouldn't be able to observe that her hands were working rapidly below the counter. Excellent, she thought, but she'd better keep her eye on him nonetheless. He was very animated now, and she could hear him cackling and telling his jokes to his patient. She listened carefully without lifting her eyes, and the instant she heard the whir of Doc's drill, she planted her key in the lock of the slotted drawer.

The phone rang as soon as she turned the key, and she was forced to answer. While she was speaking, she quietly pulled the drawer open and after hanging up, she pretended to be writing a message while her left hand sorted through the disks. There were only two of them left in the drawer today and both were missing their labels. She was at a loss. She realized she couldn't take one because with so few in the drawer, it most certainly would be missed, and she was afraid to substitute the copy she'd brought for fear that Margo might be able to detect that something was fishy. She eased the copy of the Code 1 disk out of her purse and laid it on her lap. She had to think of something before Margo returned.

The phone rang again just as Deborah was removing the disk from the computer. She dropped it into her lap and looked at it while she was speaking. Bingo! The disk was labeled "Code 2" and—wonderful!—it was for the very same time period as her Code 1 disk. This had to be what she was looking for: Hard evidence that Doc was keeping a double set of books! Telling the patient to wait, Deborah tucked the receiver under her chin and punched the hold button because she thought she'd heard a car pulling up. Through the large plate glass window of the reception room she could see Margo backing into a parking space in front of the office. Deborah panicked. She needed the Code 2 disk as absolute proof. There was no time to think! Deborah slid her copy of the Code 1 disk into the computer and slipped the Code 2 disk into her purse. She had just enough time to lock the drawer and hide her keys. When Margo was halfway up the path to the front door, Deborah grabbed the appointment book to make it look like she had been scheduling patients. Just as Margo opened the door, Deborah picked up the phone to speak to the waiting patient.

Deborah looked up to give Margo a smile and then saw the two men who were close on her heels. Nondescript men in gray rain coats. She was sure she'd seen one of them before. She signaled for Margo to turn around and then flipped the lever down. The monitor began to blink. Deborah dropped the receiver and stood up just as all three of them burst through the door. In an instant the reception area became a jumble of waving arms, flailing legs, and wobbling lamps. Margo immediately grabbed Deborah and tried to pull her away from the computer. They bumped, Margo stepped on her shoes, pushed her, and then took her by the shoulders in a failed attempt to shove her out of the way. Meanwhile, Mr. Rizzo, simultaneously identifying himself and lunging for the computer, waved a search warrant in Margo's face. Deborah heard him ordering Margo to keep her hands in the air and not touch anything. Mr. Rizzo's assistant politely asked Deborah to trade places with him.

Deborah dropped her head and stepped out of the way. In the midst of all this, Dr. Clare emerged from the patient operatory to take a look at the commotion, and Agent Rizzo slapped the search warrant in his hand. Seeing who it was, Doc grinned broadly and then after looking at the warrant—which empowered the agents to search his computer—he snickered, then exploded into gales of laughter.

"Hey guys! Help yourselves," Doc chortled, as if he were a stand-up comic delivering killer punchlines.

Margo, suddenly calm, was now back to playing the part of the hostess. With the exaggerated gestures of a pitchman's assistant, she pointed to the computer, smiled at all of them broadly and said, "Gentlemen. Pul-*lease* be my guest."

"Thank you. We'll get to work right now, madam, Dr. Clare." Rizzo spoke with elaborate courtesy. He motioned to his computer technician to boot up the program and start the printer, and then Dr. Clare, still snorting and cackling with manic elation, turned on his heel and returned to his patient.

Doc's hilarity seemed to have infected Margo because she now stood grinning at Agent Rizzo while the printer shot reams of data into his hands. Deborah, who had been keeping her back to the agents, felt a need to escape. Seeing that Margo was wholly occupied in flirting with Agent Rizzo, she backed up a step, casually reached for her purse and faded back to the laboratory. She had to figure out what to do next. Should she up and bolt? She considered this alternative and then decided against it because she knew she wasn't quite finished here yet.

While Margo was carrying on like the lady of the manor and Dr. Clare was joking loudly with his patient, Deborah stayed out of sight in the laboratory. She pulled on some latex gloves and climbed up to the shelf, grabbed the large solvent bottle, and poured some into a smaller bottle without spilling a drop. She had just climbed down when she heard Margo calling for her to make some coffee for their "guests." Margo's voice dripped with sarcasm and Deborah joined in the fun by raising her voice to a harsh falsetto to reply that she would get to it right away. Deborah hid the small bottle in the garbage bag outside the back door, then she quickly poured out some coffee and carried it toward Margo, who was waiting for her in the hall.

Margo took the cups from her hands. "Skeedaddle. Use the back door. Come back in an hour, now that's a *good* girl." Margo winked and gave her a playful bump with her hip.

Deborah had been praying for this; she grabbed her coat and purse and snatched the loaded garbage bag on her way to her car. After slipping on a pair of dark glasses and pulling her ski mittens over her rubber dental gloves, she left the parking lot from the alley and headed straight for the computer store where it took only a few minutes to place her order. Paying for everything with cash, she requested an immediate duplicate of the disk and a print-out of the data it contained, then she asked the clerk to do her a favor—would he mail a package for her?

HIGHRIDGE **Monday morning - March 4, 1974**

The room was brown, the universal dirt-colored brown often found in those tacky motels that cut corners in order to reduce their maintenance costs. Shag carpets dark as dirt, brown plaid draperies, deadwood blankets—Linnell felt as if she'd been buried alive. When she rolled over to switch on the lamp, she was not surprised to see streaks of brown tar residue coating the inside surface of the lamp shade, traceries of despair from the countless cigarettes that had been left to smolder in the tin ashtray sitting under the lamp. She sat up and stretched. Monday morning—only forty-eight hours after the glorious sunrise in Cayman—and now everything was brown and cold and foggy again.

How did she feel?

A touch queasy perhaps, but otherwise, *wonderful.* She had been delivered to herself. Made whole. She had received so little praise for bucking the system that she had actually come to believe that her very survival as a lawyer depended on her having Bear for a protector. But no longer. Now that she knew he had never been there for her at all, it meant that she had always been making it on her own.

Linnell snuggled under the covers and read all the old newspapers that Karen had saved. They were filled with articles about William E. Ivener and Project Haven Mavens. She was surprised to learn that the Intelligence Division Project, code-named "Project Haven Mavens," had begun the year before and that the case against Ivener was the first to emanate from this undercover investigation into the use of tax havens for the purpose of evading federal income tax. The paper stated that the government had already spent over $1,000,000 on this project alone, and that the public could expect to see a spate of indictments throughout the nation over the next several months.

$1,000,000 was just the beginning, she thought. What about all the judges—with their generous pensions and their bodyguards and bailiffs and attendants? And the lawyers—with their lunches and dinners and glorious weekend retreats, all of them billing for every minute at their highest rates? There would also be hundreds of court reporters and transcribers—not to mention the cost of the transcripts themselves; scores of guards and clerks and janitors—all with their salaries and pensions and perks. And the public? The taxpayers? They were going to pick up the tab, and since the government would probably spend another ten million on Project Haven Mavens before it ever collected a dime, it was unlikely that anyone outside of the legal system would recoup anything from the Ivener case no matter how much the government recovered.

Linnell was even more surprised to learn that an early date had been set for the trial. This was quite unlike Ivener. She knew him; ordinarily, he liked to stall. She read a recap of the government's case: Ivener was charged with conspiracy to evade federal income tax through his sale of allegedly phony interest and depreciation deductions to a roster of clients who had used what the IRS described as the Ivener System of Foreign Tax Planning which involved a vast array of tax haven corporations and trusts and a Bahamian bank to forward his schemes. He was also charged with selling the very same real estate under a variety of cleverly named corporate shells to different groups of ostensibly unwitting investors.

Buried on the next to the last page of the paper, was an abbreviated squib that described the Treasury Department's monitoring program as a major new component of the ongoing Haven Mavens Project: *"All those who travel to tax havens more frequently than once a year are now being placed on a "watch list" being shared with the Department of Justice and the Treasury Department."* Linnell circled the article and thought about how her room had been bugged, then pitied the hapless agent whose job it was to listen to her boring conversations. Several newspaper articles included Willy's photograph, and mentioned, but only in passing, that he was legal counsel for The Wei.

Reading between the lines, Linnell was absolutely amazed at the wealth of detailed information that the prosecutor had already acquired. Then she wondered about Harold Dolphe. Why hadn't the IRS indicted him, too? It would have served him right for cat-calling her. Well she couldn't waste any more of her time worrying about Ivener's problems, and least of all about Dolphe. She had plenty of problems of her own.

The $820,000 would be at the Canadian bank for only ten days—which meant she only had until Wednesday of this week to find it. She was actually in a race, not just with Bear, but with the IRS too. And since the IRS would be tapping her lines, they would know what she was doing to find the money. Well, they could listen all they wanted, but she was sure she could retrieve it long before the IRS could get an order served on the Canadian bank. But she needed a gimmick to buy her some time. She only needed a couple of days—and she thought she had one that would do the job: She would send Bear on a costly wild goose chase to keep him busy while she went about finding and tying up their money—and when she did, she would divert it to Cayman, then Bear would have to come begging to her.

First, she had to get a court order to remove Bear from the house and to account for their property—including the account at the Montreal Bank. If she knew Bear, he would stall; he would postpone the hearing date again and again, and then at the very last second he would get his lawyer to plead his ill health so that the matter would be forced off calendar—forcing the cycle to begin all over again. No, she would not let this happen and she had some up with a plan to stop him. Linnell called a process server and told him to go to her law office and pick up some papers and to serve them on Dr. Clare at exactly 1:30 p.m., today.

And now for the twist. Setting her briefcase on her bed to use as a desk, she laid out her papers side by side to make sure that when she drafted her wills, that they would be the same—except for two very important items: the fake corporation which she was about to invent, and her Cayman corporation, SUP Cayman Ltd. Both wills had to be entirely handwritten to be treated as valid holographic wills under California law. One will would be genuine—and the other would be a decoy. In both documents, Linnell left her half of the community property and all of her separate property to Benjy.

In her genuine will, however, she left all of the shares of SUP Cayman Ltd. to her testamentary trust in the Cayman Islands to be held for the benefit of her son. In her decoy will, she didn't mention SUP Cayman Ltd. or the testamentary trust, instead she listed the fake corporation, *Phoenix Cayman Corporation Ltd.,* as one of her assets and then stated that all shares were bequeathed to her son and none to her husband, Mark Clare. The decoy had only one purpose: that of capturing Bear's attention so that he would put all his energy into staking a claim to the red herring Phoenix Corporation. Linnell thought for a moment, then stated that the shares of the Phoenix Cayman Corporation were worth $1,400,000—large enough, she thought, to stir up his greed while at the same time not so large as to make him suspect that it was merely a ruse. And then—adding the touch that was sure to ignite a nuclear explosion—she stated that the Phoenix Cayman Corporation was her *sole and separate property.* She knew that as soon as Bear saw this, he'd no longer want to stall. He'd hot-foot it into court in order to stake a claim to the fake Phoenix corporation and then Bear and his lawyer would waste a whole lot of time and money before discovering that she'd led on them a wild goose chase. Meanwhile, this would give her the few extra days she needed to do an end-run around all of them.

She had to bring *Phoenix* to Bear's attention—but she couldn't do this in her divorce petition or else she, as a lawyer, would run the risk of being held in contempt for presenting a deliberately falsified statement of fact. So, if she couldn't draw Bear's attention to the fake Phoenix corporation in her divorce papers, she certainly could do so by way of a will. Linnell signed both of the wills, making sure that her authentic will bore the most recent date so that it would legally revoke the decoy—just in case she should be so unfortunate as to wind up under the wheels of a bus. No point in tempting fate, thought Linnell. She would mail her genuine will to her folks on her way to Bear's office.

HIGHRIDGE **Monday - 10. a.m. - March 4, 1974**

Deborah spent exactly thirty-five minutes attending to her business at the computer store and then returned to the dental office. She was now in her car, watching what was happening inside. Without making too much of it, she had explained to the computer store clerk that she had injured her hand and that she needed him to address and mail a package for her. Fortunately, she had looked so awful that he had looked at her only once while he was addressing the package in which Deborah had packed the Code 2 data. He had promised to mail it for her that evening, after work, and when she tipped him the extra five bucks, he had pocketed the cash without displaying any curiosity at all.

She hunched down behind the wheel of her car because it looked like the agents were getting ready to leave. Sliding farther down in the seat, she peeked over the dash and watched them walking to their car—it looked like the computer technician had found what he wanted because he was carrying an armload of what she knew were the print-outs of the Code 1 program.

"This is it, I'm going to chance it," Deborah thought. Waiting until the IRS agents had pulled away, she turned up the collar of her coat and walked toward the front entrance. She wanted to enter by the front door so she could immediately read the expression on Margo's face. As soon as she stepped inside, Deborah stopped to call hello. Margo was apparently ensconced with Dr. Clare because she could hear Margo's plummy voice coming from behind the door of his private office.

Deborah heard a few telling words: "Well! We *did* it . . . by the skin of our . ." and then saw his door close.

"I'm back!" Deborah called out, louder this time.

The door of Dr. Clare's private office opened abruptly and Margo's head poked out. "Debbie dear, why don't you just get the phones for a while, Doc and I are going to be busy in here a few minutes more."

Deborah was overcome with relief. It looked like the camels hadn't the faintest clue. . . she'd know in a minute. Still wearing her coat, and keeping her mittens on just in case she had to jump up and make a run for it—she sat down at the computer. With a hand that was surprisingly steady, she turned the lever and removed the disk and inserted the Code 2 disk in its place. She held her breath and looked down. Yes! It was her copy of the Code 1 disk. Incredible timing. No. *Perfect* timing . . . nobody here had discovered her switch. She hid the Code 1 disk in her purse before taking off her coat, removed only her mittens, and then she went back to tending the front desk.

When Margo and Dr. Clare sauntered back into the reception area, Deborah carefully observed their faces: Margo looked like a smug pouter-pigeon and Dr. Clare was actually smirking. *I'm home free,* Deborah thought. She looked at them expectantly, waiting to hear what Margo would say.

"Debbie sweetie, you can go work in the back now . . . you'd better stay here for lunch because Doc says he wants to give you your oral exam when he returns from lunch. Margo grinned at Doc, who was now standing next to the reception counter, holding onto his briefcase. He raised his eyebrows and waggled them at Margo and then made a peculiar face.

Deborah's face turned red; she hadn't expected *this*—at least not so soon. She grabbed a tissue and blew her nose to conceal her reaction. It was then that she happened to look out the window—a woman was walking jauntily up the path to the entrance. She was swinging a briefcase. Deborah stepped out from behind the reception counter to take a better look and then turned away. She had a feeling that this was "the wife."

HIGHRIDGE **Monday, 10:00 a.m. - March 4, 1974**

Linnell had loaded her briefcase with some tax books to give it some heft and then she had torn paper into tiny pieces and slipped them between the pages of her decoy will before sliding it into a manila envelope. With a broad-tipped felt pen, she'd written: *Last Will of Linnell Clare - A Married Woman,* on its face and then she had placed it on top of the books before closing her briefcase—and just as she'd done in Cayman, she left it unlocked. She was so certain she was going to find the eight digit code, she gave Karen the pages from the Montreal phone book which Colin had so kindly provided for this quest. In a very short while, Karen and Ray could start calling the banks—and maybe that wouldn't be necessary if Bear had been so careless as to write both the code and the name of the bank on the same piece of paper. The immediate plan was for Karen to drive her to Bear's office and to wait for her there.

They arrived at the dental center just as two men were pulling away in an old gray Chevrolet. Linnell noticed them because the driver looked briefly in her direction. The other man appeared to be holding a tall stack of papers.

"Well, this is it," Linnell said.

"Break a leg," Karen replied automatically.

"You've got to stop saying that! You know *me*. I just might," Linnell laughed nervously.

Karen stopped in front of the office; Linnell grabbed her briefcase and hopped out and walked quickly up the path to the entrance. She could see Bear standing in the reception area next to Margo. Her heart skipped a beat and then she flung open the door. "Bear darling, I'm *back*!" she cried loudly.

Bear spun around, shocked by the sound of her voice. Linnell watched him drop his briefcase on the floor next to his leg. Meanwhile, Margo stood gaping at her from the security of her spider's nest behind the reception counter.

"Good morning Margo! Good to see *you,* too." Linnell gave Margo a sunny grin, and then she rushed Bear. Dropping her briefcase at his feet, she wrapped her arms around his rigid body and gave him a hug, then raising her hand with its wedding band close to his face, she crooned: "I couldn't wait to get back to see you, honey, so I caught an early flight. Oh! And *this* must be your lovely new assistant. Aren't you Debbie? I've heard such nice things about you." Linnell addressed her remarks to the back of the frizzy-haired blonde who strode rapidly away from her down the hall.

Linnell's energy filled the room; Bear and Margo remained frozen, staring at her in drop-dead silence. Linnell waited for Bear to blink, and the instant he turned to give Margo a look, she grabbed his briefcase with one hand and his arm with the other and pulled him with her toward the front door.

"Well *darling*, I can see you are your usual busy self. I just wanted to let you know how much I missed you while I was gone. I'm going straight to my office to catch up with my work, so I'll see you later tonight. *Bahhhh,* baby!" Linnell smiled up into his face and then imitating the way he breezed out every morning, she whirled out of his office before he could speak.

Linnell rushed around the building and met Karen who sat waiting for her in her car with its engine already running. Linnell jumped in and Karen sped away.

"It's locked. I knew it would be." Linnell fumbled with Bear's briefcase.

"Why don't you try using your own briefcase key on the damn thing. They both look the same, so give it a try," Karen urged.

Linnell got the key in the lock and the briefcase popped open. "You're a genius! Forget the locksmith, now we can go straight to the copy center." Linnell found several thick folders packed with financial records, then she looked in the pockets. "It's here! This is what I hoped I would find." Linnell held up a sheet of paper and tears came to her eyes. "This is luck! And just like Colin said—it's eight digits." There was no clue to the bank however, which meant they were going to have to canvas them.

"Way to go!" Karen accelerated to top speed while Linnell rifled through the rest of the compartments. Her explorations led her to a long flannel sack and she squeezed it to see if she could tell what it was. Then she opened it.

"Karen! What's this?" Linnell held up the long rubber cylinder by its bulbous nose and waved it next to Karen's face.

"Can't look now, or I'm going to hit the speed bumps too fast." Linnell let the object slip back into its sack and when Karen flew over the speed-bumps it fell out of her hands and onto the back seat. They zig-zagged through the empty spaces and parked in front of the copy center, jumped out, and swiftly commandeered the fastest machine. Linnell unfastened the clips on each file and fed the papers into the copier while Karen reassembled the originals. Linnell scanned Bear's papers and observed that most of them were cash flow journals for the dental corporation along with several working sets of corporate tax returns. They were Bear's work-papers—the ones he kept for himself.

An embossed business card fell out of one of the files. Linnell picked it up and remarked, "Look at this. It's a card from the law office of Buster Hosterman. You know—that wannabe-cop." She sighed. Then a small sheet from a telephone-pad next caught her eye. "Bear's handwriting, I can just make it out. Willkills . . . must be a patient. Well, don't bother with it, we'll just keep it." Linnell stuffed it in her pocket, then dropped Buster Hosterman's card back into Bear's briefcase, and went on feeding documents into the copy machine.

They worked steadily without talking and when Karen next looked at her watch it was already past 11:30 a.m. Linnell knew that Bear usually called her right about this time of day, which meant he would soon be taking off for lunch.

"I'd better get this stuff back to Bear now," Linnell warned. I don't want to be anywhere near him after lunch, because that's when he's going to be served. Let's call his office—I just want to see his face one more time before everything hits the fan." Linnell packed the copies she'd made in Bear's briefcase. She knew it was going to *kill* him when he got around to discovering that she'd kept the originals and the slip of paper with the eight digit code.

Plunking coins into the pay phone, Karen motioned for Linnell to stand next to her while the call was going through. As expected, Margo answered.

"Dental office. This is *Margo* the office manager." Even at this distance, Linnell could hear the self-importance in Margo's voice.

"This is Karen from the law office of L.C. Clare." Karen, smiling into the mouthpiece, spoke softly but with a distinct British accent to mock Margo's coarseness. "Mrs. Clare is calling for her husband." Karen grinned and passed the phone to Linnell.

"Margo, I need to speak with my husband. Put him on the line." Linnell spoke crisply.

Margo's voice was all sarcasm and cloying sweetness. "Well, *Ms.* Clare, you certainly gave us a treat when you dropped in on all us-stay-at-home workers. You're always such a busy, busy little gal, traveling all over the world like you dooooo."

Linnell ignored Margo's invitation to squabble. "Where's my husband? He switched briefcases with me this morning and I just discovered the mistake when I couldn't get it unlocked, and I need my own briefcase so I can get some work done today. It looks like I'll have to swing by your place and pick mine up unless you want to drive over here."

"Well sweetie, you should know by now I can't leave the front desk. You're just gonna have to come by here and pick it up yourself. And you better do it right *now*. Doc's got a full schedule this afternoon and he can't be disturbed. I think maybe he's already gone to lunch, but if you'll just hold your horses, I'll check just for *you.*"

With the mouthpiece pressed against her well-padded hip, Margo turned to Doc. "You'd better scram. The wife's just now discovered she's got your briefcase and she needs to come back here and exchange 'em." Margo giggled. "And guess what—the dummy went all the way to her office and *then* found out she couldn't get yours unlocked! Isn't that a scream?"

Exchanging conspirational grins, Bear waggled his eyebrows at Margo in his curious new way and instead of speaking, he pointed to Linnell's briefcase which sat open on top of his desk, then he quickly slipped out of his white nylon dental jacket and made ready to flee.

Margo pursed her thick lips and simpered, "Too late, *Ms.* Clare. You just missed Doc. I'll be waiting for you, so hurry it up so's I can take my lunch break, too."

"I'm on the way," Linnell replied, forcing herself to sound civil. Then she remembered. The pills! Yes, now was a good time to do a little drilling on Margo.

"Margo, I certainly do hope you're feeling better?"

"Sweetie, I don't know about you, but *I'm* feeling just *fine.*"

"Well, I was very concerned about all that medication everybody says you've been taking. I'm just hoping you don't have a *problem.* You know what I mean? So just you hold tight and I'll be right over there to see you and then we can talk about it." Linnell managed to hang up without slamming the receiver. She had no intention of rushing back to Bear's office. Karen could drive her back to her car and then she would pick up something to eat. For some reason, she had a very good appetite today.

HIGHRIDGE **Monday - Noon - March 4, 1974**

Ma had taken him by surprise when she'd dropped in out of the blue like that. And he knew Ma had taken his briefcase just as soon as he picked up the one she had left. It was too heavy; it was also unlocked, and when he'd opened it, he'd found that it contained Linnell's tax books and the large manila envelope—which he had opened immediately. He'd just as immediately read her will . . . and he was shocked! It was an outrage. Who did she think she was? Cutting him out of their community property like that!

And then he was furious.

Bear called Buster and Buster asked him to read the part of the will that disposed of the valuable Phoenix Corporation.

"You say this Phoenix Corporation is worth how much?" Buster asked.

"1.4 mil . . . that's million," Bear replied, his voice indignant.

"You're a lucky man, Bear."

"Lucky? Why am I *lucky?*"

"First off, you're lucky 'cause the Phoenix Corporation is community property, no matter what she says. And second, . . . you're lucky because L.C.'s plane didn't go down. C*'mon,* you should know what I mean. Think about what you'd get if something happened to her *before* you got your divorce."

"You mean, like, if she were *killed?*"

"Yeah. You'd lose her half of the community property. Her half would go to your kid. I wouldn't want to be handling something like that. Fighting over her estate—maybe for years, with all those probate attorneys. Much easier for you to beat her down now and get her to settle with you—that way you can get more than your half—much easier to do that than to have to go after your kid if she croaked. Hey! I can understand why a guy in your position might want to see her get whacked—I'd gladly defend you if that came to pass—but we'd end up the losers in terms of the money . . . You following me?"

"Oh. I see. Yeah. I *see.* It's really better if she *lives.* I hadn't figured on *that.* Well, that's what I wanted to know."

Bear was thinking about the Phoenix Corporation—and how it would more than make up for the gold he had lost—when both of his eyes began to blur. He pressed them with his knuckles, hoping to put a stop to the zig-zags that flashed across his vision.

"You hadn't figured on *what?*" Buster asked.

Bear suddenly felt anxious. He hadn't meant to say that. And worse yet, Buster had caught it. He had to change the subject immediately.

"Well, how am I doing on the retainer? You need more?" Bear asked. What was the matter with his ears? The call sounded hollow. First his eyes were bothering him, and now it was his *ears*.

"I could use another $20,000 or so, for the investigator's costs. Okay?"

Bear had a sinking feeling. "What do you mean, $20,000! For what? I already paid you $5000!"

"Hey listen, Doc. You're talking big money here. I can't charge you the same. This ain't a two-bit case anymore. I have a lot of liability for your assets. See? I *gotta* charge more. No lawyer is going to work on a deal for 1.4 mil and get paid in bird seed."

"Got to go, Buster." Bear had to call Willy immediately.

"Hey, not so fast." Buster interjected. "You fiddle your books yet?"

"Yeah! I took care of 'em. Gotta *go*, Buster!"

As soon as he'd gotten rid of Buster, Bear called the Law Office of William E. Ivener. It was now an imperative—he had to call off the hit.

When he spoke with Willy's secretary he was surprised to learn that she didn't know who he was, so he spelled out his name and told her that it was an emergency. The secretary, who identified herself as Margarita, replied that *Mr. Ivener* was in conference and that she had been instructed not to interrupt him. "Sorry," she said, "but those are the rules."

"Rules! This is no time for rules! I've got to talk to Willy, *now*!" Bear begged, but to no avail.

He finally persuaded Margarita, now snippy, to take a message and she huffily promised to give it to Mr. Ivener as soon as she saw him later that afternoon. Bear carefully spelled out his message: *Dr. Clare regrets he cannot take the Advanced Wei Program this Friday. Be sure to cancel him out of the program. Important events have changed his plans.*

"And I need to have you read the message back to me so I can be sure you got it right."

"I want you to know I'm not stupid," Margarita replied. But she read the message back to him while he watched Margo out of the corner of his eye—she was signaling him. "Okay, you've got it," he said to Margarita. "You tell Willy it's important for him to understand," Bear pleaded.

"That's *Mr. Ivener,* Bear." Having the last word, Margarita cut off the call.

"The wife's on her way over here," Margo announced, "to exchange briefcases. You gotta get moving, Doc, if you want to save the afternoon for yourself. You've got Debbie at 2 p.m. and then we've got to get ready for all those special patients coming in tomorrow."

"Everything's already set up for tomorrow and I added an extra tank of nitrous. Tomorrow's going to be the last day for a while, until I get rid of the audit. I'm going to have to tell the wife about it when I see her tonight."

"Doc, don't do that. We can handle it by ourselves."

"Wait a minute. I call the shots here, not you," Bear replied. "And mind your own business."

Bear saw Margo turning around to greet a man who had just walked up to the reception desk. The man held a clip board. Bear heard him asking for Dr. Clare, saw Margo point in his direction, and watched him walking quickly towards him without waiting for Margo to announce his arrival.

The man entered his private office with a sly smile. "Are you Dr. Mark Clare?"

"Yeah, I'm Dr. Clare."

"Here! This is for you! And have a nice day."

The process server placed the papers in Bear's hand, wrote on his clipboard, and rushed out. He had added another whole hour to his lunch break by serving the papers earlier than he'd been instructed.

Bear shut his office door and then looked at the papers. The words: *Petition for the Dissolution of the Marriage of Clare* vibrated on the page.

"No!" Bear gasped, flipping the pages. "Oh no! Ma filed *first.*" He knew what people would think—they'd think he was a loser. A *loser!* Soon everyone would know Ma had dumped him. How could she do this to him? He staggered to his bathroom and gulped a glass of water, spilling some on his shirt, then he lurched back to his desk. He unlocked the drawer, grabbed his injection kit, hit a vein, and in seconds he was glowing with furious energy. Nothing could stop him now. He was going to get her! He'd get her and make her *pay*!

Bear managed to lock up his paraphernalia and then he called Buster again and was told by an answering service that "Mr. Hosterman was at lunch." Thoroughly frustrated, Bear hung up without leaving a message. He lifted his head to listen; he could hear drums throbbing softly in the distance. This time there was an entire orchestra laying out tympani in time with his pulse. He froze and then listened intently as the rumbling faded away and the words gradually emerged: *Orry-gorry-orrrry-gorrry-bloody-cutting.* Bear cocked his head and heard the sound of glass shattering inside his head. Then the static again.

He could still tell, even through this blanket of sound, that his chorus of counselors were still struggling to come to the aid of their King. *Orry-gorry-orrrry-gorrry-bloody-cutting.*

Stuffing the rolled-up divorce petition in his jacket, he had to make a conscious effort to lift his feet as he stepped his way to the reception area. Leaning on the counter, he told Margo he wanted to have Debbie waiting for him in his private office when he got back and then knitting his brow, he warned her that Debbie had better be fit for a king.

Margo looked at him, puzzled. "Doc? You feelin' okay?"

"I'm fine. I just need to get outta here. Need to get some lunch."

But he wasn't hungry at all. He drove to the park so he could study the petition. He had to read it over and over again because one of his eyes kept blurring. And then, when the words finally held still, he was able to understand that Ma was demanding an accounting from him for *all* of their money and assets and she had also requested the court to issue a restraining order to keep him away from her and the house. How in *hell* had she learned about him sending their money to the bank in Montreal! Nervy bitch wanted her half of *everything*, and yet she hadn't mentioned *anything* about the Phoenix Corporation Cayman Ltd. shares! This was an *outrage*! Buster had better get cracking on this one *immediately*. With his pulse thumping fast in his throat, Bear sat in his Cadillac and chanted his mantra until his heart stopped jumping and skipping around; then he decided that he would pass up his lunch and return to his office, where he knew he'd find Margo waiting for him like his loyal old dog. And the girl. She would be waiting for him too.

HIGHRIDGE **Monday - March 4, 1974**

After her telephone call to Margo, Linnell had allowed a full forty minutes to pass before she pulled up in front of the dental office. But Bear's Cadillac was not in the parking lot. Linnell locked Bear's briefcase and strolled to the door without hurrying, knowing that Margo would be watching her through the window. When she finally entered, after dawdling in front of the entrance, she could see that Margo's face was bubbling with rage.

"You said you'd be coming over here right away!" Margo shrilled.

Linnell ignored her and stepped into Bear's private office and traded briefcases without saying a word. She caught her breath when she saw scraps of paper underneath his chair. It had worked! He had read her will and her big to-do about having to exchange briefcases again would further convince him that it was authentic. If only she could see his face when he learned the truth! Then, out of the corner of her eye, she saw a pink swirl of nylon. She waited until the woman was almost upon her, then whirled around, forcing Margo to actually jump out of the way of her swinging briefcase.

Margo batted her false eyelashes with furious indignation. "Hey, you! Watch out! You almost hit me!"

Linnell responded by swinging her briefcase again, this time fanning Margo's legs.

Margo's expression changed. It now held a hint of fear. "You can't come in here! This is Doc's private office. And what was that crack about me taking drugs? Just what are you trying to say?"

Linnell didn't answer. She kept swinging her briefcase, forcing Margo to step out of her way until she was at the front door; then she turned toward Margo. "I didn't say *drugs*. You did. And let me break it to you gently, you old sow—you can save all your silly pig-shit for your lord and master!" Then she stepped outside, carefully leaving the door open so all the papers on the reception desk would blow to the floor.

◆❖◆

Karen and Ray were already at work when Linnell returned to her office. They hadn't found the bank yet, and they were nervous, the three hour time difference meant they had only another hour to finish their search.

Linnell nodded hello and stepped into her office. Bear's files were already on her desk and she took her first look at the inner workings of his dental practice. She spent the next half-hour examining them and forgot all about helping Karen and Ray. "It's far worse than I ever could have imagined," she thought. "He's been stealing from me in the most complex way, yet his tax evasion is so simple-minded. He just keeps a double set of books. Worse yet, it's clear he's been dealing drugs. Look at this! —"special patients"— and a list of all the drugs he's been peddling. Quaalude. Nitrous. Percodan. Cocaine. Dextroamphetamine. Valium. I . . . Benjy and I . . . we've been living in a fool's paradise God only knows for how long!" Linnell checked the time and noted that Bear would have been served. She was partly anxious and partly relieved at the thought of the battle that loomed. And then she heard Karen's voice.

"L.C.! Come here! We found the bank, but it seems there's some kind of problem. You'd better talk to the manager, he's holding for you." Karen's face held a worried expression. Karen passed the telephone to Linnell, but Linnell shook her head to let Karen know that she wanted her to stay on the line to listen in on her conversation.

"Mrs. Clare, is that you? This is Christian Journet." The manager spoke English with a discernible French accent. "Is everything to your satisfaction?"

"Mr. Journet? I've never had the occasion to speak with you before now. My husband is Mark Clare, a dentist here in California, and I'm calling you from Highridge, California, to give you instructions about my money which my husband transferred to your bank last week. As you might know, California is a community property state and the money you have is mine, so the funds must be bank-wired to me pending resolution of my petition for divorce."

There was a silence on the other end of the line and Linnell had to prompt Mr. Journet to speak.

"Madame, I am greatly concerned. As you know, this account was governed by an access code, and the lady who called this morning presented it when she informed us that she was Mrs. Clare. We bank-wired the funds to

Switzerland at exactly 8:00 AM Eastern Standard Time, pursuant to her instructions. You say *you* are Mrs. Clare? We must have confirmation. Would you kindly repeat the access code, sil vous plait?

Linnell then repeated the access code and provided him with her credentials.

"But I am astounded, Madame! Our instructions were explicit. They were provided by the chief operations officer of the Highridge Bank and we were directed to act on oral instructions upon presentation of the access code for this account."

"Did you record the call? What bank in Switzerland?"

"Madame, may I return your call? I must resort to our legal department for advice."

"That isn't good enough, Mr. Journet. Unless you want to see my lawyers and a flock of your local news reporters on your doorstep, I suggest you call the state bar to confirm my identity and my credentials, and then you had better be prepared to give me the information I've requested. It will take you ten minutes to do that, and I suggest you begin by calling the manager of the Highridge Bank. By the way, I assume you record your calls, and when I hear from you next, you'd better have that recording for me."

Linnell immediately called Bear's office, and when she heard the busy signal she cut off the call and dialed the number of the bank's Head Office in San Francisco and spoke to the president. Detecting the scent of litigation, he assured her that he would call Mr. Journet to consult with him immediately. Linnell knew that he would do as he said because of the bank's liability for negligent business practices—under the new laws, her husband could establish a bank account with community funds, but he no longer had the right to dispose of community property without her consent. And all banks in California were required to know this, especially when funds were being wired out of the country. Linnell looked at Bear's patient list. She knew there was a very good chance she'd retrieve the funds because Bear had listed the Chief Operations officer as one of his "special patients" and now she knew just how to use this information.

SAN FRANCISCO **Monday afternoon - March 4, 1974**

Jordan gazed out the grime-streaked window of the San Francisco IRS office to watch the fog rolling in and thought about Cayman and how disappointed he'd been when he'd knocked on Linnell's door, only to have it swing open to reveal an empty room. Disappointment was hardly the word. Only two days ago—wild with anticipation—he had been standing at his open window, watching the Caribbean sunrise and listening to the phone ringing and ringing in her room. The faint sound of her voice had come through the wall and he had simply stood there, on his balcony, regretting his haste in removing the bugs. He had assumed she would hang up and then take her shower, so he'd taken a long one himself. He had rented a sailboat the night before and had taken such pains to pack his duffel bag with plenty of snacks—he'd planned to take her around the island and into North Sound to search for the tame giant stingrays he'd been hearing about. But more important than that—he had wanted to gain her confidence and then tell her everything he'd learned about her husband. And so what did she do after he'd made all of these careful plans? She had simply disappeared. Jordan shrugged.

Fog blanketed the entire city. It would be a relief to get out of here—Rizzo would be taking him along on a short trip to Highridge where they planned to stake out the Ivener office. He might even get to see a little sunshine today. Jordan reached for the telephone. He had to call Linnell and alert her to what was about to come down. He dialed the number for her law office, then cut off the call after only one ring. He'd almost blown it. He couldn't *call* her—all her lines were tapped!

He didn't belong here. He had to get *out* of here, but he couldn't afford to be fired—he'd better not forget about that. Jordan closed his eyes and saw the colors—ultramarine and indigo water, cream-colored powdery sand and Linnell's warm curves packed tight inside the transparent bathing suit. Last night he had dreamt of her again. Jordan remained seated in front of the new IRS computer and daydreamed while he transferred data. Finally, Rizzo poked his head in and said, "You ready? Let's split."

It was dusk and the temperature was dropping along with the sun and it was cold by the time they pulled off the freeway in Highridge. Rizzo parked his Chevy across the street from the Ivener office, which allowed them to keep an eye on both doors.

"There's our boy—Harold Dolphe."

"Yeah. That's the same guy I saw a couple of days ago in Cayman, hanging around the hotel."

"That creep's our informant. Sort of looks the part, doesn't he? We'll follow him a couple of blocks and he'll wave us over. Let's go."

"Him? The plant in the Ivener office?"

"Sure is now. We turned him. When we got to him a couple of days ago at the airport in Houston, we showed him a copy of the indictment and told him that he'd be next if we didn't get some cooperation from him and he rolled on his back like a two buck whore. We planted the info he gave us in the papers, just to make Ivener sweat."

"Well how do you know he's not going to feed us a bunch of bullshit?" Jordan felt such questions made him appear pretty sharp.

"We'll know the score in a minute. He's pulling over." Rizzo followed Dolphe behind a shopping center and pulled behind a large refuse bin.

Dolphe rolled down his window, and yelled, "Hey Rizzo!" and gestured for Rizzo to come over to him.

"Just look at that cocky sonnavabitch!" Rizzo spoke under his breath and grinned coldly at Dolphe. Cutting the engine, he sat like a vulture in his dark khaki raincoat while he waited for Dolphe to make the next move. Dolphe, getting the point, slid out of his car and walked slowly toward Rizzo and Jordan. He carried a fat briefcase, and after opening the door to the back of Rizzo's car, he swung it up onto the seat before climbing in.

"How do I know you guys won't cross me?" Dolphe looked nervously at Rizzo and Jordan. "Hey, you. I've seen you before. You were at the hotel.

Cayman. So, *you* were the spook of the week. Nice to meet you." Dolphe laughed and extended his hand for a shake.

Jordan stared at him coldly, ignoring the proffered hand.

"Play or pay, Dolphe. You choose," Rizzo replied testily. "Now show me wotcha got."

Dolphe opened his briefcase and removed a dozen files. He described what he'd brought: Ivener's tax planning memos, each one either signed or initialed by the great man himself—and all of them describing in minute detail each step of his foreign tax shelter schemes and the dates and the names of the clients who were involved in each scheme. But, more important than that, as Harold was eager to point out, all of them pertained to the pending criminal action. "And . . ." Dolphe paused for effect while he watched Rizzo pawing through the files.

"And what?" Rizzo gave Dolphe a hard smile.

"I have the billing records." Dolphe held them up for Rizzo to see, but as soon as Rizzo reached for them, he pulled them away. "Not so fast, now you're going to do something for me." Dolphe reached in his pocket and pulled out a mini-recorder and told Rizzo that he would have to give him a statement that there were no grounds for charging him for any crime in connection with—and then Dolphe read from a document: *"Any and all matters related to Ivener's indictment, and further, to indemnify Harold Dolphe for any and all costs and legal fees that might in the future arise in connection with his having provided the IRS with his cooperation in this case."*

Rizzo thought about it for a couple of seconds. "Okay, consigliore, I'll agree to that, *if* I like the billing records."

Dolphe showed them to Rizzo, but without letting go.

Rizzo could see that Dolphe had brought the originals from Ivener's client files and he examined them with his pocket flashlight to make sure they bore Ivener's signature. He was more than satisfied. He had to close his eyes for a moment to conceal this from Dolphe.

Dolphe pushed the mini-recorder in Rizzo's face. Rizzo cleared his throat and spoke into the microphone, producing the statement Dolphe had requested. Then Dolphe grinned, and making a show of holding onto the billing records as if he were going to keep them, he laughed and then shoved them toward Rizzo's face. "Addio, Rizzo." Dolphe let them go, then he slid out and slammed the car door.

Dolphe cantered slowly back to his car. He pulled out from behind the garbage bin and when he was several car lengths away from Rizzo, he turned on his lights and drove away.

"I'd like to go a few rounds with that guy," Rizzo commented dryly. "But this time we'll let the little shithead go. At least we've got Willy nailed. By the way, how're you doing on Clare?"

"The computer print-outs show that Dr. Clare's gross receipts were a lot higher than what he was reporting and I think we can prove his intent to defraud. But I kinda wish we had something a little more. I need a little more time to examine his operating expenses and all of those phone taps, but, yes, it looks like we've got him." Jordan felt a sense of nostalgia because he was remembering

Linnell's whimsical observations about the distinction between a pirate and a privateer. And now, 150 years after the heyday of the Spanish Main, they were still at it—except her husband was now the pirate and they were the privateers.

Jordan examined Willy's client-billing records, and exclaimed, "What do you make of this? Not only does Ivener charge hourly fees, he *also* collects a percentage of all the taxes he saves his clients!"

"Yeah, I know. It's the evidence that clinches Ivener's conviction for conspiracy to evade federal income tax." This time Rizzo's smile was real.

HIGHRIDGE **2 p.m. - Monday - March 4, 1974**

"Hi, Doc. Have a good lunch? Your office is ready. And I got your briefcase back." Margo studied Bear. "You look a little green around the gills. You feeling okay?"

"I'm not feeling so good," Bear whispered in a self-pitying voice. "But that's okay. It won't change things. Just send Debbie in here, but give me five minutes. And this time you see to it I'm *not* disturbed!"

He watched Margo locking the front entrance and blocking the phones and then he dimpled at her and retreated to his office. He pushed the door until it was half-closed and then lifted the receiver off its hook to block the incoming calls on his private line. After rolling up the divorce petition and laying it on his desk, he quickly opened his drawer and found his bag of white powder. This time he simply inhaled from the bag. Wiping his face with his tie, he planted his feet in the soft thick carpet. Weaving slightly because one leg felt weak, he forced himself to stand tall.

Bear was conscious of a dull throbbing pain in his lower right leg which lagged slightly behind the syncopated pounding of the drums in his head. There was a flash of light, and the voices were instantly transformed into billions of tiny ticking feet, a universe of ants. They were marching under his skin—up and down up and down up down—in unison with the beat. And then the voices returned, even louder than before: *Orrrrry-orrygory-orry-gorry-bloody-cuttits!* Scratching himself furiously, Bear chased the waves of insects to the end of his leg. But he couldn't find it . . . where was his foot?

He willed himself to concentrate only on the pinpoint of light that twirled like a beacon before his eyes, and then the drumming receded but the voices remained. *Orrrrrygorry-cut-tits-bloody.* Singing sweetly, they begged the King to lift his great wand and to set it before them so it could be admired. *Orrrrry gorrrrry-cut-tits-bloody.* They scolded him, cajoled him Revelation had come at last and the words of The Wei sang with them inside his head: "*If it feels good, go do it and if any of you people out there don't like it, it's your problem . . .*"

Bear slid the razor-sharp surgical scalpel out of its sterile package and dropped it into the pen holder on his desk where it would be easier for him to reach. He had it all planned. He was going to get her opened up. Bear caught a flash of white in the corner of his eye and his head jerked up. Deborah had entered his office so quietly that he hadn't heard her approach. His grin now a grimace, he motioned for her to close the door. Deborah quietly pressed it closed and advanced without speaking. Bear listened to the fading drums in his head and then he motioned for Debbie to unzip her uniform and to kneel down in front of him as she had been instructed by Margo.

Moving quietly, Deborah obeyed without speaking.

There would be no blindfold today. He needed her eyes. And there was too much hair. When the King was finished he would cut that off too. Looking down at Debbie's questioning face, the King uttered his first command: "Open wide," he said, and then he couldn't restrain himself any longer—he laughed. And his laugh was a wail, a dog's wail, high-pitched and peculiar. Standing in front of her with his feet touching her knees, he loosened his belt and unzipped his trousers. She would be granted one last favor. Placing one hand on top of her head to hold himself steady, he opened his fly to expose himself. First, before everything else, she was going to worship the King.

After closing the door to Dr. Clare's private office, Margo returned to the reception counter to guard the entrance. This was such an easy way to keep Doc under her thumb. Poor Debbie, Margo thought. Such a doofus. Margo next heard the sound of Doc's high-pitched squeal and this time she actually felt a pang of jealousy—she could tell, they were doing something in there that Doc was keeping a secret. There was something about this new girl that was different from all the others but so far she couldn't figure out just what it was.

Margo stood up to listen, and heard a resounding crash. The floor actually shook; Margo held onto the counter. It felt like an earthquake—but then she realized that nothing was swaying. A minute passed and there were no sounds from behind the door. Margo was just about to go in and investigate when the door opened slowly and an ashen-faced Deborah tip-toed out.

Deborah leaned toward Margo and whispered, "Margo! I think Doc's had a seizure." Then she backed away, her hands over her mouth as if she were in a state of shock. Margo pushed past her and flew into the room and found Doc sprawled on his back across his desk. His legs were splayed open and he appeared to be holding some rolled-up papers in his hand.

"Doc!" Margo wailed. "Debbie! Debbie Brillis! You come in here this instant and help me. I think he's *dead*!"

Margo's cries for help were not met with any assistance. She froze. What was it she was supposed to do? She reached over his body and tried to feel for a pulse in his neck like she'd seen a real nurse do on television, but her heart was pounding so hard she couldn't tell whose pulse she was feeling. And Doc's face was contorted, fluid seemed to be running out of his nose and there was foam at the corners of his mouth. Hysterical, Margo pounded the telephone and screamed for help.

◆❖◆

Deborah turned to the reception counter and dropped a long, shiny object into Margo's purse, shook the handbag until it sank to the bottom, then walked swiftly down the hall toward the lab. She ducked in and turned up the flame on the Bunsen burner—it was always kept lit for melting wax impressions—until it ignited the paper towels that had been saturated with the highly flammable solvent; then she overturned a bottle of solvent on the laboratory counter. When she saw the flames leaping across the counter and up the wall, she reached for the small plastic bag filled with solvent and lobbed it against the opposite wall and watched the flames leap high in a golden arc. Picking up the bag that held all of her belongings, she slipped into her coat, took one last look at the laboratory, and calmly stepped outside.

She walked behind the large refuse bin next to the parking lot exit and changed into her loafers and pulled her mittens over her thin rubber gloves; then she threw her white shoes into her bag and walked, calmly, down the street toward her car. Heaving everything into the old junker, she climbed in and drove down a side street toward the freeway to San Francisco. Today, however, she would not use the on-ramp near Ivener's office. She had already wiped the vehicle clean of fingerprints—she had already done the same to everything in her apartment—the vehicle identification number had been obliterated long ago. She would leave the heap in the long term parking lot and the license plates would come with her—she knew that weeks would pass before anyone would notice that it had been abandoned.

While she drove, she tore up her paycheck in a ceremony of closure and fed the scraps into the wind, making sure that none blew back into the car. When that was done, she put on her dark glasses and a shapeless brown rain hat. She had exactly one hour and five minutes to make her flight to Brussels, where she would catch the express to Paris. She had obtained her passport the year before, in New York, before she had shaved off her hair. Soon she would put on her wig—not the lustrous auburn she'd worn for her meeting with Willy, but her new one, golden blonde so that it would match the color in her passport photo. This would have to wait, however—at least until she'd put enough distance between herself and the car.

Poor Uncle Willy, she would never see him again. It was really too bad, but she'd felt it would be best to leave without saying good-bye. He would never be a problem, at least not for her. She had only one small bag, which she would carry on, because she had very few belongings; she had destroyed everything that had come in contact with her—everything, that is, except the Code 2 print-outs. That nice guy at the computer store should have mailed them by now. Even Willy's gift had been destroyed—except for the diamonds. Perhaps someday she'd have them fashioned into a ring.

HIGHRIDGE **Monday evening - March 4, 1974**

When the telephone finally rang, Linnell beat Karen to it.

Linnell was annoyed—It was only a call from a cop at the Highridge Police Department. Linnell told him to get off the line, and then, remembering that this was the Highridge Police Department, she more politely explained that she had to keep all of her lines free because she was expecting an important call—then she cut him off. Linnell entered her private office and sat by her telephone to wait for the call.

The phone rang five minutes later and Linnell lunged.

"This is Journet here, my apologies for taking so long to get back to you. I received a call from your bank, and I feel comfortable speaking to the subject you raised about your funds. However, I don't like what I have to tell you."

"Just cut to the chase! How much was transferred out of the account and how did you lose control of the funds?"

"You had, not including accrued interest, the sum of $820,000 on deposit here . . . all of which was subject to the instructions of whomsoever had the access code to the account. Curiously enough, your husband established the account in what I understand is his father's name, Mark Clarichevik."

"*Another* name!" Linnell groaned. "Do you know what happened to the funds?"

"Yes and No. The funds were, I am sorry to say, bank-wired to Banca Suisse early this morning according to the instructions given by a woman who identified herself as Mrs. Clare when she presented the access code. We contacted the Banca Suisse manager at his home, and he recalls that the funds were there for only five minutes and then they were wired to a numbered account in Austria. As you know, you must retain a lawyer in Zurich to obtain an order to compel production of further information. You will no doubt succeed because you have sufficient grounds—your banker will assist you in this—to establish a prima facie case of fraud but that will unfortunately consume so much time that I fear the funds will have by then flown rather permanently into the woods. Of course, we shall do our best for you. Please accept my personal apologies."

Linnell could tell from his voice that he knew there would be litigation over this one.

"Okay. Now let's hear your tape, I want to see if I can identify this mystery woman."

Linnell fidgeted impatiently while Mr. Journet got his operation's officer on the line for a conference call. They played the tape and she listened to it several times, but couldn't identity the voice. Her mind reeled—she was a day late and a dime short. By the time she was finished with the conference call, Linnell finally felt the full effect of the news. Whoever she was, this thief, Bear must have put her up to it. And lucky for him he was still out of range because if he were here, she would happily kick him to death. Linnell stomped her foot and imagined him bleeding under her feet.

Then she decided to try something that promised to be even more effective. She would do what she'd thought she would never do: She closed her eyes and conjured up a needle, this time selecting the largest and sharpest one in the basket. In her mind, she carefully drew it out, being careful not to touch its poisoned tip, and then imagining Bear's heart, she took aim and sent the needle flying out of her hand and straight toward Bear's chest, between his ribs, and into his heart. The needle pierced it with a pop. Linnell held the vision and this time she performed the secret hand motions that Mama N'dobah had taught her.

Her ritual concluded, Linnell cleared her lungs of the spell, then left her private office to tell Karen the bad news.

Karen did her best to buck her up. "Well, at least you have a strong case against your bank and we'll nail Bear, too. You'll see. We can get to work on it tomorrow. I hope you're not thinking about going back to the house, at least not until you get your restraining order. Will you be staying at the motel?"

"Absolutely! What time is it? Anyone keeping track?" Linnell was anxious to leave. She knew she was on the edge of tears and she didn't want anyone to see her cry. Ray was saying something about packing it in for the night when the doorbell rang, followed by a loud pounding. He went to the door to investigate and was the first to see the two policemen; he opened the door a crack and they pushed it open and squeezed around him and entered Linnell's office.

Linnell examined the two cops, trying to guess what they wanted. The first officer, fleshy-faced, heavyset and the older of the two, tipped his cap and identified himself as Officer Blaine. The younger officer, the light weight, stepped back and shuffled his feet until he found the right macho stance. With his hand hovering near his weapon, he stood at the ready, as if he'd been warned in advance about encountering resistance. Linnell looked at him and was suddenly overcome by an irresistible urge to giggle.

Making it clear that he was offended by her lack of solemnity, Officer Blaine walked up to Linnell, cleared his throat and said, "You must be L.C. Clare, Mrs. Mark Clare—or is it *Ms*. Clare?"

"Yes I am." Linnell was now puzzled. The officer appeared to be holding a search warrant. She looked at Karen, and saw they were on the same wave length: Bear! The snow he'd stashed in the file drawer! This had to have something to do with it. This divorce was already looking like an all-out war! Linnell was sure Karen had followed her orders to flush it . . . she was ashamed that she had any doubts . . . on the other hand, *everyone* had been so full of surprises of late that she no longer knew what to expect.

Officer Blaine coughed nervously. "Ma'am, I'm here to inform you that your husband had a seizure. Dr. Clare was taken to the emergency room at Highridge Hospital in a coma around two hours ago. He died without regaining consciousness."

Linnell leaned on the wall and shook her head in disbelief. Seeing that the officers' expressions were hardly sympathetic, she volunteered, "I just started divorce proceedings this afternoon, he was served sometime after lunch, I think."

"Yes, we know," the officers replied in unison. Officer Blaine continued, "He apparently was stricken while he was examining your divorce papers. I called you a little while ago, but you were allegedly too busy to speak with us, so we presumed you would want to know. And since we have some *other* business to perform here, we're giving you formal notice of his demise."

"Oh for God's sake! Kindly get to the point. What's your *other* business here?"

"We're sorry that we have to intrude under these circumstances," the look on Officer Blaine's face said just the opposite, "but we have to search your office. Here's the warrant."

Linnell read it and showed it to Karen. "Not my *office* . . . Looks like it's just for inspecting my filing cabinets. Okay. Go ahead, search. But first, let's have you roll up your sleeves and open your hands before you begin." Linnell spoke courteously, enjoying the way Officer Blaine's face reddened. She'd heard stories about how some rogue cops planted drugs, and she wasn't about to take any chances because she was sure the warrant had something to do with Bear's foray into her files.

The officers pawed through the filing cabinets and came up empty-handed. The younger officer apologized profusely and said, almost inaudibly, "That Buster, he must be nuts."

Linnell heard what he'd said. And then she remembered how she'd found Hosterman's card in Bear's briefcase. Everything suddenly clicked: Buster Hosterman—part of the old guard at the Highridge Country Club, counsel to the Highridge police department—had something to do with the warrant. Linnell decided it was her turn to have fun. "What did you say? Did I hear you say 'Bust her *nuts*'? Are you *crazy*?"

The older officer glared at the younger officer, who stood sheepishly silent. Concealing her anger, she smiled and told Officer Blaine to give her regards to Buster Hosterman and to be sure to tell the old frog he'd be hearing from her soon. Blaine's reaction told her everything she needed to know. He immediately gave Linnell such an obviously insincere apology for his intrusion that she was sorely tempted to give him a shove. Instead, she gave him a dirty look. Nevertheless, he tipped his hat to her when he closed the door.

There now were blue circles under Linnell's eyes and Karen and Ray looked haggard. Linnell struggled to sum it all up. "Well, it's been just one hell of a strange day, hasn't it? No condolences, please. I'm not exactly a grieving widow." Linnell yawned. "I'm shot, I have to get some sleep. Well, now that I don't have to worry about Bear, I guess I should go back to the house tonight. If something comes up, just give me a call."

"You want us to come with you?" Ray asked.

"No, I'm fine. Thanks."

"No you're not," Karen asserted. "I'm coming with you."

"No thanks. There's no need for you to put yourself out." Linnell yawned again. Ray and Karen yawned next. "Are you hungry?" Linnell asked. "I'm starved. Let's get some pizza and then you can drop me off at Bear's office, I'll get his Cadillac and drive it home. I can leave my Jag here, where it's safe, and then tomorrow morning, first thing, I can search his car . . . maybe I'll find some clues."

"I don't think you can do that," said Karen. "In the first place, you don't have the keys to the Cadillac. Right?"

"Right you are. You always think of the things that matter. And you know what?" Linnell had suddenly remembered the spider. "I think I'm going to stay at the motel after all."

◆❖◆

Linnell felt sluggish. She'd had too many slices of pizza and she had also dropped—the curse had returned—some tomato sauce in her lap and she could still smell the garlic on her fingers. But this time she wasn't upset. In fact, the whole thing made her laugh, and she realized she was cured. Who knows? she thought, someday I might even find there's a good use for this curse.

By the time she returned to her brown motel room, she was feeling almost jolly and now she wished she'd gone home after all. Then she told herself that she'd better be mighty careful about what she wished for. Talk about having the power! Wow! Hadn't she just conjured Bear dead? And now *poof* . . . he was *gone*! He really *was* dead. She'd called the hospital to double-check. Mama N'dobah was right—just as she'd promised, when the time was right, the power would be there and working like mad! Linnell caught herself on the verge of exulting, and stopped. Maybe it would be the best thing for her to just leave it alone; there was no point in taking it farther, especially now that her reason for desiring such dark arts had departed this world. Feeling almost virtuous, Linnell closed her eyes again and this time saw herself putting all of the think-needles back in Mama N'dobah's basket. "No more negative thoughts," Linnell prayed, "from now on I'm going to focus all my energy on learning the best way to use my new fortune."

Linnell took a shower and fell into bed shortly before midnight. And then, for no particular reason, she felt an urge to call home and leave a message on her answering machine. She couldn't say why she had to do this; maybe it was just that she needed to do something to mark the occasion, like say, perform a ritual for Bear's death, or an exorcism, she thought. Linnell dialed, listened to the phone ringing, heard the answering machine as it picked up her call, and then in a dark and spectral voice, as if she were addressing Bear's ghost, she growled: "It's me*eeeee*, L. Ce*eeeeee*. It's midnight. Hoo-hoo HOOOooo. Get out of the house! BEeeeeeGoo*ooone*. Get out of *my* house!"

Heaven forbid anyone should hear her doing this. How could she possibly explain? And then she realized with a start that explaining herself was another thing she no longer would have to do.

HIGHRIDGE **Tuesday - 12 a.m., March 5, 1974**

It was the hour of the bones, when the evil Loas rise up to grab the ankles of the tender children whose feet dingle-dangle from under their bedcovers. Drag the little chosen ones under the bed and down through the hole in the floor and then deep deep *deep* under the dirt to eat them alive. Claude-Claudine had believed every word of this story when he was a boy. He still told himself this was nonsense for children. *He* had attended Secondary school in Jamaica and he knew better. But still, to keep himself strong and brave, he would also tell himself that behind every ghost was the hand of a man.

That was why he'd had the courage to return to the house. He had to learn its ways. To study it like he'd studied that small picture of his target. As he had studied the note the police left in the door which said there would be no more lights and wailing sirens. Now it was safe to wait for her here. In her bathroom, perhaps? Or maybe in her bedroom, underneath her bed. She would return at night and he would be waiting to surprise her.

Claude-Claudine found the bedroom by flashing his light through the windows and then chose the window behind the flowering bush. Prying the screen loose with the back of his knife, he unscrewed the bracket that held the window and lifted it out. He climbed in by swinging a leg over the sill and then by crunching his abdominal muscles, he lifted himself up in a single smooth move. With his flashlight in his teeth and his rope coiled over an arm, Claude-Claudine dropped to the floor and swarmed toward the bed. Narrow as a blade, he flattened himself to slide under the bed like a snake. Swinging his leg, he lashed into something that felt like a solid brick wall. And indeed, when he turned on his flashlight, he saw that it was. He sat up to explore.

The strange woman slept in a stranger bed. He reached up and pressed a fist into a warm bladder that sprang back from his touch. But there was no under to this curious bed. Claude-Claudine lay on the floor at the side of the bed, thinking about where to hide next—but only for a moment, because this time, instead of a siren, the telephone rang in his ear. He pulled himself up and sat on his knees, staring at the blinking red eye of the machine, while the telephone rang three more times.

And then the voice of the pale blonde butterfly floated into the room as if her spirit was staring at him through the bright red eye. This was not a natural woman. She was in league with the underground demons. Her spirit howled and threatened. It warned him to leave. But she would never catch Claude-Claudine. Clutching his rope and his flashlight, he sprang for the window and cleared it without touching the window ledge. No! No more house. Claude-Claudine picked up the window, set it back in its frame, and slipped away into the darkness to find Grande Charlus.

HIGHRIDGE **Tuesday morning - March 5, 1974**

Linnell awoke before sunrise the following morning. The time had come for her to go home.

When she arrived at the house, she wondered if she'd just had some visitors because the turnaround area looked freshly disturbed—as if a car had backed up too fast in the gravel. Linnell studied the curved tracks for a moment—one section cut deep—and then hauled her belongings up to the door. When she stepped inside, her eyes immediately fell on the coins scattered across the floor: The remains of her blackjack. She remembered the spider, this time wondering if tarantulas ever traveled in pairs. Carrying her suitcase at her side like a shield, she walked swiftly down the hall toward the bedroom and thought about the last time she'd been in the house with Bear. She could still see his eyes glittering at her from the medicine cabinet mirror. Now the stillness made her uneasy. It was too quiet, as if someone or something was holding its breath in order to listen to her. Linnell held hers and stood without moving to see if she could detect anything different about the silence.

Nothing seemed out of order.

She stepped into Bear's bathroom—her bathroom now. And truly, whatever remained was all hers. Linnell sat down. She was warmed by the thought that he really was gone—and it seemed like a hundred years had passed since she'd sat in the dining room, looking at the view and thinking about how their paths had crossed. She washed her hands in Bear's sink—*her* sink—and while drying them on the towel, for the first time realized that she'd overlooked something—the security system. The sirens. Hadn't they been blaring and howling when she beat her retreat?

She returned to the living room and looked out to the patio through the French doors. It was a misty morning and the sun had not yet cleared the hilltops. But it was light enough for her to see what had happened Saturday night: A faint trail of soot ran from the fireplace box to the side of the fireplace and then across the marble hearth to its edge just above the carpet. The wind had apparently blown the tarantula onto the chimney cap and from there it must have tumbled down the sooty chimney to the ashes in the firebox and then crawled into the room through the open screen. Shuddering at the thought of encountering another, Linnell bravely stuck her hand in the fireplace and closed the damper and then the screen. After removing the light from the floor, she carried it with her to the utility room and stored it in a cabinet.

While she was exploring the utility room in search of the fuse box, she happened to glance out the window and caught sight of something white and slightly soggy fluttering at the door—a sheet of paper had been tucked in the screen. Unlatching the doors, she quickly grabbed the paper—now soft with moisture—and just as quickly closed and locked them again. It was a handwritten note from the police department, letting her know that they had been up to the house to trip the alarm at the outdoor junction box in response to complaints from the neighbors.

Well, mystery solved, Linnell sighed with relief. By her watch it was only 6:45 a.m.—too early to make any calls. Just then, the sun rose over the tops of the hills on the other side of the valley and the mist disappeared. She couldn't resist; she had to visit her roses to see how they had survived the winter. On her way, Linnell found the junction box at the back of the house, opened it and located the set-switch for the burglar alarm and decided to leave it turned off so it wouldn't scare her again. That done, she headed toward the back garden. She saw at once that the Bougainvillea and flowering plums were recovering nicely from the December freeze. The sap was rising, buds were bursting into bloom, petals would soon be unfurling. She closed her eyes and again felt the man with the kiss of a rose. Stunned by the vividness of her recollection, she stood there and relived her short saga with Roberto. And then deliberately put him out of her mind.

Bear and drugs. How to account for his behavior? He must have been possessed to have wanted money so much that he'd be willing to destroy his own life to get it. As for her life and Benjy's? They had never been a part of the equation. And yet he'd still had the gall to tell her that everything he did he was doing for her! Linnell punctuated her disgust by booting a pine cone into the bushes. And then her eyes were drawn to her feet—there were footprints next to the ones she had just left. It looked as if someone had stumbled and taken a few steps off the path. She knelt down to examine them. The footprints looked fresh. *Someone was up here. No. Not one, two. One, a man—had to have been quite a heavyweight because the tracks are so deep. The other, I can't tell . . . might even be a woman because the prints are shallower and appear to have been made by a narrow foot.*

Then she remembered: Of course, it had to have been the cops.

Knowing what to look for, she followed the tracks left by the smaller foot back to the bushes at the edge of the garden behind the swimming pool.

Linnell examined the house from this vantage point, something she'd never had reason to do before now, and saw that she could look into every window of the house. Then she saw the plastic waste bucket and the broom—the pillow was lying loose—and remembered the door handle. She was about to cross through the flower bed to see what needed repair when she heard the telephone. Linnell sprinted back to the house and picked up the kitchen extension before the answering machine had a chance to intercept the call.

Breathless, she answered, "Hello?"

"Ahhhh, Yessssss. Hello. L.C., is that you? *Pretty* L.C. Please, I hope this is you . . . Am I speaking with pretty L.C.?" The man's voice was unnaturally seductive and teasingly soft.

"Yes. Who is this?" she replied. The call was cut off.

The melodious cadence. It reminded her of the West Indies—Cayman or Jamaica; in fact, it reminded her of the dive master's accent—he was born in Jamaica and had worked in Haiti for a couple of years. But this voice was different because there had also been the trace of a British accent. Yes, the person who'd just called had to be from one of the islands in the Caribbean. And she could tell from the absence of nasal twang that this caller was black. Well, this was the first time the caller had made voice contact with her. Strange. In the past, the caller had confined himself—or herself—to breathing.

Linnell walked into her bedroom to check the answering machine. She rewound the tape, punched "play" and listened to the calls that had come in since Helene and Benjy had left. There were calls from the hospital, asking her to call about the bill, the ambulance company, asking where the bill should be sent; Nancy, of course; and a message from Helene to tell her that everything was fine, and interspersed amongst all these messages were numerous hang-up calls—too many to count. Then Linnell listened to her own voice and winced with embarrassment. She had managed to sound spooky and silly all at once, but following her own message, there were six more beeps indicating additional "no-message" calls. Linnell looked at her watch. It was already 7 a.m. Then it dawned: Someone had called the house *six times* between midnight and 7 a.m.

She thought about this while she fried an egg—could someone be keeping tabs on her? Were they trying to track her whereabouts? If so, this was more than a simple case of harassment. Determined to shake off this uneasy feeling, she put herself to work and spent the rest of the morning cleaning Bear's bathroom. She hauled the filthy towels out of the laundry bin, hid the Percodan vials, and then called the hospital and made arrangements with the pathology department to have the pathologist, Dr. Herman, perform an autopsy on Bear.

Her last call was to Karen, to tell her that she would be heading over to the dental office to get it closed up. The instant she set the receiver down, the telephone rang again. She answered it the same as before, but this time no one spoke. She waited in cold silence until she heard the caller hang up. Linnell's hands turned clammy and a *frisson* of fear climbed the back of her neck. This had been going on for months, but now she was certain—somebody *was* keeping tabs on her! Linnell seized the telephone directory and searched through the listings to see if anyone named Willkills was listed. She found Willits and

Willkilts, but no listing for Willkills. It was all very strange, but there could no longer be any doubt: she was indeed being watched.

HIGHRIDGE **Tuesday - March 5, 1974**

Margo Callahan had just finished parking her car next to Doc's Cadillac when she saw a white Jaguar pulling into the parking lot. "Oh shit, here comes the *wife*!" grumbled Margo. She had wanted to get into the office to do some more scavenging. Dental supplies were good as gold, better than money in the bank, she thought. Margo folded her large canvas shopping bag, tucked it under her arm to keep from looking too obvious, and raced toward the entrance.

Margo glared at Linnell, then forced a smile. She knew she had to get into Doc's private office before the witch had a chance to check it out because there had to be something really valuable in that goddam desk—why else would he have always kept it locked up like that? Margo smiled broadly, put her key in the lock, then beckoned to the widow and waited until Linnell was almost upon her. Then quick as a cat, she unlocked the door and stepped inside and held the door until Linnell was at the threshold before letting it swing back in Linnell's face. Without making a move to assist her, Margo stood looking at Linnell through the glass and watched Linnell catch the door with her foot to keep it from closing.

Clumsy fool, thought Margo. She stepped back and smoothed down her dress. Spanking new, it was a classy red and white rayon ensemble with red plastic cherries for buttons and a nice pattern of matching red bubbles. She'd gotten herself all dolled up special today because she was heading for the Red Dog Inn right after she unloaded some more dental instruments at the flea market. Come to think of it, she might as well take the large tape recorder, too—if she could just get her hands on it. And after she got her wad, she planned to take it to the lounge and maybe get herself hooked up with that nice new bartender while she tied one on.

Margo watched Linnell as she struggled to let herself in. She smiled wickedly. "Well. Hello there, Ms. Clare."

Linnell ignored her greeting and stood in the doorway while she sniffed the air. "What's been going on here? I smell smoke."

"Yeah. There was a fire. In the laboratory. It started right after Doc had his stroke."

"You and Debbie were here when Bear had his stroke. Is that right?"

Margo was puzzled at first and then harrumphed noncommittally. She had forgotten that the widow was referring to her Doc.

Linnell walked toward Bear's private office, then stood in the doorway. "Okay. What *really* happened?"

"Debbie and me," Margo spoke imperiously, "*we* were setting up an operatory for a patient, when we heard a loud crash. Like something falling. At first I thought it was an earthquake. We called for Doc, and when he didn't answer, we went into his office and saw him lying there on his back, across the desk. I called the ambulance and then right away there was that fire back there, in the laboratory and I can't remember what else, because we both were so upset."

Margo didn't mention that Debbie had run off and left her. Nor did she mention that she'd removed all the used cassettes from Dr. Clare's desk and the teeny-tiny pocket-sized tape recorder she'd found next to the large one in the drawer and that she had tossed all this stuff into the fire. And that new scalpel she'd found on the floor in Doc's office? Well, that was a godsend because she'd used it to cut out all the wires, and the microphone in his bathroom, too—and of course she had sent all the rest of the computer disks to the hole underneath the building. The fire was actually just what she'd needed; she'd pitched everything into the blaze—along with all those secret papers she'd found in his briefcase. Passport, too. She'd burned it along with everything else. After that, she'd stuffed her bag full of dental instruments and then she'd had just enough time left to grab all the cash she'd been hoarding in her special drawer. So! Nobody would ever find even one little thing to pin on her and now all she had to do was collect all that money Doc had been socking away for her in her pension plan. She'd been a damned good employee and she knew to the penny how much she had coming.

Linnell interrupted her reverie. "You knew about the divorce?"

"Well, of *course* I did. You're always so busy, always traveling and pretending you're one of those fancy jet-setters. I knew about the divorce all right. *I* was the one who was with Doc, every day for the last seven years. I knew *everything*." Margo's rubbery red lips spread into a sarcastic smile.

"What was that? You knew *everything*?"

"You didn't know," Margo pushed her face closer to Linnell's, "but Doc was going to dump *you.* What do you think about *that?*"

"Nice try—but for your information, it was the other way around. Not that it's any of your business. Anyway, I've had quite enough of you and your antics. I want you out of here! Give me your address so I can send you your final paycheck. And that new assistant, Debbie Brillis, I need hers too. And the keys. Hand them over. You're out of here *now*!"

"You can't do this! You're gonna have to pay me to leave!" Margo wanted to stick out her tongue and call Linnell a dirty name, but instead she put her nose up and gave Linnell her haughtiest look. She would show the bitch that she was a lady too. "And don't you bother yourself about ol' Debbie, I already paid her and then *I* let her go."

"You heard me. I want Debbie's address NOW!" Linnell snapped her fingers.

Margo, surprised by the scary edge to Linnell's voice, was even more surprised to find herself obeying. She pulled out a file from under the counter, copied an address onto one of Bear's prescription pads and slapped it down on the counter.

"Give me the keys." Linnell reached out and it looked like she was going to grab her purse.

Margo jerked her purse away and accidentally banged it, crooked, against the counter so that it fell open and spilled its contents at their feet.

◆❖◆

Linnell saw a long glass cylinder fall out of Margo's purse and roll across the carpet, but before she could make a grab for it, Margo was in her face again, this time so close that she could detect the rank odor of fear on the woman's breath.

Margo was now sputtering strangely. "You're not going to get away with this! *You're* gonna hear from my lawyer you stupid . . . you slut!" Hunching her shoulders, she pushed her face into Linnell's.

Linnell suddenly burst into laughter. "Hey! Nice talk, there, Margo. As if I give a damn about what you think. Say, looks like you dropped something. What's this?" Linnell pointed to the floor.

Margo lunged for the cylinder.

Linnell allowed Margo to pick it up and then she landed a sharp chop across Margo's fat wrist. The glass cylinder flew across the room and landed on the padded seat of a reception room chair and for the first time Linnell could see what it was: a large syringe with a very long and evil-looking needle.

Margo held her wrist—a shocked, self-pitying expression stealing across her open-mouthed face.

Linnell spoke very quietly. "Very well then, now we can discuss your unfortunate abuse of narcotics. Let me be the first to remind you that your use of Percodan and this other junk you're apparently injecting," Linnell nodded her head in the direction of the syringe, "not only violates your employment agreement, but also terminates your rights to a pension."

"What are you talkin' about! Are you crazy! *I* don't use Percodan. I only do soft stuff, like nitrous."

"Well, that's nice to know. Yes, I already know about that and I know about you . . . and all the so-called special patients. I found proof of everything I need to know about what you two were doing in here because your name's on that secret list Bear was keeping. As for all that Percodan? It sure looks like you're a user, all right. Oh? Didn't you know? Bear had been prescribing it for *you*. Or were you too busy with him every day to know about *that*? I have a whole box full of pill bottles and your name's on every one. And frankly, I want you to know I don't give a rat's ass about whether you really use it or not because there's plenty of evidence to make it look like you did. So, if you still feel like making some trouble for yourself, have that so-called lawyer of yours call the DEA and find out first hand what happens to medical personnel who dip into their employer's narcotics. And now that we're having this pleasant conversation, we can also explore the matter of your tax evasion and drug dealing. Bear set you up. In fact, he had been setting you up all along. Do you want to see the records? They're very detailed. I found them yesterday morning. In his briefcase. I can prove you were stealing cash. And I can prove you were dealing drugs and doing a little hooking on the side. And I have the originals of all his papers, I want you to know, just in case you hoped you had destroyed all his records in this oh-so-convenient *fire*. All things considered, it sure looks like you had a strong motive for arson—and maybe something far worse than that. Did you know you could get twenty years just for arson alone?"

Linnell was bluffing, but from the look of furious dismay on Margo's face she could tell she'd hit the nail square on the head.

"That *bastard*!" Margo shrieked, spittle flying.

"Oh *thank* you Margo, I couldn't have said it better myself. Now, you'd better ankle out of here while you still can or else I'll call the cops and have them carry you out feet first. But first, I want the keys. Hand them over."

Margo picked up the keys she had been carrying for the last seven years and dropped them on the reception counter. Without saying another word, Linnell held the door open and Margo ducked out without looking at her. Linnell couldn't resist: she timed it perfectly so that the door would close on the woman's heels.

When Linnell saw that Margo was walking without her usual sashay, she knew she had won. Then she got a tissue and picked up the large syringe so Margo's fingerprints wouldn't be smudged. The needle was lethally sharp. Linnell tore an eraser from a pencil, stuck it on the needle tip, carefully dropped the syringe into a plastic bag to preserve Margo's prints, then hid the instrument deep in her hand bag. Now that Margo was dispatched, she could inspect the rest of the damage at leisure.

The fire department had extinguished the conflagration only after it had consumed the entire dental laboratory and most of the back bathroom. The floor was a mess of charred wires, burnt paper, tarred and cracked bottles soaking in soot-blackened water; what was left of the ceiling was charred and still wet. Water still dripped to the floor from the large sheet of plastic that had been placed over the roof. While she was inspecting the debris, she heard voices in the reception area—Bear's first patients for the day. Linnell sped to the front of the office to tell them to leave, then she prepared a notice for the door to announce that the office had closed. She had to know she would be undisturbed because she needed to give the office a thorough search. When she tacked the sign to the glass of the front door, she had a sense of déjà vu—as if she were revisiting Ye Olde Banke.

Linnell sat down at the desk and tried all the keys. She found the key to the right-hand bank of drawers, but there were none that fit the drawers on the left. No matter. She had never mentioned to Bear that her grandfather's desk had a secret. As with most desks of this era, there were alternative ways to access the drawers. Linnell found the levers underneath the opposite side of the desk top and jiggered the panels out of the slots carved underneath the ornate beaded trim. When the panels were removed, she had easy access to the drawers which she could remove from the opposite side of the desk.

She found the money in a thick envelope. She bounced the packet in her hand and guessed that Bear had amassed around six thousand dollars, now all in 100s. She'd have plenty left after paying for his funeral. Then she had a more sobering thought: The audit! The skimming! She gripped the large wad of bills, less thrilled now because she knew she couldn't spend them openly. In fact, if the IRS was in fact investigating Bear for criminal tax evasion, which was what she suspected, she had better be very careful to not give them any reason to think she had benefited from it or else the agency would be all over her like a wet blanket. "Oh dear!" thought Linnell. Now she'd have to keep all that SUP Cayman Ltd. money hidden offshore as well. Dammit! Why was it that everything always had to turn into such awful mixed blessings?

Linnell pawed around in the drawer and found one of her discarded bath powder boxes wedged in the corner of the drawer; it was heavy and extremely difficult to move. Using both hands to pull it toward her, she yanked off the cover and found gold scrap of every description: everything from old bridges and crowns to shiny planchets of 24 karat dental gold. The drawer also held an empty glycine bag containing a trace of white powder, numerous small syringes and a small black kit in the front of the drawer. His drugs. Linnell quickly searched the rest of the drawers. There was just the tape recorder, which didn't much surprise her given Bear's love of recording equipment, and several packages of unopened cassettes. Linnell removed the gold and the money and then reassembled the desk.

Linnell puttered around the reception counter. It was obvious that Margo hadn't paid any bills—a big stack of them still sat on the reception counter. Linnell sorted through them, selecting the ones from the telephone company—she had a sneaking suspicion. Then she examined the keys she'd received from Margo and saw that Margo had even been given a key to his car!

Linnell unlocked the Cadillac and searched it eagerly, plunging her hands deep into its many velvet pockets, sure they would yield some important clues. She was hoping to find a telephone number. There had to be something! Some key to the puzzle of the mystery woman's identity. But except for another pair of very dark sunglasses, she came up with nothing but rolled up match book covers. Not even so much as a hair pin—the usual tell-tale message. The SOB was dead—and she couldn't find one single clue to the identity of the thief who'd stolen her savings. Well, at least she could rule out Margo as a suspect. Anyone who had just ripped off $820,00 wouldn't be hanging around risking arrest just to rip off a few hundred bucks worth of dental supplies.

SAN FRANCISCO **Tuesday - March 5, 1974**

Although he knew from the morning papers that Dr. Clare was dead, Jordan continued to listen to the tapes from the telephone taps. He'd completed his examination of the computer print-outs and they proved Rizzo right: Dr. Clare's skimming and drug dealing had been a bolder enterprise than anyone had ever imagined. This had been borne out by the most amazing event: the arrival of a large package this morning. The address had been printed, as if by a child, and directed to the attention of Mr. Rizzo—at the correct street address but without any reference to the IRS. The contents of the box would have convicted Dr. Clare had he lived: It contained print-outs of spreadsheets that gave the IRS hard evidence that Dr. Clare had been using his computer to keep two sets of books. Rizzo had shown them to him this morning, saying, "See? You never know what's going to turn up in this business." Jordan wondered which one of the two women had supplied the material; Rizzo laid odds on the young one—the one with the awful hair and a face like an unseasoned veal patty.

But it was the tapes of the dental office telephone taps that still held his attention. He listened to the recording of Margo's frantic voice one more time. He was curious about the sounds recorded shortly before the fortuitously fatal event. The tap had been activated when someone, probably Clare, removed the receiver from its cradle. But then he was mystified: He could hear something that sounded like the rustling of paper, then a few moments of silence, and finally, Dr. Clare saying, "Open wide," and then the man's mad laughter . . . a pause . . . and a chucking noise—quite possibly the dentist's death rattle—followed by the thunder of his body dropping. The sounds following after that were fainter and reminded him of the sound made by a fingernail being scraped down the teeth of a plastic comb, then there was a brief moment of silence again, a door slamming open against the wall, and finally Margo Callahan's hysterics when she called for the other assistant to come in and help her.

However, the telephone calls Clare made earlier on in the day interested him even more. There was Dr. Clare's call to his lawyer. To his way of thinking, the peculiar nuances of their last conversation strongly suggested that Clare had been plotting to murder Linnell. Something bothered him about his choice of words—he'd said *killed,* not *died.* Jordan took out the tapes and searched them until he found Dr. Clare's last conversation with Buster Hosterman: *"I can understand why a guy in your position might want to see her get whacked—I'd gladly defend you if that came to pass . . ."*

Jordan listened carefully to Dr. Clare's voice—his reply was both candid and spontaneous: *"Oh. I see. Yeah. I see. It's really better if she* lives. *I hadn't figured on that . . ."* Jordan was convinced that such talk—coupled to the fact that Clare had just planted cocaine in Linnell's office—was the talk of a would-be killer. Then he listened once again to the tapes of the calls that had been made to the Clare residence. Especially the call that had been made to the Clare residence early in the morning. He wasn't sure, but he thought that it could have been Willy Ivener himself. It was followed by a spate of hang-up calls to the Clare residence shortly before Linnell returned home. He also noticed that just today, early in the morning, a man with an accent, similar to those he'd heard on the island, had also contacted Linnell at her residence. The caller hadn't identified himself, but had addressed her as *pretty L.C.*, then he'd cut off the call in a most peculiar way. And the fact that Ivener and Clare had been in touch during the time of the IRS surveillance was another interesting twist. Harold Dolphe, Ivener's associate, had called Dr. Clare's office to confirm a "private meeting" between Ivener and Clare—and Dolphe had mentioned something about photographs.

Photographs? What was *that* all about? he wondered. Edgardo had observed Dolphe accessing Linnell's room—but he'd said that Dolphe had left empty-handed. He hadn't known what Dolphe looked like when he'd first arrived on the island, but now that he did, he knew that Dolphe was the one who had been staring at him when he first arrived. Jordan tried to recall whether Dolphe had a camera. Damn! He just couldn't remember because he hadn't been focusing on him. And then, on the heels of Clare's odd conversation with Hosterman, there was Clare's near hysterical call to Ivener's office to cancel his attendance at The Wei—something to do with the advanced training program that was scheduled for this upcoming Friday. There were all these contacts between Dr. Clare and Willy Ivener. What was really going on?

Unfortunately, the wire taps had not extended to Dr. Clare's telephone at the club. There seemed to be plenty of excuses for that—for one, in his absence, the phone taps weren't being reviewed on a daily basis, so when it was discovered that Clare was staying at the club, someone, not Rizzo, had decided that it was too late to bother. A terrible slip-up to his way of thinking. But now no one cared because it looked like the Clare case was about to be closed. Jordan wondered what significance, if any, Rizzo would attach to Clare's meeting with Ivener. Rizzo had already let on that he thought their respective cases were completely unrelated, since the two men had been fishing in different ponds. But Jordan remained curious. Ivener and Clare seemed to have only two things in common: The Wei and Linnell Clare.

Jordan waited for Rizzo to return to the office because he needed to discuss what was bothering him.

◆❖◆

Rizzo and Jordan were holed up in Rizzo's office and although it was getting late, Rizzo took the time to explain things to Jordan.

"First, you've got to look at things logically," Rizzo said. "Let's look first at the calls between Ivener and Clare. There's nothing mysterious about *that* connection. Ivener might be crooked as the proverbial dog's hind leg, but he's still a brilliant operator. Clare had to know he had his ass in a sling, so it's only natural that someone in his position would want to pick Ivener's brains. No pun intended, but Ivener has been beating us off for years. They probably were in contact with each other long before we ever thought of installing the wire-taps. And remember how Clare tried to make it appear that his wife was cooking his books? That probably was Ivener's idea, because that's fairly typical of his style of thinking. Give up trying to discover what they really discussed. You know what Ivener would say? He'd say their conversations were protected by the lawyer-client privilege.

"And Harold Dolphe? Sneaking into her room? You already know how much the mavens like to play games. They check each other out every chance they can get. Except Ivener is the sort who is willing to go one step further and Dolphe is the sort who would be happy to oblige, plus, he probably gets off on sniffing her underwear drawer. He just likes doing little things to make her feel paranoid—given half a chance, the mavens will head-trip each other when they can't find one of us.

"As for Clare? He was an addict. His judgment was shot, which explains why he forked over his computer print-outs without putting up any kind of resistance. You weren't there to see how he carried on when we showed him our search warrant. Man! Was he flying high! He thought the whole damn thing was a joke. I wouldn't be surprised if the guy took a dose, once it hit him that he'd hung himself out to dry."

"You mean you think he took his own life? Suicide?" Jordan asked.

"I had a case like that once—the guy took a dose right after he saw that he'd backed himself into a corner."

"Oh," Jordan said quietly. The thought of Bear committing suicide had never occurred to him. "Well, then what explains the conversation between Dr. Clare and this Buster Hosterman? The part where Buster tells Clare that he'd be glad to defend him if Mrs. Clare were whacked and Clare replies that it's better she lives. It sounds to me like Clare had been doing a whole lot more than just wishing her dead."

"You've never been married, son, so you don't understand. Let me tell you something—they were married a long, long time and there was lots of friction, what with her working and traveling and him being doped-up half the time. He was just talking crazy. That happens, let me tell you. It doesn't mean squat. Her old man was under pressure and just blowing off steam. On the other hand, even if you *do* have a point, what's the problem? There *is* no problem, not anymore, because now her old man is dead."

Jordan was half-convinced, but he had one more question. "Why do you think Dr. Clare hired a shyster like Hosterman? He's more of a criminal defense attorney than anything else, and everyone knows he's wired to the police department. So, why him?"

"Hosterman? Yeah, I know about him. Thinks he's a power broker—he's got connections in some very high places. Brags about 'em, too. Clare probably had plenty of legal problems with his patients, so Hosterman would be a natural for a guy like him." Rizzo paused for a moment, then said, "You know? Maybe I'm partly to blame for this—I *did* tell you the sky was the limit just so long as your *actions* wouldn't jeopardize our case—but, I think maybe you somehow got emotionally involved with this L.C. Clare in ways you don't quite understand. See here! You gotta look on the bright side—Clare's suicide saved us a whole lot of trouble, you did your job, the case is set to be closed, and you've got to let go and get started on a new one. Get my point?"

"Yes sir. I understand," Jordan replied.

"Jordan? I don't think you do, so I want to make it clear that I don't want you to even *think* about L.C., let alone have any contact with her. The Intelligence Division has already shelled out over $1,000,000 on Project Haven Mavens, and that's just for Ivener. We can't afford to have that sort of investment jeopardized by any leaks that might reveal how we go about doing our business. A leak would blow all our cases. You be sure to remember that. But I'll give you this much—we're not going to be the ones to tell her that her husband was a Dr. Feelgood.

"We're gonna spare her that, 'cause it's clear she never knew anything about anything—and she sure didn't benefit from her old man's tax fiddling and the taps show she never knew anything about him peddling drugs. Mrs. Clare is off the hook. She's not only clean, she's been cleaned-out; her old man's dead; she's got a nice kid to raise . . . so, now you know why the Clare case is heading for the dead files.

"As for Dr. Clare and the money? It looks like it's all been dragged away by another rat, so what's left is the house, and *that's* probably mortgaged up to the hilt. Mrs. Clare can keep it. Say, remember that loony Cayman bank that failed? That's what clinched it—I think that's where her old man was socking his cash, and definitely, that's where he was buying his gold."

Jordan was relieved to know that Linnell Clare was off the hook. Under these circumstances, he felt right about his other decision, too: He wouldn't say anything to anybody about the Phoenix corporation that Dr. Clare had been complaining about to Buster Hosterman. Besides them, he and Linnell were the only ones who knew anything about it, and after everything Linnell had been through, she deserved to keep the whole ball of wax for herself.

He decided to erase all mention of the Phoenix Corporation from the IRS tapes the next chance he got.

◆❖◆

Rizzo watched Jordan rewinding the tape recordings and stacking the Clare files on the top of his desk so they could be packed and sent to the archives. "He's a good guy," Rizzo said to himself. "A bit wet behind the ears, but still, we don't want to lose him. I think I'll send him to Miami to toughen him up . . . and I'll get the order extended to tap Mrs. Clare's lines for another couple of weeks. If anyone's going to locate the Clare fortune, it's gonna be her and that'll save the service from having to spend anything more on this case. And if she locates the missing money? We can always reopen the case and file a claim against Dr. Clare's estate—and if she doesn't, then I guess we can pack it in for good."

◆❖◆

Jordan left the office feeling a little let-down, he still had this gut-feeling that there had been a whole lot more going on than what Rizzo thought. But he couldn't afford to keep pushing Rizzo for answers, especially on a case that was about to be closed. He had only one more concern: that maybe Dolphe had been snooping on Linnell because of some kind of sick obsession with her.

Well, it was time for him to stop daydreaming about Linnell. Like it or not, he had to face up to reality. And there was also the new girl he'd been dating these last several months. Suzanne. She'd called him every day while he was gone, leaving messages on his answering machine about how much she missed him—and would he come over for dinner tonight? Ordinarily, he would've dropped in on Suzanne without thinking twice, but now he had a problem with this. And the problem was that ever since he'd first laid eyes on Linnell he'd stopped thinking about anyone else.

All things considered, maybe it would be best to cool it with Suzanne. And Joanne, and Mary, and all the rest of them for that matter. On the other hand, he was really hungry and there was nothing in the fridge but a rotting tomato and some dried salami. A home-cooked meal would be nice for a change. Joanne had called him a couple of times, but Suzanne had called and left word everyday. Maybe it wouldn't hurt to pick up a bottle of wine and drop in on her for a quick bite to eat. That might not be so bad, and just maybe it would help him get his mind off being dumped by Linnell.

HIGHRIDGE **Wednesday - March 6, 1974**

Linnell felt something was odd because she had slept until her alarm had gone off at 8:00 a.m. And then she remembered—she was a *widow*. She rolled out of bed, did her usual stretches and bends, then stepped into the shower while she listened to the beep-whir-'n'-click of her answering machine as it picked up more calls. But she wasn't paying any attention to any of this because she was so deeply engrossed in thinking about how to tell Benjy about his father's death.

Dressing quickly and then locking up the house, she tore off the hill and then on a whim, stopped in for breakfast at a coffee shop near her late husband's office. The waitresses seemed very friendly, until she paid her check with her credit card. Then she noticed the small group of waitresses who were standing together and whispering, giving her dark looks. She wondered if she was imagining things, but it seemed like the temperature dropped to zero after they saw who she was.

By the time Linnell arrived at her office, Karen was already there.

"You see today's paper?" Karen passed the newspaper to Linnell just as the phone rang again.

Linnell grabbed it and read:

"POLICE DEPARTMENT SOURCE REPORTS ELUSIVE TAX HAVEN ATTORNEY WANTED FOR QUESTIONING IN DENTIST'S DEATH. Gouged to death by greedy lawyer? Prominent local dentist apparently shocked to death when wife, the elusive tax haven attorney "L.C." Clare, serves divorce papers demanding he vacate their luxurious Highridge estate. A reliable source has informed this reporter that the lady lawyer is wanted for questioning."

She couldn't believe her eyes. After composing herself, she studied the entire news article: Bear was being described as Highridge's noble benefactor. The reporter repeatedly referred to him as the *wealthy and generous* Dr. Clare, and then the article went on to weepily describe how poor Dr. Clare had been rushed to the hospital in a coma—where he was said to have died without regaining consciousness. The man was being portrayed as a saint! As for her, the article reported that this same "reliable source" had speculated that Dr. Clare's wife—"the lady lawyer!"—had sprung the divorce on "the doctor" upon her return from her trip to a "tax haven," most likely because "the doctor" had already begun to suspect that she was plotting to take him for all he was worth. The article concluded with a description of *tax havens* and how they were becoming notorious for *tax evasion* and the *laundering of dirty money.*

"This is ridiculous!" Linnell exclaimed angrily.

"Please. Don't let them get your goat," Karen commiserated. "The good ol' boys club is just giving you flak. You know how they are—they fix the system so they can skim the cream off the top and then they carry on like their ordure-don't-odoriferate. They're jealous of you, so you'd better get used to it. And the phone calls! I'd like to forward them straight to the editor—let *him* waste *his* time. Oh yes—now you're getting calls from the phonies who want you to hide their money in Cayman." Karen reached out a scarlet-taloned hand as if to strangle the ringing telephone.

Karen handed the receiver to Linnell. "It's Helene, she hasn't heard, so you'd better tell her yourself."

Linnell listened in frustration as Helene told her about all the fun they were having and then she had to interrupt to tell her about Bear's sudden death and to warn her about the newspaper's attempt to create a scandal. Helene assured her that she and Benjy would catch the next plane to SFO and then take the shuttle straight to the house.

Linnell retreated to her office, closed the door, and switched off the intercom. She was livid—who had planted that scandalous article? And what really set her teeth on edge was the possibility that this sort of reporting might affect the outcome of her negotiations with the bank—it might inspire them to take the position that Bear was merely protecting himself from her "plotting" when he had shipped off their money, then they would argue that they ought not to be held liable under these "unusual circumstances." Could it be that this outrageous newspaper article was Margo's revenge?

Buzzing Karen, Linnell instructed her to make two calls: First, to call Chief Sommers and to tell him in no uncertain terms that she expected an explanation from him, and then to call long distance in Chicago to see if she could find a listing for Bear's father, Mr. Clarichevik—and if she could, to put him through to her right away.

Why did Bear use his father's name on the Montreal bank account? Weren't they estranged? She'd get to the bottom of this; first, she would break the news to his father, and then she would try to finesse some information from him about the Montreal Bank account. While she was thinking about how to go about doing this, to her great surprise, Karen buzzed her back immediately with Mr. Clarichevik on the line. Linnell recognized a middle European accent. Linnell told Mr. Clarichevik who she was, and inquired about his health.

"I'm old," replied Mr. Clarichevik.

Linnell tried her best to be gentle. "I have some sad news about your son," she said.

"So you're the wife. That boy! I haven't talked to him for *many* years. So what's new? Is he dead?"

Linnell was taken aback by his bluntness. "Yes, Mr. Clarichevik, he died. I thought you should know." There was silence on the line and Linnell wondered if he was still there.

"Not surprised. He was sick, you know. Sick like his mother. She died young too."

"I beg your pardon, did I hear you say he was *sick*?"

"My son, he's dead. Now I can tell you. Yes. My boy, he was sick like his mother. Her head was sick. Beautiful woman. Now she's dead a long time. The doctors, they tell me she was polar. They took her away to the hospital."

"Polar? What's that?"

"Yes. She always was talking to voices. They took her away. Long time ago."

Linnell stood up, shocked by the news. She could only say "Oh."

"So I never hear from him." Mr. Clarichevik sounded resigned.

"Mr. Clarichevik, have you received anything in the mail for him or from him . . . like from a bank? It's very important, please think."

"No. I'm an old man. No one writes."

"Mr. Clarichevik, do you have a nurse? A woman who helps you around the house?"

"No. No woman is ever here. No one comes to see me. Not since his mother. So you be a nice girl and you bury him. I don't travel. Too old. You be a good girl and you say good-bye to him for me." Mr. Clarichevik hung up without saying good-bye to her.

A strange sickness in the head, he'd said. What did she know about mental illness? Not much. In fact, nothing at all. And this was the first time she'd ever heard of an illness called "polar." When Karen stepped in to hand her messages, she asked, "You ever hear of some kind of a mental illness called "polar"?"

"Oh, I think you're talking about something called bi-polar manic-depression." Karen fell silent. She looked worried.

"Well. Is that all? I just spoke with Bear's father and he said Bear's mother had it and that Bear had it, too. So what is it?"

"Severe mood-swings. First a high—the patient has this irrational sense of superiority. Delusions of grandeur, loss of judgment—at its worst, the patient hears voices and hallucinates and offers weird explanations for his anti-social behavior, and then there's a crash and the lowest of lows, depression, sometimes suicide. It tends to run in some families, so it's probably got something to do with genetics. Ray's sister-in-law—she committed suicide in her late twenties—she had it bad, that's how I know so much about it."

"Oh God. Could a person with this bi-polar condition still function? I mean, get up, get dressed, go to work, that sort of thing?"

"Sure. Just so long as the condition doesn't get too bad. Sometimes the manic part is exciting, I understand. Some really brilliant people, like Josh Logan, the playwright, and Prime Minister Churchill were afflicted. But in other instances it can be awful, and others worse off can go totally bonkers and be very, *very* dangerous, so I guess it all depends . . ."

"Yes. I see." For a moment, Linnell felt faint.

It was all clear to her now: For fourteen years she'd been trying to connect with a guy whose wiring had been all screwed-up. Fourteen long years doing the woman-thing: Trying to fix things and hold things together and then blaming herself when nothing would work—when in reality this all too large man was crazy. She felt just a bit sick to her stomach to learn—only after the fact—that after years of thinking that she was merely caught up in an endless, lame comedy, that in fact she had been blithely skipping along on the edge of an abyss. Truly, it had to be luck that had kept her from being dragged with him over the edge.

She pretended to study the stack of pink slips that Karen had handed her. Most were condolences from colleagues and clients; there were also comforting messages from all of the "Cs", —it looked like her friends were going to stand by her. The rest were either hang-up calls or crank-calls that blamed *her* for Bear's sudden death, and to top it all off, there was a call from the hospital about paying Bear's emergency room bill—and the coroner's office. Which reminded her: she still had Bear's telephone bills in her purse. She pulled them out and asked Karen to review them to see if any of the calls from his office matched up with their cat-call records.

"L.C., you've had enough. I think you really ought to go home and get some rest. We can finish tomorrow. It's okay. I'll check the telephone log and we can look at it next week."

"You know, that sounds like a good idea. In fact, let's work really hard tomorrow and then we can take a three-day weekend."

Linnell stepped into her office and called the pathology lab herself. It was located at the Highridge Hospital and Dr. Herman, the coroner and black-humored chief of pathology, was an old friend and client.

The doctor picked up the phone in his laboratory and in his typical fashion got straight to the point: "Hey baby. I just read the paper. You're a big celebrity now. By the way, I just fressed your old man. I think you'd better come over here, I need to talk to you right away."

"Herman, I can't. I've got to meet Benjy. So, can you *please* tell me now?"

"I've been reading all that stuff about the IRS and Project Haven Mavens. Now that you're this famously elusive tax haven shyster, how do I know *your* lines aren't being tapped?" Dr. Herman loved to kid around.

Linnell laughed even though Dr. Herman's observation made her nervous. "Oh, cut that stuff out. Please, *please* tell me *now*."

Dr. Herman's voice abruptly changed to a cold clinical tone. "This has to do with the autopsy. You don't really want to know more about what I found, and I'm sorry L.C., to have to tell you this stuff on the phone—I would have preferred meeting you over a cup of coffee. But here goes: When your old man died, he was loaded with drugs. Cocaine, morphine, Dexies, the works. Massive cerebral infarctions—the junk just blew out his brains—although I must add that his final stroke was preceded by several smaller ones over the last several weeks. The moderate arm tracks indicate that he had recently begun to inject narcotics, and the nasal mucosa and septum were eroded and suffused with a rare strain of bacteria, indicating a long-standing habit of cocaine inhalation. I'm going to have to report that his death was due to a drug overdose."

"In other words, you mean he was suicidal . . . and a drug addict to boot."

"That about sums it up."

"What made you think of doing a narcotics panel on him?"

"Oh, I'm always the first to pick up the rumors. My colleagues seem to be treating an increasing number of your late husband's patients. So, in addition to being a habitual user, it's fairly certain that he was peddling drugs to them as well. And my sources, I want you to know, *are* reliable. I was sure you wouldn't know this stuff about your old man, because when a doctor or dentist gets hooked on narcotics he invariably keeps it a secret, especially from his wife. In fact, the wife's usually the last one to know. Well, that's about it. I would have enjoyed seeing you, though. One of these days we'll sit down and have ourselves a real talk. Meanwhile, you listen to *me,* widow Clare—*you* have no reason to feel guilty about anything!"

"Herman, Don't hang up yet. I want to run something by you. Today, I just learned that Bear's mother had gone mental. Bi-polar manic-depressive. Died in an institution. Could it be possible . . .?"

"Yes indeed! Latest research shows a correlation between certain mental illnesses and genetics, and bi-polar is one of them. People with this affliction are usually aware that something's going wrong and quite often they turn to drugs either to medicate themselves or to use drugs so they can point to them as an explanation for their weird behavior. That's probably why your old man got so interested in them in the first place. Well, we can talk later, but now I've got to take care of the paperwork."

"Thanks for the info. I'd appreciate it if you could keep this under your hat until later this evening. I want to talk to Benjy this afternoon."

"You don't have to ask. But I couldn't muzzle the ambulance attendant. He got his hands on your divorce papers. Bear was holding them when he keeled. He either accidentally overdosed or else he intended to kill himself. Odds are from the amount of all those other drugs I found that it's the latter. So I have to report this as a suicide. It looks like he was snorting his own pharmaceuticals. That stuff is murder—the potency's close to 100%."

HIGHRIDGE **Wednesday evening - March 6, 1974**

"Ma! I'm home!" Benjy ran into his mother's arms, and Linnell was so relieved to see him she almost wept. He was so happy and so full of stories about his adventures that she decided to wait until they had all finished dinner before telling him that his father had died.

Benjy seemed unmoved at first, then he asked her how this had happened and she told him his father's heart had stopped because he had been careless about taking some medicine and that she'd tell him more when he was older. Benjy looked around, as if he was afraid Bear was still there, listening, and finally, he spoke: "Well Ma, it's hard for me to say what I feel, but I didn't know him very well. We never talked. Are we going to have to move?"

"Don't worry Benjy, everything's been taken care of so we can live here as long as we want. But we may go to an island every now and then and play pirates and privateers. Would you like that?"

Benjy looked at her with a wise expression too old for his years. "Ma, I thought we were playing that *here*. Come 'n look. I wanna show you something!"

Taking her hand, Benjy led her out of the house, down the path, and into Bear's garage. "Now I can tell you my secret. I followed Bear here because he was walking kinda sneaky, like sorta creeping over the gravel so no one could hear. He was hiding things, like the pirate in my treasure book, so I followed him on the other side of the bushes, just like in the story, and I saw where he was hiding his treasure. He looked so scary I never told anyone I was spying on him. But when he was gone, I looked. Stay here. I want you to watch me!"

Benjy climbed up on the boxes stored in the garage and pulled on a box which he couldn't move. On a hunch, Linnell told him to wait until she got a flashlight; then she got a ladder and climbed up next to him. Linnell let Benjy pull open the folds at the top of the box. The flashlight revealed many large cotton bank bags and smaller ones tucked in between them. As soon as she tried to pick up one of the bags she knew from the weight that it had to be gold. Benjy told her he had found treasure inside most of the big bags but that there was pirate's powder in some of the others. Pretending that the pirate's powder was of no consequence, Linnell sent Benjy back in the house and told him to close all the curtains and window blinds so nobody could see in.

They spent the next hour hauling the heavy bags into the house and piling them on the kitchen table. Linnell kept the small parcels away from Benjy. After carrying them into the guest bath, she opened them carefully and finding pills and powders of every description, flushed a drug lord's fortune down the toilet. As for the dental gold—she guessed there was more than a 100 pounds, similar to the gold scrap she'd found in the desk—it appeared that Bear must have latched onto every bit, no matter how small, that had ever walked into his office.

Helene watched them count and pack the gold. "That gold—it's an invitation to robbers and I'm not staying in this house unless you get that stuff out of here," she announced. Then she made Linnell and Benjy wash their hands.

After everyone was asleep, Linnell crept into her bathroom and closed the door. She wanted to scream from the strain of pretending—for Benjy's sake, mostly, but also for Helene's—that this had been a normal household. Bear might have been crazy, but he had also been very cunning. He had fooled them all. She intended to be the wiser for it.

SAN FRANCISCO **Thursday - March 7, 1974**

Even though the fraud case against Dr. Clare was for all practical purposes a closed-down case, Jordan had been assigned to the final task of reviewing the tapes of L.C.'s telephone calls because Rizzo was still looking for leads to the money that had vanished from the bank in Montreal. When he was finished with this, the tapes would be crated with all the rest of the regional cases, then stored in the archives for seven years until they were either lost or destroyed. Especially the tapes, nobody would ever admit to their existence because of the irregular circumstances under which they were made.

The conversation between Dr. Herman and Linnell came as no surprise. It was old news about Dr. Clare dipping into his drug inventory, and their discussion confirmed that old Rizzo had been right all along. This was all very interesting, of course, except it did not provide any leads to the missing money. Listening to Linnell's disembodied voice, however, again persuaded him to worry—it was obvious, at least to him, that there was something about that house that frightened her, so much so that she was using some kind of exorcism to cleanse it. He listened to her midnight call, and thought it was very strange. Linnell had an unusual side to her, he realized, one that you'd never expect.

Jordan removed his headphones and stopped the tape. All of this made him think about what might have been, could have been, had only he acted upon his instincts. He should have knocked on her door that night. Or perhaps if he'd called her, late Saturday night, he might be with her now, instead of ending up trapped behind the scenes and listening to her recorded voice. He turned on the tape again and after finishing his review of the more recent taps, he suddenly realized that something was turning peculiar: The hang-up calls—to her home and office lines alike—had increased dramatically and there also were some pretty odd crank calls, too. Could it be that there was somebody else keeping tabs on her too? He remembered how she'd joked about being under surveillance and how he had assumed she was referring to the IRS spooks. But he knew something she didn't—that one of Ivener's lawyers, Harold Dolphe, had been in her room. And furthermore, one caller—a man who would not give his name to Linnell's secretary—had even told her in no polite terms "that L.C.'s whoring was the real reason why Dr. Clare was driven to kill himself."

It was this that caught him up short—had somebody on the island been spying on them? How could that be? The only person who could have was Dolphe, and according to Edgardo, Dolphe had already left the island by the time he and Linnell actually got together. So maybe Dolphe was keeping tabs on her, but Dolphe wouldn't know about them, that they'd met. On the other hand, maybe somebody local, somebody who had it in for Linnell, like Hosterman obviously did, was rattling her cage—that would explain things. Hosterman would say anything, so if it was just Hosterman, then he could dismiss his call as nothing more than a nasty coincidence.

But what really bothered him, in fact more than anything else, was the way the press had gone on about Dr. Clare's death. The newspaper was deliberately creating the false impression that Linnell was in some way responsible. This was ridiculous. And such outrageous headlines. It looked like the real reason they were hassling her was simply because she had rebelled, she had refused to slide into the non-threatening subordinate slots that women were given, and had chosen a profession, instead, which apparently made her fair game for all sorts of abuse.

All of it—the media hype, the lurid headlines and all the rest of the blather—offended his sense of justice. He had to do something. And now that he didn't have to work through his lunch break, he would. Jordan slipped into his jacket. Then, on impulse, he rummaged through the tapes again until he found the one that contained the information about the Phoenix Corporation and Bear's lamentations about it to his lawyer, Hosterman.

No. He couldn't tamper with evidence. He'd had a chance to think about doing something like that and he knew that he couldn't destroy the tape. But he *could* sort of lose it in the files. Jordan quickly removed the label from the reel, crumpled the label into a ball, mixed the tape into a mislabeled box for a different case and then pushed all of the crates to the back of the gurney so they could be sent to their final resting place—most likely an incinerator in the desert somewhere.

Jordan left the office at noon and headed out for a phone that he knew wouldn't be tapped. He placed a call to the Highridge News and caught the editor for the evening edition. He gave the editor enough facts to convince him that he was a reliable source but told him that he had to remain anonymous, and then he gave him some background about the IRS and Dr. Clare's tax problems. In addition to that, he told him in no uncertain terms that Mrs. Clare had no knowledge of her husband's criminal activities or his drug habits—and that a good place for the two-bit news-agitator of a reporter to start earning his Pulitzer prize would be with the autopsy report and the drug panel performed on the late Dr. Clare by the coroner's office.

As soon as he finished with the editor, Jordan finally placed the call he'd been longing to make. He listened to Linnell's secretary announcing "Law office of Linnell Clare. Who's calling, please?" But when he opened his mouth to speak, the words he so much wanted to say became stuck in the back of his throat. He was flabbergasted. This had never happened before. Jordan tried to clear his throat and suddenly, out came an ugly, embarrassing noise.

"Just who *are* you? You'd better stop bothering us, you damned idiot!" Karen sounded menacing.

By some obscene twist of fate, when he tried to speak, Jordan's tongue thickened into a cotton wad. This time he coughed a dry squawk. Surprised by the weird noises he was producing, Jordan finally managed an embarrassed laugh which had the unfortunate effect of enraging Karen even more because now she was shrieking at him to get lost. With Karen's angry words still ringing in his ear, Jordan hung up without speaking.

Jordan returned to the IRS office, walked into Rizzo's office, and handed him his notice of resignation.

Rizzo appeared to be taken aback by the suddenness of his decision, and asked him to think it over for a while.

Jordan agreed to stay until the following day.

When Linnell returned to her office on Thursday, she was greeted by another stack of pink message slips. Karen had placed the most troubling one on top. Linnell saw the name on the slip and froze: Chief Sommers. He hadn't personally returned her call, his desk sergeant had; the message requested her to come in ASAP to see the Chief. Karen had checked the box marked *Urgent*.

"He wants to *see* me? Did he say why?" Linnell suddenly remembered something—Margo's syringe, she had been carrying it around in her purse for almost two days. Oh my God! What if the syringe had something to do with Bear's drug overdose? But if so, then what was it doing in Margo's purse? And now it was in *hers*. What should she do? Destroy it?

Karen replied, "I asked what was up, but the desk sergeant wouldn't say. But *I* think it has something to do with that newspaper article."

This time, instead of feeling a nibble of pain underneath her ribs, Linnell felt sick to her stomach. Nauseated. Nerves, she thought. But why should she be nervous? She had nothing to be nervous about. She was glad he was dead. But so what? That was no crime. The wave of nausea passed but the anxiety remained.

"Okay. Call Sommers back, and this time emphasize how much I'd appreciate his immediate explanation for that scurrilous newspaper article, and leave word that I'll be in to see him after the funeral." Linnell breathed deeply and tried to stay calm. What new ugliness awaited her now? she thought angrily. She waited until Karen had left the room and then picked up the phone and called information in Michigan for the number of Michigan State University. A minute later she was dialing the records department to see if the admissions clerk could tell her the date of graduation of a student named Robert Roberts.

"Robert Roberts you say? How old?"

"Oh, I think he would have graduated sometime within the last ten years—I think he said he was in his late twenties. Thereabouts. "

The records clerk told Linnell to hold the line.

Two minutes later, the clerk was back with the news. "We've checked out records for the last twenty years—Robert Roberts did not attend here."

"Well, how about just the surname, "Roberts"? You must have had someone . . ."

"All five of us clerks—we've already checked. No males in that age group. Coupla gals with that surname. But the only guy with that name we've ever enrolled would have to be in his fifties. You said this guy's in his twenties. Right?"

"Right." Linnell wasn't surprised. "Well. Thanks for your trouble."

Dejected, Linnell set the receiver down in its cradle. Now she was sure: He must have been just like her—married. Wasn't that *exactly* what she'd first thought? Except—unlike her—he'd been smart enough to keep it under his hat. But still, she didn't regret what she'd done, not for a minute. Linnell sighed when she recalled the way he'd told her about looking for her all his life. It was *such* a corny line, and she would sooner die than admit it—but it had made her feel so good just to hear him say it. Maybe things would have turned out altogether different if she'd stayed through Saturday. Linnell allowed herself one tear, blotted it carefully so as not to smear her mascara and then opened the door and told Karen that she would be going home.

But what she really had in mind was finding Debbie Brillis.

At first Linnell drove aimlessly, enjoying the weather and the novelty of feeling genuinely free, until she realized she was idling in front of Willy's office building. It was just her luck that the signal had changed, forcing her to stop at the crosswalk opposite the window of his private office. She wondered if he was on the other side of the glass, swiveling to and fro in his chair and staring out the window like he usually did when plotting one of his intricate tax schemes. She hoped he could see her now. She tried to look in his window, but the sun shone brightly, transforming his windows into mirrors that threw back her reflection in long wobbly lines. Giving her hair a toss, Linnell put on a brave face and thought: Take a good look at me, Harold; envy my toys, and I've got my own practice, too. So to hell with you *and* the Highridge News—I'm free at last. Are you?

As soon as the signal changed to green, she peeled out; then she dug in her purse to find the piece of paper with Deborah Brillis' address.

Linnell was puzzled when she found that the location of the address was an automobile repair shop in the industrial district. She checked the map to see if she'd made a mistake. But she hadn't, and there was no other street with a similar name. Then she had the strangest thought: What if there was no such person as Debbie Brillis? What if the woman she'd seen in Bear's office had been somebody else? Linnell told herself to stop being so silly, but still, she kept remembering how she'd felt at dinner, when she thought the ground was slipping away from beneath her feet.

She had the same feeling now—except now it was people: Bear was dead, Roberts had vanished into thin air, and now so had this Debbie Brillis person. Linnell drove home very slowly. As soon as she got in the door, she called the telephone company for the listing of Debbie Brillis. The operator told her their records showed that the woman's telephone service had been disconnected. Linnell hung up, relieved to know that at least Debbie Brillis was real. She told herself she was being anxious over nothing, and then she spent the rest of the day with Benjy, packing the gold so that she could store it until she could have it assayed. She planned to keep it until the gold restrictions were lifted and then sell it into a rising market.

There were more cat-calls later that afternoon. Helene got two of them, which persuaded her to stay overnight so that Linnell could get some rest.

SAN FRANCISCO **Friday - March 8, 1974**

Robert Jordan returned to his office and killed time by cleaning his desk and making lists of major accounting firms. He selected only those with international tax departments; he was on the phone making appointments for interviews when Rizzo poked his head around the door. Jordan pretended to be working and Rizzo walked in and held a newspaper under his nose.

"Take a look at today's headline, kid. What you think about this?"

Jordan froze, then cut off his call and while Rizzo stood waiting for his reaction, he read the article on the lower half of the front page:

"POPS PILLS AND PULLS PLUG The Highridge coroner reports that Mark Clare, a local dentist, died from a self-administered cocktail of cocaine and narcotics. The dentist faced criminal prosecution for tax evasion. When interviewed, the dentist's office manager, Margo Callahan, confirmed that he had been struggling with a long-standing drug problem and that two special agents from the IRS criminal division visited him several hours before he took his life. When contacted, the IRS stated that the Privacy Act of 1974 prohibits them from commenting, however a reliable independent source confirms this information. The dentist's widow, a well-respected Highridge attorney, remains in seclusion."

"You sure had him figured right," Jordan replied.

Rizzo grinned at Jordan wolfishly then picked up the newspaper and gave him a friendly whack. "Sure hate to see you go, kid. That's okay, go ahead, use the phone. Any one of the Big Eight would be more than happy to hire one of my guys. See you later—we'll have couple of brews after work."

Rizzo closed Jordan's door on his way out.

Jordan called Buster Hosterman's office and the lawyer was immediately available when Jordan informed the secretary that he was the president of a silicon valley electronics company. Recalling one of Linnell's vignettes about lawyers' tricks, Jordan scheduled a meeting for the entire day—he could hear Buster telling his secretary to pencil out all his existing appointments—and while Buster launched into a rhapsody about his fee, Jordan focused on the background noises, and by the time he was ready to hang up, he knew beyond any doubt that Linnell's worst crank call had been made by Buster, himself.

HIGHRIDGE **Friday morning - March 8, 1974**

Linnell was grateful to Helene for changing her mind—now she was willing to stay for the entire weekend instead of just for one night. Linnell decided to keep the phone off the hook to block the calls.

By noon, however, Linnell felt isolated, so she restored the connection and to her great chagrin it seemed as if her mysterious caller had never left because just as soon as she set the phone in its cradle, it rang again. She picked it up immediately and was treated to yet another bout of heavy breathing. Linnell whispered a few impolite words before hanging up and this time she was careful not to let Helene know it was another one of those crazy cat-calls.

She was truly worried now. How do you fight a cloud? First there had been that rotten article in the newspaper, and now there was *this*. Perhaps she'd better take some precautions. How did she know that Bear didn't have an accomplice? And what if he was the one who was calling her now? Trying to figure out the best time to rob them? She'd better get the gold out of here fast—it might be worth as much as $100,000 today, but if the gold market opened to U.S. investors, the price of the metal would soar and the gold could be worth ten times as much . . . so maybe whoever was watching her was aware of this, too.

Linnell was careful to keep her concerns to herself while they all carried the gold out to her car. She was anxious to leave, but then, to her great dismay, when she turned the ignition switch, Charles just sat there and clicked. His electrical system had gone on the fritz again. She had no choice—Charles would have to be towed back to the dealership. All of them carried the gold back into the house, and while Linnell called for a tow truck, Helene hovered nervously at the front door.

It was only after the Jaguar was towed away and the three of them were packing the gold into the Cadillac, that Linnell noticed how irritable Benjy had become. He had begun to whine about being too hot and even Helene was edgy. Linnell didn't feel so good herself; her stomach felt queasy and she was strangely short of breath. To make matters worse, as soon as they pulled onto the freeway, Benjy began to bounce around in the back seat, constantly asking: "Are we there yet?" It was so unlike her to be so short tempered—but she wanted to smack him. Fortunately, they found a bank with a large enough safety deposit box halfway between San Francisco and Highridge, and by 2 that afternoon, the gold was safely stored. Helene was at last finally satisfied that they were no longer in danger of being killed in their beds—and Linnell was relieved to be rid of the large syringe. She'd swaddled it inside a large padded envelope and sacked it with the empty vials of Percodan that Bear had prescribed for Margo Callahan; then she'd placed everything in the safety deposit box along with a note explaining the circumstances, just in case something should happen to her. Best to err on the side of caution, she thought.

By the time they returned to the house, the weather had turned warm enough for a swim—but one quick toe-dip was all they could stand because Linnell hadn't gotten around to turning on the pool heater. Benjy began to complain again, and Linnell was seized with a desperate urge to escape. If only she could take another walk on the beach.

"Cabin fever?" Helene asked. "Sure. That's what it is. You better get out of here, go to the club. Get some exercise." Helene reached out and patted Linnell's arm. "You'll see, this will blow over and things will be fine. Besides, right now you should be with your friends. Go show 'em you're not going to hide."

"I guess you're right. Their pool is heated. I can swim laps and maybe get in a few sets of tennis."

"Good," replied Helene. "That's more like it. Now you go and change into something nice. Wear your new tennis whites. You have such a good tan you should go show it off. And don't worry, I'll take good care of Benjy."

Linnell picked up another newspaper on her way to the club. She was amazed as much by the flippant headline as by the suddenness of the restoration of her respectability. It was all so puzzling. Now she was being described as a "*widow and well respected Highridge attorney.*" Maybe they were afraid she'd sue; she'd been thinking of it. "Pays to be a lawyer," she said to herself. Tossing the paper aside, Linnell let the Cadillac glide into the parking lot and once again saw that there was a space for her, right in front of the entrance. She glanced at the clock in the dash: It was nearing a quarter to three. She looked around to see if her friends had arrived and saw only one other car that she recognized—the new white Jaguar, Larry's gift—parked as before at the side of the building away from the other cars. Well, it wasn't her favorite C, but it was reassuring to see that at least one of them was there. Linnell wondered where the rest of them were and then she remembered it was Friday, and Nancy would still be at the bank and Cee-Cee would be picking up her daughter from school.

Linnell entered the club and said hello to the couple who stood in the foyer, but instead of a reply, she got a cold stare. Linnell shrugged and walked through the lounge and sat down at the end of the bar. She noticed that people seemed to be avoiding her eyes and yet she could feel their eyes burning holes in the back of her head. Something was up. She could feel it. And sure enough, when she caught their eyes again, in the mirror over the bar, she could see heads turning away from her glance.

Linnell was relieved to see that a favorite of hers, Dan, was tending bar.

Dan approached her but kept his head down when he spoke. "There's been a lot of talk about you," he whispered.

Linnell took this head-ducking to mean that he didn't want people to see that he was being sociable with her. "You mean I'm a pariah because of that damn newspaper article?"

"Yeah! I mean, no! It wasn't just that . . . see, it all started the week you were gone. I heard talk about you. You forget your husband was staying here?"

"To tell the truth, I did. So, tell me more."

"Don't you go shooting the messenger, you hear? But your old man was in here practically every day, telling everybody within ear-shot that you'd snitched on your former boss, you know, that Wei guru. Wotsisname? Yeah, Willy Ivener. A lot of people here take that Wei stuff like it was the gospel—

they're hard-core believers. They go to all the life-training courses . . . so, when the word got around that you were fingering Willy, well, quite a few people around here now think you're a total shit, to put it politely. And the reports about you going to tax havens didn't help you much, either."

Linnell's face felt on fire. "Fingering Willy? What's *that* supposed to mean! You say *Bear* started this rumor?"

"Bear, and then, after that, that new pal of his picked it up. You must know who he is—he's the lawyer for the club—Buster Hosterman. Him."

"I'll bet this has something to do with the "Cs" and that feeble-minded old dork on the board of directors. Well, I want you to know I'm nobody's snitch, and you can just tell that ass Buster to go pound a cork in it or else I'll do it myself. He'll understand what that means." Linnell tossed her hair angrily. She had never talked like this before. "And besides, even if I *did* have some info about Ivener's business—which, for your information, I don't—I'm forbidden to tell anyone, let alone testify about it, because of the lawyer-client privilege."

"But that's not all," Dan interrupted her rant, "Bear said he was really *frightened* for you—like he was afraid that maybe Ivener had some connections that could do you in."

"Oh, that's incredible! That's nuts! Now I *know* Bear was crazy. You read the papers today? I just did, and I have to tell you, the media knows more about Bear's problems than I ever did. I didn't know he was doing drugs, and I was his wife!"

Linnell was now so amazed and so furious, she ordered a gin and tonic. And then she gave Dan a five and told him to spread what she'd just told him around. Ordinarily, not being the drinking sort, she would have taken a few sips and left the rest of her drink nearly untouched on the bar, but today she had Dan pour her drink into a plastic cup so she could carry it into the pool area.

Without looking back at the members whom she knew were still staring at her, Linnell Clare picked up her drink and flounced out of the lounge and into the gym. Linnell cut angrily through the weight room and entered the fenced-in pool area. There was no one around, which was fine with her because she wanted to be alone. Finding a padded chaise set up next to the pool, she kicked off her shoes, tore off her warm-up pants, sat down and chugged half her drink. Laying back on the cushions, she began to think about Mr. Clarichevik's comment about Bear's mother. Insanity in the family—all of them, *bonkers* . . . and Bear had kept this crucial piece of information a secret. The bastard! No wonder he hadn't wanted to tell her anything more about his family!

It was warm by the pool and her stomach felt queasy. Linnell rolled over and flipped her towel over her head. She had just begun to doze when she heard someone entering the pool area from one of the rest rooms. She felt too sleepy to look and see who it was—and besides, she didn't need to look, gin always sharpened a different part of her mind—she could tell without looking it was only one person. The report of hard leather on concrete told her that it was a man and by the echoes and vibrations she could tell he was big as a couch. She listened to his footsteps as he walked past her chaise. She could tell that he'd stopped. No surprise. He would be taking another look at her legs. She could hear him turning around to stare at her. Well, let the overstuffed buffalo have an eyeful! What did she care?

Linnell fell asleep underneath her towel and didn't hear a sound of what happened next.

HIGHRIDGE **Friday Evening - March 8, 1974**

"Where's *Ma*?" Benjy croaked. He was still at the dining room window, watching the driveway. It seemed like he'd been there all afternoon, and now he was standing there, eating a cereal snack and waiting for his mother to come up the driveway.

"Honey, I think your mother would be a lot happier if you called her "Mother." Or "Mom."" Helene, who was standing at the kitchen sink, chopping lettuce, didn't want to be interrupted.

Benjy banged on the window with his spoon as if he were trying to scare away something on the other side of the glass. Hearing the noise, Helen yelled. "Stop that racket, I can't hear myself think. You *know* your mother's just gone to the club. You hold your horses. She'll be here soon. She's never late for one of *my* dinners!"

Benjy started to wail.

"Benjy? What's the matter, dear?"

"I want my *mother.*"

"Oh, honey, don't worry. She'll be here any time now. You know she just got back from her trip and she hasn't had any time to rest since your father passed away. It's been real hard on her."

"Yeah. But where *is* she? It's getting dark." Benjy, his chest heaving, looked like he was ready to burst into tears.

Helene glanced at him, then rushed into the dining room and fell on her knees so she could look into his eyes. She gave him a hug. “C'mon now, don't you cry,” Helene comforted. “I'll tell you what I'm going to do. If your mother's not here in fifteen minutes, then I promise—I'll call the club and I'll find her for you. Everything's fine. You'll see."

Benjy began to cry. "Something's happened to her."

Helene, seeing that she was getting nowhere with him, finally took Benjy’s hand and walked him into the kitchen, where she pulled up a chair and had him sit next to her while she finished making their dinner. Then she looked at Benjy's tear-streaked face and announced: "Okay, okay. You just sit here with me, and if she's not here in another five minutes we'll call the police."

THE BAY AREA **Early Sunday Evening—March 10, 1974**

Avoiding her face, he finally looked at her body, then he squeezed his eyes closed and his mind's eye was again overwhelmed by the sight of a huge black-shelled cockroach. It was clattering straight for him, picking up speed, but this time he could see its gargantuan mandibles swinging wide open and then, at the very last second, when it was almost upon him, he saw it suddenly veer and slip into the shadowy foliage, where the flowery tufts at the ends of its antennae slowly waved at him from the darkness like frightful daisies. Inviting him to follow. To make a mistake and be eaten alive.

Chief Sommers' eyes flew open to banish his waking nightmare. He struggled to breathe and while his head fought off echoes of crunching bones, watery images of her kept rising up before his eyes. Then he swallowed and realized it was his own hand at his throat that was cutting off his air. Oh God it was awful—he was actually seeing her twice: in the flesh, in the more gripping here and now, and then mercifully superimposed over this horror was a pastel dream of her sitting with her pretty, rich friends; all of them stretched out underneath those bright blue umbrellas at the Highridge country club. He could actually see their long sun tanned legs—glistening in the heat while the four blondes sipped on iced tea and waited for courts.

The shimmering blue umbrellas and summery faces gradually faded away as Sommers got a better grip on himself. He stared at the body. She'd been a stunner all right. And used to the good life, too—as anyone could easily tell from her expensive apparel and the even tan of her incredible legs. Her perfect legs, now bent double, were tightly tucked underneath the rumpled white pleats of her tennis dress. But her face was what gripped him, it was frozen in shock, and her hair, fanning into a silken corona around her head, was sprinkled with a few fresh eucalyptus leaves—a useless clue since this rambunctious tree grew in thousands of groves all over the Bay Area.

His officers had found her like this. Late this afternoon. Trussed up and straining against the cords that bound her because rigor mortis had already set in. After the photographers and reporters retreated, Chief Sommers slipped his hands into thin plastic gloves, then stood frozen before the open-mouthed trunk of the otherwise spotless luxury sedan. First he made himself take a couple of long breaths, then avoiding her face, he forced himself to lean over the body to examine something his officers seemed to have missed: a small mound of what looked to be curdled brown pudding, pressed into the coarse, tweedy trunk liner.

Reaching down with a gloved finger, Sommers dabbed at the crusty mess and then, nose crinkling with anticipatory disgust, held his finger up close to one nostril and sniffed. Expecting evil-smelling skatole, he was greatly relieved when his finger presented only a metallic odor reminiscent of freshly turned loam. He stepped back, took another long breath, then leaned even closer to examine the curious spot and this time he saw something that looked like a delicate crab's leg, near invisible because it blended so well with the dark fabric lining. One leg. Brownish-black and prickly looking.

He lifted it gently and held it up to the light. Wondering if something so large could have come from a spider, Sommers set it down on the top edge of the trunk lid to study its articulated joints for a moment, then he noted his discovery on his list—*spider leg?*—and put it back where he'd found it. He slowly peeled off his glove and while he was busying himself with his notes, a cool breeze gusted suddenly and the faint trace of black powder that had been deposited by the leg on the edge of the trunk lid first fanned out—for a second it resembled the pattern made by the victim's hair—then disappeared into the wind entirely.

What he knew of the facts was very disturbing. For instance, it was clear that robbery was not the motive here because she still wore her heavy gold wedding band. Worse yet, her valuable wristwatch—its filigree guard-chain now torn—was still there on her wrist. Was there some kind of message intended by this? The thought made him choke. Sommers coughed to conceal his distress and held the field report out at arm's length before eyes that still yearned not to see: Skull fractures. In what order, he didn't know for sure, but there had been a blow to the back of the head. And then she had been pithed. Like a frog. Stabbed with a long narrow instrument from the base of her skull underneath her thick hair, clear through her spine and into the anterior cortex.

Wooden-legged, like a wounded stag, the Chief stepped back to lean on the wall. There'd be plenty of time to think later on, but right now it just felt as if something inside him had torn and he was bleeding internally. He was alone. There wasn't a soul he could talk to. And there hadn't been a murder in Highridge for fifty years, so where, exactly, was he supposed to begin? He couldn't consult with anyone about any of this, because if he did, in no time at all it would get back to that filthy cockroach of a city attorney—God! He hated him, Buster Hosterman—and then he'd have Hosterman and any number of the man's hard-shelled protégés crawling all over his back. He couldn't let that happen, there already were too many problems as it was.

Sommers closed his eyes and counted to ten and this time, when he opened them, it was as if everything had miraculously snapped back into focus. First the rope caught his eye. Then the knots. A blue water sailor himself, Sommers recognized the special way the cords had been tied—they were the sheep-shank knots of a seaman. Could it be that the perpetrator of this nasty business was a stevedore? Or a wacked-out sailor from one of the larger vessels that had recently entered the Bay?

He thought about this; then decided no. Crimes like these were most often committed by somebody known to the victim. It had to be somebody local—somebody who sailed—and of course he would interview the husband first. Even so, from what he could see so far, it looked like the killer was someone so obsessed with control that the murder seemed almost—he struggled for a word. Ceremonial. That was it. The way she was tied. The unnecessary stab wound. Like a ritualized slaughter. A cult? Now that was a real possibility. He'd better order his lieutenant to get cracking; have him review the weekly Coast Guard logs, then get him to report back about what was happening cult-wise around the bay.

And he'd better make sure that forensics got back here immediately to see if she had been molested . . . in any unusual ways.

HIGHRIDGE **Late Sunday Evening - March 10, 1974**

For the first time in years, Linnell enjoyed Sunday dinner. She sat next to Benjy and felt truly blessed. She was so lucky to have such a wonderful son, and soon they would have a wonderful life. But he'd sure been a handful on Friday night; he'd literally clung to her for the rest of the evening and they had ended up eating dinner in the kitchen, because Benjy refused to go into the dining room. There was something in the bushes, he'd said. Something big as a bear. And then later she'd had to peel him off her to get him to go to bed. She had tried to get him to explain what was upsetting him and all he could tell her was that he had been scared that something bad had happened to her. So then she'd explained that it was only natural for a child to have these scary feelings when a parent dies. But he'd kept on insisting that this wasn't it; that there really were monsters in the bushes. Well, one thing was clear—the boy had definitely inherited her imagination.

Linnell tried to remember if anything strange had happened this past Friday. She could remember her conversation with the bar tender, Dan, and then falling asleep by the swimming pool. It was only because the temperature had dropped so suddenly that she'd awakened. With a headache, of course. Nothing strange about that. She'd swum a few laps and when she finally looked at her watch she realized she'd been asleep for nearly three hours. Afraid of being late, she had flown half-dressed through the lobby, and then there had been even more aggravation when she couldn't find precious Charles.

She had walked through the parking lot in a state of shock. Hardly any cars remained—and *her* car was *gone*. Hijacked! Then—and feeling like an absolute fool—she finally recalled that she'd driven the Cadillac. And there it was, right in front of the entrance. She had also noticed that Elsie had already left, because her car was gone, too. She knew this for a fact because she had been looking for a white Jaguar instead of the Cadillac. That was all she could remember, and none of this seemed extraordinary.

The next day, at Bear's graveside funeral—a swift, private burial, Saturday morning—she had stood dry-eyed at the grave and Benjy had held her hand tightly all during the service. At its conclusion, she had pitched a handful of dirt on the casket, feeling nothing at all because she realized that the Mark she once thought she knew had never existed. Now, with her arm around Benjy, Linnell picked at her dessert. It was Sunday evening; and a very peaceful and tranquil evening because there hadn't been any more of those troubling hang-up calls. Linnell sighed—it was near overwhelming to think how much things had changed over the past two weeks.

Helene, in the meanwhile, had finished her dinner and was glued to the television, watching the news. Linnell heard the newscaster mention something about the woman whose body had been found in the trunk of her car. A new, white Jaguar sedan. Discovered in the parking lot of a funeral parlor, high in the hills above San Francisco. When Linnell heard the word *Jaguar* she paid more attention, but by then the newscast was over.

After Linnell put Benjy to bed and Helene had retired, Linnell went into her bedroom and closed the door, turned on television, and waited for the ten o'clock news. The report opened with the camera panning the scene, then zooming in on a white Jaguar sedan that looked exactly like Charles; the crime scene was yellow-taped and surrounded by a half-circle of squad cars. The camera cut to the reporter, who gravely intoned:

"We have an update. The woman found late this afternoon in the trunk of her car, apparently abandoned sometime this weekend in the parking lot of the Switser Funeral Parlor, has been identified as Elsie Baron. She was last seen around five in the evening at the Highridge Country Club. The police think she was abducted from the parking lot because witnesses say they saw her sitting in the passenger seat of her vehicle as it was driven away from the club by a slender, middle-aged, Afro-American male. Her distraught husband, Lawrence Baron, told investigators he'd just given her the car for her birthday two weeks before. Please call the number you see on your screen if you think you have any information that might relate to this crime."

Linnell shivered and pulled the comforter up around her shoulders, she was glad that she wasn't all alone in the house. Then she rolled out of bed and checked all the doors and windows to make sure they were locked. When she climbed in again, she piled all of the pillows behind her back like she'd once done as a child. Except this time she wasn't worried about witches and werewolves. She fell asleep sitting up.

The phone rang at 11:30 p.m. Linnell looked at the illuminated dial of her bedside clock, surprised that anyone would be calling the house so late in the evening. Her hand shot out to grab the instrument before it could ring again and pressed the receiver to her mouth and quietly said hello.

She heard a muffled voice repeating her name: "L. C. . . . L.C. . . . Is this *you*?" The voice sounded anxious and surprised and vaguely familiar.

Linnell, still groggy, responded automatically as if she were still at her office: "Yes, this is L.C. and how may I help you?"

The caller hung up without saying anything more.

Linnell bounced upright in the water bed. Now she was wide awake. She'd just been struck by an incredible thought: *Linnell Clare, L.C. . . . L.C. married to Bear . . . Elsie . . . Elsie Baron.*

"Oh no, that can't be! Linnell hugged her pillow to her chest.

HIGHRIDGE **Monday - March 11, 1974**

"If I'm so damned rich, then why aren't I smart?" Linnell complained to Karen. She was aggravated. Even though the Sea Urchin Project had been set up to take advantage of what mavens called "governmental incentives"—"loopholes," according to the popular press—she still couldn't share the good news about her success. And she wouldn't, at least not until she was sure Bear's audit was closed. But her secrets were safe because Colin and his bank were barred by the newly enacted Cayman banking regulations from revealing any information about its customers. Better still, these new statutes made violations of the colony's privacy laws a serious crime. That left only Karen, and she knew that Karen would never tell.

But discovering the whereabouts of the rest of her money was proving impossible. Thanks to the magic of wire-transfers, $820,000 had been sucked into the void and if it weren't for her secret cache, a loss of this magnitude would have been devastating. Linnell reminded herself once again that she'd better not forget to pretend she was devastated, especially on the telephone, where the IRS most assuredly was lurking to record her every word.

Now frustrated in every respect, Linnell instructed Karen to block her calls, retreated to her private office and closed the door. She needed to be alone so she could think in peace. Linnell found a yellow legal pad and sat down at her desk. The late-night telephone call was still on her mind.

She thought about Elsie's dreadful murder, then about Elsie herself and felt a sense of remorse because it was only now, when it was too late, that she had finally grasped that her friend's imitation of her was simply Elsie's childlike way of expressing her admiration for her and all the rest of the "Cs". Linnell felt a terrible emptiness. Poor Elsie. Now it was too late to tell her anything.

Linnell, thinking about all the various losses and vanishings and disappearances of the past few weeks, felt even more despondent and now terribly alone. Whom could she talk too? Karen, of course. But Karen had her own life to lead and besides, she didn't want to burden Karen—possibly make her feel uneasy, and for no good reason—with what might be nothing more than figments of her imagination. No—it would be best to keep Karen out of this. Leaning over her desk, Linnell picked up a pen and began to doodle on her legal pad, allowing her hand to wander freely over the page.

There was something underlying the events of the past several weeks that bothered her and this frustrated her, too, because she couldn't say exactly what it was. She wished there was somebody around to give her a reality check, perhaps tell her that her imagination was veering a bit too far afield. But she couldn't help it—she couldn't stop wondering. Why, for instance, would anyone want to kill Elsie? As far as she knew, Elsie wasn't the sort to have or even make enemies. She'd been a stay-at-home housewife. The mother of a boy the same age as Benjy. A threat to no one; basically, and outside of being a bit too boisterous, she had otherwise been—win or lose—a good sport. Likable—albeit a trifle immature. Sociable. So, who on earth would want to kill her?

Now as for herself—*she* was a different story. Making enemies was an unfortunate by-product of her profession. She'd never shied away from this. She liked to win, and over the past three years she'd met her share of kooks who really resented this. So, could it be that this wasn't a random killing? What if there had been a mistake? After all, Elsie and she looked so much alike.

Linnell suddenly thought about Bear. Part of her lingering malaise had a lot to do with that evil look she'd seen on his face. And his eyes . . . glaring at her as if he were wishing her dead. Linnell finally allowed herself to form the thought:

Is it possible? Could I have been the intended victim?

There, she'd finally said it. The idea had first flashed through her mind, when, groggy and half-asleep, she'd answered the phone the night before. Why would somebody call her like that? In the middle of the night? *To see if she was still alive, that's why.* And even though he had whispered to conceal his identity, she was sure she'd heard that voice before—the voice of a man—whispering.

Frightened by the sound of *her* voice.

As if her hand alone was intrigued by such thoughts, the pen it held produced a name: *Willy Ivener*. Linnell stared at the name on the yellow pad. He's amoral, she thought, and murder would not be beyond him, but the big question really boils down to just this: Why on earth would he want to kill her? He wasn't crazy—and he certainly wasn't stupid. Furthermore, if Ivener had gotten wind of the lies Bear was spreading about her being a government witness, certainly Ivener's lawyers would have landed on her by now—hard and fast. All lawyers knew that the law strictly forbade any lawyer to divulge any confidences acquired through his or her employment. So Ivener would have to know for a fact that she was well aware of her ethical obligations and the penalities attached to violating this rule. Furthermore, so far as she could tell, there had never been any contact between Ivener and Bear because Bear had disliked him so thoroughly. Witness the fact that Bear had gone to such lengths—been willing to spend money, even—to get her away from Ivener. So, scratch Ivener, he would have no motive for wanting to kill her. Linnell printed, in large capitals: IVENER—NO MOTIVE.

Linnell told herself that this would be a different picture entirely if Bear had somehow been more acquainted with Ivener, or if Bear had made friends with somebody at Ivener's firm. Yes, something like that would definitely change the picture. However—and she'd combed through them thoroughly—Bear's secret accounts of his drug sales did not hint at any contacts with Ivener or anybody else at his firm. So, despite her strange feelings about Ivener, she nevertheless had to stick with the facts. Yes, scratch Ivener, Linnell thought. She crossed out his name and paused—the slip of paper she'd found in Bear's briefcase—did this mean something? Why did Bear write Willkills? Was this a name? Like Willy? Or was he trying to leave a message, or maybe a warning . . . and if so, then to whom? Were these even rational questions?

And what about Bear? Linnell wrote his name in big letters and thought about what Margo had said about him wanting to get a divorce. Maybe that's why he'd hid their money like that—this could very well have been part of his plans for divorce. And from what she'd learned of his secret life, there was no question about his capacity for crime. He also had plenty of motives:

He was greedy. Greedy enough to kill, she was sure. But, if he was still sane enough to try and hide all their money—would he want to kill her just for the house? That didn't make any sense, especially since it looked like he still needed her as a patsy to take the rap for his tax fraud. On the other hand, maybe he was afraid she would discover his side-business selling drugs. If she were dead he wouldn't have to worry about her exposing him. Now, that looked like a *really* strong motive for wanting her dead. And he could have been even more afraid of what she would do if she'd ever caught him stealing from her. Yes, this also made sense. There was one problem, however . . . he had killed himself before the hit had taken place. *Nope. That rules him out.* Linnell printed in large square letters, next to Bear's name: STRONG MOTIVE—NO OPPORTUNITY.

And then she thought of another hitch: Bear had killed himself *before* he could have learned she was on to him.

So, she was back to square one. And then there was the mystery woman who'd whisked all their money away. Who was she? A lover? Would Bear trust anyone, let alone a woman, to help him hide so much money? She answered her own question: *No. Certainly not. He'd never let anybody, let alone a woman, gain so much control. Not even if she were his mistress.* Could this woman have been blackmailing him? God knows he had plenty to be blackmailed about. *Blackmail—now that really makes sense. She threatens to spill the beans to the wife so Bear hires a hit man to off me? But why me and not her? After all, he needed me as his patsy. Or, maybe she hired some hit men to get rid of me? Or, he kills himself when he discovers she's stolen the money? No! Really! All of this sounds too farfetched.*

Exasperated, Linnell finally gave up. There were far too many angles and nothing seemed to hang together. At least, not for long. She wondered if perhaps the killers had been after Elsie's car and things had simply turned ugly. Perhaps so. Linnell carefully folded the yellow paper now covered with names and arrows and notations and locked it in the drawer where she kept her rudder. It was time for her to get moving. She hurriedly looked at her watch and saw that she only had fifteen minutes to get to Elsie's memorial service.

HIGHRIDGE **Monday evening - March 11, 1974**

The chapel had been transformed. She, Cee-Cee, and Nancy had chipped in and bought all the white roses at the San Francisco flower mart, as well as hundreds of long white tapers which now sent their flickering tongues into the darkness, creating the odd effect that the flowers were alive and trembling in the golden half-light.

Larry Baron stood at the head of the reception line at the entrance, his face a combination of leathery puffiness and bloodshot eyes. Linnell approached him with mixed emotions, part sympathy, part disgust. When she reached him, he first clasped her hands to pull her toward him, then threw both arms around her shoulders and hugged her while he whispered in her ear: "Stick around. I need to talk to you. And John needs to talk to you, too. Look for him." Larry released her and nodded in the direction of the chapel. "Thanks," he said. "Thank you all. The flowers are terrific."

Linnell had little time to be surprised by Larry's behavior because someone in the crowd behind her had reached out to pat her shoulder. Linnell heard a familiar voice.

"Looks like the room is filled with clouds, doesn't it?"

Linnell recognized Nancy's voice. Nancy whirled to stand in front of her. Slack-jawed with amazement, Linnell could only stare—it looked like Nancy had first ironed her hair, then lopped it off on a paper cutter. It hung, uncurled, barely covering the nape of her neck, with one thick strand tucked carelessly behind an ear. No lipstick. It was Nancy, plain.

"*This* is the new you?" Linnell made no attempt to conceal her shock; then a thought instantly flashed: A year from now who would even remember that the "Cs" had once looked so much alike?

"Yep. No more "Cs"." Nancy whispered in dead seriousness. "This is so awful. I feel so bad. And just wait till you hear what happened to Cee-Cee! John will fill you in, it's better he tells you himself."

"I don't see her. Where is she?" Linnell asked.

"She's home. In shock after what happened to her this morning. Maybe she's just getting exactly what she deserves. No! I'm just kidding."

Linnell felt a heavy hand on her shoulder and a man's voice whispered angrily overhead: "I want you to sue the bastards!"

"John!" Linnell exclaimed, trying to keep her voice low. "What happened? Why isn't Cee-Cee here?"

"It's incredible. *She* was hauled in for questioning this morning. The cops even gave her a polygraph test. It's goddam outrageous!"

Linnell still didn't get his meaning. "What are you talking about?"

"I'm talking about Elsie's murder!" John, ordinarily a placid, easygoing man, was red-faced with anger. "And, see? In the back. He's *here*."

"Who?" Linnell was even more puzzled.

"John! Keep it down," Nancy warned. "We'll talk after the service. It's beginning and I've got to sing."

Nancy left them to step behind the piano and began to accompany herself while she sang Amazing Grace. Linnell felt disembodied, as if she were floating above it all. Still stunned by the news about Cee-Cee, Linnell searched the room and spotted the large man in dark aviator glasses. It was Chief Sommers, his tan face a dark blotch against the banks of delicate blooms. Linnell ducked away from John, and after cadging a cigarette from a stranger, she stepped outside and had her first smoke in years. The odor of burning tobacco reminded her of law school; she took another drag and immediately felt sick to her stomach.

Linnell wondered: *Why is he here? Does he think the suspect's in here? And what's this about Cee-Cee? Could she possibly be involved?*

John, spotting the smoldering eye of her cigarette, stepped outside.

"That was Chief Sommers, wasn't it?" Linnell asked.

"Yeah. That's him all right. Nosing around."

"Who else knows about this Cee-Cee stuff?" Linnell snuffed out her cigarette in a planter box.

"Not counting the police and no doubt Hosterman, then only the "Cs", the rest of the guys and me."

"What about Larry? The police question him?"

"They questioned both of us. We had to account for the entire weekend. And the cops were all over the club Sunday night," John was now whispering angrily, "until the club's lawyer, Buster Hosterman, came sashaying in. I hear he made a big show of throwing them off the premises. Curiously enough, the only dirt they picked up was that old nasty rumor about Elsie screwing around with me! So what do you think those idiots did next? After I left for the office this morning, they hauled Cee-Cee in and questioned her about carrying a grudge against Elsie . . . and whether *she'd* hired the hit-men!"

Considering the irony of all this, Linnell could scarcely speak.

"Yeah," John continued, "they even made Cee-Cee take a polygraph test before they'd release her. Sent her home in a cab. She's still in shock."

Linnell, preoccupied by the thought of two killers, had to force herself to converse. "John, without question, it's not only crazy, it's terribly *stupid.* Who do you think is behind all this stuff?" She had a good idea who, she just wanted to hear it from somebody else.

"It's gotta be somebody on the board of directors at the club. Remember that old fart you gals used to tease? I think he had something to do with it, and I swear that lousy bastard Hosterman had a hand in it, too. I heard he interfered with the investigation, wouldn't let the officers interview the members who might have seen something, you know, those witnesses who first spoke to the reporters."

"Hey? What was that stuff about hit-*men*. I think the paper mentioned only one man."

"According to what Cee-Cee picked up from the cops, there were two of them. Had to be—'cause one of them would've had to drive the other one to the club. The police know one of them is an Afro-American male, and maybe the other is, too—anyway, the man seen driving Elsie's Jag was black and sorta delicate looking . . ." John gave a big hiccup and changed the subject back to his wife. ". . . then, after questioning Cee-Cee, she said they told her they would swear under oath that they had read her Miranda rights and that she had given her consent to being questioned without her lawyer being present. Can you believe that something like this could happen right here in Highridge?"

"Sounds just like Hosterman to me. You're going to need an attorney who's not wired into this town—there's a large firm in Oakland that would love to get their hands on a case like this. Call me and I'll refer you to them. John, excuse me, but I have to sit down and digest all of this." Feeling dizzy, Linnell sat down on the edge of the planter box and foraged for the cigarette. She picked it up and rolled it between her fingers while she sat, rocking to and fro, trying to sort things out: *Two men, one of them 'fragile-looking'. Two sets of footprints in the garden—one of them very narrow, could have been a woman or a very small man. Hang-up calls to my house and my office . . . a black man who calls and says pretty L.C. and then Bear and drugs and Buster Hosterman's card in Bear's briefcase . . .*

Linnell murmured softly, concentrating, trying to fit things together, and therefore didn't notice that Larry had crept up and was now standing almost on top of her, offering her a fresh cigarette.

"What's that you're saying?" Larry waved the pack under her nose. "John tell you what happened?"

Feeling sick to her stomach Linnell mashed the unlit butt into the dirt and shook her head, nauseated by the smell of tobacco. Finally, she was able to speak. "Larry . . . how are you doing? You okay?"

"Thanks . . . I'm maintaining. But don't worry about me, you've had more than your share of stuff to handle, yourself. Here, I have something for you." Larry dug in his coat pocket. "It was Elsie's. I know she'd want you to have it. She really admired you, you know. She used to say you were way ahead of your time. So I think she'd be happy if you took this." Larry held out a ladies gold watch with a braided gold wrist band.

Linnell could tell, even in the darkness, that it had cost a fortune. "Larry. I can't accept this. I mean, I'd be proud to wear something of Elsie's, but this is far too valuable." Linnell shook her head no.

"That's no reason. Here. You take it. It's brand new, I guess she just got it. It would make me feel better if you had it. Besides, *I* want you to have it because we didn't have a daughter for her to leave it to."

Over her protests, Larry managed to slide the watch into Linnell's pocket.

"Thank you, Larry. I don't know what to say, except I wish Elsie was still here to wear it herself. I hate having to ask, but was this . . . found on her?"

"Yeah, it was, and that's exactly what I want to tell you about. Sommers said something strange. I can't repeat his exact words but his point was that robbery couldn't have been a motive in Elsie's murder because her personal effects weren't stolen. And since robbery wasn't the motive—maybe that explains why Cee-Cee was hauled in and why John and I were questioned. Anyway, there's one more thing I'm going to tell you even though Sommers told me not to say anything: She wasn't molested. And I'm telling you this because I think you should know."

"Larry, you *must* tell me. How . . . how did she . . . die?"

"Sommers said he couldn't tell me, at least not till the case is closed."

"I've been wondering. About the cars. This bothers me a lot—did Sommers say anything about our cars being the same?"

"Now that you mention it—he didn't. But *I* did."

Without saying anything more, Larry patted Linnell's shoulder and then turned to hide his eyes. Linnell watched him walk away, shoulder's slumped, back into the chapel and his slow steps made her wonder if he could be thinking the same thing as she: *Why was it her and not you?* Then Linnell looked up at the sapphire spring sky and searched for some stars between the high clouds: *Could it really be true? That only a glass of gin and a towel over one's head is all that separates the quick from the dead?*

HIGHRIDGE **Tuesday - 12 a.m., March 12, 1974**

Linnell untied her bathrobe and stood before the mirror in what had once been Bear's bathroom, staring at her stomach. It felt warm and just a tiny bit distended, then she realized what she'd been forgetting! Linnell ran to her cabinet in her old bathroom and dug out her calendar and counted the days. Her period! She was already eight days late. And she was always so regular, to the day, to the hour! Oh good lord! Her nausea, her dizziness, the upset stomach. So many important things had happened over the last two weeks that the thought of being pregnant hadn't once crossed her mind.

Linnell dashed back into the bedroom and yanked the comforter off her bed. Thank heavens she'd been too busy to attend to such mundane things as changing the sheets! Grabbing the table lamp and holding it at an angle like a flashlight, she searched the bedding for tell-tale dried spots, rubbing her hand across the fabric while she searched for stains of dried semen. She was hopeful:

From what she could see, and from what she had already deduced about drug abuse, she was almost certain that Bear had not baked his meat loaf that Monday night. But she had to be sure . . . *Oh please, not Bear's.*

She returned to the bathroom to examine herself more closely: Her breasts were tender but only slightly enlarged, there would be no way for anyone to know how far along she might be. Linnell prayed again, but not to any God of her fathers. *Roberto.* He just had to be the one. He was young, strong, and healthy. Why shouldn't she do as she pleased? She was thirty-five, and if she were to bow to convention and wait until she found a man whom *she* wanted to marry, it would most likely take years. She would be out of time.

She would do one more test.

Linnell set up the ironing board in the bedroom, nervously pacing until the iron was hot. Then she ironed the sheets at the highest temperature—hoping against hope that no spots of seminal protein were there to scorch and turn brown. She held her breath while she ironed, perspiration beading her forehead and cheeks. The heat did not bring up any stains. So far so good. Linnell next found the silk pajamas she'd worn on her last night with Bear. She got a scissors and cut the fabric so it would lie flat and then held the pieces up to the light. She took her time, adjusted the temperature of the iron, and then carefully pressed every inch and every seam and found no charred traces of Bear's last remains. The odds were looking good and it was her call.

Linnell decided: She would go with the odds and choose life, because even though it would be *no* to Bear, it would be *yes* to the man she'd known only as Robert Roberts.

HIGHRIDGE **Tuesday - March 12, 1974**

The old newspaper had been lying on the floor of her car for over a week. If only she had read it more carefully: "POPS PILLS AND PULLS PLUG?: . . . *a reliable source states that Clare was facing criminal prosecution for tax evasion* . . ."

She'd been laboring on her theory of the Baron case, looking for someone or something that would tie all the tantalizing clues together and here, all this time, there was this *reliable source* who might hold the key to this mystery. And Chief Sommers wanted to see her? She wanted to see *him.*

She would see if he could meet with her today—and, come to think of it, since he'd been so hot to see her last week, why hadn't he called her back to set up the appointment he'd wanted? Well, now she had to see him—he might have a crucial piece of information and not realize it. Linnell pressed the intercom and told Karen to call the Highridge Police Department and make an appointment for her to meet with Chief Sommers.

Ten minutes later, Karen got back to her with a message from Chief Sommers: Would she come in today?

Linnell jumped on it. She tucked her outline in her purse and remembered to grab a photograph of the "Cs"—a picture of all of them standing together at the club—that had been taken earlier that year at the tennis competition. Before leaving, and in honor of Elsie's memory, she removed her old Timex and fastened Elsie's expensive gold watch around her left wrist.

"I'm going to tweak the old lion's whiskers," Linnell said on her way to the door. "And thanks for the sleuthing you did on those telephone logs. Good work! Solves at least part of the mystery."

Karen had compared the telephone bills for Bear's office with her log of cat-calls and had found that over the last several months all had come from his office, as had many—but not all—of the more recent ones. What had driven him to do this was hard to fathom; he would start in the morning, around 9:00 a.m., sometimes making as many as four calls in a row from the telephones in his office. Then he'd perform the same ritual, again and again, in the afternoon—sometimes he'd even call the house and do the same thing. Apparently, he'd just listen to her voice on the answering machine and then hang up without leaving a message. He'd had some crazy compulsions, all right. Linnell shuddered at the thought of him. However, the more recent cat-calls were a mystery because none of them could be matched to Bear's telephone bills. So the question remained: Who was out there doing this to her? And why? She had a theory about this and she wanted to discuss it with Chief Sommers.

Driving through Highridge on the way to police headquarters, Linnell rested her arm on the top of the car door so the sunlight could strike Elsie's watch. The ruby that sat in lieu of the numeral two looked genuine. A very unusual, very attractive watch, Linnell thought. Made in France, she observed. Wasn't there a custom in France? Something about meeting your lover at two? Or was it Spain? Funny, now that she thought about it, it was about that same time that she had first met Roberto. Linnell sighed at the thought, then willed herself back to the less pleasant present.

Now she was nervous. She had to make sure her conference with Chief Sommers wouldn't slide into a confrontation; all she wanted from him was some information, something to help set her to rest. And thank heavens she had never expressed her loathing for Bear—now people would simply assume he was the father. She would have to learn to live with this for the sake of her forthcoming child, whom she did not want to be branded with the stigma of illegitimacy. On the other hand, it was equally important that her child not be tainted by Bear's sordid reputation. Another balancing act, though Linnell. She consoled herself with the thought that people were people, and that absent a new scandal, they'd soon enough forget all about Bear.

She reviewed what she ought not to get into with Chief Sommers. Then she decided to wait until she had a chance to read him—she couldn't forget that she would be dealing with the man who had allowed a hack like Buster to worm his way into the police department. Sommers had to be either very cagey or very dense to allow something like that to happen. So, for the time being, all she could do was hope that Sommers would prove to be, as some people around here said, a fair-minded man.

The Highridge Police Headquarters building was the round-cornered concrete growth that seemed to have mushroomed from the west side of the courthouse. The ugliest building in Highridge, it had been constructed during the late Fifties and nothing had been done to it since. The interior was just as gloomy. A narrow hall lined with small offices for the beat cops ran the length of the building; the other side, with its slit-windowed walls, harbored the holding cells. Befitting his rank, the Chief had the largest office in the annex; it faced the main entrance, which allowed him to keep track of the more favored lawyers who were permitted to use the annex as a short-cut to the courthouse.

Since she was a tax attorney, she'd never had cause to visit the criminal courts before now, thus she had never actually spoken to Sommers until their encounter, when he'd stopped to inspect her car. He had looked large and leathery then. She'd had only a brief glimpse of him at the funeral, where he had impressed her as a man too big for his suit—but now, standing at the door and waiting to greet her himself, he appeared less threatening. In fact, he seemed rather personable. More to the point, she could tell that he thought she was attractive.

After a warm, firm handshake, Sommers escorted her into his office and then, without so much as a murmur, he poured two cups of coffee and handed one of them to her. This wasn't at all what she'd been expecting. She could see for herself that Sommers was rather handsome—in a thick sort of way. His features were exaggerated, like those of a character in a Norman Rockwell illustration, and without his dark glasses, she could appreciate the blue eyes that twinkled at her from under his bushy salt-and-pepper eyebrows. She could feel her reservations about Sommers melting away and she decided to eliminate all the chit-chat—not mention any of the occasions she'd seen him before.

"I hope you can help me, Chief Sommers." Linnell smiled prettily, then thrust the newspapers toward the chief. "Who, may I ask, are these *reliable sources*? Can you tell me?"

"Ms. Clare, I sure do wish I could tell you that." Sommers voice rang with sincerity. "By the way, before we go any further, I want you to know I had nothing to do with any of those crazy stories about you in the paper. And so far as I can gather, neither did anyone in my department. In fact, that's why I called your office—to assure you of that. Sometimes I have to wonder about those guys over there at the Highridge News. Seems like these days they're all too willing to stir things up just so they can have something to report."

Holding the newspaper at arm's length with one hand, Sommers leaned back in his chair and scratched the back of his head with a thick thumbnail. "In fact, I'd like to get acquainted with this reliable source myself. The department's hit a brick wall on this one. Seems as if California's determined to stay on the cutting edge when it comes to protecting the confidentiality of news sources. Reliable source? Hell, it's for sure *I'll* never know who it is and the newspaper has a squadron of lawyers who are damned and determined to make sure that I never will. But, see here, I'm still very interested in anything you have to say about the Baron case."

A dead end, right off the bat, thought Linnell.

Overcome by equal measures of relief and disappointment, she leaned forward to rest her left arm on Sommers' desk and slowly unfolded the yellow sheet where she had outlined her thoughts just a few days before. When she looked up to speak, it was as if to a different man. Chief Sommers eyes were blue saucers and he was staring at her as if he'd been stabbed and struck dumb. She wondered if she ought to continue. Was he having a seizure? Then, just as suddenly, Sommers coughed and patted his generous mouth with a plaid handkerchief and then he was back to normal again.

"Chief Sommers, are you okay?" Linnell was genuinely concerned.

"It's nothing. Just the coffee—pretty awful, I guess."

Linnell thought she'd better press on: "From what I've heard, this doesn't seem to be a crime of passion—does it?" She was curious about that. As far as she knew, Elsie hadn't been living a double life, but one could never tell.

"Oh no! It appears to be quite the opposite." Sommers replied somberly, but his voice was uneasy.

"I'd assumed as much." Linnell felt awkward. She sat quietly, examining her outline, which listed the names of the players and their possible motives and relationships—and then she showed it to Sommers, twice mentioning that she had been wondering how Buster Hosterman fit into the picture since she had found his business card among her late husband's personal effects. She also pointed out that everyone knew that Hosterman had interfered with the police investigation at the club.

Sommers looked at her, startled, and exclaimed: "What's that you say? He interfered? How so?"

Linnell described what she'd learned about Hosterman. The Chief's reactions to her comments about Hosterman convinced her that he hadn't known about Hosterman's meddling. Encouraged by the fact that Sommers made no attempt to rise to Hosterman's defense, Linnell described how certain unpleasant rumors had been started about the "Cs," and then she recounted how the "Cs" had traced the rumors back to a member of the club's board of directors whose errors involving the identities of the "Cs" had led him to spread gossip about them which in turn caused him to become the butt of their taunts. Linnell reached in her purse and pulled out her photograph of the four women.

"See? We really do look alike."

"Yeah. You really do. You mind if I keep this?" Sommers asked.

"It's yours." Linnell watched Sommers eyes feasting hungrily on the photograph. Sommers placed the photograph on his desk, and then tearing off a fresh sheet of paper, he opened his file and took notes while Linnell described the peculiar events of the previous two weeks.

Linnell thought he seemed very interested because he kept her for over an hour, taking copious notes about the personalities involved: Willy Ivener and his amoral nature and paranoid habits; Harold Dolphe's fascination with her; Buster Hosterman and his activities at the club and how he and Bear had spread lies about her being a witness against Ivener at his forthcoming trial; Bear transferring their money to Canada and the unidentified woman who had accessed the numbered bank account; her belated discovery that Bear was mentally ill and nearing the edge of a nervous breakdown and her speculations about how this might explain why he'd turned to drugs.

Linnell watched Sommers write everything down as she spoke. The one thing that seemed to impress him the most—he was the first to mention it—was the fact that her automobile was the same as Elsie Baron's. Linnell told him that she had first seen Elsie's new Jaguar the day she'd departed on her trip, and that she had been immediately concerned about how this might someday lead to a mix up. Seeing that Sommers understood the significance of this, she described the sudden flurry of phone calls she had received around the time that Elsie was murdered.

"I remember one in particular. It was a man with an accent. I know he was black and from somewhere in the Caribbean, maybe Haiti." Linnell said.

"Did you record the call? A tape recording would be invaluable!"

"No, I'm afraid I didn't. But the reason I kept a log of these calls," she hastened to explain because now she felt foolish, "was because I had been receiving so many hang-up calls over the past several months. To make a long story short, I now have proof that most of these calls were being made by my husband. But, not all of them . . . I'll get to this in a minute. But as far as my husband is concerned and maybe it was a symptom of his illness—just as soon as he got me on the line, he would listen to me saying hello and then he'd hang up without speaking. And then, all of the sudden, the calls changed."

"Changed? How so?" Sommers asked.

"The hang-up calls continued after Bear's suicide, and then, for the first time, the caller made voice contact with me. That's how I know it was a man. I'm sure he's from the Caribbean."

"I'm not sure I get the connection here. What does this have to do with the Baron case?"

"Don't you see? The last person to be seen with Elsie was a black man. I know that at least *two* different men were cat-calling me. One of them was my husband, the other was, well . . . someone else. Maybe the murderer."

There. She'd said it aloud to another person.

"Ah. Now I see. You mean—the murderer—he was keeping track of your whereabouts . . . and then he stumbled upon Elsie and mistook her for you because the two of you look so alike."

"Exactly." It seemed like a plausible enough theory to her, but still, she couldn't tell from Sommers' now impassive face if this sounded reasonable to him. Maybe he was beginning to think *she* was crazy for having come up with a theory like this.

"How do you suppose the assassin would know to look for you at the Highridge Country Club?" Sommers now stared at her, his blue eyes blank.

Linnell was sure he thought she was crazy. She raised a hand as if she were about to twist her hair, then catching herself, quickly dropped it to her lap. "I don't know exactly. I have to guess he already knew something about my usual haunts and that was why he was calling me—to see where I was. Or, and this is more likely, the person who hired him was familiar with them."

Sommers suddenly stopped writing. "Did your husband, Bear, did he do any sailing?

"Sailing? No. He hated the water."

"Did he know you were planning to divorce him?"

"No. Not at all. What I mean to say, is contrary to that newspaper article, I hadn't been planning to divorce him, I acted on impulse . . . I just knew, when I returned from my trip, that I just couldn't live with him any longer."

"Now I hope you'll forgive me, but I need to ask you a few quick questions. I don't mean, you know . . . to embarrass you, but I have to ask if you and your husband were still having, uh . . ."

"Relations. I think that's the word. Yes. In fact, just the day I left on my trip . . ."

"That's okay, I understand," Sommers quickly cut her off. "So, you take a trip, think things over, and then you come home and presto!—you file for divorce. Yeah, I get the picture." Sommers, who had been apprising Linnell with admiration all this time, now looked embarrassed. "And then your husband, he kills himself—the same day you have him served. Hmmm. Did your decision to divorce him have anything to do with his problems with the IRS?"

Linnell wondered if Sommers was just fishing around. She'd better not lose sight of her own agenda: She'd come here to get information, and furthermore, she didn't owe him any answers about the IRS.

"No," Linnell replied. "I didn't know he had all these problems until I read the paper. He'd kept them a secret from me. It was just like I said, I just couldn't stand being married to him anymore. He was—at least as far as looks were concerned—a handsome man, but underneath it all he was terribly moody and secretive. And I need someone who isn't."

She had to avoid all discussion of the IRS and what she had discovered about Bear's skimming, because his audit was still open and she feared that loose lips on her part might trigger further activity along those lines, especially if Sommers was in the habit of passing information along to a known meddler like Hosterman. As for her discovery that Bear had been selling drugs to his "special" patients? She couldn't risk mentioning *that*. Her knowledge about such things, even though innocently acquired after Bear's death, could be too easily twisted against her, lending credence to the scurrilous insinuations that had already been published about her and her trips to tax havens.

Linnell changed the subject by mentioning that she hadn't driven her Jaguar to the club the day Elsie was kidnapped because it had been towed to the mechanic for repairs. This bit of intelligence apparently took Sommers by surprise because she saw his eyes widen and his shoulders tense. Linnell decided to tell him about Bear's close relationship with the convicted drug dealer, Davie Merino. Perhaps, she thought, this little tap in the head would send Sommers off in the right direction so he could discover Bear's unsavory side-business for himself. Sommers asked no further questions, however. He continued to write, and when he was finished, she finally asked the question that disturbed her the most:

"How was Elsie killed?" Linnell was now so convinced that Elsie had been killed by mistake that she squirmed at the thought of hearing the answer. Why had she asked? She really didn't want to know.

To her great relief, Sommers replied that he couldn't reveal this information. Perhaps he'd let her know after the case was solved. Then he laid out his notes in front of him, folded his hands and told her that he would sum things up for her, given the information he could share: "Yes, Elsie had most likely been the victim of hired killers."

He also told her—and Linnell listened keenly to this—that it was entirely possible that Linnell could very well have been the intended victim. Linnell's entire body flushed when she heard him say this. At least Sommers didn't think she was crazy. On the other hand, this wasn't exactly the kind of news she wanted to hear.

"However," Chief Sommers quickly interjected, "there's *no* hard evidence of this. If only you had made a tape recording of this black man's voice, or had some hard evidence that your husband was in touch with any of these other characters—say, for example, this Ivener guy—that would certainly firm things up. Then we'd have something to go on. But, you don't . . . and neither do we. That's the big problem here—there's no hard evidence. But I have to admit, there sure seems to be a lot of interesting things going on here." Sommers' thick fingers drummed on his notes.

"What if I'm still being stalked? What can be done to protect me?"

"I'm afraid our hands are tied until a crime is committed. All you can do is keep your eyes open and be sure to keep good records of what's happening to you. And you can always call me if you've got real trouble."

Linnell watched him with mixed emotions as Sommers listed the names of the people they had discussed: Mark-Bear-Doc-Clarichevik-Clare; William "Willy" E. Ivener; Buster Hosterman; Harold "the Hyena" Dolphe; and finally, Davie Merino, the drug dealer with all his contacts in San Quentin. Sommers specifically noted that all of them would most likely have known that she had a white Jaguar sedan.

Well, thought Linnell, it's always best to leave them while they're still begging for more. She lifted her wrist to look at her watch and again noticed the way Sommers stared. Yes, her resemblance to Elsie was uncanny; she knew that. She yawned discreetly behind her hand. It was already 4:30 p.m.—she had been with Sommers for over an hour and now she was drained.

"Just a few more quick questions and then I think I've got it," said Chief Sommers.

Linnell stiffened.

"Tell me, were you and Elsie real close?"

"Very close," Linnell replied. She was about to mention that the watch she was wearing once belonged to Elsie when Chief Sommers interrupted.

"I mean, she *confided* in you?"

Linnell was deeply disappointed. She hadn't obtained any more information, and basically, it looked like she was back to square one. She looked at him wearily, hoping he'd take a hint that she'd had enough. She was immediately rewarded: Sommers seemed to be pushing his chair away from his desk. Linnell stood up and collected her material to let him know she was leaving.

"She was one of my best friends. And thanks for your time," Linnell replied.

"Thank you for coming by, Ms. Clare," Sommers said, standing up. "We'll keep in touch."

Linnell left, disappointed. She was half-way home when she remembered the book. André Gide. Lafcadio's Adventures. Linnell turned around and headed for the library.

◆❖◆

Sommers swung around in his chair to watch Linnell as she pulled out of the parking lot. She hadn't answered his question about Elsie confiding in her. Why not? Did that mean that she knew? Lawyers! They were the absolute shits. You could never tell what they really were after.

And God! What a shock. He'd thought he was going to stroke out when he saw that gold watch. How'd she get her hands on it? Had to have been from that damn fool, Larry. He'd like to know why, but he couldn't ask. It might open up a Pandora's box if anyone ever began to suspect that he had a personal reason for wanting to know. He should've tried harder to get it lost in the evidence room. He'd thought about that. He'd even thought about switching it for something less valuable. But too late—it had already been too carefully detailed by his officers. Cost him two month's salary, too. He'd had it customized for his sweetie, thank goodness not around here, to remind her of their first afternoon together. All those years of denying himself—exercising, keeping himself fit and in shape—had led to her teasing him, throwing her arms around his neck and climbing all over him as if he were a tree. Later she'd called him an old-fashioned sentimentalist, but not an old man. And then his gift to her had been turned over to that damn Baron idiot.

As for Linnell . . . "L.C." . . . His sweetie was right—the "Cs" looked the same. Especially in that photo—it really captured their similarities. But he'd had one of them for himself, so he knew the difference. But still, it was spooky how much they resembled each other. Damned spooky. So now the big Sixty-four Dollar Question was whether L.C. knew. Was there any way for her to guess? Had Elsie told? That day, Monday, when he was out on the road, scouting for Elsie, and he had mistaken the lawyer's car for his sweetie's—had L.C. attached any significance to this? And today, the way she flaunted his watch like that, when she was questioning him—*This doesn't seem to be a crime of passion—does it?* What was she trying to do? Torment him? Play games with his head?

Yet, maybe not. L.C. seemed a straight arrow, the sort who would speak her mind, just like Elsie said. On the other hand, his sweetie had been naive about a lot of things, especially about that husband of hers. Too bad the asshole had such a tight alibi. He'd looked into that first. He had also looked into the Baron telephone records to see if Larry had been making any unusual telephone calls, but he'd found zip there, too. Sommers wondered what to do next. How should he handle L.C.? Should he ask her to go for a sail—maybe cruise across the bay and have a quiet dinner in Sausalito? This would give him a chance to find out what she really was thinking.

Sommers pondered the idea and then decided against it. First, it was too soon after her husband's death, and second, L.C. was a bit too sharp. Maybe it would be best to just leave her alone. Avoid her. He'd better concentrate on what was best for himself. Right now L.C. had it in mind that she could have been the intended victim. This was a very good thing; so he'd better not do anything to discourage her from this train of thought because it would sure keep her mind off of him.

Sommers sighed dejectedly. Well, wouldn't you just know it! The first murder in Highridge in fifty years and it turns into a hot potato, worse yet, one he could never afford to pass on. And he'd better watch his step, too, because if he didn't, he'd be the next one to star in the headlines of that filthy Highridge rag. He could just see the headlines now: *"POLICE CHIEF IN LOVE-NEST WITH MURDERED HOUSEWIFE!"*

HIGHRIDGE **Tuesday - March 12, 1974**

By 5:00 p.m., Buster Hosterman was finished with the hearing on the annoying battery case—the one filed by the wife of one of his boys. Like usual, the bored judge had simply let him carry on as if he were the witness, so it had been the usual exchange: First he stood up and told his usual lies about how the wife had provoked her husband; then the wife had jumped up to call him a dirty liar; then he'd huffed and puffed as to how *he* was an officer of the court who had *sworn* to uphold the law—and then the judge had ruled in his favor. Like usual. Having won another easy battle, Buster now strutted through police headquarters with his usual proprietary air, on his way to his car, which he always parked next to the squad cars. Saved him from having to walk clear around the block with the rest of the jerks in the briefcase brigade.

Buster looked in on Chief Sommers' office and wasn't the least bit surprised to see the man beckoning him to come on in. As soon as he entered, Buster chose the chair with the padded arm rests, sat down, and then tried to guess what sort of mood the Chief was in. Today, for some reason, he couldn't read him.

"Well, Buster, you sure look like you've had yourself a good day. I just want to run something by you, see what you think. This has to do with the Baron case and maybe the late Dr. Mark Clare as well. I just spent an hour with Mrs. Clare."

"Oh yeah. That's "L.C."—that's what they call her around here."

Like most lawyers, Buster could read upside-down. He leaned forward slightly and tried to read Sommers' notes, but the chief kept pushing his papers around and moving his hand to cover them up.

"She's come up with a plausible theory. She thinks it was a professional hit and that it could've been aimed at her. As you might have noticed already, "L.C." and "Elsie" sound exactly the same, and they do look alike, so maybe somebody got 'em mixed up and kidnapped the wrong woman. You ever do that? Get 'em mixed up?"

Buster didn't know if this was a question that had a right answer. He took a stab at it. "Uh. Sure. I guess a lotta people did."

"Who knew that both of them drove white Jaguar sedans?"

Buster was alarmed. Shit! He was slipping! This was the first time he'd paid any attention to the cars. And that itinerary of L.C.'s movements that Bear had given him . . . *the itinerary that his office had typed up!* It would be just as useful to a kidnapper as a process server!

"Well?" Sommers demanded.

Buster knew he had to say something. "I guess the whole damn club must've known." Had Bear known that the cars were exactly the same? Could it be that Bear had been playing him for a fool from the very beginning? This same thought had crossed his mind once before; which was why he'd persuaded his boys to stop nosing around at the country club. You never could tell what they might have picked up if they had been allowed to hang around any longer. But if, as he had all along suspected, Bear had hired hit-men to do L.C., then he had to be mighty careful not to get sucked into this mess; he sure didn't want to end up being charged as an accessory. Hell! He was Buster T. Hosterman, just a plain country lawyer, not some cold-blooded killer.

"You ever say anything to anyone about Mrs. Clare testifying against this Ivener guy?"

Buster gave Chief Sommers a boyish duck of the head and then gazed up at him with a practiced look of wide-eyed innocence. If he'd had a forelock to tug, he would have done that, too. "Me? Hell, *no!* All I know about this Ivener fella is what I been readin' in the papers."

"I hear you're acquainted with the Clares. That true?"

Buster wondered if Sommers was questioning him and he could feel his armpits getting sticky. He quickly replied, "You wasted your time with L.C.? Come *on*, everyone knows what she is—she's a *nut* case! Here. I wanna show you something." Buster reached in his jacket and pulled out a packet of photographs and handed it to the Chief. "Those pictures were taken on her last trip, you know, to that little Caribbean tax haven. The Cayman Islands. The IRS is investigating all them thieving pirates right now. It's been in all the papers." Buster pointed to a photograph. "Okay, look! Here she is—boozing it up with this real young fella. And just have a look at her, there—near bare-assed on the beach! Makin' out with all those half-naked bucks in the water—and look, here she is again! All tangled up with this huge black dude. Here's the best—see that? She's goin' topless on her bedroom balcony. You can see with your own eyes what she's up to! Pictures don't lie."

Buster saw no reaction from Sommers. This was not a good sign.

"Great tits. I can say that much for her." Buster sniggered.

"Yeah. Okay. So how'd you get your hands on these?"

"At the club. They were floatin' around and I happened to snag them."

Buster looked at Chief Sommers, who was staring at him with his flat blue eyes. Now he was sure he was being questioned. "Bear, I mean Doc, Dr. Clare—he was fed up with all her fooling around. He told me he was going to dump her and get on with his life. He said he'd already filed the papers, done it all by himself. So, you wanna know what I think? I'll tell you, Chief—she's a *two*-timer, an' *I* wouldn't believe one word she said."

Buster knew he was talking too fast, but he couldn't afford to let anyone get the idea that Bear had been his client. Not only would it get him drawn into this case, it might get back to L.C. and then she might start asking the sort of questions that would reveal his hand in getting her offices searched, not to mention all the strings he'd pulled to get that reporter to slap her down. Things could snowball and then maybe she'd find out about all that cash Bear had paid him—

and then for sure there'd be some tax problems with that nice wad, not to mention all the problems L.C. could stir up for him with the State Bar and the IRS.

Buster wondered what might have happened to him if he had not filed Bear's divorce papers. Bear was plenty cunning all right, but not as smart as he thought, because Bear hadn't noticed that his lawyer's name had been left off his divorce papers. So, after Bear signed and handed them over to him, he, Buster Hosterman, had simply added the words "in propria persona" right underneath Bear's signature to make it look like he had no lawyer and was representing himself. And then, that Saturday, just as soon as Bear left his office, he had mailed the papers—he'd enclosed them in Bear's nicely engraved envelope—to the court clerk's office so they could be filed first thing Monday morning. Hell, all he'd had in mind was to get the show on the road, but now it was beginning to look like he had accidentally saved his own ass.

Chief Sommers' face slowly settled into a resigned expression. "No kidding. You say *he* was planning to divorce L.C.? And then she finds out and gets her papers served on him first. Is that it?"

"It sure *looks* like it happened that way." Buster hoped his voice didn't sound anxious.

Buster watched helplessly as Chief Sommers set the photographs down on this notes.

"You don't mind if I keep these, do you?" Chief Sommers said in a way that gave Buster no choice. "And another thing. I want you to keep that damn mouth of yours shut about what we've been talking about here. And I don't want you to go interfering with this investigation. You hear?"

Buster almost saluted. "Yessir!"

"Oh yeah, there's something else I want to discuss now that you're here. I understand you're still the lawyer for the Highridge Country Club. That right?"

"Right."

"Then tell me something Hosterman, why did you have my investigators kicked off the premises? Can you tell me why in hell you did something as stupid as that?"

Buster again opened his eyes very wide and pulled another innocent face, the way Bear used to do with him.

"Oh *hell*, Chief." His voice slid smoothly into the whine he used when he was signaling the judge to cut him some slack. "You *know* I take my orders from the board of directors. I didn't have a choice. They're paying me to protect their interests."

"Well, we might go out there again, and next time I don't want any trouble."

"Sure, Chief. I'll be glad to take it up with the directors. Your boys won't have any more problems if I have my way."

"And Buster . . . I hope I'm not gonna be hearing anything more about you and your doings."

Buster remained silent but nodded his head. He felt more confident now. If word ever got out about the little favor he'd arranged for his pal on the board of directors, then he would just have to swear under oath that he'd had absolutely nothing to do with Sgt. Blaine hauling that broad in for questioning. What was her name? He was always getting them mixed up.

"And there's something else I want you to do for *me*."

"Whatever you say, Chief."

"Get yourself a good pair of track shoes. You're going to need 'em, because I don't want to see you *or* your boots scooting through my building anymore. Hear me? Go park on the street like everyone else." Sommers' eyebrows were now bristling; he glared furiously at Buster, then motioned for him to get out.

◆❖◆

Chief Sommers was satisfied to see Buster shrink and creep out. He'd handled him fine. The old cocksucker wouldn't be nosing around *this* case anymore and besides, he never did like the way the man strutted around the station. You'd think he owned the place. Well, not any more. Sommers jotted orders for the desk sergeant to keep Buster clear of the building and out of the parking lot, then he waited until he saw Buster climbing into his car before opening the Baron file. He didn't care much for tattle-tales who started rumors about somebody else being a snitch—especially if the tattle-tale was already the biggest snitch in the county. In large letters, Sommers added another name to his list of suspects: *"B. Hosterman—Mark Clare D.D.S./ L.C. theory."*

There was just one more thing he had to do before he was through for the day. Picking up his private line to the records division, he asked Marsha, the clerk, to take a peek at the files to see if by any chance a Dr. Mark Clare had filed for divorce. Draining the last drop of his cold cup of coffee, he waited for Marsha to give him the word.

A few seconds later, Marsha had an answer. "Yes, Chief. The papers are here in the files. Dr. Clare filed for divorce—his papers came in here by mail. Let's see. They arrived here last Monday, But he didn't request service on Mrs. Clare. Probably because he was representing himself and didn't know how to go about it."

"Thanks Marsha. That's all I need to know." He was disappointed—but he was still sure that Buster was lying about something, just not about that.

Sommers knew he was going to have a hard time adjusting. His affair with Elsie was the best thing that had happened to him in years—and now she was gone. It was a nightmare. He didn't want to think about how she had met her end. And the only thing he had left of her was this case. No, that no longer was true. At least now he had a photograph of her that he could bear to look at. Sommers picked up the photograph of the four women. They certainly did look a whole lot alike—sure, maybe to a stranger they looked like dead ringers—but as far as *he* was concerned, there was only one Elsie. He did not want to be disrespectful to the memory of that fine person who had once been his wife—but Elsie was the most wonderful woman he'd ever had in his life. Chief Sommers' large fingers gently stroked the file, then he folded his hands behind his head and leaned far back in his chair.

It's hard to tell who or what to believe. It's like climbing in bed with a bunch of weasels. But I know old Buster. He's sure acting guilty about something. Humph . . . carrying L.C.'s pictures around like a dirty old man! I don't believe a word he said about finding them floating around at the club. I think Doc Clare had a detective on her case and then paid him to sneak the photos around to all the Family Court judges. I guess it's this thing Buster has about women—and it's for damn sure he doesn't care much for lady-lawyers!

And L.C.? What about her? Her reasoning's good, at least on the surface. But it's kind of funny she didn't say anything about her husband filing for divorce. Maybe she didn't know. Or maybe they were in a race for the courthouse and he pulled the plug on himself when he saw she'd beaten him to the punch. After losing all that money this was probably the last straw. Damn it all anyway, but L.C.'s theory sure would make a whole lot more sense if her old man had killed himself after Elsie was murdered. See, if a guy's going to put up the dough for some hit-men to snuff his old lady, then you just know he'd want to stick around long enough to see that they did the job right. But here, L.C.'s old man goes and kills himself before the kidnapping ever took place. It just makes no sense.

And all those unexplained telephone calls to L.C.? That newspaper article probably brought them on, so it could be most anyone; could even be one of the guys in those photos. If I were still young, and a friendly, sexy gal like L.C. just happened along and smiled at me, I'd think about calling her, too. As for that tax guy, Ivener? It's like L.C. says—he just doesn't seem to have a real motive for wanting her dead. And besides, from what she just told me about Bear hating Ivener's guts, there couldn't have been any connection between the two gents..

He sat for a little while longer, trying to sort out the motives of all of the players, but he only ended up with a bad feeling, deep in his gut, that the Baron case might be the one that would never be solved. Feeling even more distraught, Sommers studied the photograph of L.C. and the big black man who stood next to her with his arm around her shoulders. It didn't look to him like they were fooling around, at least not with each other. The man's face held a fatherly expression. It looked like they were just hanging out, kidding around and cleaning fish. Just *who* did old Buster think he was kidding?

Sommers held the photograph up to the light—he could see all the cases of booze and fishing nets and dirty buckets piled in the background. Looked like a typical bait house to him. He'd just seen L.C. up close and personal, and even though it was obvious that she had a wild streak or two, it was ridiculous to think she was the kind of gal who would have to sneak around in some stinking fish house to get herself laid. He'd bet dollars to donuts that Dr. Clare had hired some kind of weird dick to prowl around on that little island out there and that the weasel had tried to earn his keep by making it look like he'd gotten the goods on her. It was no secret—plenty of unlicensed investigators pulled stunts like that to guarantee getting paid. And even if she *was* screwing around. So what? She was a good looking dame, married to a useless drug addict. He wouldn't blame her a bit . . .

Sommers gathered up all the photographs and attached all but two of them to the notes of his meeting with Mrs. Clare, then he folded everything into the file.

Since homicide files were the sort that remained open until the case was solved, he thought it would be best to keep that photo of L.C. on her balcony locked up in his desk, just to make sure it wouldn't accidentally go floating around. And the other one—the one of Elsie surrounded by her friends—this he carefully tucked away in his wallet.

SAN FRANCISCO **Tuesday evening - March 12, 1974**

Jordan had spent all day Tuesday submitting applications to the accounting firms on his list. The ones with high-flying international divisions. So far nothing has changed his mind—he still felt he'd done the right thing by calling the newspaper, then giving Rizzo his resignation. Linnell Clare might have been off limits to him—she still was as far as the Special Services Division was concerned—but he hoped that by leaving the service he would keep Rizzo's respect. And maybe his friendship, too. Rizzo hadn't said anything, but Jordan sensed Rizzo had known something had been going on. Anyway, now it was over and all he wanted to do was to be alone so he could recover from his exhausting three days with Suzanne. Saturday, Sunday and Monday with an insatiable whirlwind. He was spent.

Suzanne, twenty-three, was a nurse at San Francisco General Hospital and he'd been seeing her only for a couple of months and certainly not exclusively. But after three days with her he could already see those small warning signs—that she hoped to be "the only one"—even though he had always made it clear that there were and would always be others. In fact, he had been very careful, as usual, not to say anything to get her to thinking there would ever be anything here that was going anywhere. This had always been okay with Suzanne. She would even say so. In fact, she had just said so. But still, he'd better be careful. "She's a good kid," he thought. He was definitely not in love with her and he was fairly certain she wasn't in love with him.

But there was one thing he now knew for sure: Suzanne sure loved a good romp in the sack. Early Saturday morning, she'd surprised him by pulling up to his dump in her red Corvette to tell him that she just wanted to get out there into the great outdoors and would he come along? For protection. Just three days, her treat, she'd said. And she'd drive. He'd agreed. She wanted to use him? Fine. That was okay. He had actually hoped that a small diversion with the energetic Suzanne would force him to get on with his life. They would use each other, which was not such a bad thing just so long as they both understood.

Jordan stepped out of his loafers and padded over to his answering machine to check his calls. He had four from Mary Jo, two from a Kim whom he didn't know, and already a new call from Suzanne. She must have called while he was out picking up the evening paper. Jordan shrugged, then went to the fridge to get himself a beer. Beer seemed to go with a dump like this. The flat had come furnished with Salvation Army junk and even though his landlord had assured him that everything had been cleaned, he always felt dirty as soon as he sat in his chair. Now, whenever his thoughts turned to the beach, and the wind, and the starlit skies of the Caribbean, it felt even dirtier. He had to find a new place, and soon, because he knew he couldn't take it here much longer.

He was feeling sorry for himself. Really down. He kept thinking about Linnell and how she'd pushed him away and then how she had disappeared on him without saying good bye. He'd even checked at the front desk to see if she might possibly have left him a note. There had been nothing. Well, if dumping him was what she really wanted to do, she couldn't have done a better job. No cruel lingering withdrawals, just one sharp cut and he was out of her life. Right? So what difference did anything make? He might as well screw his brains out.

How this had happened was really all Suzanne's doing. In fact, it now looked like she'd had it all planned in advance because as soon as they started driving north for their weekend getaway, she got this bright idea about visiting the baths at Calistoga. And before he could even say whoa!, there they were, planted together in a tub of warm mud and he was having an experience as different as anything you could imagine from what he'd been doing in Cayman.

"Baby, you don't have to worry about *me*," she'd crooned. "I know what to do—I'm a *nurse* for crissakes." So he'd decided it would be okay just to let nature take its course and that was the only reason why things had happened the way they did. Right now, however, when he thought about it, he felt disappointed in himself—he sure hoped he hadn't made a foolish mistake.

Jordan settled down in front of his old television set and clicked through the channels. He was even more restless than before, and despite everything he'd just done, Linnell was still there, keeping him company in his head. He adjusted the color. A dull Tuesday night: It was either the Cleavers, with this chirpy doll in her ruffled apron having orgasms over those double-fudge cookies she always baked, or else it was Watergate, and he couldn't stand anything more about Nixon and those cruddy damn plumbers. Jordan picked up his paper. He knew what he wanted. He wanted to read something more about the Clares. But there was nothing more about them; now it was only Watergate, kidnappings, pot busts, bank robberies, and another murder—this time it was a beautiful blonde who had been snatched from the Highridge Country Club this past weekend.

The Highridge Country Club?

Jordan's interest was piqued. Linnell was a member. She'd told him all about the club. He read on: Elsie Baron, the wife of Lawrence Baron, had been kidnapped from the club early Friday evening, March 8, 1974, and her body was found Sunday afternoon, in the trunk of her white Jaguar sedan. The article described her clothing as a white tennis dress and a new navy-blue warm-up jacket which she'd just purchased from the club's gift shop. She had not been molested, the paper was quick to report. The immediate survivors were listed as her husband and their seven year old son. The article continued on the back page and when Jordan turned over the paper the victim's photograph leaped up at him from the page. The young woman was a dead-ringer for Linnell! Wide-set, inquisitive eyes. Blonde hair falling in soft waves around her face—that was how Linnell wore her hair. And the navy blue warm-up jacket—why, Linnell had one just like it! Jordan held the paper under the lamp. Same insignia on the pocket. Exactly. In fact, Linnell had worn this very same jacket at the beach bar, the day of the bank failure.

Jordan read and re-read the article. It speculated that the kidnapper was the slender, middle-aged black man who had been seen driving Mrs. Baron away from the club in her new Jaguar sedan. Several witnesses had also come forward to say that they had seen the suspect at the club—a soft-spoken, well-dressed black man. They thought he might have been inside the bar, making inquiries about the victim. Jordan suddenly recalled Linnell's conversation about her name when they first walked together on the beach. He stared at the newspaper, his lips moving slightly as he focused on the sound of their names: *Elsie Baron; Elsie; L.C. Clare . . . L.C. Clare with a husband called Bear.*

The two women had so much in common. The same looks—this was obvious. The same club. Similar sounding names. And they both played tennis. Jordan wondered if the victim might have been one of the women Linnell had mentioned. Part of a clique called the *Four Cs.* He could remember this because she'd joked about them. And the Baron boy was the same age as Benjy. Another odd coincidence. Now he could remember even more: Linnell had mentioned something in passing about how all her friends looked alike and how their names made a rhyme like the one he was thinking of now: *Elsie Baron . . . L.C. Clare with a husband called Bear.*

Jordan reviewed in his mind all the data gathered by the Special Services Division—data that would be known only to the agency. First, there was Harold Dolphe—his behavior had been unusual, to say the least. According to Edgardo, he had been spying on Linnell, even going so far as sneak into her room. Then there had been his mention of photographs and his telephone call to Dr. Clare to set up a meeting with Ivener. There were also all those strange telephone calls that Linnell had suddenly begun to receive—they were all there on the IRS tapes—and one of these calls had come from someone who sounded an awful lot like a soft-spoken black man. He had called her *pretty L.C.* And there was also that call to Dr. Clare from a man who said he was calling on behalf of The Wei. Whoever it was, his voice was right there, on the IRS tapes. Add to all this the fact that Linnell had prepared a trust that would take effect only on her death—a trust that excluded her husband. And then, later, there was the will Linnell had prepared—a will that would cut her husband out of the Phoenix Corporation—he had learned about this on the telephone tap. All of this had led him to thinking that she was getting herself prepared for possible trouble with her husband.

That's right! he thought. The Phoenix Corporation—the 1.4 million dollars! Jordan wanted to kick himself. Outside of Linnell, and Bear—who was now dead—and Buster Hosterman—who couldn't tell—*he* was the only one who knew about the Phoenix Corporation, because he was the one—the *only* one—who had reviewed the tapes of Bear's conversation with Buster. There was also that highly suspect conversation between Bear and Buster, followed by Bear's near hysterical call to Ivener's office about bowing out of some kind of training program at The Wei. If he remembered right, all this stuff was on the same tape! Jordan's stomach churned. He had hidden the tape in the files—in all probability, it was now lost—and there was no way for him to get back into the IRS archives to set things right.

As far as he was concerned, all of these fragments seemed to fit into only one picture. Problem was, he couldn't get it into focus. And no matter what Rizzo said, it sure sounded to him as if Bear and Buster were skirting around a subject that both men knew better than to mention directly. He didn't care what

Rizzo thought, it *still* sounded to him as if Bear had murder on his mind. And the victim's body—stuffed in the trunk of her car like that—it sure looked to him like a professional hit. A professional hit that had gone awry. So the big question was whether or not the hit-man screwed up. Had he? Could it be that he was really after Linnell? He wondered how crazy he'd sound if he told anyone what he was thinking.

What's the use? thought Jordan. Today, and for what seemed like the millionth time, he was still asking all the same questions and getting the same old answers: Would Linnell really want to have anything to do with an unemployed bean counter? Seven years her junior? Worst of all, one who had been spying on her for the IRS? Not a director on any bank's board of directors, but a person who seldom if ever even visited a bank because he had so little money. He was a man who had nothing to offer except himself. And she was a woman who could have any man she wanted.

So, the answer was no. Not a chance. A smart woman like Linnell would most likely take him for a schemer. A juvenile schemer, one who'd learned all these secrets about her while spying on her for the IRS and who was now going after her for all that money she had stashed in the Phoenix Corporation. That's what she'd think. See? No matter what he did, whether he leveled or not, he'd still come away looking like a stinking rat! She'd *never* trust him. Besides, the whole thing between them had probably been, for her, nothing more than a game. He'd better not forget—in fact, he'd been warned—playing games was what mavens did best.

But it had been real enough for him. He couldn't stop thinking about her. And now he wouldn't be hearing her voice any more, either, not even on tape, because he had left the service. So what should he do? Even if she didn't want him, he still wanted to do the right thing. That was part of the problem. What *was* the right thing? Should he go to the police? Tell them what he suspected? Jordan wrestled with the idea while he changed into his warm-ups.

A chilling thought suddenly crossed his mind: what if that 1.4 million dollars he'd just learned about had something to do with Bear and the money he'd skimmed? Could this be possible? Could it be that Linnell had out-gamed them all? Jordan suddenly felt hot and cold all at once. He told himself no, not Linnell. Then he began to argue with himself: Yes, she was clever enough to have pulled such a stunt—but would she? Anything was possible under the sun.

On the other hand, his heart told him that even if she could, she most likely wouldn't. Not something like that. But still? He couldn't forget that she was one of those haven mavens . . . so how could he ever be sure? How could he discover the truth about the Phoenix Corporation? Now he just had to know, and there was nothing he could do—he couldn't very well call and order her to spill the beans. And by resigning from the Intelligence Division he'd cut himself off from all of his investigative tools.

Fighting against the thin snake of pain and suspicion that had slithered into his imagination, Jordan stood up and began to pace. So, what should he do? Should he go to the police? Should he leak all the information he'd learned through listening to the tapes?

If I leaked it would blow the whole Haven Maven operation. And they'd blame Rizzo and he'd end up taking the rap for me because he was my sponsor. I can't screw him like that . . . not after he went to bat for me so I could have the offshore assignment. Besides, if I told the cops what I knew, then it would have to come out that Linnell and I were together and then she'd be tarred and feathered all over again—I can just see that old bastard Buster, he'd be the first one to destroy her reputation. Besides, I can't get at the tapes and without them I don't have any hard evidence, so the cops would think I was nuts, especially if I showed up empty handed, babbling about all my theories. I know I'd risk everything if Linnell were in any kind of danger. But she's not—because, it's like Rizzo said: her old man is dead. Besides, there's a chance that maybe I've remembered things wrong, so this whole thing might really be nothing more than a complicated fantasy I've cooked up in my head because I still want Linnell to see me as some kind of white knight . . .

There, now that he'd thought it through, everything really did sound rather ridiculous. He also felt a slight sense of relief because he'd at least made a decision. Well, thought Jordan, the good thing about this was the fact that Linnell was still okay, and so long as she was, maybe he'd get a chance to see her again. There was hope. Jordan dialed her number, and then remembering just in time that her lines were still tapped, he quickly cut off the call. He suddenly felt very sad. Damn the Phoenix corporation, thought Jordan. Why did *he* have to be the one to know about it?

POWER

HIGHRIDGE **Friday evening - August 9, 1974**

Linnell sat in front of her new large-screen color television and fiddled with the buttons, hoping to find a channel with something more besides Watergate and half-listening to the commentators' remarks about how Nixon had used the IRS to pursue his enemies. This led her back to her usual question: Why hadn't the IRS followed up on Bear's audit? It really was odd, but it seemed as if they'd actually dropped it. Same for Chief Sommers. He hadn't gotten back to her, either. Well, she certainly wasn't about to remind any of them to keep in touch. Actually, she was rather glad that Sommers hadn't called her again, especially after what she had gathered from her later reading of the book, the one she had discovered shortly before her departure to the Cayman Islands. She'd almost forgotten about it, but for some reason, immediately after her long session with Sommers, she had remembered Lafcadio and her curiosity about his adventures, so she had headed over to the library to check out the book. And to tell the truth, had she read it beforehand, she wouldn't have bothered to meet with the Chief because, after studying Gide's astute portrayal of the motiveless crime, she had ended up convinced that the same thing had happened to Elsie. Poor Elsie, just like Lafcadio's *camel*—Gide's character regarded his randomly selected sacrifice in this cavalier manner—she had simply had the horrific misfortune of crossing paths with some evil-doers possessed of the same mad narcissism as Gide's twisted murderer.

So, after stripping the situation of all of the coincidences she had once thought so significant, she was finally able to view the matter in a colder yet far brighter light: Elsie had not been molested; nor had she been robbed; there had been no attempts to collect any ransom, and as everyone knew, Elsie had never been involved in anything the least bit dangerous or illegal. By eliminating all those freakish coincidences involving herself, she could only conclude that the slaying was not the result of a "motive" somehow missing its target. No, Elsie's murder was clearly one of those unspeakable motiveless crimes. Which also explained why the police hadn't made any headway. She would have to wait and see, of course, but right now she was willing to bet that they never would.

So, yes, in one sense—if one thought along supernatural lines, if one could imagine time being run in reverse so that "cause-and-effect" was forced to stand on its head—Gide's book had indeed been an answer; just not to any question that pertained to herself. Quite incredibly, as things turned out, it had been Elsie, or rather, and to put it more bluntly, Elsie's death—not her own—that had always been the big question.

Yes, it had to be that all those thoughts in her head about Mama N'dobah's magic had skewed her perception and this explained why her imagination took off on such wild flights of fancy. Her, the intended victim? Really! This now sounded so silly! So it was an altogether good thing that Sommers had not kept in touch because it would have been near impossible for her to explain, especially to a man like him, all the mental gymnastics that had led her to getting things so wrong. In fact, now that she could think about the entire situation more coolly, like a good lawyer should, she had even come up with a corollary to her original maxim: *If miracles are simply physics unexplained . . . then it surely follows that coincidences are nothing more than accidents over-explained.* That sounded pretty good; it was sort of poetic. Made sense, too, thought Linnell.

Finally satisfied that she'd summed it all up as best as she ever could, Linnell decided to let it all go. In fact, she could actually feel the mystery of Elsie's murder slowly floating away into darkness, like the sand that had once drifted out of her hand. As for the IRS—the local district was happily occupied with Ivener at the moment. His trial had just begun and it looked like it would be governing the news for the next several months. And the cat-calls? They had stopped too. Though strangely enough, today, for the first time in months, there had been three. One, earlier this morning: Karen buzzed her to say that a man who refused to say who he was kept insisting that he had to talk to "Ms. Clare." But then, when Karen put the call through to her, she was greeted only by silence and then a loud click. The same thing had happened at noon, and then, just a little while ago, it had happened again here at home. The calls were annoying. Who on earth would want to do this to her?

On the other hand, she had to confess that sometimes she wondered—no, hoped—if it might be Roberto. In the past, when she more freely allowed herself to think about him, she had wept bitter tears of frustration. But then, as the days passed, she had learned how to put her feelings away. This had been near impossible at first, but now, after so many long months of steeling herself, the pain had finally begun to recede. Besides, considering the way she had practically climbed out of her skin to escape him, why on earth would he want to call *her*? So, no; it couldn't possibly be him because he had already melted into the soft dream of blue water locked away in her heart.

Linnell's hand, resting lightly on her belly, felt the stir of new life. "But this is no dream," she declared aloud. She'd had plenty of time to think about how she had broken the rules. Rules made by men for the governance of women. But she had learned—and the first inkling of this had come to her on the beach—that she had the power to change the rules instead of changing herself to fit them. After all, it was her life and she alone would be paying the price for her choices, so why not make her own rules? Besides, there was no one to stop her now. Best of all, she no longer had to appease anyone in order to get what she needed, and she would, too, because she now had her own tools: one was money—her own—and the other was knowledge.

"A woman is the final arbiter," thought Linnell. "Her thumb turns up—the world gains new life; thumb's down—and it doesn't. Rape or no, seduction or no, a knowledgeable woman will always see to it that this is so." Linnell thought about the Zulu Queen in the ladies room at O'Hare Airport and what she had said: "The power . . . Use it or lose it," the woman had warned.

"Well," said Linnell, "now I've learned how."

Linnell felt, if not entirely at peace, then at least more at rest because she had finally accepted the fact that there would always be a few mysteries in life that could never be solved. And then, with a pleasant start, she realized there was something else about herself that had changed as well: her urge to kill. It had quieted. "In fact, come to think about it, ever since Bear killed himself, it seems I haven't once thought about killing at all!" Linnell marveled. Then, just as a test, she tried to conjure up a basket of Mama N'dobah's needles, but this time all she got was a faint image of them floating high in the air on the edge of her vision. Perhaps it was all nonsense—she was sure others would no doubt tell her so if they knew—nevertheless and although she would never, ever, breathe a word of this to another soul, she was still sure in her heart that one of Mama's needles must have somehow found Bear.

The telephone suddenly shrilled. Linnell jumped in her chair and listened to it ring three more times and then stop before her answering machine could pick it up. "Okay," said Linnell, "that's it! I'm going to clear out of here if I get any more of those calls."

There was no one to hear her; Benjy was already fast asleep and Helene had gone home. Linnell inched her chair closer to her television set just as the cameraman zoomed in for a close-up of the president's face and she was momentarily distracted by the large pores in Nixon's glistening nose. Linnell leaned forward, then spoke to the screen. "I mean it. If I get *any* more of those cat-calls, I'm moving back to LA."

She had been thinking of moving her law office to Los Angeles for the past several months. Now that she no longer had to worry about money, she had begun to think about building an entirely new life for herself. Besides, she no longer felt connected to anything in Highridge. The house no longer felt like her home, the Highridge Country Club crowd was a drag, and Nancy and Karen would always be her true friends no matter where she lived. She was free! Free to do as she pleased, and she had a feeling that wherever she was, she'd do very well. And her practice was thriving. Her article on foreign foundations had just been released and she had already received two large retainers from reputable charitable organizations in New York.

Linnell scanned the pages of the Highridge News. The paper had long ago dropped all mention of Bear's suicide and Elsie's murder. The reporters, looking to a future without a Nixon to kick around, had begun to obsess about Willy and *"The Tax Trial of the Century."* Linnell read a recap of the government's case and saw that half the charges had already been dropped, and that Willy, predictably enough, was painting himself as the victim of selective prosecution—arguing that the government had charged him with tax fraud in order to persecute him for his political beliefs. She had to laugh. The rabid old anarchist was now doing his best to obscure the issues by posing this time as a staunch socialist. He had even rounded up some loud demonstrators to make rude noises and wave their red flags in front of the court house. This was all just so *him.*

Willy's photograph showed him surrounded by a phalanx of lawyers on their way into the courthouse. His face was unsmiling and his lawyers looked tired and Linnell recognized Harold's face in the group. The photographer had captured his self-satisfied expression: fat and sassy, and much too relaxed. She knew the Hyena—she could tell from his face he was up to no good.

SAN FRANCISCO **Friday evening - August 9, 1974**

Robert Jordan leaned against the wharf's rough wooden guard rail and ran his fingers along a top edge rubbed surprisingly satin-slick by the countless hands of all those who had arrived here before him to gaze across the bay. Travelers from every corner of the world, wanderers who had reached the end of the line by riding the cable car over the hill and down to water's edge. Perhaps some of them had even stood here just like himself, trying to figure out what it was all supposed to mean. And tomorrow? Tomorrow was the last leg of his C.P.A. exam and he was in no mood to cram. Jordan leaned far out over the rail to look down, then he lifted his feet and tottered. How far down to the water? Thirty feet? Forty? In the darkness it was hard to tell.

Bright mercury vapor lights high over the wharf cast long wavering shadows of him onto the surface of the oil-slicked water that wobbled darkly beneath his feet. But the pay phone was only ten feet away. Just close enough to give him a peculiar sense of security, as if it were the phone booth itself that was keeping him tethered. He stood down to let the feeling pass through him. He'd give it another ten minutes and then if he still had enough change, maybe he'd try calling again. Jingling the remaining coins in his pocket, this time Jordan stepped up onto the lower rung of the rail and stared where the harsh light pierced the surface of the water, making the top six inches glow ghostly gray like a moonstone's eye. Then he leaned farther out and focused on his ink-black shadow and watched how it flickered in the wavelets before splitting in two, leaving him swaying with vertigo until he would close his eyes.

He had played a more innocent game of this sort once before: When he was twelve he had stood on the high suspension bridge over Silver Bow Creek.

And he had leaned far over the rail—same as he was doing now—so he could spit into the water below to seal his pledge to leave Montana and search for adventure upon the high seas. To be a blue water sailor and sail the atolls of the Pacific. That's what he once wished for. A fantasy born to his land-bound child's soul from reading too much Nordhoff and Hall he supposed.

He no longer cared. Jordan sighed and leaned over the rail again.

He had tried to reach her a couple of times over the last several months. It was torture, knowing that she was actually so close at hand yet so far beyond reach. But what point was there in trying to see her? Still, every now and then he would dial her number, hoping against hope that maybe this time he'd find the right words. But then, just as soon as he'd hear her voice, his would disappear in his stomach. It had never been worse than today. Yeah. He was probably cracking up. He'd been working too much. Fifty, sometimes sixty, hours a week and then up all night studying. And he'd really screwed up today; when he'd first dialed her number he'd talked to her secretary okay, but then, just as soon as he heard her saying hello, his tongue had once again fused to the roof of his mouth. Maybe he was afraid he'd blurt everything out—all his fears, his uncertainties, his terrible doubts—and then she'd be lost to him forever.

This was all so totally weird he could scarcely believe it was happening to him. But still, he needed to talk to her. He wanted to tell her that he did not, not, not! want to marry *any* of them. *Definitely* not Suzanne. Nor Mary Jo—nor for that matter even Elizabeth, the attractive new receptionist. But each of them wanted to marry him. The pressure was on. He was even getting it from the head of the International Division who'd made it plain to him that only a family man would be eligible for that important corner office. "And the sooner you stop chasing around and settle down, the sooner you'll be in line for getting one for yourself. Otherwise, who knows?" He had understood the warning.

With his eyes fixed on blackness, Jordan saw a sea lion pop up and glide through an oil slick, leaving a silvery-green whorl in its wake. Everything looked so unreal that sometimes it was hard for him to believe that this dark and here filthy fluid actually sheltered the planet in one single film. That it curved and wandered around the earth in an unending dance with the moon until it was magically cleansed and could lick once again sweet and clear against the powdery white edges of that tiny island, thousands of miles from this raggedy shore. But it did. And thank God for that, because this was exactly what filled him with hope.

All right! He'd done enough wallowing for one night. Jordan pulled himself straight, then despite himself, called out her name. *Linnell!* And then, just as her name fell from his lips, like magic, a bluish light flashed from inside the saloon on the other side of the boardwalk. Jordan smiled, amazed, even though he knew it was just the bartender turning on the television.

Robert Jordan focused his still perfect eyes and saw the image flicker, turn bright, and then offer a tight close-up of Richard Nixon's face. The patrons, now sitting motionless before the large screen, were watching another broadcast of the president's resignation speech. Now. This very instant. He knew where she was. She was sitting in front of her television set . . . If only . . . if only he could reach out and touch the fluorescent face of the cathode tube, reverse the photons and send her the rest of his soul.

A sea lion barked. He looked at his watch. Almost 10:30 p.m. He would try one more time. Jordan dropped his last four quarters into the slot and then holding his breath, dialed her number.

HIGHRIDGE **Friday evening - August 9, 1974**

Linnell yawned sleepily and put down the paper. The phone rang at exactly 10:30 p.m. and Linnell once again found herself saying hello to dark silence; then she heard the click of the call being cut off. Linnell patted her belly to send it a message: "Okay honey, that's it—you, me, and Benjy—we're all going to L. A."

HIGHRIDGE **Monday, August 12, 1974**

The settlement documents had been sitting on Linnell's desk for almost a week. Negotiating with the bank had turned into a real hassle because she'd decided not to use the sensitive information she'd discovered about their former operations officer and Bear—she'd thought it might reveal too much about what she'd learned about Bear and his drug dealing. She now thought this might have been an overly cautious decision, because it had forced her to bang heads with them and now the cheapskates were offering her only 70 cents on the dollar. They could do better, she thought.

Linnell tried to conjure up help, but the best she could do was a single needle. A blunt one. She closed her eyes and pointed it at the president of the bank. Then she crossed out their offer and wrote in $656,000—80 cents on the dollar—with the proviso that they pay her through their offshore affiliate in Cayman. She was sure they would, because this way the bank would be saved from embarrassment and all the bad publicity. As for her, it would preserve her privacy and save her the costs of litigation. The deal wasn't perfect, but the gold she and Benjy had found would be more than enough to make up the difference.

As for Mr. Journet's recording of the mystery woman's call to his bank? She had listened to it maybe a hundred times; so had Nancy and the now discharged operations officer. Like everybody else, Linnell had wracked her brain, but so far she hadn't a clue who she was. The mystery woman sometimes spoke in breathy, self-conscious syllables, as if she were holding her nose and doing a send-up of Jackie Onassis. Then the voice would change and sound almost like Linnell's. It was truly eerie. Obviously, the mystery woman knew exactly what she was doing—and then she and the money had vanished without a trace.

And besides this aggravation, there were several others. Minor loose ends that still remained to be tied—for instance, Bear stealing a copy of her article. She'd finally discovered it in his private bathroom at his office, under some white linen rags—in a towel drawer, of all places! What had he done with the first forty pages? And why had he hidden it like that? And then there was also the door handle, at home. She was sure she'd seen it break off and go flying across the patio, and yet a month later, when she'd finally thought about examining the door, there was the handle, perfectly intact. All unanswered questions, albeit they were all topped by the larger mystery of Elsie's death.

But, quite apart from all this, the most bizarre twist had come from the thing Ray and Karen had found in the flannel sack, underneath the back seat of their car. Ray still got his kicks by teasing them about it.

It was so embarrassing to learn what it was! I would never have dreamed! I don't want to think about what Bear might have been doing with something like that! But leave it to Karen, she was truly inspired: She wrapped the darn thing in brown paper and then we flipped coins to see who would get it, and that's why it wasn't sent to the Hyena. Instead, we mailed it from San Francisco—anonymously of course—to the law office of old Buster Hosterman. I have to give myself credit, too . . . It was my idea to enclose Bear's note—the one he sent me along with those roses.

Linnell buzzed her secretary. When Karen picked up, Linnell asked, "How'd you like to go to the land where the lotus grows?"

"You mean L.A.?" Karen squealed. "Hey baby, sounds great to me! When we leaving?"

FLYING HOME TO ROOST

HIGHRIDGE **November, 1974**

Jordan passed the last leg of his California CPA exam in late August of 1974, and then after only three months, the accounting firm transferred him into the international tax department. He now had an assistant and a secretary and a generous expense account, and best of all, he did a lot of traveling because his clients were some of the major players up and down the West Coast. Every now and then he'd get a call from Chief Agent Augustus Rizzo, who would fill him in on the Ivener trial, now going into its fourth month. Rizzo had asked him to meet him in Highridge so they could look in on the proceedings. Jordan had time to do that today.

Jordan met Rizzo on the steps of the courthouse. "This is why I stay in the service, to see things like this," Rizzo announced by way of a greeting.

"You mean you actually get off on seeing Ivener sweat?" Jordan was surprised, he hadn't thought of Rizzo as being the kind of guy who would nurse a grudge against someone who was already going down for the count.

"No. Not Ivener—he's a goner. I'm talking about Harold Dolphe. Just wait, you're gonna see what I mean."

"You mean he's here? At the trial?"

"Sure he's here; he's *still* with the Ivener firm."

The trial was being held on the first floor and Jordan and Rizzo entered the hearing by different doors and pretended to accidentally bump into each other in the back of the courtroom. Rizzo leaned on the wall and Jordan stood slightly in front of him so he could listen to Rizzo's commentary. Willy Ivener was already on the stand, and it looked like the prosecutor was laying the foundation for showing him some documents.

Rizzo whispered, "Look at that weasel, see him sitting up there?"

"You mean Ivener?" Jordan queried

"No, kid. Dolphe! Harold Dolphe."

Jordan finally saw Dolphe, who was sitting at counsel's table with Ivener's lawyers. Just then, Dolphe stood up and requested the court's permission to hand Mr. Ivener a glass of water; then Dolphe approached Ivener and humbly held out the glass and waited at Ivener's feet like a servant, then took the empty glass and returned with it to the counsel's table.

"Hard as a frozen turd, that guy." Rizzo folded his arms and leaned back.

Jordan saw the prosecutor hand Ivener a pile of documents. Jordan knew what Ivener was examining, because he saw Ivener's face blanch as he flipped through the pages, apparently recognizing his signature on every one.

There was a sudden commotion in front of the counselor's bench: Ivener was down! And then there was bedlam. The judge was slamming his gavel and calling for an ambulance while the bailiffs pushed against the crowd of onlookers who were crowding in to gawk at the frail body that lay motionless in front of the witness stand. The word buzzed back to the rear of the courtroom that Mr. Ivener must have had a stroke. Rizzo and Jordan pushed their way to the end of the aisle and watched a still motionless Ivener being wheeled away on a gurney. One of Ivener's blotched hands rested limp on his chest and an oxygen mask was clamped to his face. Dolphe, however, was a sight to behold. Standing proudly erect, with his shoulders thrown back, he now strutted behind Ivener's gurney, staring back arrogantly at the crowd.

You think Dolphe slipped him a dose? Or is Ivener just pulling a fast one?" Jordan asked.

"Well, I wouldn't put anything past Dolphe, but I suspect Ivener's not pulling a fake-out. I can tell from those purple blotches that he's really sick. But hey, this trial was *his* choice. He could've plea bargained his way out of this mess and gotten off with a penalty. 'Course, it would've cost him at least a cool million."

"I assume Ivener's got the money. So why did he risk a trial?"

"Hell, I dunno. Maybe bad judgment. Or maybe just for the business. Every time the IRS goes after him he thumbs his nose at us in the press, then he gets a big spread in Newsweek and Forbes and hundreds of new clients beat a path to his door. You know what he's always said, don't you? He's always said that it's the Treasury Department that's made him a millionaire—and ten times over."

"You think things will be different with Dolphe?"

"Him? *That* shit-head? Things will be different all right. He thinks he's smarter than Ivener. What a joke! He was so busy shagging L.C. all over Cayman that he didn't pick up on the fact that we were shagging him. We've been biding our time and now we know where all the bodies are buried. We learned he was in charge of shipping tons of documents out of the Bahamas and we've found where he's stored them. He rented a warehouse and we've already been in it a couple of times and the dummy hasn't caught on that we know it's the new headquarters for The Wei."

"In Cayman?"

"Right. Edgardo was put on his tail. That's why we sent you there, you had to take his place for a while. Well, Dolphe's gonna be in for quite a surprise because he's been so busy setting up Ivener that he hasn't guessed that we've got something cooking for him. By the way . . . I want you to take a look at this. It came out a couple a months ago, so I brought you a copy." Rizzo pulled a manila envelope out of his briefcase and handed it to Jordan.

Jordan ripped it open and found the Universal Tax Journal of International Operations. He flipped the pages and saw that the lead article had been written by Linnell Clare—on the subject of the Foreign Foundation and United States Taxation.

"There's stuff in there that even *I* never knew. Let's just say this: It's going to be the knife that cuts off that guy's little watering-spout." Rizzo jerked his head in Dolphe's direction. "We're going to let him spin himself out and then we're gonna string him up to high heaven. He's gonna to be indicted as soon as we're through with Ivener and I'm *personally* gonna nail his ass to the ground. Anyway, I thought you might want to take a look at this thing since I have this hunch that one of these day you're gonna be running into Ms. Clare."

The color rose in Jordan's cheeks. But it was too late for something like that. He had just married Suzanne and the baby was due any day now.

BEVERLY HILLS **November, 1974**

Linnell sold her house on the hill and left for Los Angeles in August of 1974. A month later, Karen and Ray decided to join her. Karen continued to work for Linnell's law firm—Linnell now had two law associates of her own—and then Helene joined them because both women needed her to help them manage their soon-to-be enlarged families.

Linnell had kept track of the "Tax Trial of the Century" through her daily tax bulletins and somehow she was not at all surprised to read that it had ended with Willy Ivener's near fatal stroke. The episode had left him paralyzed from the neck down—it was reported that he'd crushed several cervical vertebrae in a fall from the witness stand. In fact, Linnell observed, Willy was now at the same hospital where Bear had passed away. Perhaps if she flew up to see him he'd be so touched by this gesture he would be willing to talk to her. Maybe he had some information about what Bear had been doing at The Wei. And with whom. A woman, perhaps? It was worth the risk.

The tax bulletin went on to report that when the prosecution moved for a retrial, Ivener's lawyers quickly stipulated to a judgment for $2.5 million dollars, to be paid either by Ivener or his estate if he died. The settlement had been promptly approved by the court and the judge gave Ivener a suspended sentence.

"He's finished," thought Linnell. "The Treasury has finally won and he can't block this, not even by dying." The rest of the article left her feeling profoundly disappointed. It reported that Mr. Ivener had made Harold Dolphe the managing partner of the Ivener firm and that *Mr.* Dolphe—it was grating to observe the respect now being shown toward the despicable creature—would now serve as tax counsel to The Wei. Linnell dropped the bulletin and called out

Karen. "I know you're going to tell me I'm crazy, but I want to make peace with Willy. How about booking me a flight up to Highridge for tomorrow morning."

"Okay. You're nuts!" Karen shot back. "You really shouldn't be flying around in the state you're in—you're big as a barn. And you're backing off from your promise to let go of this thing."

"Yes. I know. But I have to go. The mystery of the missing money—this is my last chance to search for more clues."

HIGHRIDGE **November, 1974**

Green-gowned and infuriated, William E. Ivener lay helpless in his hospital bed. How did he feel? Well, if he were to borrow some mumbo-jumbo from The Wei he would have to say that he was simply *Overflowing with Knowing.* The thought made him laugh. He couldn't feel anything below his chin, so he could only listen to the odd gurgles and guess that they rose from his throat. Ha! Overflowing with knowing? That was his spit! He was literally drowning in it. Yeah, and right now he knew more than he wanted to know: He knew that the intubation tubes were keeping nothing more than his mind alive while the rest of himself was slowly rotting away. He'd be long dead before anyone would ever know why. God knows, his doctors had tried. A rare cancer—Kaposi—was all they could tell him, and here all this time he'd thought it was just a bad cold. And he already knew what the nurses wouldn't say. But they didn't have to tell him. Nobody had to tell him that this was definitely a one-way trip and that any day now he'd be checking out, for good.

Willy Ivener closed his eyes and relived the exact moment he'd first learned how to worry: *Everything began to slide the night I called L.C.'s number and I heard her voice . . . my worst nightmare . . . she was still alive! See? Even the best laid plans can be ruined by a few lousy details. Like the fact that all those damn women looked so much alike. I never thought about that. Worse still, that crazy-sonnava-bitch-coked-out-dentist—I never figured on him pulling the plug like that. So when he bailed, I couldn't stop worrying about whether the bastard had left any clues behind to point things my way—like a diary, or a suicide note, some thing or another that might turn up some day and tie me to the murder, or—worse still—blackmail! And it was always on my mind—that Deborah took off like that because she'd figured things out . . . and that she was out there somewhere, waiting to pounce. Oh God! I shoulda kept her under tighter control. Yeah, I know, I know . . . I shoulda called off the hit as soon as I read about that SOB killing himself. But I didn't. I couldn't. I just wanted to get rid of L.C. I had to get rid of her . . . for the sake of The Wei. Oh, I was so damn close to having it all . . . my own tax haven . . .*

Ivener bit down on the intubation tube and finally managed a few words aloud: "They caught me . . . Those . . . damn fuckin' pirates . . . from the . . ."

Linnell, now great with child, walked slowly through the corridors and arrived at Willy's room along with the hospital respiratory technician. They entered together and Linnell asked permission to approach the patient.

"I just want to say a few words to him," she whispered.

The tech whispered back: "Go ahead. But you'd better make it quick."

Linnell tip-toed over to Ivener's hospital bed and being so big, had to lean over sideways to look into his face and saw that Willy was struggling to speak.

"Mr. Ivener? Willy? I've come to see you. It's *me*, L. C. . . . Linnell Clare." She glanced at the nurse's records suspended from a clip at the end of the bed and read the most recent notation:

Total Immune System Collapse—ETIOLOGY UNKNOWN.

Ivener blinked with shock when he saw that he was staring up into Linnell's face. With his last burst of strength, he lifted his head, and his eyes, feverish lakes at the bottom of sunken craters, opened wide with horror.

It was Linnell who caught his last word:

" . . . *Eyeaarress!* . . ." Ivener gurgled softly, then his head sank down and he died.

LONDON **Summer - 1979**

When she thought about it, which she seldom did anymore, Deborah Graff was still overcome by a sense of wonderment. What were the words her dear Uncle Willy always liked to say? *The best way is always the easy way?* Something like that. Well, he didn't know the half of it. There were no accidents in this life—none at all. It was all meant to be; that's why it had all been so easy.

And even though Uncle Willy had been dead for five years, she could still hear him preaching: *My dear, you really can have it all . . . you merely have to find the right path.* Well, she certainly had—her most recent box office bonanza was proof enough of that. Her gross receipts were absolutely staggering—just this past week alone she had banked over four mil because this time she had demanded a percentage of the *gross*.

She turned up her dressing room lights and approached the full length mirror to give herself a cold-eyed appraisal. She had to admit, she was perfectly gorgeous. Uncle Willy had been right—a little bit of plastic surgery here and there had worked wonders and now her profile was perfect from every camera angle. But she had done her share too: She had kept the weight off, not by dieting, but by exercising relentlessly so that she would be flawless in full body shots. Her complexion, always tops, was still perfect—no frosted lenses or trick lighting was ever required for the stunning Ms. Graff!

Critics applauded, admirers said she was more stunning than Ava or Grace in their prime and more compelling than Hepburn and Davis rolled into one. And when it came to sexual charisma, men and women alike agreed that she had it all over the Marilyn. Women waited for her movies so they could see what she wore. Men proposed marriage with offers of yachts. With fifteen films to her credit—four in Italy, two in France, and the rest in London—she could well afford to branch out. And that's what she had planned. She would be the first actor to control—in total secrecy, of course—her own production company. She had never been a stranger when it came to keeping her own secrets.

It's so amusing to hear people say, when they meet me, that they would kill to be in my shoes. I'm sometimes tempted to tell them I quite agree . . . because that's exactly the way I got to be me.

Deborah shuddered when she thought about where she had been, five years before: . . . *On my knees in front of that beast.* She had long ago blotted his name from her mind, but she could very clearly remember all the rest. *The beast! He ordered me to open wide . . . he gave me his ugly worm to eat . . . Evil irrumator . . . but I was ready for any move he would make . . . and I killed it before he could kill me . . . found the dorsal veins with the tip of my tongue. The cocaine blocked all his sensations of pain and so swiftly he didn't know what I was doing until it was way too late . . . Hit him up with a speedball . . . a kiss to the fold and the syringe was emptied. No one will ever know how, but I did it. And in a way that no coroner would be likely to imagine since I had the presence of mind to zip up his pants. Then I placed all those rolled up papers in his outstretched hand and Margo, that fool . . . she did all the rest.*

Deborah thought about her very first day at the dental office, when she had been ordered to scrub dental trays. It was this that had led her to discovering all those discarded injection sets. Actually, the idea of learning how to use them had been inspired by Uncle Willy's concern over her hat pin, which had got her to thinking that if a hat pin was a good weapon, then a hypodermic syringe would be and even better defense. So she'd carried them home and had practiced with them for days on end, first with all those oranges, and then on a pineapple—aiming for all those eyes. And when her hands had stopped shaking, and she was sure she could handle one deftly, that was when she knew she was up to using the giant hypodermic syringe she'd found behind the can of plaster of paris—the one that looked like it could deliver a dose that would drop a rhino.

And that day in the lab, when she'd discovered the beast was already injecting narcotics? Well, *that* was what clinched it—that was what made her so sure she would be able to get away with it all.

And all that money?. . . it was almost an afterthought; something that had come to mind once she remembered that she had the beast's tape recording. And to think she'd almost forgotten about it. But it had been there all along, same place she'd ditched it—underneath the front seat of her junky old car! When she finally listened to it she realized it was the key to a fortune.

Deborah twisted her long auburn locks into a smooth chignon while she paused for a moment to remember: *The beast must have been so bedazzled by the sight of my heavenly heinie that he left his recorder on when he called the bank. And so it ran on and on until every bit of information I needed was there on the tape . . . I can still remember the eight digit code. It all fell into place once I got the idea that I could pretend to be Mrs. Clare. And listening to her outgoing message on her answering machine was such a big help—it made it possible for me to mimic the way she spoke. As soon as I got the money out of that Canadian bank, I just wired the funds to Switzerland and then I kept on dividing it into smaller and smaller accounts in all those different countries. Poor Uncle Willy. It's too bad he's no longer here—he'd be so proud of me.*

And he was such a splendid instructor . . . I always learned so much just by watching him.

Deborah had intended to practice some new facial expressions but found herself smiling instead. A wicked idea had suddenly popped into mind: *I think I'll give L.C. a chance to earn back some of her money! My accountant says she's still tops when it comes to international tax planning. I know she's still practicing law, somewhere in California. Next month, when I'm in Hollywood, I think I'll just look her up—I've always wanted to meet her to see what she's made of. Besides, there are so many clever things she knows how to do. She can start by forming a holding company for me in the Netherlands Antilles. And then she can fix me up with an Anstalt in Liechtenstein. Yes, I think it's high time that we met . . .*

BEVERLY HILLS **Summer - 1979**

Woe, woe unto man. The great libraries of Alexandria were razed to eradicate Her every last word and through such perversion was history artfully snipped to fit male form alone. Thenceforth did Church and clergy alike declare itself the Mother and Him the bearer of reborn life and through such cunning devises did they advance the fancy that man need no longer venerate Her. Woe, woe; sing woe unto man, for he shall pay dearly for these sins.

Seventh Song of Efik; translated 1974 - The Book of the Deep.

Linnell's daughter was born in November, 1974—the day after Linnell paid her final respects to Willy Ivener—at the same hospital from which he and Bear had departed. Linnell named her Marina Dawn in memory of the beautiful morning she'd missed on Seven Mile Beach. She had also managed to outwait the IRS, and instead of having her Cayman trust pay out its income—and her pay all that tax—she had followed the usual practice of allowing it to lend her its funds. She still practiced law, and her fortune, once small, had now grown very large in mysterious places all over the world. As for her gold, now worth a million, she had transferred it to her foreign foundation. Now she could play Lady Bountiful at will, which to her credit she was more often than not. And so, as a result of her flight from all memories of routine, she had ended up in this land of make-believe, where she had practiced for almost five years—and not always the law.

Her experiences had brought her to thinking that life was nothing more than a series of accidents, all of them strung together by time, creating an illusion of cause and effect. As for Kismet and predestination? Nonsense! There was no such thing. Nothing in life was preordained. Her life was a perfect example: all zigzags and whimsy from beginning to end. Life was uncertain. You never could tell, because at bottom life was simply a roll of the dice.

Tax law was a workable puzzle, however, and that's why she still liked it so much. To her, a tax law was a fortress with a gate marked *no entry.* Thus, like a good detective, she would nose around in the tax code until she found a back door through which she could enter in order to launch an attack. And whenever she tired of these puzzles or needed a touch of comic relief, she would set her law books aside and exercise her strange talent for attracting chaos.

It seemed she had found a fine way to put it to use: by setting it loose on those Hollywood film producers who annoyed her the most. Especially those who featured women as prey or objects of sexual abuse. To a lesser degree, she was also piqued by the endless fantasies where women were portrayed as twittering nitwits in fluffy aprons, pampered kitchen queens with little more to their lives than baking all those endless trays of peanut butter cookies—this, while the real women of Hollywood were still struggling to make it on minimum wage. So, destroy a sound stage? No problem. Burn the studio to the ground? Okay! Such things were but child's play when compared to modifying a Venturi pump.

It was inexplicable to others, but it seemed that all *she* had to do was to visit a studio and—surprise! surprise!—before anyone could say *boo!* racks of cameras and lights would come tumbling down to her feet. Entire productions would instantaneously turn into toast. Pipes would burst; sets would flood as if under an evil spell. Until finally, under the weight of so many mysterious afflictions, the offending production would be forced to fold. Linnell smiled at the thought of how much she had done.

Well, enough of this silly stuff, thought Linnell. She looked at her watch. Two major events had already happened today, and these now required her careful attention. One was the impromptu meeting with the famous actress, Ms. Graff, scheduled for 2 p.m. this afternoon, the other was the telephone call she'd received earlier that morning. The actress was due to arrive in ten minutes so she had time to think about the telephone call.

Linnell sank into the huge down-filled couch that filled one corner of her glass-walled office. Swinging her feet up, she leaned into its gray velvet cushions and for the first time in months took stock of her life. Nothing that thrilling. She had been seeing a director—a hardworking man, not unhandsome—who was always after her to tie the knot. But she had been unwilling to make a commitment because she still wasn't sure what she wanted to do. Watching Benjy, now twelve, surf his rising hormonal tides gave her as much family life as she could stand right now, and Marina, nearly five, was no less enthralling.

Marina, a tow-head until she was two, had ended up with a head of lovely light brown hair and sunny eyes that brimmed with her father's light. Who would ever know? Everyone had been so carefully tactful. She had decided not to burden Karen with any confessions, and Karen—bless her heart—hadn't asked any questions. Linnell knew that Karen had long ago understood that Marina's father wasn't the late Bear Clare, because Karen knew better than anyone else exactly what Linnell would have done if she'd thought that he was.

Yes, thought Linnell, she had been very lucky. For almost five years now, things had been almost too tranquil. She should have known that things were too smooth to last. Because something was coming. She could feel it in her bones: A sea-change was coming, an unknown wave was bulking up just over the horizon. And inside her, where her heart had once thumped, she had felt a new stirring.

Linnell jumped up suddenly, hurried to her carved mahogany desk to knock on wood, then turned away to face her window, where she caught a glimpse of herself in the thick plate glass. She smiled and her reflection showed clear happy eyes that for an instant revealed, and for first time in years, just the faintest trace of bewilderment. She studied herself. Well, no matter what might be happening inside, it was still reassuring to see that gravity had not yet taken its toll on the mask she had fixed between herself and the world.

But the telephone call—now *that* was a cruncher. She was still stunned. He had simply called her, early this morning, out of the blue. He wanted to tell her his real name: "Robert Jordan," he'd said. But that wasn't all. "Oh Linnell, *please* see me," he'd declared with a passion she still found most attractive. He'd said that he needed a chance to explain; he'd told her that there was so much he wanted to say, then he'd said that his divorce was now final. He got her attention with that. Yes, yes, yes . . . she remembered the man very well—although she had pretended otherwise—but the name? Robert Jordan? For some reason it sounded vaguely familiar. Karen had thought so too, but neither of them could say why, exactly. So, he'd begged. But still she'd stood firm. Then he'd said he just wanted her to talk to him. And again, she'd said no.

Now she was wondering if she'd made a mistake.

Linnell stared at her rudder. She had worked so hard to forget him. Why leave herself open to any more pain? That had been her first thought after recovering from the shock of hearing his voice. Linnell looked down and spotted a chauffeured black Mercedes rolling into her underground parking garage. She glanced one more time at her watch; the small gold hand lay exactly on top the ruby.

"Here she is, the famous Ms. Graff," Linnell whispered to herself.

Linnell knew this encounter would be particularly fascinating because, ever since her fiasco with Bear and her mishap with Robert Jordan, she had made it a rule to compare her now more astute first impressions against the detailed reports that were inevitably produced by her private investigator, a highly protective, persistent man who routinely delved into the background of all those who sought her attention. He'd be relentless—simply out of his mind with joy to be assigned to the fascinating task of digging through all of Ms. Graff's delicious dirt.

Linnell thumbed through her leather-bound rudder until she found a blank page and then for some unknown reason, she suddenly thought of her rose garden. In her mind's eye she could see all her roses unfolding at once, with their soft pink petals billowing around her like ruffled confetti.

Linnell picked up her pen, but the words wouldn't come. She should have said yes. But it was too late now because, as before, she hadn't thought about asking him for his telephone number. Her sad thoughts were interrupted by the commotion in her reception area and the delight she could hear in Karen's voice made her feel even more irritable. "The famous actress is here," Linnell grumped to herself, "and now she's going to get everybody stirred up."

Linnell straightened her black cashmere knit, took another look at her reflection in the small mirror on her desk to be sure she didn't have lipstick on her teeth, then turned around so that Ms. Graff's first glimpse would be of her back. Then she held her breath and listened to the sound of Karen opening the door. Glancing quickly over her shoulder, she saw Karen looking back at her visitor with a vivacious smile. Linnell went back to staring moodily out the window and waited for Ms. Graff to make her grand entrance.

Linnell finally turned around, then froze to the spot. An incredibly handsome man now stood on her threshold. It was him. Roberto. Linnell stared, her face an eloquent palette of astonishment and delight. He was older and smoother and extremely well-dressed and with one glance she could tell there was not a single tuft of eaglet fluff to be found amongst his glossy feathers. He was a soaring eagle now; a man in his prime.

"You said no." Robert Jordan's face held a determined expression. "Well, nobody says no to me unless they say it to my face. But first, let me remove all the guess-work for you—I'm alone, I'm going for a swim, and then I'm going for a walk on the beach. Okay?" He stepped toward her and then his face lit up with a smile. "I won't settle for anything less than a yes."

He's changed, thought Linnell. All of his hesitation is gone. And he wants me to know that he remembers every word I've ever said to him. Linnell felt a familiar dizziness when she gazed at his face; then barely managing to keep her presence of mind, she stepped lightly around him to lean through the door and grin happily at Karen. "When Ms. Graff arrives, tell her I'm in conference and that it's going to be quite a long while before I can see her. I think it would be best for us all if she scheduled her appointment for another day."

With that, Linnell closed the door, turned around slowly to face Robert Jordan, and even though she wasn't the least bit at a loss for words, this time she made sure to say only one: "Yes!"

END

9 781893 335097